Life in 1984

JC Akends

Published by Houck Publishing, 2026.

This is a work of fiction. Names, characters, places, and incidents are the product of the author's imagination or are used fictitiously. Any resemblance to actual events, locales, or persons, living or dead, is coincidental.

Website: https://houckpublishing.com

The publisher is not responsible for websites (or their content) that are not owned by the publisher.

Dedication

Life in 1984 rough draft was written over ten years ago in a major state of depression, when one can't see life ever getting better. The protagonist friends always help the protagonist find heart and soul of life and make this book reality.

Thanks to Kathy Houck, Tom Deimer, with technical points of rules we live by although many have changed in 2026 compared to 1984. This is a fiction novel but the realism of life in a small country town in Michigan.

Thanks, and gratitude to my writing associates from Florida Writers Association, Oxford Group. Chris Coward, Mark Pryor, John Mallon, John DeJordy, Margaret Agard, and Bobbie Calhoun, who have endured years of rewrites. I want to add a special thanks in the early years to Su Gerheim who passed before seeing the completed book but always had encouraging words.

Course my wife Sue Dahl who has reread and endured every rewrite. I take full responsibility for anything that is still in the book that doesn't make sense.

Copy Editing, Alexandra Ott

Book Cover Design: Eliane Lee, forthemusedesigns@gmail.com

One

February 11, 1984

The needles of air sting my face, when I open the old black steel door of Maggie's, sliding the piece of wood under the edge. The Friday night party is over and cold seeps in around my Carhart jacket but can't deter my swagger across Main Street. Twinkling stars and the misty clouds float past a full moon in the dim streetlights as if they know it's a night to remember. The old Ford F-250 groans before the diesel rumbles out bellows of smoke. The frosted windshield, do little to keep me from making a perfect U-turn and negotiate the truck in front of the bar door. Leaving it to warm up, I head towards the alley for Laura's car.

What the hell? A kid walking towards me, dressed in teddy bear pajamas sticking out of a pair of black rubber boots, with his hands stuffed in his pockets, squeezing his jacket closed. *He can't be four, maybe five.* It's three a.m. I drop to one knee in front of him. "Where're you going, son?"

His deep brown eyes pierce my face and he spits out. "I'm looking for my Aunt Laura."

"I'm a friend of hers." I stretch out my hands. He shifts a small step towards me, then freezes. I quickly pick him up. "She's inside. I'll take you to her." He feels like a log as I carry him inside and sit him on the bar.

I say, "Everything's going to be okay." *Where in hell is your mother?* I yell toward the office in the back. "Laura, we have company." No answer and the kid still squinting with a defiant stare, sending a chill through me. "What's your name, son?" I lightly rub the top of his legs and say, "Laura will be here in a minute." Finally, the office door closes. "Someone's here to see you."

"Yeah. Smart-ass, who?"

I'm staring at her when she comes around the corner. "Someone looking for his Aunt Laura."

Her eyes become darts, and she runs towards us. "Johnny, oh my God, what happened?" Pushing me away pulls him tight, rubbing his back. He lays his head on her shoulder and sobs. She cradles him until his crying becomes a whimper, then wipes the tears still running down his face with her hand.

"Where's your mother?"

"Mommy fell asleep, and the heater started blowing cold air."

"We'll go get her." She moves him to a chair, and wraps her coat around him and says, "You stay at the table. We'll find your mommy."

"Aunt Laura." The kid's eyes roll up at me he leans towards her and whispers. "She doesn't want anyone to know what happened."

She kisses his forehead. "Don't worry, it will be okay."

I give her my coat. "I didn't see a car. The kid was walking up the sidewalk."

We turn down the alley beside the bar and parked next to Laura's car, it is an old Pinto.

Laura opens the driver's door. "That bastard, son-of-b..." The dim light exposes a woman collapsed against the console. Laura gently shakes her. "Marilyn, wake up. Marilyn—"

I put my hand on Laura's shoulder. "Let's get her inside." She moves away, her green eyes watery. I squat down, pull the girl upright and try to zip her cheap winter coat. It's stuck. I pulled it closed over the ripped blouse and her exposed chest. A small dignity. Then lay her head on my shoulder and pull her tight to me. A faint breath tingles the hairs on my neck. Her swollen eye, and the dry blood smeared across her face—*suck it up*. I swallow, slide my arm under her legs, draw her close, and lift her from the car.

Laura scurries ahead, pulls the bar door open, then runs and slides a couple of chairs together.

Limp as a rag doll ... *I'm choking up and my eyes are blurry.*

"Sit her down. Let me get a warm towel."

"She needs more than a towel." I keep my arm around her, keeping her head on my shoulder. *Damn it, kid, quit staring at me. I'm trying to help.*

Laura pulls a chair in front of the girl and wipes the dry blood from her face. Her dark brunette hair is matted with more blood. "Marilyn, can you hear me? Marilyn!"

The kid says, "Aunt Laura, why's Mommy not answering?"

"She's still asleep, dear."

I sit holding her limp body, and motion for the kid to sit by me. "We'll take care of your mom. No one is going to hurt her anymore."

The kid doesn't move off his chair but the vibes. He wants to punch me.

"Marilyn, can you hear me?" There is still no response. "Marilyn." Laura closes her eyes.

I lift Laura's chin and whisper, "She needs to go to the hospital."

The kid moves and yells, "No. No. Mommy said they will take me away."

Laura holds out her hand. "Come here." She hugs Johnny. "We won't let them take you." Laura keeps rubbing the girls' legs.

I keep her tight, adding body heat but seems little for what this girl needs ... Laura knows her, but more than a bar friend and haven't I seen her? Would've remembered ... This jealous asshole messed her up on purpose, he needs to pay.

The girl pushes Laura's hand and swings wildly with the other, hitting me in the face. "Get away. Leave me alone."

The deep brown eyes that are twins of the kid's, glare at me with fear or hate, I can't tell.

"Marilyn, it's Laura."

Her eyes shift to Laura. "Oh my God, I am so sorry. Where am I?" She winces when the kid hugs her, and says, "Johnny, are you all right?"

"Yes, Mommy, I was so scared."

"I know, baby." She glances at Laura. "We had a fight—I didn't know where else to go."

"You did the right thing." Laura's eyes are glossy. "We'll figure out something as she keeps rubbing the girl's legs. "We need to warm you up."

The girl with such a softens voice says, "I'm sorry. I didn't mean to hit you."

"Thought it was a love tap."

Laura wraps my jacket around the girl's legs. "You're still freezing."

"I'm so sorry to ... It's my problem—"

"We're going to help you. Keith, get her a shot of schnapps."

The girl says, "I don't need anything."

I'm instantly behind the bar pouring a shot and handing it to Laura. The vibe—we need one too.

Laura hands Marilyn the glass says, "Marilyn, this is Keith. Keith, meet Marilyn and Johnny."

I reach out my hand. "Nice to meet you."

Marilyn cautiously moves her hand.

The softness touches me as I slowly let it slip away.

Laura is staring at Marilyn and says, "Drink. It will help warm you up."

Marilyn sips the schnapps, and her eyes ...

Queasiness grabs me. "I'll be back, girls." I make the bathroom and up chuck. Gaining some composer, I wash my face, rinse my mouth, and look at blurry image in the mirror. Emotions are for the weak and wimpy. The mirror stares back. The game face.

Don't get all caring ...

It was a great night now stored in my secret memoirs. The beef-feeding-frenzy starts in a couple of hours, and I turn into a farmer. There is no time for emotional affection.

Two

February 11, 1984

The small sip of schnapps burns Marilyn's throat. She winces when Johnny slides onto her lap and leans back into her, but she still pulls him close.

Laura scurries around the bar and brings ice wrapped in a towel. "Here, hold this on your eye."

Marilyn says, "All I could think was run before he kills me or starts beating on Johnny."

Laura slides the chair close and says, "You did the right thing."

"It was the worst." Marilyn looks around. "The place looks different from what I remember."

"The new owner made improvements. It's been almost three years. Keep drinking your schnapps. It'll help you warm up and relax."

Johnny moves. Marilyn winces.

Laura slides a chair close to the table. "Johnny, move over here, and I'll get you some pop. Your mommy is hurting too much for you to sit on her lap."

Marilyn leans ahead, keeping the ice on her eye, trying to get a grip.

Must be Laura's boyfriend?

Laura says, "Okay, so what happened?"

"The norm promised to be home right after work but went to the bar. The lie, I believed it again. I fixed mac and cheese, read Johnny a story, and tucked him into bed. Having a heart-to-heart with myself at the kitchen table, saying I should've gone to Mom's for the night at least to scare him.

"He strutted in carrying a twelve-pack and said, 'What's for supper?' Without hesitating, I answered him. 'Cold macaroni and cheese. We saved you some. You can warm it up.' Course he spits trying to talk. 'Funny. I don't eat mac and cheese in case your feeble mind forgot.' I calmly glanced at the clock. 'Remember, I was getting groceries at four when you supposedly got home? Guess the alcohol blurred your sense of time. Supper was at six; it's now ten, we assumed you ate.'"

Laura leans back in her chair.

Marilyn says, "I couldn't let it rest. 'We understand your bar friends are important.' His jaw tightened, but I continued. 'Did you save money for food or rent?' He went ballistic, pulled out a wad of money, waved it around. 'This is all you care about, isn't it? Well, isn't it? Answer me, you—'" She glances at Johnny; he's playing with the straw and his ice cubes. "He threw it on the table, dug out the change, threw that which some of it hit the floor. He pulled his pockets inside out. 'You got it all ...' I sat completely still." She closes her eyes and recollects herself.

"He opened the freezer and found the hamburger I had planned for Sunday. Threw it on the table, it slid and hit the floor." Marilyn takes the ice away from her eye. "He's laughing. 'You've been waiting to take care of your man, right?' I picked up the hamburger, never looking he left to watch TV."

Keith walks back over to us. "You want me to go start the cars?"

Laura nods and says, "Yes, we need to go."

Johnny sucks air from his glass.

Laura finger-combs his hair. "You need a haircut."

Marilyn looks at Johnny and says, "He does, but it would be another fight. John thinks he looks tough with his scraggly hair."

Laura is rubbing her face. "So, he got mad because you wouldn't cook him something to eat?"

"No, I cooked the hamburger for his worthless ass."

"Mommy, that's a bad word."

"Sorry." Marilyn is shaking her head.

Laura rubs my hand. "You're still cold." She gets up and refills the glasses. "Johnny, don't drink too fast; there's no more."

Johnny says, "Thank you, Aunt Laura."

"You're welcome, dear." Lips to me, "It's mostly ice."

Marilyn sips hers. "I'm still worried—no grocery money, the landlord coming in the morning for the rent that is past due, the electric bill is due on Tuesday, which we have no way of paying."

"His problem. You're on to your new life."

"Sounds like a dream ... I don't want you involved any more than you are I'll go to my mom's in the morning." She gazes at Laura. "My revenge, I left him a dime and a penny with a note. 'You can call someone, and you're still not broke.' I took the rest of the money. He gave it to me, right?"

Laura smiles. "Definitely the right thing to do."

"He is going to come after me and anyone who helps me. You understand that."

"We'll find someplace for you to hide. Till we get him locked up." Laura is rubbing her mouth.

"Even if I press charges, his mother will bail him out. I'll go to my mom's till I figure out what to do. She won't be happy, but at least she didn't have to drive to the hospital in the middle of the night."

"I tried to follow what they said in counseling, make minimal eye contact, agree to whatever he said, and stay calm. But I had to defend myself." Marilyn holds up the empty glass. "Think I'm over my one-drink limit." Tears are forming. She stares at Laura. "He moved his hand up my leg. I pushed it away and said, You should've cuddled with your bar friends."

Marilyn closes her eyes. "He quipped back with his smirk, 'I always come home to you.' I was going to add, no one wants you there either, but I didn't dare say it. He goes into this big explanation about his unwinding time, everyone having a few laughs on a Friday night. He continues to whine, justifying how I'm making a big deal about it. Tell's me. 'The girls realize I'm married, and a caring husband.' I wanted to gag."

"What bar do they go to?"

"They go to Jack's in Peck. Says the bars here in town are too snotty."

Laura smiles. "I'm sure we are. So, what set him off?"

"I kept reading, ignoring him. He droned on how he brings his love home and I sit around being Miss Prissy reading a love story but won't give him any.' Then jumps to how I am teaching Johnny to be a sissy."

Johnny turns in his chair and says, "Aunt Laura, I'm not a sissy, am I?"

Laura puts him on her lap and gives him a hug. "You're mommy's hero." Turns to Marilyn. "So, he's pissed because you are reading?"

"Yeah, but hates being ignored and says, 'Maybe if you give me some, it would help me relax.' I'm not forgiving you. Watch TV."

"Mommy, what did Daddy want you to give him?"

Marilyn catches her breath.

Laura pipes in. "It's an extra kiss."

"You can see what else happened. I'll finish telling you later; the rest is ugly. I'm vowing not to cry anymore." She wipes her tears on her sleeve.

"What's your friend going to say? I feel so repulsive."

"Keith, is part family. Your secret is safe." Laura's eyes light up. "You can stay at the farm."

"What are you saying? Whose farm?"

"Uncle Keith's, as Chad calls him. He has a quaint old farmhouse with extra rooms."

"Laura, I'm not really in a joking mood."

"It is perfect."

"You're telling me to go home with a guy from the bar with a quaint farmhouse? Think I've had enough guys for one night."

"You're not sleeping with him."

"Laura, be serious. I don't know him. I'll just go to Mom's."

"Remember how that worked out? It'll be the first place he goes when he sobers up. Trust me; the farm is the perfect hideout."

Marilyn closes her eyes and lets out a breath. "I should've worked out a real plan."

"You can't work out a plan when you are living in hell and getting the shit beat out of you every day."

"But staying with another guy?"

"I've known him for over ten years. It'll be your hideout for a while, till we can figure out something."

"This is not a fairy tale."

Laura grimaces. "Not all guys are slimebags and beat up women." She nervously glances at the bar door. "Keith should've been back."

Marilyn says, "It's after three, you should be home." A tear drops off her cheek.

Laura picks up the glasses. "Some quick history about Keith. He's a teddy bear, who will turn into a grizzly if someone goes after his friends."

"He goes around taking care of abused married women?"

"No." Laura looks off into space. "He's a stand-up guy." She smiles. "Don't get me wrong, he wants it ... but he wants you to feel good too. John doesn't know it yet, but he should be worried about Keith beating the shit out of him. Remember, when I started working here? I had everything under control."

"Yeah, so."

The door closes.
Marilyn whispers, “He’s coming.”
Laura leans close to her ear. “I’ll tell you later.”

Three

February 11, 1984

Some kind of hypnosis takes over me, planting me into a war novel, a mother cuddling her child, with the building wreckage behind her. A softness emerges from Laura as she holds Marilyn's hands, both with tears running down their faces.

I step into the icy wind. Forgetting my coat slaps me back to reality. The Ford, the diesel purring, waits to go home, as I jog by the alley towards the girls' cars. Sliding sideways in the Pinto, turn the key, and a dim red light shows on the dash. The gas gauge doesn't move. *Walk mode.* I turn the key, a small groan before *click, click, click.*

Shit.

Grab her purse, throw it in Laura's car and push the seat back, swing my legs inside and close the door. The Cutlass makes a low moan, sputters, and comes to life. Light frost covers the windshield. I roll down the window, stick my head out. Park, facing Main Street, turn the defroster on full blast, and leave it running in the middle of the alley.

The sheriff patrol parks in front of the car, such timing, he shines his spotlight towards the car, and waits as I walk up to the passenger side. He shuts the light off. "You're a little late leaving. Is everything okay?"

I squat down, keeping some distance from them. "Just some extra work to finish up."

"You work at the bar?"

"Help the girls close, make sure the stragglers are gone. Where's Sid been?"

The passenger cop, with tight-trimmed hair and mustache, says, "Can we see your ID?"

"Sure, I'm Keith Larson." I dig out my license. They're looking at it; thoughts race into my head. *Something is not right, although they stay in the car.*

"So, what kind of private after-bar party did we miss out on?"

"The party is over. You missed out on the cleanup."

The driver snickers. "You own the beef farm out on Baily Road. Rumors you're a heartthrob for the women in the county. What kind of seeds are you planting?" He raises his arm and looks at his watch. "At three-twenty in the morning?"

I say, "Making sure the women are safe. It's a humble job."

Passenger cop says, "Along with winning Jock of the Year or something."

The driver says, "You beat my kid's team ... Yeah, I remember, thirty-five to nothing. I can't recall any humbling."

Passenger cop turns to the driver with a grin. "Should we check out his story? Or whose wife he's secretly taking care of?"

The driver leans ahead. "Sid gave us a report about the troublemakers in town." He chuckles. "My hypothesis is he's doing the bartender."

I grin. "And the rule of the bar is, the bartender never tells."

He hands me my license. "We need details. Who is she? Measurements, quality rating, all of it?" He glances at the driver. "The crucial details for our report. Her husband's name, how long, where she lives, it saves time when we come back."

"I see Sid is keeping abreast of my farming secrets."

They are both laughing as they peer down the alley. "Or maybe he has more than one?"

"The battery is dead. She needed a ride home." My neck tenses. "Haven't seen Sid in a while. I miss him harassing me, although I can tell he sent quality replacements."

"He's on day shift. We'll tell him you're missing him."

"Tell him to stop by the coffee shop on Sunday morning. I'd like to thank him for keeping me in his caring thoughts."

The passenger cop grins. "We don't believe your tale, now get her home." He's laughing and starts to roll up the window. "And put a coat on; you're making me cold."

I stand up. "Pass my best on to Sid and thanks for the advice."

He loses his grin. "You be careful."

"Always." My heart is racing. *Should I've told them?* I rub my arms, return to game face and walk into the bar.

Laura's eyes squint. "What took you so long?"

"Had a friendly chat with the sheriff patrol."

Marilyn's eyes dart to the door. "They can't find me. I need to hide—"

I raise my hands. "Calm down girls, everything is fine."

"What did you tell them?"

"I was helping the bartender––"

Laura says, "I'm surprised they didn't want to check it out."

"They did, but I told them it was a secret, and better if they didn't know who. Besides it was more fun sitting in the warm police cruiser watching me freeze."

Marilyn's voice is trembling. "You didn't tell them ...?"

"No, they didn't think anyone––"

"I can't ... go through that again."

Laura says, "Some of them are just nosy. Why aren't they out catching criminals instead of checking who's still out past curfew—"

Marilyn is gasping. "Please—I don't want anyone—"

"Don't worry, I took care of it. They don't know you're here. The bad news is Marilyn's car has a dead battery and, I am assuming, is out of gas."

Silence, which seems forever. Laura motions for me to follow her. Once we're in the office, she bears hugs me. "I hate to put you in this mess."

I feel her shaking. "Got that part. I'll straighten him out."

"No, we will talk about that later." She puts her arms on my chest. "Can she stay at your place over the weekend, till we figure out what to do?"

"Sure, anything to help ... She's okay with that?"

"We're short on options, but don't let your ego knight-in-shining-armor image swell your head too big. John, her husband, is nasty, more than the normal jealous husband you have pissed off before."

"And life was getting so boring."

Luara shakes her head. "I'll update when we have more time. She's been through hell. John, her husband, the asshole, and Bob, his butt buddy, they'll be drilling me tomorrow. Her mother is so wishy-washy it's hard to tell what she'll do." She pinches her lips together. "It's a mess, and I'll owe you for helping."

"Seriously, you won't owe me." I grin. "On second thought, I have a fun repayment plan."

She gives me a gentle slap on the arm. "The fun's over. Be serious. Please."

"I can't be getting all serious. Next thing, this caring emotion will be spilling out and ruin my reputation."

She hugs me again. "You can't hide it from me. She has to break free from her slime-bag husband. Hopefully, this gives her enough willpower to leave him."

"I'll do whatever. You know how I hate guys that beat up women."

"Let's get home. I don't need Ace to ask why I'm late."

"Someone needs to teach her husband you're not allowed to beat up on women the modern world," I mumble under my breath. "I'd like to feel his face at the end of my fist, hearing bones crunch."

"You can't, remember? He doesn't realize you exist. That's why your place is perfect until we can figure out what to do." She looks up at Keith. "And your gigolo status ends. You are now Uncle Keith." Tears well in Laura's eyes and she kisses me. "Take care of her, please. Let's go tell her."

Four

February 11, 1984

The anguish rips my heart when Marilyn looks up at me. *The kid is holding on to her like a baby cub.* She is rocking him and winces in pain, motions towards my coat. "You're gonna need that."

I pick it off the chair. "The truck is nice and toasty."

Laura sits across from her, their knees interlocking. She takes hold of her hand. "You're going home with Keith."

Tears stream down Marilyn's cheeks. "All I do is mess up everyone's lives."

Calmly, I say, "It's not a problem for a girl to stay overnight at my house."

Laura spits nails at me. "Damn, be serious for once?"

My stomach is churning again, just shut off the emotion.

Marilyn gradually gets up. She rejects the offer to help he up.

I'm choking spit out. "Honestly," I pat my heart. "Just want to help." I flip the chairs onto the table and kneel in front of Johnny. "I'll take care of your mom. No one's going to hurt her anymore."

He just stares with those deep, penetrating dark eyes.

"Did they tell you we have tractors and a snowmobile, a toy box that is part of the living room, and most of all, Jake, my purebred farm dog, loves to play with kids. Do you like dogs?"

His head barely nods. "I don't have one."

"Well, you do now. Jake will be your new friend."

Laura picks Johnny up. "We've got to go." She looks at me and raises her eyebrows. "Before someone promises his cows can jump over the moon."

Johnny glues his eyes on me and says, "Can Mommy play too?"

"Well, of course, they're for everyone that visits."

I hold the bar door and Marilyn follows Laura out.

I ran quickly in front of her and open the truck door. She declines taking my hand even with pain etched on her face when she pulls herself up.

Laura sits Johnny on Marilyn's lap. "Johnny, your mom is hurting. You should sit next to her on the seat."

Marilyn pulls him close to her and says, "He'll be fine."

Laura closes the door softly. I wrap my arm around her shoulders and walk her to the car. Tears fill her eyes as she gives me a hug. I kiss her on the cheek.

"I'll take care of her."

"I wish there was ... She's scared to death."

***

I have clever, sexy lines once I have the girl in the car. Beads of sweat break out on my forehead before we're even out of town. I turn the fan down too low. "Are you warm enough?"

"Yes, you must've been freezing without a coat?"

"It's supposed to impress my toughness."

"You don't want to be involved in my life."

"Damsels in distress enhance my knight-in-shining-armor status, and I just showed up."

Johnny is sleeping before we are out of town.

"You've taken girls home as nasty as me before?"

I glance over. *Say something to cheer her up.*

"You could do anything you want. I wouldn't even make an ugly whore statistic. You should think of yourself. I'm not that good, according to John. And he'll want revenge, so you'll—"

I pull up to the stop sign and glare at her. "You're a friend of Laura's, Laura is a friend of mine, and caring farm hospitality is priority."

"You should stay out of my life; nothing good for you can come from it."

The humming of the tires fills the silence. *No smooth talking is making this better.*

I pull onto the gravel road and park the truck right up beside the house. "The farmhouse is nothing fancy, but you'll be able to rest. Wait here and let me open the door."

Jake bounds outside and does his tire check. I slowly reach out my arms sliding them under Johnny, her eyes penetrate my soul. "You're both safe," I whisper finally feeling her release him. "Stay here. I'll come back and help you." I cradle Johnny in my arms, my heart is pounding as I lay him on the couch, and cover him with the quilt off my chair.

She is still in a trance when I return. She clutches my arm tight as she slides out of the truck. The pain on her face gives me shivers. I lead her through the kitchen into the living room. "Would you like another drink?"

She closes her eyes and shakes her head slowly. "I'll sleep at this end of the couch."

"You're the guest you can sleep in the bedroom." I feel her tense up. "There's no sleeping for me the beef must be fed. How about a hot shower?" She stands motionless, tenderly I walk her to the bathroom. Dig out a clean towel, washrag, and a new bar of soap, adjust the water and say, "It takes a bit to warm up."

She is still in a trance. "I suppose it's time for you to strip off my clothes."

I fold her petite hands into mine. "Promise." My voice trembles. "Cross my heart down-to-earth farm care." I close the door.

I dig out the smallest sweats, a t-shirt and flannel shirt for her wardrobe. They'll engulf her, but it's the best I can do. Steam rolls out when I crack the door and set the clothes on the vanity with one hand.

I turn on the headboard night-light and pull back the blankets. Not quite what I planned for Friday night clean sheets. Change into work clothes and throw the dirty ones in the corner. I gently carry Johnny into the waterbed. At least he'll be warm and won't fall out. Jake lies at the end of the bed. Digging in my closet, I found my keepsake teddy bear my mother insisted I save and tuck it in under Johnny's arm. He instantly squeezes it tight. I leave the door open enough for Jake to get out.

The night's excitement and pain swirl through my mind as I pour coffee and sit down in the lounger. Better not get too comfortable. She finally came out of the bathroom with her sleeves rolled up, the shirt buttoned to the top, and her wet hair wrapped in a towel. Panic on her face as she takes in the surroundings.

"Don't worry, I tucked him into bed." I point to the bedroom. "Jake is watching him."

She slowly takes a seat on the couch.

"Nice outfit."

"From what I heard, surprise, this is the sexiest thing you could find."

"Thought the flannels were the best for today. You want something to drink?"

"No, I'm over my limit." She glances toward the bedroom again.

"He's sound asleep."

She put the ice pack on her eye. "You have a nice place."

"An old farmhouse with country hospitality."

She sits in silence.

I sip my coffee. "You can sleep on the waterbed with him. It's a lot more comfortable than the couch."

She has her head propped on the ice bag. "I'm not sleeping in your bed."

"Might as well take advantage; it's warm with clean sheets. Besides, there's no sleep for me tonight. The beef feeding frenzy starts shortly."

Softly, she says, "I don't understand."

"People call them cows, but it's beef on the hoof, worth so much a pound. The bigger they are, the more they are worth." I rise out of the lounger and hold out my hand.

She closes her eyes, shakes her head.

"Time for me to go to work and for you to get some sleep."

She takes my hand as I guide her to the edge of the bedroom.

She trembles, staring at Johnny. "Where did the teddy bear come from?"

"It was mine when I was a kid. He was so restless ... seems like it helped." I hold on to her as she lies down. "Rest." I point to the light on the headboard. Her eyes reach my soul.

She touches my arm. "Thank you."

"You're welcome. Glad I could help." I motion for Jake and close the door.

Five

February 11, 1984

The wailing starts at the first sound of the John Deere roaring to the silage bunker. I scrape off the top layer of frozen silage and begin the sixteen trips to fill the feeding trough. The flashbacks of the night—eyes of fear, piercing my soul. It's not a magazine story.

I'm still trying to grasp the emotion running through me, Laura instantly snapping out of fun mode, into taking care of the crisis. *Where's the girl's family?*

Girls like Leslie are my type. Has a depressing moment. Stops for the weekend or on a weekday afternoon. Flaunts her gorgeous chest, and I give her a pick-me-up with a booster. We return to our lives and see you next time.

The bawling stops and turns to slobbering beef, money from heaven I say when Mom's not around. What's the rest of Marilyn's story? You marry someone who is incompatible and a lowlife; you become one yourself or get divorced. I squeeze the tractor tight against one side of the tool shed and plug it in, leaving enough room to park her car beside it.

***

It's after seven when I call Jason. When he answers I instantly say, "Glad you're up."

"Waiting for your call."

I lower my voice. "This is out of my norm."

"That's hard to believe."

"This one is serious. Someone's car is at the bar, and we don't want the world to know."

"And our hero steps in to comfort another damsel in distress."

"It's not me this time, but one of Laura's friends needs a hideout. And Mr. Mean will be looking for her today."

"That's the norm." Jason breaks out laughing. "And you are helping a deprived girl needing hospitality and exceptional care."

The phone cord is stretched to end as I let Jake in. "Couldn't leave her to fend for herself on a record cold night."

"Your help is in the cosmos, girls in distress drawn into your charming spell. So, you have her all tucked in and sleeping comfortably now?"

"Yeah, her kid too."

"Oh, this is interesting. She brought her kid?"

"I'll fill you in later, but she wasn't stopping for a social drink."

Jason says, "When are you going?"

"I'm going now, been up for twenty-four hours. I'll crash if I stop. I'll leave the truck at the bar and we can pick it up later if you want."

"I'll meet you—can't believe the trouble you find when I leave early."

"It'll be a Friday night for the history books."

Jason says, "A top secret fun winter day in 1984."

"Don't think she's had fun. Her old man is nasty, and she should be at the hospital. See you a half-hour."

I set cereal and bowls on the table with a note.

Marilyn

Went to retrieve your car. Help yourself to anything else you need. Make a list of what you like to eat, and I'll run up town later.

Keith

I grab coffee, pull the truck around by the toolshed, and grab some tools, cables, gas, and head to town.

I nose the truck up to her Pinto. Attaching the jumper cables and examining the four-cylinder lawn mower engine, I tried to grasp how small it is. The right side of the windshield reflects a spider crack from my flashlight. The mini trunk, not even big enough to hold a beer cooler. *Who's going to buy these puddle jumpers?*

I slide my leg halfway in, with my knee rubbing the steering wheel, and struggle to release the seat. With one leg outside, I turn the key. It cranks, but nothing except the whine of the starter. I pull myself out, grab the gas can. Headlights shine up the alley.

Jason parks his truck and walks around mine. "Okay, so what

kind—shit—" He freezes. "This belongs to the girl down the road from me."

"Oh, yeah."

"She's cute. Her husband—a top-notch jerk."

"We'll add wife-beater to his resume." I keep pouring gas into the car.

Jason glances at the windshield. "Remember when the hydraulic line blew and dropped the plow in the road?"

"Yeah."

"This is the guy. When I explained why you couldn't move the plow until it's repaired, he went into a tirade. 'Typical dumb farmer,' he pointed, 'it's sitting on wheels.' I bit my grin, asking if he has a license to drive a tractor."

"That was cocky of you." I add a splash of gas to the carb. "He was clueless?"

"I said it with a face that would've won me an Oscar. He stomped off, screaming something about being an ass."

"You probably were."

Jason sticks out his finger. "I learned from the best. The kid always stops playing and waves when I drive by with the tractor. Considered asking him if he wanted to go for a ride."

"Too late now. I already promised them both a ride." I squeeze into the car.

He leans around the hood "You move quick, that's why you get all the girls." Jason says, with his half-grin. "The interesting part, the next day she came and apologized. Opposites sure fit—such a dick and her trying to smooth everything over."

"Let's see if it'll start." Damn thing sputters as I flutter the gas pedal and kept it running.

Jason unhooks the cables and closes the hood. "So, do I dare ask how you--"

"I'll fill you in, but let's get out of town before anyone comes looking for a white Pinto. Follow me in my truck. We'll sneak out the back side of town."

"Okay."

The warm air and the twenty-mile-per-hour drive down the gravel roads of glass make this a dumb decision. I roll the window down halfway to keep some sub-zero air blowing on my face, freezing my eyelids open. I squeeze her car into the tool shed beside the tractor.

Before I uncoil from the car, Jason walks up beside me. "What's in the garbage bags?"

I stand, working the kinks out of my legs. "Clothes, I believe."

Jason jumps in the truck, with a grinning still plastered on his face. "She runs away from home, goes to the bar with her kid?"

We drive by Dad's house before I say, "Much as I can figure, she knew Laura would be working and would help her. The unbelievable part was seeing the kid in doggie-print pajamas walking up the sidewalk, looking for his Aunt Laura." I glance at Jason. "She was unconscious when we found her and lucky she didn't freeze to death."

Jason turns the radio down. "So, how did you end up with her at your house?"

"This John is a buddy of Bob's and they will be looking for her today." I glance quickly. "Doesn't know me. The vibes from Laura. Bob's days are numbered even as a renter. She needs a babysitter if you're interested."

"Surprised you haven't stepped up? Jason pauses before adding, "Laura was extra short with Bob the last time he stopped at the bar."

"Being we're all friends, thought you'd watch Chad and I'll take care of her other needs."

"You hadn't worked that out with Bob already?" He is grinning and shaking. "Your greedy self, you're probably already planning on taking care of them both."

"See, you're getting the wrong idea. Laura asked if I could hide Marilyn for a few days. Not sure Marilyn agrees, but—"

"She melted into your arms." He grins. "And you whisked her off her feet, and now she's sleeping in your bed."

I quit grinning and say, "Laura knows how sweet and caring I am. Personally, I thought she was dead when I first saw her. Way beyond my caring skills."

"Has to be a first. Did you tell her you're a certified gynecologist?"

Silence overcomes me as I visualize helplessness. "I can't shake the image. She had some old blue jeans with a ripped blouse exposing a bruise above her breast. Her old Kmart coat had the zipper jammed so it wouldn't close." My voice gets shaky. "Her eye was swollen half shut with dried blood under her nose when I lifted her out of the car."

Jason looks at his watch. "We've got time. Let's go kick the shit out of him."

"I wanted to do that last night. Figured he should wake up with a hangover, he would be days recovering."

"Why didn't she call the police?" Jason asks as he waves at Hank crossing the street to the coffee shop.

"Not sure, but the county sheriff stopped for the nightly check, and I stretched the truth about taking care of the bartender—"

"This week—or just today?"

I flip him off. "I should've told them; they would've arrested him. But the strange part is she went into panic mode when I said they stopped."

Jason says, "Last summer, her car was gone for at least a couple of months."

"Had a feeling about this not being the first time."

"Don said they're always behind on the rent. He feels sorry for her, or he would've evicted them."

"She seems too nice to fit the bitch category. Her husband John didn't just slap her and realize he shouldn't." Her swollen black-and-blue face made me pause. "The kid flinched when I wiped a tear off his face. She is in major pain; he hurt her bad." I pull into the alley and put the truck in park. "She must trust Laura." I glance at Jason ... "She went home with a complete stranger."

"So, your elegant reputation." A slow grin absorbs Jason's face as he says, "A woman leaves her husband in the middle of the night. You take her home, and she's sleeping in your bed by morning."

"I tucked her and the kid in the waterbed, perfect gentleman status." Intensely I hold my gaze. "Even God would have been proud."

"You're lucky he doesn't know everything."

"Went and fed the cows. Smart ass."

"I promise not to ruin your reputation." He raises his right hand. "Your secret is safe with me." Jason climbs out of the truck. "Are you going uptown tonight?"

"Was planning on it—going to need sleep, eventually."

"You'd better stay home with the wife and kid. They say that's how it happens. Most eligible bachelor in town one day has a one-night stand, finds love, wakes up with a wife, and you are always outdoing everyone, adding a kid too."

"Thanks for the help. Just go home, asshole. When I'm looking for the next life critic, I'll call."

"I'll tell everyone there is an extra barstool. You became a family man." He closes the door.

I roll the window down. "Shit seriously, don't tell anybody."

He sticks his head in. "Your secret is safely tucked in at the farm."

"Yeah, the worst part..." I drop my grin. "Is trying to explain to my old man."

"You're saying he won't believe you're not sleeping with her?"

Six

February 11, 1984

Light shines through a crack in the curtain as Marilyn tries to focus. The waterbed rolls as she moves slightly to see the clock, 11:07 A.M.; the scattered money, lying in the dust, holds her attention when the clock flips 11:08.

She sits motionless, not wanting to wake Johnny, looking around the room. *I am in a man's water bed whom I met a few hours ago. No way to leave. No clothes to wear, and what's his last name? How come I'm so calm?*

Johnny is sleeping peacefully with the teddy bear tucked under his arm. *How many women have slept here?* She stares at the drawer in the nightstand. According to Mom, every guy has secrets in the nightstand, and then hearing her say, 'You stayed overnight with a guy from the bar!'

Just has a teddy bear? Has Johnny ever slept this peacefully after John threw his in the fire? The stream of light reveals a walnut-colored dresser with a pile of clothes on the floor beside it.

Johnny wakes up and rubs his eyes. "Where are we, Mommy?"

"Someplace safe."

He holds the teddy bear up in front of his face. "Mommy, look! Can I keep it?"

"No, it belongs to Uncle Keith." She tightens her lips.

"Why does he have a teddy bear? He's all grown up?"

"I don't know but make sure nothing happens to it." She sits up straighter and says, "We're not here for handouts, and don't start asking for stuff."

"I wish I still had my teddy bear."

"I know, dear."

Johnny moves close. "Mommy, I like sleeping with you."

"I like sleeping with you, too." She hugs him, feeling the pain in her ribs.

"How come this bed feels all mushy?"

"It's a waterbed."

"What's a waterbed?"

"It's filled with water instead of springs."

He pushes down, and the bed moves.

"That's enough."

He rolls, watching it move. "Mommy, I have to go potty."

Marilyn rolls out of bed. "Okay, just remember to be quiet."

Jake perks his head up when she opens the door.

Johnny says, "Look, a doggie."

She puts her finger over her lips and whispers, "Yes, dear, he was guarding your room." She guides Johnny to the bathroom while stealing a quick glance at Keith, sleeping in the recliner. His mouth is open, but his shoulders and arms stretch the white T-shirt tight.

The mirror reveals the reality of a black-and-blue swollen eye. She rolls her puffed lip, exposing a nasty cut inside. Next, trying to improve the fit of the oversize flannel shirt, she pulls and tucks it in the sweatpants and ties them tight. She fingers the matted side of her hair, trying to match the frizz mess on the other side. Her clothes from last night are still arranged in a neat pile, making sure her underwear is out of view. She takes the toothpaste out of the holder with only one toothbrush. She turns to Johnny. "Hold out your finger." She puts a dab of toothpaste on it. "Rub it on your teeth."

"This is a funny way to brush your teeth. Why don't we use the toothbrush?" Johnny points to the rack.

She cringes, remembering using hers to brush Johnny's teeth before. "You can't use someone else's toothbrush." She motions to be quiet when they go through the living room.

Johnny pulls on her shirt and points to the toys. She pushes him along toward the kitchen. Jake trots to the outside door and looks at them. She whispers to Johnny, "I think he wants to go outside." The icy wind hits her in the face when she cracks the door. They watch together as Jake runs towards Keith's truck.

Johnny giggles. "Look, Mommy, he is peeing on the tire."

"Boy doggies do that."

"Mommy, how do you know it's a boy dog?"

She lets Jake in the house. "I just do."

Johnny gives Jake a hug. "He is cold." Johnny's eyes are glassy as he says, "When are we getting a doggie?"

Marilyn looks away and takes some hard breaths. *A place to live first.*

"Someday, dear." Marilyn reads the note stuck under the cereal bowls. "Guess he knew he'd still be sleeping."

Johnny says, "Can I have the Sugar Pops?"

"Yes, Uncle Keith set them out for us to eat."

"Mommy, he was really nice to me."

She digs the milk out and fixes Johnny a bowl of cereal, hoping it will slow down the questions. She picks up the empty coffeepot, ponders, opens the cupboard above it, and finds the coffee and makes some. Her hands are shaking when she realizes she just helped herself.

The questions from Johnny continue to bombard her, and her questions with no answers. *Where's the car? And where's my purse?* She goes over to her coat and boots to check on them. Nothing. *Why does he want to help me, us? How will I ever pay him back? You realize the answer.*

Johnny is staring at her the whole time and says, "How did we get here without your car?"

"We rode in Uncle Keith's truck." *It sounds strange calling him an uncle.*

"I like his truck. It has big tires. Is that why the dog peed on them?"

"I don't know."

Johnny finishes his cereal. "When are we going for a ride on the tractor?"

"Johnny." She lowers her voice. "We can't be asking ... Uncle Keith to do stuff for us."

"He said he would give me a ride, and we could see cows."

"You have to be patient; Uncle Keith was up all night taking care of us." She pours coffee and adds milk. *You can live without cream.* "He had to feed the cows before he could go to sleep. We can't be making more work for him."

"Can I play with the toys?"

"No, Uncle Keith is sleeping, and you must ask first." Marilyn shakes her head.

"Does he have kids who live here?"

"No." *I don't think so.*

"Why does he have so many toys?"

"I don't know."

"I was scared last night."

"You were very brave, and I'm extremely proud of you."

"Uncle Keith helped me find Aunt Laura. Are we going to live here?"

"For a few days." *Wonder when he'll quit asking so many questions.*

"How come we never visited Uncle Keith if he is part of our family?" The phone rings.

Marilyn rests her arms on the table to keep them from trembling.

Johnny's eyes are staring. "Mommy—why are you not answering the phone?"

Seven

February 11, 1984

The ringing phone brings me to consciousness as I stagger to the kitchen. Click and a dial tone. The smell of fresh coffee and my guest's brown eyes transfix me. I mumble, "Someday, I'm going to buy me one of those answering machines." Jake is wagging his tail and runs to me as I scruff his ear. "Do you need to go out?"

Marilyn, slightly above a whisper, says, "I let him out. Hope that was okay?"

"The coffee made. The dog let out. You're trying to impress me?" I walk to the counter behind them and pour some coffee.

"I won't be impressing anyone for a long time."

"No disbelieving allowed." Neither of them moves as I take a seat. "How were the accommodations?"

The kid's brown eyes matching hers are penetrating my heart. She says, "It's very generous of you to give up your bed."

Johnny says shyly, "The bed is all mushy."

I break into a grin.

Marilyn says, "We've never slept in a waterbed."

"It has a calming effect, even better with ..." I shake the Sugar Pops box, hearing a few. Look at Johnny. "Did you have enough?"

He nods slowly.

Marilyn whispers, "What do you say?"

"Thank you."

"I'll get more." I nod towards him. "Teddy didn't wake you up, did he? He used to get up early."

He looks at the bear. Marilyn answers, "It was nice of you—"

"My daddy threw mine in the fire—" Johnny's voice trembles. "Said men don't sleep with dolls."

I wink at him. "We all need someone to sleep with. Teddy sleeps with me when I am lonely."

He is trying not to giggle. "You're grown-up."

"I pretend to be grown-up, trying to fool everyone. But it's a secret, so don't tell anyone." He is still staring, but I can see a small smile develop. "Did you see the toys?"

Johnny looks up at his mother.

"You can answer."

His eyes dance from his mother and then to me.

"You want to play with them?"

He holds his gaze on Marilyn.

"Come on." I wave for him to follow me. "This is the playroom." I point at the center of the living room over to the other wall. "Kid's side, with a mini toy farm, tractors, and trucks in the toy box. By the wall there's more Lincoln Logs. Tear down the log cabin and build anything you want. The fun part—no picking up the toys; leave them out for the next time."

He sets the teddy bear against the toy box and opens it. "You have a lot of toys." He pulls out the tractor.

I say, "My kid image."

Jake lies down, and Johnny drives the tractor toward the log house.

"You watch Jake while I visit with your mom?"

He never looks up but says, "Okay."

I watch him for a moment before I turn to the kitchen. I pick up my coffee cup, motion if she wants more. She looks at her empty cup.

I hold up my hand. "Sit. I'll get it."

She leans back.

"Relax." I pour some.

She stammers out, "Thank you."

I sit back down and slowly say, "The kid must like tractors?"

She nods. "Yes. He has a plastic one with a wobbly wheel. He always stopped and watched when the neighbor drives by, but we don't expect to be entertained. And he'll live without a tractor ride. We've imposed on you enough."

"Anything to impress how cool I am." I lean back in my chair. "It touches my heart seeing him so excited. Although I'd deny the heart thing in public."

Caring creeps onto her face as she looks away. "Caring for us will only bring trouble to your life. I'll find someplace to go."

"You found a place. Sit back, relax, chill, drink some cocktails, tell stories, snuggle up till spring. You'll want to leave before planting starts; life becomes all work."

She seems to relax. "I wish life could be so simple, but John will—"

"Get an ass kicking he'll never forget."

"Please, he can't find out we stayed here." She holds her breath. "He's crazy enough to go buy a gun and come after you."

"He won't find out, but if he did, I know cops and other caring people. We'll make sure he gets the proper message." I touch the top of her hand. "Trust me, nobody is messing with you."

She doesn't move it. "I can't remember parts of what happened last night. How did I get into the bar?"

"I carried you."

"I just let you carry me."

"You were unconscious."

"I must have looked—"

"Like you needed help. You should be proud of your kid. He knew you were in trouble and was determined to find Laura."

"The hell he's been through—everything is my fault. It was closing time. Figured Laura would be out soon. I must've fallen asleep."

"Your car ran out of gas."

"Is it still there?"

"No, I called my friend Jason. He met me, and we put it in the tool shed. Needed some gas and a jump is all. According to the world, you officially vanished."

"Jason." She rubs her chin. "He didn't ask why?"

"He's known me long enough not to ask questions. The white Pinto surprised him, not many around." I pause and say, "Jason is your neighbor."

"Oh, my God. Everybody in town will know. What did you tell him?"

"The truth. You had a disagreement with your husband. I offered you a cozy farm house charming hospitality, hot coffee, a warm waterbed, and you couldn't resist."

Terror stream down her cheeks. She says, "When am I scheduled for the exam?"

My voice gets shaky. "Sorry ..." I straighten up, focusing on her demeanor. "People say I'm a little suggestive ... but trying to express my caring is all."

Her eyes acquire sadness. "You can do better than me."

"Priority is to get you healed up. Think of me as your dedicated butler, nurse, cook, and nanny. Life will look better. When Laura gets here, we'll put a plan together."

She closes her eyes, sipping coffee. "You're not afraid of me becoming too bossy."

The phone rings. I answer it on the second ring. "Hello?"

"How is everything?"

"Everything is great here. She's already decided I'm the greatest guy she's ever met. She made coffee this morning. Jake and Johnny have become best friends. True farm hospitality, taking care of her every desire."

"I hope part of it is true. Bob's uptown getting a new battery for his car and is beyond his normal piss-ass self."

"You can be awfully demanding, making it hard for a guy to satisfy you."

"Oh, shut up."

"She squeaked out a complaint about the wardrobe options; the cozy flannel shirt and sweats weren't her size. I added some cheer suggesting clothes are optional."

Laura says, "Keith—damn you, it's not the bar—let me talk to her."

I walk towards Marilyn. "Her first night in a waterbed was beyond her wildest dreams." Letting my hand linger on her soft hand.

Marilyn says, "Hello," And gazes at me. "He's trying to cheer me up. He's been a perfect host. Did you call earlier?"

"Yes."

I head to the living room with my coffee.

When I return for more Marilyn is still on the phone. "John should be in raging bull mode by now; can't believe he hasn't called or showed up." Marilyn pulls the phone away and gazes at me. "I heard something in the background and then a click. She hung up."

I take the receiver and hang it up. "Give her a minute. She'll call back." *Bob was going uptown. She would've waited till he was gone.*

Fear overwhelms Marilyn's face. "John's there—"

"Laura knows how to handle herself." I lay a pad and pen in front of her. "Why don't you make a list? I'll run up to the store." *And check on Laura.*

"We can get by with peanut butter and jelly."

"You're at a farm that grows the best beef money can buy. I have a whole freezer full. Mom has all kinds of homemade canned fruits and vegetables. My cooking is nothing like Mom's, but as you can see, I'm not starving, and Mom refuses to cook for me during the week."

She looks up from her list with slight smile. "Seems like you're managing fairly well. I hate to ask but we could use toothbrushes. I have some money in my purse."

"I put your purse in Laura's car, thinking ..."

She looks away. "Sorry for involving you."

"Glad I was there." I open the fridge door. "Since you're hanging out for a few days, add food you like." I look over her shoulder. "We'll need more Sugar Pops, and what do you normally put in your coffee?"

"We don't need the extras."

"Let me ask Johnny what he needs, like his favorite ice cream and cookies."

She looks down with a small smile creeping out. "Laura said you spoil Chad, too."

"Kids are easy to make happy. Show them the toys, offer rides on the tractor and snowmobile, buy ice cream, and I'm a legend."

"You have some magic Johnny is normally clinging to me." Marilyn's dimple comes out. "I don't expect you to support us."

A grin seeps out. "I live to save damsels in distress, and don't worry, there's extra bedrooms." Quietly I say, "Have you thought about seeing a doctor? The way you're wincing, I'd guess you have some cracked ribs. Can't do much for them, but you should have them looked at."

She says, "We went to the hospital last summer, after one of our fights. They called the police, of course. Made out a report. The hospital admitted me and took it upon themselves to call foster care. They arrived to take Johnny. I completely lost it, telling them they weren't taking him. Four o'clock in the morning, the police drove me to my mother's. She wasn't pleased and lectured me about what I should've done. It was a nightmare." Marilyn goes silent. "Her great wisdom would approve letting a guy take me home is better than waking her up, although she would deny it."

The phone rings. "Laura's calling, be my guess. Hello."

"Sorry I had to hang up. I had a visitor."

I look at Marilyn, who is staring at me. "Everything okay?"

"Yeah, is Marilyn freaking out?"

I stretch the cord towards the table. "She's forgotten her past life and is dreaming of the glorious life at the farm."

Marilyn takes the receiver and says, "John showed up, didn't he?"

I walk into the living room. I sit on the floor by Johnny, put my finger over my mouth, and whisper, "What kind of ice cream do you like?"

He looks at the kitchen before saying, "Chocolate."

"Good choice. I'll add more Sugar Pops and chocolate ice cream to the list. They're both my favorites." I give Jake a pat on the head.

Johnny's dark eyes are lasers at me.

"What's the matter?"

He whispers, "Are we going on a tractor ride?"

I grin. "Tomorrow, hopefully your mom will feel better."

Marilyn is still at the table talking. I hold up the list on the way out the door.

Her face has a soft glow as she lips, "Thank you."

My body quivers. *Shouldn't I give you a kiss?*

Eight

February 11, 1984

Laura blinks the sleep from her eyes, trying to compartmentalize her messed-up life. The smell of stale, empty beer cans, a plate with leftover bread crust on the coffee table and Bob's bedroom door closed. *Must be sleeping off a hangover.* She dials the farm, but no one answers. Glancing out the window, Bob is bent under the hood of his car.

She pours a cup of coffee. The joy still tingles in her thoughts, but Marilyn's crisis and dealing with Mr. Slob ruins the memory quickly.

She laughs to herself, the romantic dream world before going to sleep. When Mr. Right waltzes into the bar, buys her a drink, makes love to her, *takes me home and the fireworks continue.* Only in the movies. She fights to add a kick to the coffee, instead of the reality. *Bob's un-wowing excitement, so why did I ... then again. You're such a fool.*

Bob comes in from outside and sets his boots on the tray.

"What are you doing?" Laura squints, trying to shake off yesterday.

"The car won't start. Battery is dead." He is rubbing his hands together. "Must have been a wild after party, a little late getting home."

"It's winter. Everyone is stir crazy. We had a few drinks, nothing out of the ordinary."

"Seems to be a new habit." He pours coffee. "Without Chad, we could have fun together?"

"We are now. Enjoy the quiet."

"We have alone time, and you want to sip coffee? Do you remember the last time I saw you naked?"

"Don't plan on it ever happening again."

"Maybe if you had a daytime job, we could spend the evening like normal couples."

"Well, none of them will pay me enough." She closes her eyes, trying to block the ugliness, and says, "We're not building a bonding relationship."

Bob leans forward and says, "The flirting at work seems to have changed your priorities at home."

"I told you to forget it how long ago?" Laura shakes her head. "Thought you were coming to check on my flirting?"

"I had a couple of beers after work at Jack's, and the car wouldn't start. Decided to come straight home. Waited up ... thought you'd—"

"You're shutting me off?"

"If that's what you want to call it. More like it never happened." Laura rubs her hands under the table and glares at him.

Bob drops his head and goes into sad puppy-dog mode.

Laura holds her glare. "This arrangement didn't include fringe benefits. Pack it away in the forgotten memories."

Bob sets his cup in the sink, grabs his coat and her keys off the hook. "Not taking your car, need to jump mine and go get a battery."

Laura sits in a trance. "Leave the keys in it. I'm going to go uptown later."

Five minutes later, Bob comes back into the house, carrying a purse. "Awful trusting, leaving your purse in the car." He throws it across the table.

She freezes, her heart pounding.

"Don't panic. I didn't look at your secret phone book."

She catches her breath. "I was exhausted."

"Or extra buzzed?" He is standing in the doorway with his wet boots. "Who was there?"

"Shirley and Keith." Laura's heart is still pounding.

"He spends a lot of time there."

"It's winter. He's always there." She's rubbing her hands. "When are you cleaning up the mess you're making?" She stares at the water on the floor. "Remember the living room too."

"I know Keith." Bob exhales a long breath. "Was too cold for a quickie in the parking lot ... so you girls do him right on the bar, make a lasting threesome."

"Only in your dream world does it happen. He doesn't date waitresses, and we made a pact years ago ..." *Why am I defending myself?*

He stares at me. "You with a buzz, and Keith's phony macho woman charm, which makes me want to gag, women can't spread their legs fast enough—"

"If it makes you feel better—he suggested the threesome. But we weren't in the mood."

"Which of you took care of him first?"

"He was joking."

"Yeah right." A smirk forms on Bob's face. "You both said, think you can handle us, and humble Keith says, 'Not tonight girls, I'm too tired.'" Bob says, "I don't live in the bar like you, but I've been in a bar and it's professional bullshit—" He turns and leaves the water puddle.

"You are such an ass—"

***

Laura throws in a load of laundry and is screaming profanity, walking by the coffee table of crumbs, empty beer cans, with a half a bag of chips—on the floor. Finally, grips her emotions enough to dial the farm.

Keith answers, and his joyful good morning makes her heart flutter. He rambles his normal sexy small talk as she scolds him, but it lifts her spirits.

He puts Marilyn on the phone.

Laura relaxes as she can feel Marilyn's calmness. Horrified, she hangs up as John crashes through the door, and she screams. "Get out of here."

John walks past her as if she is not even there, leaving his wet boot tracks across the kitchen floor. "Is Marilyn here?" He stands in the kitchen doorway studying the living room.

"Get out of my house."

John turns inches from her face, his jaw tight. "Where's my wife?"

"She's not here. Take your worthless ass out of here before I call the police." She grabs the receiver.

He grabs her hand, pulls the receiver out of it and hears the dial tone. "Where is she?" He slams the receiver.

He pushes Laura against the wall, his stale beer breath gagging her. "Another fight?"

"Yeah, if it's any of your business, she was bitching because she had to fix her working husband something to eat, which any halfway decent wife would do. No 'thank you' or 'glad you're home.' No, just continue bitching on and on and on. Who were you talking to?"

"None of your business."

"You're overly calm." He relaxes his hold. "She had this planned. Goaded me into hitting her."

"I'm proud of her." A small grin slides out.

"Yeah, funny—you're not worried she could've frozen to death; it was sub-zero weather last night. Her mother is ready to put out a missing-person alert. I told her to wait until I talk to you."

"She must've handled it, or she would've called."

"You're lying to me. She does nothing without your approval."

Laura quips. "My guess is she went to the safe house and reported your worthless ass."

"It was a couple of slaps."

"Well, then you have nothing to worry about except starving to death before you find someone to feed you."

"Yeah, right, she took the money. We needed to pay the landlord."

He steps inches from her, blocking her from slipping by him.

He grabs her wrist and says, "The landlord is pissed. Gave us an eviction notice to be out at the end of the month."

Laura grins. "It's terrible; you need a cook and a place to live."

"I'll find her, and people are going to pay. You're at the top of the list."

Laura spits out, "Case you forgot, I have friends tougher than you, and after you're out of prison, I'll have them stop and visit your wimpy ass."

He squeezes and twists her wrist.

"I'm happy she is planning a life without you. Now get out of my house."

He pushes her against the wall, his face inches from hers. "I should bend you over and teach you a lesson."

She turns her head, trying to keep from gagging. "Let go of me."

"You're a teasing bitch." He twists her wrist harder. "If Bob weren't my buddy, I'd teach you what we do with women who are teasers." He pushes away. "Better if he teaches you."

Laura is shaking.

He slams the door.

Laura opens it and screams, "Stick that ego, you worthless piece of shit."

He turns, straightens up, and puts his hands on his hips. "You want it—don't you?"

Nine

February 11, 1984

Laura is shaking as she walks away from the door, digs out the bottle of tequila, and takes a swig. She fills a shot glass and carries it to the table. *Bob could be home anytime.* She takes Marilyn's purse and swaps the wallet and throws her purse in a paper bag. Runs to the bedroom, grabs whatever is on top for clothes. Holding up the bra, she smiles. *She'll lose a couple of sizes squeezing into it.* She adds an extra sweatshirt and pants to her beach bag. She scouts the road for cars before running outside and tossing it in the trunk of the car. Sets Marilyn's purse where she keeps hers. After a few long breaths, she downs the shot, and calls Keith's.

"Hello."

"I had a visitor."

"Is everything okay?"

"Yes, made his threat and left." And says, "I'll be over soon. Let me talk to Marilyn."

Marilyn pauses and says, "Is everything okay?"

"Yes, he's so predictable. He went to your mother's and then my house."

"Did he hit you?"

"He fears the consequences." Laura is pacing the kitchen as far as the cord reaches. "Bob went uptown to get a battery. I'm finishing the laundry, and then I'll be over."

"Just what you need on top of your problems is my problems."

"I'd be great if I could spend a couple of weeks in the Bahamas. I've packed you a few clothes and have your purse."

"Keith said he left it in your car."

***

Laura fixes something to eat, fighting the urge ... shaking, she puts the bottle away. Bob's car pulls in, she takes extra deep breaths and a bite of her sandwich.

Bob storms in with the same foul mood he left with and says, "Fixing lunch for yourself only."

Laura lifts her eyebrows slowly. "I'm not your mother, and I don't see you carrying any groceries."

"Sorry, it's a shitty week. A short paycheck and getting ripped off for a new battery haven't helped."

"And with your superior money management skills, make you anger dipping into your savings."

"You could show a bit of sympathy."

"Because you're a slob and won't learn to manage money. Everyone is devastating for you."

"You're seeing someone else?"

"Where did that come from?" *As if I would tell you.*

"Because you decided and forgot to mention something so trivial to me."

"Us was a bad idea, which became shitty. Because of some sex, now you are in love." Laura takes the last bite of sandwich. "We're not living in the fifty's."

He sits rubbing his chin. "Are you throwing me out?"

"No, but you better start cleaning up after yourself or I'll bill you for maid service."

His face tightens. "There's a lot of shit happening."

"Let me add to your happiness." Laura straightens. "Your asshole buddy John showed up here. She exams her wrist. "Some advice for him and you, is to convince him not to let that happen again."

Bob becomes stoical and doesn't answer.

"And in case you're not caught up on the social happenings. Marilyn left him, and now he's harassing and blaming everyone except himself." Laura rinses off her plate. "My guess is he beat her up again, although he denied it. Once I talk to her, I may go take care of the problem myself."

Laura finishes the laundry, and Bob picks up his beer cans, but moments later he makes a sandwich and plops in front of the TV. She walks by him, shaking her head. "I'm going uptown to get groceries. You should pry yourself off the couch and run the vacuum."

***

Laura goes to Keith's, gives a soft knock, Jake makes a small wolf, and is waging his tail as she pets him and she follows him into the living room. Johnny glances up from the toys. Marilyn is on the couch, sleeping.

She waves at him and whispers, "How are you doing?"

"I'm having fun. Look at the toys."

"I see you are taking over the living room."

Marilyn stirs and looks around.

Johnny says, "Uncle Keith ... said it was okay."

Laura smiles. "Chad loves to visit." Laura's heart skips a beat as Marilyn puts the ice pack on her eye. She looks dreadful with her bruised face, her eye swollen shut, and the oversize flannel shirt.

Laura looses her smile and says, "How are you feeling?"

She leans close, whispering, "As bad as I look."

Johnny comes over carrying a tractor and the teddy bear. "Aunt Laura, this is like a real tractor and my teddy bear."

"Johnny, it's not yours to keep."

He scowls. "I know, Mom."

Laura says, "You must like Uncle Keith?"

"He went to buy me ice cream. Tomorrow we're going for a ride on a real tractor."

Marilyn blurts, "Johnny, I told you not to be begging for stuff."

"He told me, Mommy."

Marilyn brushes his hair back. "Okay, we'll see. Johnny, let me talk to Aunt Laura. She can't stay. You can tell her the stuff later when she comes back to visit."

He goes and plays. Jake tags behind him.

"He's made himself at home." Laura watches him and slides closer to Marilyn. "Snuck out a few clothes when Bob was gone. At least you have something to wear until Monday."

"What happened with John?"

"Scared and confuse, would be my first assessment."

"I feel terrible getting everyone involved."

"We're friends, so quit worrying. Where's Keith?"

"He went to get groceries, adding to my guilt, him taking care of us."

"He loves it although hidden behind his ego most of the time."

"He keeps apologizing." She smiles. "His remarks should be offensive, but they make me feel like some special babe—"

"Don't be afraid to tell him to stop—he gets carried away. Good bet John will stop at the bar tonight, and we can add to his confusion. Did Keith say he was coming up?"

"He didn't say what he was doing."

"You getting settled in yet?"

"I can't stay here, but I'm not in panic mode. When was the last time you saw Johnny not clinging to me?" They glance over. "I haven't known Keith for a day, yet I feel safe. I can't explain it."

"He has a gift ..." Laura scans his trophy case. "I told Bob our mini-relationship was over again." She takes some calming breaths. "I'll smooth it over a bit, so he stays at least until the end of summer."

"Laura, this is crazy, me staying here."

Laura shakes her head. "We'll take a quick trip to your house on Monday and get your clothes."

Marilyn flinches when she moves. "You think my wardrobe needs help?"

Laura smiles.

"You heard the suggested alternative?" Tears form. "He was trying to cheer me up, but the ugliness ... I'll never be able ..."

"Give it time. We should go on Monday and file assault charges."

"Not sure I want to live through that again, and John will go ballistic with more reason to come after you."

"Quit worrying; I would love to see him in jail. John knows my dad would make his life a living hell if he does anything to me."

"Keith's friend Jason helped get my car this morning. He was my neighbor."

"I forgot he lives down the road." Laura rolls her lip. "Perfect. We'll move your stuff down to his house."

"Laura."

"Ponder that thought, love yah. Your clothes and purse are on the table. If I can get out of the house without Bob asking too many questions, I'll come see you tomorrow."

Marilyn winces as she tries to move.

Laura gives her a hug and says, "Rest, gotta run."

Ten

February 11, 1984

Johnny glances from his make-believe world as Marilyn walks by, on her way to the kitchen. She gazes through the kitchen window above the sink, absorbed in details of farm picture. A two-car garage with peeled white paint. Farther is the tool shed and, across the driveway to the right, the barn, and pen for the cows.

Still in her picture, grabs the bag of clothes, walks to the bathroom, unbuttons the top buttons of the oversized flannel shirt, and lets it slide to the floor. The dark purple, green consuming her right side, including her breast. She grips the counter, the punch that made her gasp and give in to hell. Quiet tears flow; she turns away and puts on the blue jeans. She hooks Laura's bra, which brings instant pain, and she puts it back in the bag. The torn strap and bent clips on her bra, the nightmare of it being ripped off. Trembling, she sits on the edge of the tub buries her face in her hands and cries.

There's a knock at the door.

She grabs the sweatshirt—covering her.

"Mommy, are you okay?"

She sucks in a scream from the pain, yanking on the sweatshirt. "Yes, dear. I'm okay."

"You are crying."

Jake is whimpering.

"I'm fine, dear." Wiping her face, she takes another look in the mirror. The horror. She opens the door.

She kneels, hugs Johnny, and pets Jake. "He's your new friend."

Johnny pets Jake and says, "Why were you crying?"

"It's my happy-sad cry. Now go play." She lies on the couch with a new ice pack. Trying to breathe so that it doesn't hurt.

***

Marilyn hears whispering, awakes out of her sleep. Keith was lying on the floor, his head propped up with his arm. Johnny is pointing and giggling. She is hallucinating, Johnny talking to a guy.

Johnny sees her and says, "Hi Mommy. Uncle Keith is showing me how to put the Lincoln Logs together."

"I see that." Marilyn chokes back the tears. Keith sits up with an overwhelming kid grin.

Keith says to Johnny, "You work on the barn, and I'm going to find your mom something fun to do."

"Okay."

Keith turns to Marilyn. "I made coffee." Keith holds his arm out, never losing his rugged grin on the way to the kitchen. "I was telling Johnny when spring comes, I'd teach him how to drive a real tractor. He's excited but wanted me to teach you too."

Marilyn laughs but winces with pain and whispers, "I don't think you want us hanging around until spring."

"He declared me his favorite uncle and figured you'd want to stay for the next couple of months of partying." He sets the cups on the table. "When the non-stop work begins, you could qualify for a promotion to agricultural assistant, and Johnny is your helper."

Marilyn is shaking her head, trying to hold back a smile. "You've made big plans."

"The dream job, the likeness of being at the beach. Playing in the sand, dirt blown and sticking to every body part, adding a daily picnic and a tan. There are no set hours; you just hang out until the sun goes down." He is grinning. "The tan is a stretch, and the pay ... comes with a room, meals, and the bonus is all the beer you can drink."

She pours cream into her coffee. "Two beers were my limit, and I haven't drunk anything since I was old enough to drink."

"Great, we won't need to expand the budget to cover two beers. And with no hangover, you'll be crisp and ready for the next day."

She bites her lip and winces.

"The little dimple is coming out." He points at her.

"Stop making me laugh." She catches her breath finally. "Talking about beer, Laura was asking if you were going to the bar tonight."

"Kind of rude to leave my new guest."

"Please..." Marilyn bites her lip. "I don't want everyone messed up in my shit life. Laura said she's not afraid, but he'll show and ..."

"When the time comes, we'll take care of it. I can lay on BS and become his bar buddies—"

"No—he's been in lots of bar fights. I don't know what happened earlier today, but Laura was rattled when she came here. Promise me you won't—"

He reaches for her hand. "Wimps that can beat up women don't scare me. I played football and broke all kinds of records." He grins and raises his voice an octave. "The inside of football, they didn't play fair. The realistic truth is a lot of testosterone competing for the hottest girls and bragging about who is the best." He stares at her. "I was. That's a threat in guy talk."

"Even more reason to be careful. He hated ... athletes." She peers over her cup. "Can I ask a favor? I need to call my sister's, and it is long distance."

"Sure, it's included with the rent."

Marilyn calmly raises her eyes and holds her gaze at Keith. "You add too many free comforts, I'll become a leech."

"You don't fit the type. Besides, you'll be tired of me telling you how great I am after a month and run away. When the sixteen-hour days start, with no time to ... I become moody and stressed."

She gazes at him and says, "Johnny is having fun and won't want to leave." *Me either.*

"Yep, he was wondering why you never talked about me or came to visit before."

"What did you tell him?"

"The truth. You wanted to but his dad doesn't like me." Keith tips his head up slightly. "You updated your wardrobe."

She crosses her arms over her chest. *He noticed no bra.*

"The flannel shirt had a certain appeal at the right moment, of course." Keith finishes his drink. "Scheduling to eat about four thirty, if that's okay with you."

"We'll adjust to your schedule."

"After we eat, and I feed the cows. We'll catch up on our juicy history."

"Mine is ugly and you don't want to be caught up in it."

"It's the next game to win. I'll go meet this nemesis of yours and set a plan to take him out of your future."

Marilyn stares at him. "I remember when you won the championship; I was a freshman. For a ... star football player, you were always nice to everyone. I'm surprised you are not ... never mind."

"Married?" Keith leans forward.

She stutters. "It's none of my business. Sorry—"

Keith waves his hand. "Relax. I thought the whole town knew. The homecoming king is dumped by the queen to marry a doctor or lawyer, not a macho farm boy. Been telling the women since, just looking for a good time, no commitments. I can be your prince tonight, but I turn into a farm boy in the morning, and they're running to town." Keith refills the coffee. "So, what kind of charm did your husband woo you with?"

"You mean the wisdom of my mother continually saying, 'You'd better hurry. The good ones will be taken'? Then, my sister Ann slips on a low-cut blouse and adds a charming word, guys stumbling and drooling over her." She glances out into space. "It was sickening some days, but she found herself a rich husband, has two kids and a nice suburban home, with a fenced-in backyard."

"Young, we don't do much listening?"

"I had to get out of the house after my sister left, college was out of the question. John wooed my mom and ... My stepfather is another ugly story ... with no money or place to live." Tears come to her eyes. "A frog comes along and promises me a happy home." She takes a drink. "He never turned into a prince." She says, "I can't believe you're ..."

"Glad I can help."

"I am so thankful but the risk you are taking ..."

Keith winks at her. "Quit worrying, it keeps life exciting."

She says slowly, "I hate to ask you, but Johnny's clothes are in the car—"

"Relax." Keith drains his coffee. "I'll move your car into the garage and bring in the bags."

The room takes on an eerie silence once he is gone. Marilyn wanders over to the trophy case.

Johnny pulls on her hand. "What are you looking at, Mommy?"

"The trophies Uncle Keith won playing football in high school."

"Wow, he has a lot of them."

"Yes, he was the best player we ever had, and they won the state championship." She points to the top. "That big one is the trophy."

Johnny just stares.

Eleven

February 11, 1984

I walk into the cement block two car garage behind the house, with the Vette on one side the Polaris and a mess on the other. Pulling the Polaris out first and put it in the toolshed alongside the tractor. Then three trips filling the bucket on the tractor and stacking that stuff in the tool shed. I pull the Pinto tight against the wall, leaving a nice space between the Vette.

I'm still smiling at myself as I set the bags of clothes inside the door. Hang my Carhart's on the pegs. Jake comes to get his pat, and Johnny stands in the doorway, examining everything. Marilyn finally walks through the doorway. I say, "That took longer than expected. Someone made a mess in that garage."

Marilyn relaxes. "I'm sorry we are causing you extra work."

"It's not extra, just overdue." I look down at Johnny. "Are you getting hungry?"

He nods slowly.

"On it." I dig out the potatoes and get ready to peel them.

Marilyn walks beside me and says, "I can help."

I hand her a knife and slide over to share the sink.

Marilyn breaks the silence and says quietly, "I remember the girls in high school all wanting you."

"Most of them wanted the image."

"I remember one night when you came off the field. Someone in the crowd behind me yelled, 'I love you, Keith.' You stopped and scanned the crowd. Suddenly, you stared at me and blew me a kiss. My girlfriends teased me for months afterwards."

"And you did, I assume."

"Have to admit, I played it for a few weeks." Marilyn stops peeling. "It wasn't me. I was a shy, skinny little ninth grader."

I stop peeling. "You're still trying to deny it?"

"You had far better options than me, as you still do." She glances at me. "I didn't realize it last night, but you still have that patented grin."

I work on the rest of dinner seeing pain on her face each time she moves and convinces her to sit. We both make small talk about life, before she calls Johnny to come eat. I turn from the stove, Johnny is frozen and staring at me.

Marilyn glances at us both. "Uncle Keith is fixing us something to eat."

"Just plain farm food. Hope you like it." I set the food on the table.

Marilyn says, "Come here. Uncle Keith has your seat at the head of the table."

He cautiously walks towards the chair, watching me the whole time.

The room becomes silent. We all take bites of food. I look at Johnny and say, "Not comparable to your mom's cooking, I'm assuming?"

Marilyn takes a bite. "It tastes great. Uncle Keith did an excellent job, don't you think, Johnny?"

His dark eyes hold me in a trance. He finally says, "Yes."

Marilyn says, "It was better not to talk at meals."

***

When I finish the chores, and get showered, they are snuggled up together at the end of the couch. I sit at the other end. "You might as well take the bed again tonight. We'll get more organized tomorrow and open the room upstairs."

"We're not taking your bed again."

"Johnny, did you like the waterbed?"

He looks at Marilyn before he answers. "Yes, the bed is warm and squishy."

Marilyn says, "We're not sleeping in your bed. We'll be fine on the couch."

Johnny says, "Mommy, we can share. It has lots of room."

"That's a brilliant solution." I'm grinning.

Marilyn says, "You are being very manipulative."

"The comfort of my guests is my top priority. I glance at Johnny. The rule is, one who does chores in morning sleeps on the couch and makes coffee. Once your mom gets healed up, then we'll reevaluate."

Johnny watches silently. I ask him, "What'd you think about the farm?"

"I like staying here."

"The farm resort has fun things to see and do. You'll be eating premium beef, take tractor tours, rides on the snowmobile, have hot chocolate with marshmallows, and homemade cookies baked fresh by my mom."

His face gets a glow to it. "My mom makes chocolate chip cookies, too. They are really good."

"Can't wait to have some. The spa farm treatment. Memories for a lifetime."

Marilyn is shaking her head. "You're making big promises." She holds back a smile. "What about your other girlfriends?"

"My dream world, they want me?"

"I can't believe you're not seeing someone." Her face tightens. "Forget I said that—how long have you lived here?"

I say, "You've heard it's winter, lonely women needing comfort, and you're receiving priority status."

She is taking quick breaths.

"I have a couple of girls on the string, but it's a secret."

"And none of my—" She wraps her arms around herself.

I say, "You have joined the secret farm paradise."

Her dimple appears. "Don't your parents bug you about starting a family?"

I'm grinning. "So, you think it's time too?"

"No, I didn't mean..." She looks towards the kitchen. "It's none of my business."

I lean back in my chair. "Mom and Dad believe I need a disciplined, hardworking, churchgoing farm girl. My dream girl is free-spirited and wants a beer. You can see my dilemma a wild party girl, that goes to church. So here I am, a free spirted bachelor."

Marilyn winces, holding back a laugh. "Do your parents care if someone stays at your house?"

"We'll work on that tomorrow."

"They're not going to be happy?"

Serenely and quietly, I say, "It won't be bad if you promise when you're healed up that you won't jump in bed and take advantage of me." I get up without looking at her.

Marilyn holds her chest as tears come to her eyes. "Quit making me laugh."

"My mom's tender heart is a sucker for little kids. Johnny needs a place to stay and that little magic that melts your heart, will melt my mom's."

She follows me and leans against the doorway.

"Get some sleep. I'll play fly on the wall and give a full report in the morning."

With her arms folded across her chest, she leans against the casing. "Be careful."

I pause at the door. *You want a kiss?* "Don't worry."

Twelve

February 11, 1984

When I enter the bar, queasiness hits me, as if I never left, but a cold beer is waiting at my bar stool.

Jason, interjects. "You, okay?"

I take a sip of beer. "Other than everyone started without me."

"You're late. Laura filled me in on the details between customers. John showing up at her house, rattled her."

"She sounded out of sorts when she called." I'm gazing across the bar, taking a slow drink before saying, "The kid wants to stay, and gave me permission to sleep with his mom."

"You're moving fast even for you. Day one welcome to the sweet life on the farm."

"She has a sweetness, can't quiet...."

Jason gets a big grin.

"What? I'm the official Uncle Keith."

"I want to congratulate you."

"On what?"

"Woman brings her kid on first date and single life is over."

"I'm the uncle helping out not the boyfriend."

"Yeah, secret family incest." Jason raises the bottle for Laura to see. "I have this vision of dirty face kids running around in the yard... What do you think, six, eight—"

Laura brings two beers without a smile. "I'm sure John will be here tonight—"

"We're ready to explain to the asshole he's messed with the wrong people."

She picks up money. "Not today. The secret is a top priority. How is everything at the house?"

"Everything is great. The kid volunteered to help with the chores. She wants to cook. The kid said he thought we could share the waterbed."

Laura turns, points her finger at me. "I will kick your ass. Remember, she is a guest—"

"Speaking of your friend ..."

"Yep, that's him. Now promise no fighting. You know nothing about what happened."

John and Bob take the stools on the corner and signal Laura for two beers. Bob squirms as he introduces us. John's steely squint gives me the creeps.

Jason says, "You're my neighbor. Your kid always stops playing and waves when I drive the tractor by your house."

John's steely eyes didn't blink. He says, "Ever seen anyone else at my house?"

"Not one to keep track of the neighbors but no." Jason motions his hand toward him. "I work during the day."

Laura sets a beer in front of John. "Make sure you don't cause any trouble."

John answers, "I could leave now if you will tell me where my wife is."

"No one here knows about Marilyn. Go home and sob no one here will feel sorry for you either." Laura turns, her eyes on fire.

John's eyes dart around the bar and then focus on Laura walking away. "Wife packed up the kid and ran off last night." He tips his bottle towards Laura. "Her best friend, and claims she has no idea, where she is, which any sane person knows is a lie."

"She seems awful pissed." I lean forward so I can see Bob better. "What else happened?"

Bob sets his beer on the counter. "She isn't talking to me except to bitch, about everything even the crumbs in the living room."

John says, "My wife called her and gave her the exaggerated sob story about our fight, probably left out about her trying to kick me. All I wanted is a warm meal, and minor caring, at the end of another week of hell."

Jason stares. "You slapped her around until she saw reality."

"She does it on purpose, just keeps bitching."

I take a slow sip. "The girls got the winter blues." I study his reaction.

John scowls. "What do you mean, the winter blues?"

Mellow as I can, I say, "The winter blues—starts during hunting and football season, then takes on full depression right after Christmas. Women couped up in the house with no one to give them attention, besides a whiny kid. I have a light work schedule during the winter, so I spend some time, tell them they're gorgeous, take care of their desires, add a romantic dinner, and send them home feeling good."

John says, "You're surveying married women? So you can get laid? You're sick."

I break out laughing. "Jason, did I say anything about getting laid? When's the last time you took your wife on a date?"

"We're married. We don't do teenage dating stuff."

"Take her out ... show her off." I pause. "Even if she's not good-looking."

"Better than what you'll find in here." He digs a picture out of his wallet and passes it to me. "I've carried that picture since we got hitched."

I respond, "She is gorgeous. I'll help her, and she'll be feeling good in no time."

His body strains. "You're disgusting. That's my wife."

Bob puts his hand on John's shoulder. "Settle down. Keith packs a lot of bullshit; he thinks women love it."

John is burning a hole through me. "You are part of the reason she doesn't go out. You'd better hope I never find you talking to her."

I put my hands up. "It was a compliment to your good-looking better half; not everyone qualifies."

Laura brings Jason and me another round, picks up the money, and never makes eye contact.

John says, "We could use another round too."

She turns around. "Do we have a please?"

She brings their drinks, and John says, "I didn't hear your friends say please."

Laura winks at me. "If you'd tip like him, you wouldn't have to say please." She grins and leaves.

John glances at Bob. "How do you stand her flirting? I can't imagine what happens when you're not here."

Bob is a statue.

John flags Shirley one of the waitresses and shows her his wife's picture. She shrugs, looks at me, and shakes her head no. He moves down the bar asking others.

***

Leaning close to Jason I whisper, “It’s time for me to socialize.” I grab my beer. “I’ll be back.” I say hi to Rob and his wife, he was right offensive guard, nicknamed Mr. Bulldozer when we won the championship.

Rob says, “What's going on with the guy whose wife is missing? First time I ever saw the guy, and acting like we are best friends.”

“Bar buddies. His wife is a friend of Laura’s. I’m sure he told you he beat her up last night, and she split.”

“He didn't mention that part, but I knew something wasn’t right.”

“Heard it’s more than a love tap. She should’ve gone to the hospital, not that I’m a doctor.”

Rob puts his hand on my shoulder. “I could accidentally bump him and see how tough he is.”

“Laura doesn’t want any trouble, so we’re tolerating the guy today. I offered to take his wife out and cheer her up.”

Rob’s wife interjects. “You'd better not be taking someone else out—you promised me last year, and I’m still waiting.” She squeezes a smile, puts her hand on my arm.

Rob says, “The pretty boys are flash and bullshit. No action.”

She kisses me on the cheek and says, “Sorry I have tonight covered.”

“Get Rob to quit being so greedy and give you a night out.” Ginger is waving me over to her table. “Gotta run. Duty is calling.”

I pull up a chair and say, “What brings you girls out on the town?”

Ginger says, “The guys are home trying to get lucky playing cards. We told them, no trying for us; we’re going to get lucky.”

“You came to the right place.” I wave to Jason to join us.

Jason and I, hanging out with the girls, introduce them to the drummer between sets, laughing and teasing about our desires. Ginger asks me for a slow dance. Her breasts are pushing against my chest and out of her blouse, the rest of her body moves tighter. *Let’s do it.*

“There’re people watching.” Ginger slips a napkin into my hand. Give me a call next week. I’m home alone in the mornings.”

“Will do.” Returning to my barstool John’s squinting eyes intersect mine.

With a slimy grin he says, “You seemed to have the run of the bar?” He drops the smile his eyes reduce to slits. "Laura knows where my wife is hiding. And it's impossible to believe someone else in your group doesn't know."

"You know the story the bartender never tells and doesn't approve of my extra carrying ways." I put my hand on his shoulder. "If I hear of something that will help, I'll get hold of you." I continue to my stool. *He wants to kick my ass, but doubt overwhelms him.*

Laura brings drinks and smirks. "You're making promises for tonight—"

"I thought we were on for tonight—"

John blurts, "You shut Bob off to sleep with Mr. Macho?"

She stares at Bob. "What the F are you talking about?"

Bob is stone-faced.

I say, "Damn, Bob, trying to help."

She walks over to Bob. "Not getting enough at home, you tell your lowlife friend?"

His face is blank.

I poke Jason, whispering in his ear. "He's not getting it tonight."

Laura's face is getting red. She says to John. "Now that you have become kiss-ass buddies, go home; with Bob, he needs company."

I can feel John's hostility, my arms tense.

Laura's face is beet red. "Maybe you can take care of each other." She pats my hand. "I'll see if Mr. Macho can cure my winter blues; works for everyone else." She struts towards the other end of the bar.

I flip my hands up, watching Laura but waiting for him to explode. "They want me, my curse of life."

The evening is winding to a close, but John's glare hasn't left. "I can't believe you haven't had your ass kicked the way you carry on with women." He finishes his beer. "Stay away from my wife and kid."

"Sounds threatening, but don't worry. Your wife must've had a plan and found someone, but I'll put the word out."

"Forget it." John stands. "You're a real ass."

"Trying to extend my caring."

Bob gives him a small shove towards the door.

Jason leans close. "Had to get the last twist."

Thirteen

February 12,1984

Marilyn rolls slowly out of bed to keep from waking Johnny, and pauses by the recliner. His clothes are folded and stacked neatly on the mahogany end table. The scuffed walnut coffee table has a scattered collection of farm and hot rod magazines, with dust covering the open spaces.

She pours coffee, looking out the kitchen window, the tractor smoke trail curls into the air. Her thoughts race. *Does he intend to add me to the list? A dream you don't rate above slutty.* And how is it that Johnny cowers around men, but Keith is an instant superhero? A playboy image—yet no serious relationship or clues of such and half the living room, a toy room.

She is startled when Keith comes through the door. Hangs up his Carhartt jacket and coveralls and says, "Good morning. I assume you slept well."

Marilyn snaps to reality. "Of course, haven't adjusted to someone up working and having the coffee made for me."

Keith goes to the coffeepot. "Definition of farming: the first half-day of work completed before the world is awake." He sits at the table.

Marilyn anxiety over takes her. "How did it go with John?"

"You mean after I explained I'm the top dog and take care of the women?"

Marilyn's dimples come out, and she says, "Yes right after."

"He showed us your graduation picture and I told him you're gorgeous." I glance over my cup. "Promise if I found you, I would make sure you were taken care of."

Marilyn's eyes open wide. "I can't believe he—"

"Stayed calm—he was a caged tiger, but smart enough to realize engaging the bar wouldn't turn out well for him."

Marilyn says, "He would threaten guys who glanced at me."

"Like I said, you're safe. Lots of this is coming at you awfully fast but I usually have Sunday breakfast at Skippy's." He sets his cup down, and his face loses its expression. "My friend Sid will be there."

She sets her cup down. "And is there a reason you're telling me?"

"He's a cop for the county sheriff—"

"No, please—they can't find out—I'll get out of your hair." She tries to catch her breath. "Thank you for your help."

Keith slowly touches the top of her hand and says, "How long are you going to keep running? I know people, police, lawyers, and friends ... and they tell me, you can't fix everything yourself."

Marilyn grips her cup. "No."

"You want to return for the next beating?"

"Stop it. What are my choices, Mr. Big Shot?" Marilyn glares at him. "No job. No money. My new home is the last guy in the bar. Who promises his magic wand will fix it." She covers her face and sobs.

Keith retrieves a box of Kleenex.

"I'm sorry." Marilyn dabs the tears off her cheeks and gazes at Keith. "You didn't deserve that tirade. I wouldn't forgive myself if something happened to you." Marilyn shakes her head slightly. "I'll talk to the sheriff."

"Quit worrying. I've upset a couple of guys before in my life." Keith is grinning. "It comes with my shining knight image."

"I can't believe I'm letting you talk me into this."

"Tough, but the right decision for your kid and everyone else." Keith leans on the back of the chair. "Help yourself to breakfast and tell Johnny we're going on that tractor ride later." He winks. "He'll be asking."

She says, "Thank you." He heads out the door.

***

Marilyn gets more coffee, snuggles her face in the oversized housecoat, and lets his scent linger, driving crazy feelings ... Johnny breaks her dream as he makes his way into the kitchen, his teddy bear squeezed tight and Jake trailing along.

Still half-awake, says, "Mommy, when are we going on a tractor ride?"

She smiles. "Later, Uncle Keith went to restaurant for breakfast."

"Why didn't you make him breakfast?"

"It's Sunday and he's meeting friends."

"When does he work?"

"He works every day. He was up early and fed the cows."

"Does his boss tell him how to do everything?"

"He doesn't have a boss."

"How does he know what to do?"

"He grew up on the farm and learned when he was young."

"Mommy, I'd like to live on a farm."

"Yes, dear."

"Do you think Uncle Keith will let us live here? I'll promise to be good and do my chores."

"He's only helping us until we find our own place."

"Who cleans his house and cooks his food?"

She kisses him on his forehead. "He does it himself."

Silence for a moment, and Johnny asks, "How does he...? Dad said it's a woman's job."

"Your dad ... Never mind. Do you ever run out of questions?"

Johnny continues, "Do you like Uncle Keith?"

"Yes."

He wraps his arms around her and whispers, "I love you, Mommy."

"I love you too. You want something to eat?"

"Yes, I want the Sugar Pops."

"Okay, go wash up."

Fourteen

February 12, 1984

The vibes and rumors are more than normal from the coffee drinker's table. I pick the farthest front corner booth. Jason arrives shortly, and we order breakfast. I say, "Sid is meeting us."

Jason says, "You're telling him about Marilyn?"

"Yeah, she had a mini meltdown but agreed, mostly out of fear."

Jason says, "You ever wonder how nice girls get mixed up with such assholes, then worse, stay with them?"

"I can't explain it, but she's different from the norm."

Sid enters with his partner. I wave him over. He examines everyone in the restaurant before he sits. Connie, brings coffee and takes their orders.

I held my hand up. "I'll buy these boys' breakfast."

Sid glances up at Connie and says, "Separate checks. We're not owing him because of a free breakfast."

Connie winks. "I've heard the girls fall for it at the bar."

"Just my friendly nature."

Sid introduction of his partner, Les Simmons, who chimes in on the normal banter.

I lean closer to them and say, "I have a friend who had an ugly argument with her husband."

Sid curls his hands under his chin. After a slow pause, he asks, "Have you slept with her?"

I flip my hand. "No. The first question and why does it matter?"

"Background information."

Les is choking back a smile.

Sid finishes chewing a mouthful of food and stares at Jason. "You believe that?"

Jason breaks into a grin. "Yeah, this time."

Sid smirks. "No one else will."

I hold up my hand. "My new image."

"She heard of your monk status and knew it was a safe place to stay. How long have you known her?"

"Two days."

He's shaking his head. "The first piece of advice is, get her out of your house. When she goes back with this creep—"

"She—not doing that again."

"Yeah—that's what they say, but they never stick to it. What's her story? How did she end up at your house?" He stops eating. "And she wanted to sleep with you."

"You're such an asshole."

Sid rubs his forehead. "Two, three weeks, guilt will consume her, she'll kiss and make up with the asshole. Telling him how you got her drunk and took advantage of her. What is this guy's name?

"John Desmond."

Sid glances out the window and then at his partner. "I remember the guy, got squinty dark eyes. Repeating a hundred times. 'I barely hit her.' Then added, 'She faked the bruises.' Not their first time."

"Admitted she panicked at the hospital the last time, said they wanted her kid taken to foster care."

Connie takes our dirty plates and fills our coffee.

Sid stares at me the whole time until she leaves. "Where is the kid?"

"He's—"

"Don't answer." Sid closes his eyes. "This Desmond character knows how to manipulate the rules. When he finds out his kid is at your brothel, we'll be reading you your rights and then arresting you, because you endangered his kid, and he had to take the law into his own hands."

"I can't throw the girl out on the street."

Sid looks at Jason, points at me. "What's up? He found a caring gene?"

Jason says, "He's been dreaming of this sweet family life, and she shows up with a kid. Thinks it's divine intervention."

They break out laughing.

I flip them off. "Someone has got to help her."

We pay and stand by the police car. Sid says, "We'll stop in a couple of hours." Simmons slides into the passenger side of the car. "If she doesn't want to talk, we'll leave, and we can pretend nothing happened." Sid puts his hand on my shoulder. "You're in a no-win situation. It's not worth it for a piece of ass."

I take a breath, shaking my head.

They drive off. Jason says, "What's the plan for saving your new damsel?"

I look at the sunny day, the winter air whipping light snow. "I met a couple of tough dudes in college. He isn't close, and I'm not putting her out on the street."

"Figured." He pats my shoulder. "Let me know if you need anything."

***

Leaving the truck running in the driveway at my parents, I slide in the side garage door. Slip off my shoes in the entry.

Mom is in the kitchen preparing food. She wipes her hands and gives me a hug. "You want coffee or something to eat?"

"No, I have to get home." I say quietly, "Won't be able to make dinner today. Something came up."

"There'll be leftovers." She becomes serious. "Something you need to tell me?"

"Yes, but not today. Need to borrow the space heater."

"It is in the spare bedroom closet."

I return, and Dad says, "What are you doing with the heater?"

"Taking the chill off the bedroom."

"What was going on yesterday morning? Jason driving your truck, following a car into your driveway."

"I'm helping a friend."

Dad's jaw tightens. "Where did this girl sleep last night?"

"What if it wasn't a girl? I slept on the couch, being it is your business."

"A low-life bar friend?"

I stare at him. "It's Laura's friend who needs a place to stay for a few days."

Dad's face is getting red. "Oh, that clears up the vagueness. A girl comes to the bar, goes home with Mr. Stud." He points his finger and waves his hand. "Oh, she not a gold digger, just upstanding white trash?"

"Why don't you go over and tell her and her four old they can't stay a few days because it won't look good in the neighborhood."

Dad's neck tenses. "Even better brings a kid."

Mom is gripping the counter. "Earl, stop it."

"Pardon me for complaining about the one-night stands."

"You're always so worried about the family image, and not if someone needs compassion or a helping hand."

Mom says, "Earl—" She turns towards me. "Keith, you understand how immoral and wrong this is."

Dad catches his breath. "Mother—I hear of his helping at the coffee shop. You can only laugh at his sexual episodes for so long. He's the laughing stock living like a big-time city gigolo. I'm embarrassed to show my face at the restaurant. The first question they ask me: Who's your son f'n this week? Someday he'll knock up one of those so-called sweet girls, and she'll own half the farm."

"I'm not—if you could bring yourself to believe me, for once in your life. Sorry, Mother."

"Stop it, both of you."

"We raised him better. His winter comprises drinking beer and getting laid. Carla would make a great wife. He ignores her. You said that yourself. Oh, that's right, she is old-fashion, marriage before jumping in bed."

"Earl. Remember what the doctor said about your stress?"

"Now he brings married women home, with a kid in tow. He's a disgrace to the family."

"Dammit, I'm not sleeping with every girl I know. I've already talked to Sid. He's coming over this afternoon, and we'll work out something."

Dad's fine veins on his face are bright red. He storms out.

"I'm sorry, Mom. I couldn't leave her out in the cold. Her little boy's brown eyes melt your soul."

"Promise me you are not trying to sleep with her."

"Believe me, I am not."

"We'll talk more later. Does she need anything?"

"Not at the moment, Laura brought her clothes, Sid is coming this afternoon to talk to her, and I'm opening the bedroom upstairs is why I need the heater."

"Stop back before you feed the cows. I'll save you some casserole."

I give her a hug. "It's not the normal domestic BS; he beat her up bad. They were lucky they didn't freeze to death."

"Do the right thing."

I give her another hug. "Thanks, I will."

Fifteen

February 12, 1984

Jake woofs, and Johnny runs to the window, yelling, "Mommy, Mommy, Uncle Keith is here." Running to the door.

She hears Johnny ask, "Uncle Keith, when are we going on the tractor ride?"

Marilyn raises her voice and puts the magazine down. "Johnny."

Johnny doesn't look at her, and Keith has his smirk grin as they continue into the living room.

Marilyn says, "Johnny go play, I need to talk to Uncle Keith."

Johnny pulls Keith arm and says, "Mommy says she could cook and clean your house—"

"Johnny, go play!"

Keith breaks out his patented grin. "We'll find her a list of fun things to do."

Marilyn feels her face turn red.

"The place needs some cleaning?"

She tenses. "Everything is perfect."

"I drink beer, and feed cows perfect. The rest of me needs sophistication."

"I'm not the girl for that. I'll ... I'll help more once I get moving better." She rolls her lips tight together.

Keith sits beside her, takes her hand, and whispers, "On to the serious matters. I talked to Sid this morning. He is coming around one. Something else to consider: do you want me to take Johnny on his tractor ride when Sid comes? Give you some privacy."

She bites her lip. "Johnny is scared to death of the police taking him away."

Keith says, "I noticed." Keith squeezes her hand.

"Thanks for the caring. So, you realize John hates Laura because she corrupts my thinking, and hates guys because he believes they can talk me into anything."

"That is good to know."

What did I just say? She stares at the wall. "Remember, his fantasy world how he is doing everything to save his marriage." She leans toward Keith and says softly, "Next he and his mother will be saying Johnny is traumatized and need counseling."

She looks into his hazel eyes. "Full disclosure, my options are extremely limited, but I can't let Johnny live in that hell anymore. I'm never going back, no matter." Marilyn takes a deep breath, fighting the pain in her ribs. "I'm not the innocent girl you winked at in high school." *He's better than John.* "And I'm not taking advantage of your hospitality. Set up a tab, room, and board, add consulting and childcare." Her lips tighten. "I'll pay you. Some way."

"How many guys did you date before John?"

She closes her eyes. *I should lie.* "John's the only one."

"When you get healed up, we'll evaluate the extended stay options. We can work something out."

She muffles the crying with her hands. "Don't tease me. Your standards are above my white-trash life."

Keith, picks her chin up, gently turns her toward him, and says, "You're not white trash unless you choose to be. It was life yesterday. Hell will be trying to drag you back, but you are at the farm, living in paradise."

Marilyn flinches, biting her lip. "You should show me my room before I make more of a fool of myself."

Keith gets the heater and follows Marilyn up the stairs.

She is taking the steps, leading with her left foot each time. Halfway up it dawns on her what Keith is observing. *Why doesn't it feel offensive?*

The cool air hits her as he opens the door. Keith moves the boxes out of the center of the room and connects the heater. "I'll move this junk over to the other bedroom tomorrow." Keith stands staring at her.

Marilyn says, "What?"

"I can't believe you want to give up a nice warm waterbed to sleep in the cold bell tower."

"Your other friends may be jealous."

Keith laughs. "I'll check." He holds out his arm. "Least wait until tomorrow for it to warm up. The tractor ride is priority today."

"How could I forget." Marilyn holds his arm going down one step at a time.

Keith says, "You don't appear ready to climb stairs either."

Sixteen

February 12, 1984

I'm making coffee when Marilyn comes out to the kitchen. "My feeling is Sid won't be here long, but just in case. Did you tell Johnny yet?"

"No, I'm procrastinating."

"Not sure I'm much help I'm terrible at serious conversations in case you haven't already realized." I warm up the soup and put the sandwiches out on the table. "Johnny, lunch is ready." I sit him in his chair.

Marilyn says, "You believe me that I won't let anything happen to you?" He stares. "The police are going to be here to talk to me, they're friends of Keith and are going to help us."

After a long pause, Johnny says, "I want to live here—Uncle Keith, can't we stay here?"

"Of course." Stumbles out of my mouth.

"Johnny, men, and women can't just live together."

"Johnny there is some adult issues to work out." Keith is grinning, "But we'll work on it. When the police leave, we'll go on a tractor ride."

The rest of lunch is spent in silence and Johnny goes back to play.

Mairlyn says, "Do you spoil all the kids?"

"Kids, they're excited and happy with simple stuff. How many diamonds would it take to make a woman that happy?"

Jake woofs, and Johnny runs to the window. "Mommy, the police."

"It's okay." Marilyn hugs him as he grips her.

I'm tilting my head looking at her. "Remember, Sid has to be official but is dedicated to doing right." I answer the door. "Welcome to the farm." Sid kicks the snow off his boots.

I motion to the table. "Don't worry about the fancy linoleum floor. Nothing has hurt it in the last fifty years." I ask, "Where is your partner?"

"This is an unofficial visit, and I didn't see you both here together."

"Come in, sit down. Made fresh coffee."

"Thanks, but I can't stay."

With an official straight face, Sid heads to the table, and hands her a business card. "Mrs. Desmond, correct?" Turns and reaches his hand to Johnny. "You must be Johnny nice to meet you."

Marilyn says, "You can shake his hand, he is here to help us."

He shakes Mairlyn's hand. "Sid Avery. "Do you realize you need help?"

"Yes." She looks at Johnny. "Go run and play."

"What I see is minimal of spousal abuse." Silence absorbs the room. "If you remember, I was at your home last summer. How many times has it been now?"

Marilyn is taking deep breaths, her eyes darting in every direction. "To many."

"I'll do the police part, but you must commit. None of want to waste our time."

Her lips are trembling. "I know." She has a death grip on the table. "I'm so scared. It's not just me, he'll come after everyone."

"And that to will get worse." Sid stays standing and glances at me. "Then your son will grow up just like him?"

Marilyn is squeezing her coffee cup. "What do I need to do?"

He softens his voice. "Tomorrow come to the station and file a report. Chris Sanders works with spousal abuse cases, and she will walk you through everything."

Marilyn closes her eyes.

"You do need a good mailing address. Your parents or good friend. Next, find a place to stay." Sid looks at me. "Here may be safe, but the court frowns on shacking up with a new guy after leaving your husband. It doesn't reflect well on your decision-making." He looks at Marilyn. "Do you have a girlfriend or family you could stay with?"

"I don't ... I didn't want anyone involved in my mess." She looks up at me.

I wink.

"Move to the safe house that's why we have them." Sid glance. "We will help you with a restraining order, and the court would order him to leave your house."

"We're behind on the rent, and I can't afford to pay it."

"I understand the hassle, but the safe house has upsides."

Marilyn drops her head.

"Further advice, if I didn't know Keith, I would assume everything is a lie, and you've been seeing Keith, and your husband found out—you're trying to make him jealous, to prove he loves you."

Marilyn yells, "No, I wouldn't do that," and stares at Sid.

"Mrs. Desmond, I'm taking your word, but the world won't. Guys who can't control their temper never improve without major psychological help. Staying with them or teasing them makes it worse." He raises his head. "I think you know the consequences."

I jump in. "No one is going to connect us."

Sid scowls.

Marilyn sits in silence. "I'll come in the morning."

"Mrs. Desmond." He quietly says, "Around nine or ten o'clock. Ask for me and remember we didn't have this conversation."

We walk out the door together, and whispers to me, "I'll help her." He glances at Marilyn. "Hope she's ready."

I put my hand on his shoulder. "You're a little rough on her."

"It's not going to be easy, and she needs more than sweet talk."

I close the door.

Marilyn sits in a daze, a complete blank. *Do I give her a hug?* "Sid put on his tough act, but he'll make it happen."

She raises her gaze. "He is right, about it getting worse. I shouldn't be dragging you into my mess probably already too late to fix it."

"No quitters at the farm. The cows demand to be fed. Whether I'm hungover, run over by a truck, it doesn't matter. One gets up and does it." I give her shoulders a small massage. "Time for a nice, calm ride around the farm."

"You don't believe him, do you? That I would—"

"Nah, and don't believe all the crap. The vibes say you're tough enough. You're safe, and your secret is safe. Sid's trying to make sure."

Johnny runs over to Marilyn and hugs her.

Without breaking stride, I say, "Think it's time. Grab your coats. I'll be back with the tractor."

***

I unplug the heater and back the tractor out of the toolshed. *Why do I feel all quivery? Quit.*

They have their coats on and are waiting.

"Jake, stay." He sits by the door, whimpering. "Sorry, bud, there's not enough room." I open the door and lift Johnny onto the first step. He scurries up as if he's been doing it all his life.

I smile at Marilyn. She says, "Are you lifting me up too?"

"I can't show off too much. Let me get a stepladder." I hold the ladder and watch her climb up. After different seating combinations, Marilyn decides sits on the arm rest. I set Johnny on my lap.

"Johnny, you ready?" Excitement glows as scans the gauges and levers. I take his hand in mine. "Push this lever up." I let out the clutch. "We are off." I steer the 4020 John Deere into the lane. We hit the first snowbank behind the barn, the snow flies.

"Mommy, did you see that?" Excitement breaks out on Johnny's face.

"Yes."

Once in the straight part of the lane, I scoot up to the front of the seat, so Johnny can reach the steering wheel, and say, "Johnny, you ready to drive?"

I position his hands on the wheel and point in front of us. "Keep it between the little weeds sticking through the snow." I'm still doing most of the driving. Then, I raise my hands. "Look, Mom, no hands."

"Mommy, I am driving the tractor."

I glance at Marilyn, and her face is also aglow. I say, "When you're healed up, you'll be able to have a turn."

She rubs Johnny's hair and says, "You are doing a great job."

I slow the tractor, help him turn the corner, and we continue along the back fence. We hit snow drifts, blowing snow over the tractor and Johnny's eye light up like one's first carnival ride. I stop the tractor at the edge of the woods and point to the other end. "A deer is looking at us."

Johnny says, "Let's go closer."

"He'll run if we go too close." I pull the binoculars out of the glove compartment and adjust the focus. I lift them to Johnny's face. "Now line it up with the fence and then turn slowly along till you find the deer."

He is holding the binoculars like he knows how. "I see it. It looks so big."

"He's looking for food under the snow." I point to different things for Johnny to explore through the binoculars, chilling with the peaceful hum of the diesel. Marilyn sits quietly.

Johnny takes them down and says, "Mommy, do you want to look?"

"No, we need to return home, Uncle Keith has to feed the cows."

"Yeah, the chores need to be done every day." I glance at Marilyn. *And your thoughts?* Johnny hands me the binoculars. "We'll have more rides."

Johnny says, "Uncle Keith, what are these for?" He reaches for the levers.

Marilyn instantly says, "Johnny, don't touch those."

"It's hard to explain, but they move the equipment up and down." I point to the other ones. "These levers make the tractor change speed."

He points. "What do the little ones do?"

"This one turns on the lights. We can work all night. This one is for air conditioning. In the modern age of farming, we turn on cold air, crank the radio up, and sip champagne all day."

"Uncle Keith, what is cham...pagne?"

Marilyn smirks. "And the answer?"

"It's something to celebrate with on special occasions."

"We should've brought some."

"Yes, we should've."

Johnny says, "I like driving the tractor. Can we go again sometime?"

"Of course."

"Johnny." Marilyn keeps leaning tight to me.

I look at Marilyn, and there're tears running down her cheeks. She whispers, "Thank you."

"Two more farmhands. One needs a booster seat, and one can ride on my lap."

Her dimples break out. "Do you impress other girls with tractor rides?"

"No, you're the first."

Seventeen

February 13, 1984

I have my morning coffee, pondering my new guest. The mystifying brown eyes of her and Johnny, each with their own intensity. How am I setting up a date with Ginger is what is should be asking myself.

Marilyn drifts to the kitchen wrapped in my housecoat. The swelling has gone down a bit in her eye, replaced with dark green and black.

"Good morning. Want coffee?"

"Yes."

I wave my hand. "Sit."

"Thank you. Not used to someone waiting on me."

"Just trying to impress the houseguest." I pour her coffee. "While you girls are gone, I'll take the boys out snowmobiling."

"Johnny would like that." She holds her gaze at me.

Love or fear, I can't tell.

The phone rings.

"Hold that thought." I answer, "Hello."

"Good morning. And how is everyone?"

"Laura, you won't believe how much our new friend has taken to me." I wink at Marilyn, stretching the cord towards the table.

"Let me talk to her and find out the truth."

I hand the phone to Marilyn, pick up my coffee, and head to the living room. Adrenaline picks up as I flashback to Ginger and the priority for this week. Johnny shuffles out of the bedroom, with Jake following. I let Jake out and watch Johnny give Marilyn a hug. *Kids, someday. Rule no women with kids.*

"I'll be ready, goodbye." She hangs up. Hurriedly goes to the cupboard and flinches reaching for a bowl. Laura's on her way."

I touch her hand. "You need help?"

"I need a shower, and he needs breakfast." She glances at Johnny.

"I can help. Which one first?" *You're such an ass.* "Woops, sorry. Johnny, let's cook up some Sugar Pops."

Johnny grins, "You can't cook Sugar Pops."

"That's what makes them pop."

"Uncle Keith, you're silly."

I ruffle his hair glance at Marilyn and say, "Your personal shower helper is busy, can you manage?" Lifting Johnny onto his chair.

She bites back a smile. "Thanks."

***

Marilyn is dressed in her sweatshirt and jeans. I say, "You should eat too." She doesn't answer, but I grab cereal and a bowl.

"Thank you. You're waiting on me again."

"It's for the brownie points." I sit with my coffee.

Jake woofs and goes to the kitchen door, with Johnny behind him.

"Laura must be here."

Chad runs into the house with Laura yelling, "Take your boots off."

Chad and Johnny run off to the living room.

> Marilyn evaluates the hug Laura gave Keith—a bond more than friendship?
> Laura lets go of Keith and looks at Marilyn. "Let's go do this."

They make their way to the door, and Laura says, "Depending on how long it takes, we may retrieve Marilyn's clothes."

Marilyn glance towards the living room. "I can't believe he not in panic mode."

Keith says, "Just the guys hanging out for the day."

***

They pull out of the driveway, Marilyn instantly ask, "What happened with John? I've been so worried."

"He poured out normal profanity trying to appear tough."

"He'll be back."

"Yeah, don't worry. It must be the weekend for fights. I had it out with Bob, too."

Marilyn asks, "Is it because of me?"

"No, not everything is your fault. He's like every whiny guy, not getting enough. We agreed when he started renting, it wasn't a long-term relationship with benefits." Laura takes a quick glance. "He's not that exciting in bed."

Marilyn glances out at the snowy field. "Not sure sex can ever be fun, even when the chance of forever ..."

"The unfairness of the world. A guy can have sex, and no big deal, but if a girl does it, then she's a whore."

"Not sure I'll ever be able to ..." Her eyes water.

"Give it time, and don't get hung up on my self-made issues."

"Takes my mind off my problems. How do you feel about Keith?"

Laura never looks over. "What do you mean?"

"My vast experience with guys." She smiles at herself. "The normal sexual comments men say, with Keith there's an aura of affection, takes me out of my beat-up white trash mentality."

"Quit—you're not white trash just because you ended up with a deadbeat husband. I am living with a deadbeat. We make mistakes. Trust the lies. It happens. Correct it, move on. Many question Keith's morals. The other night he was hot on Ginger, or more, she was hot on him. The bar scuttle is her husband's been fooling around and between you and me, they're hooking up somewhere." She glances at Marilyn. "Makes me jealous, her flaunting her tits and picks who she wants, but who do we judge being wrong?"

"I was dumbstruck this morning when I walked into the kitchen. Keith nonchalantly poured me coffee, making my heart patter." Laura smiles, and Marilyn continues. "Then he fixes Johnny breakfast. What guy does that?"

Laura says, "His mother demanded old-fashioned manners, church each Sunday, yes sir, treat women with respect, and some of it stuck. She is a darling. Have you met her yet?"

"No, she has made food for the last couple of days. She's making roast beef tonight, and Keith is grilling steaks tomorrow. Spoiling us."

"Trust me. You've never had a steak that good. Being a guy, everyone presumes they're more than a friend. He jokes about how much sex we're having ... when I started my divorce, but the true friendship was how many times at the last minute he or his mother would watch Chad for me. Like part of the family. That's why we started calling him Uncle Keith."

Marilyn takes a breath. "None of my business, but why doesn't he have a steady girlfriend?"

"He will deny it but the ugly breakup with his high school sweetheart." Laura looks around as if someone were eavesdropping. "This is our secret. He's scared to death of a real relationship. The girls he dates are stacked, wild, carefree, and add a little airheaded."

"I might qualify for the airheaded part. Flunking the rest of the equation." They both laugh.

Laura glances over. "Once you get out of those bulky sweatshirts and flaunt how carefree and wild you are, three out of four, you will be reeling him in if you want to."

Marilyn shakes her head. After a couple of miles of stillness, Marilyn says, "John will be an irrational animal, after they arrest him."

"Ain't he always. His parents will post bail, I assume?"

"Yes, they can't have their son looking bad in the neighborhood. John will be sneaking around, so be careful if you come to Keith's. I worry about Keith, does he realize how nasty John is?"

"Quit dwelling on it. Keith will kick ass if he gets the chance." They pull into the police station. "Use my address for your place of residence, and we'll juggle where you're staying."

"What's Bob doing?"

"Skipping out to leave me hanging. Date and time to be determined. I saved rent ahead. Quit worrying about me."

***

With my aid, the boys expanded the play area around the furniture. I call Mom to fill her in on details. "Do you have a kid's snowsuit?"

"Yes, Jenny's extra suit."

I rub my chin, visualizing the last time I saw Jenny wearing it. "Little girlish, but we'll make it work."

"When are you coming over?"

"About an hour."

Mom volunteers to make lunch for us. I act like she doesn't need to, but she added fresh-baked cookies and hot chocolate. I thank her and call Ginger. "Morning, how's life treating you?"

"Cold and lonesome."

"Some hot companionship coming your way."

"I've heard the promises before."

"The challenge is on. I'll bring refreshments. Is Thursday about ten good?"

"Yes, Joe is going to the city and won't be back till later. I'm watching my parents' house while they are in Florida. A nice, secluded spot to spend the afternoon in front of the fireplace."

"I am ready to relax."

"There's no relaxing. You'd better come rested." She is laughing. "My crazed anticipation is how much and how long can you last. Do you know where my parents live?"

"Yep, the house in the woods, just past Willis Road."

She exhales. "Can't wait for some company."

"See you Thursday."

Next, I call Jason. We have our normal bantering about my new family. Then updates on George Marilyn's landlord was at her house.

"That's interesting. Wonder where John is hanging out?" I say quietly. "They're planning on picking up Marilyn's clothes today."

"Keep me posted." Jason makes a small laugh. "I'm sure there's a reason you're telling me."

I'm grinning. "See yah."

***

"Boys, are you ready to ride the snowmobile and have some homemade cookies?"

Chad jumps. "Yes, I brought extra clothes." He turns to Johnny, and says, "Grandma L makes the best cookies."

Johnny's bottom lip quivers. "We didn't bring my suit."

"Don't worry, Grandma G has an extra one." Chad is digging out his stuff. "Don't put your suit on yet. You'll be too hot."

We pile into the truck with Jake sitting on the seat between them and

Chad with his extra clothes on his lap. They are squirming, and their eyes are dancing. We crash into the kitchen of my parents' house. Dad is sitting at the table, quieter than normal. I introduce them to Johnny. Dad is friendly, but ... *Is he still pissed? Strange, he was always over it and complaining about the next thing I hadn't done correctly.*

My mom crouches, hugs the boys, and introduces herself to Johnny. "I'm glad you came to visit. Let's try on the snowsuit." She takes his hand and goes to the bedroom. The suit, which belonged to my niece, fits Johnny but I see tears in his eyes.

I kneel and whisper, "What's the matter?"

"It's a girl's suit. I don't want to turn into a girl."

"They are farm clothes, and anyone's suit. We share and wear what is warm." I whisper. "Your mom is wearing my clothes. She's not turning into a guy."

He's quiet, but then a tiny smile forms.

I wink. "Let's go have fun."

I tie the toboggan to the Polaris with a ten-foot tow rope and demonstrate how to lean into the curve. I put them on the toboggan. "Chad, what's the rule to stop or if you are hurt?"

He raises his hand. "Hold your hand up, straight up, no waving."

They were non-stop laughing, Jake chasing them, they'd fall off, and he would run and bark at them. Once they learn to stay on, I speed up, swinging in a big circle. Jake finally gets tired and lies near the barn. Last year, he could go all day.

I ask, "Are you getting cold?"

Through red cheeks they say. "We want to go faster."

How would they know when there're cold? After two more laps making bigger loops in the field, then around the barn, I drive by the house and stop. "Let's go check on the hot chocolate." Excitement flows through me as I help them take their suits off. I say to Johnny, "Did you stay warm in your suit?"

Johnny nods, and I gave him a hug.

The aroma of cookies and hot chocolate warming on the stove put be back to my childhood. The boy's excitement consumes me while they explain how to lean into the curves.

I glance into the living room. "Where's Dad?"

"Lying down, he's been under the weather."

"Is he okay? He never naps during the day."

"His new winter routine." She whispers as she observes Johnny.

"A real mess."

"You are doing a lot for her. Remember, she is married."

"I understand how it looks, but nothing is going on, just helping her until she gets on her feet."

"You're not making her cook, are you?

"No." I scrunch my face.

I'll make extra roast beef, so stop before chores and pick it up."

"Thanks, my guess is she has cracked ribs." Although Mom wants to ask more questions. We leave and I say when walk in house, "Boys, let's take a mini nap." I put one at each end of the couch, throw quilts over them and pull the recliner lever.

Eighteen

February 13, 1984

They enter the police station and ask for Sid Avery. The officer stays emotionless. "Take a seat." He points to the wooden bench by the wall.

"Try to relax," Laura says. "We'll check off this mess, grab your clothes, and be having a beer at Keith's before chores."

Sid opens the door at the end of the hallway. "Follow me." They follow him down a grimy, painted-green hallway to a conference room with a rectangle table in the center and brown metal chairs on both sides. There are portraits of police officers lining the dull walls. "Wait here. I'll be right back."

Marilyn is rubbing her arms. "Laura, let's leave."

"You must end it. There's no quitting. You can't let him use you as a punching bag every time the mood strikes him."

Sid comes through the door and introduces them to Chris Sanders. He motions for everyone to sit. "We understand how hard this is." He nods. "Ms. Sanders is a domestic violence counselor and is damn good."

"He brags me up. My education I've been there." She pauses. "So, relax and tell us everything that happened."

She prods Marilyn through all the ugliness again.

"How long?"

Sid pipes in, "We were at their house last summer—"

Marilyn drops her head down. "I'm sorry—I dropped the charges." She looks up at Sid. "I thought ..."

"Mrs. Desmond, you don't have to apologize, but I assume you want to end the hell you're living?"

Marilyn whispers, "Yes."

Officer Sanders studies Laura. "Have you witnessed any of these attacks?"

"No." But she holds up her wrist. "He told me I'd be next if I didn't tell him where she was."

"He bruised your wrist?"

"He grabbed me."

Marilyn glares at her. "You didn't tell me."

"I didn't want you to worry."

"You should report that too." Leaning towards Marilyn, Sanders says, "You need counseling. You're not the only women who's been through this hell. Where are you staying?"

"A friend's."

"I recommended that you go to the safe house, at minimum until you receive the restraining order."

"He doesn't know where I am staying. The safe house was so depressing before, but I'll consider it. The added ugliness, John's out doing whatever, and I go to prison."

"I know it's not a perfect system. We'll process the paperwork and then arrest him. Figure late this afternoon or tomorrow." She folds up her papers. "I realize this is tough, and you should've gone to emergency, but you need to see a doctor today."

"I can't afford too."

She walks over to the phone and dials. "Sending a woman over—a victim of spousal abuse. Cracked ribs, could be internal bleeding ... think so ... Marilyn Desmond. Okay ... I'll send her over." She hangs up the phone. She writes the address on a piece of paper.

"Mrs. Desmond, we need pictures." Sid rises, glances at Sanders, and says, "I'm sending Lucy."

Tears are rolling down Marilyn's cheeks. They guide her to a private dressing room.

Sanders walks them into the hall. "Once the judge looks at the case, you can have your lawyer file a PPO (Personal Protection Order)." She touches Marilyn's arm. "You probably doubt, but I will do everything I can. Don't be afraid to call." She hands Marilyn her card. "Someone answers that number."

Laura says, "We'll keep her safe."

Ms. Sanders holds the door. "You girls be careful." She looks at Laura. "Take her to the doctor."

Marilyn is sobbing uncontrollably when they reach the doctor's office. "I ... can't."

Laura goes around the car and helps her out. Marilyn tries to regain some composure before going in. Laura goes to the check-in window.

A nurse comes out and instantly takes them into an exam room. Marilyn feels Laura holding her. When the nurse comes in, Laura leaves.

Marilyn is in a daze as the nurse helps her undress and get into a hospital gown.

"I want to leave."

"Dear, it's going to be alright. You want your friend to be with you?"

Marilyn stays in a daze, "Yes," blocking out the world, feeling like she is falling off a cliff in slow motion.

***

The twelve miles of barren brown fields with patches of snow stretch endlessly. The humiliation keeps crawling over her skin. They drive through the parking lot at the factory, and John's faded burnt orange Chevy truck is there, and Bob's car parked beside it.

"He went to work," Laura says. "They could do the world a favor and become butt buddies."

Marilyn keeps staring out across the parking lot, never looking. Laura heads to Marilyn's house, as a creep silence engulfs the car.

Marilyn finally glances at Laura when they pull into her driveway. "More ugliness, stealing from my house?"

Laura looks at her. "Breathe. We're getting the asshole out of your life."

Marilyn, in a partial daze, sticks her key in the lock, and it still turns. She's looking at the mess—beer cans stacked on the side table, dishes piled in the sink, with stuck-on macaroni dried on the top. Clothes hung on the back of the kitchen chair. Unthinkingly, Marilyn reaches to pick them up.

Laura grabs the pants and throws them on the floor. "You're not cleaning his mess."

Laura grabs clothes from the dresser and closet and stuffs them in garbage bags. They dig her makeup out of the trash can. In Johnny's room, the drawer is open, the bed unmade, the same as when Marilyn left. They clean out the rest of Johnny's clothes.

Laura is making trips to the car when the landlord pulls into the driveway. He walks to the door and faces Marilyn. "Leaving?"

Marilyn puts down the bag of clothes. "I'm so sorry. I meant ..."

He keeps staring at her and blocking their path. "I never trusted your deadbeat husband, but you ... you're all lying deadbeats." He reaches into his pocket and takes out a paper. "Eviction notice. I should've served this before Christmas, when you were only a month behind, but I fell for your pathetic story."

Laura steps in front of the landlord. "Mr. Pathetic, we're happy she is alive, and you're worried about your damn money. We're getting her personal stuff. She left a long time ago. Come to think of it, you didn't see us today."

He stares over Laura's shoulder at Marilyn. "Low-life's. I should've evicted you the first time you were late. Now you're sticking me with three months' rent."

Laura grabs the paper, jams it in his shirt pocket. "Give Ace the papers. He'll be here shortly. He has the rent money. Excuse us, we have to go." She pushes past him.

They head to Keith's. Marilyn still in trance but mutters. "All I do is apologize, but there's no way to repay him or make it right."

Nineteen

February 13, 1984

Marilyn and Laura meet Jake at the door wagging his tail but he didn't wolf. Marilyn leans against the archway, letting the moment of Keith and the boys sleeping soak into her heart.

Laura glances and says, "Let's not interrupt nap time." Laura walks over to the fridge and grabs a beer. "You want one?"

Marilyn slowly walks to the table and shakes her head. "You can put me away in a loony house if I start drinking." She leans forward. "No way I can scrape up money for a divorce or even a restraining order. Even that costs something. And you heard the doctor. No lifting, which means no work."

Laura savors her first mouthful. "Forget all that crap." Sets her beer down. "We're going to make this happen. First thing, John's not paying the rent, he'll leave your stuff or destroy it, just to be mean. When they lock him up we'll move you."

"Sid said I shouldn't be living here, which I understand. Mom's will be an endless rant, and without the restraining order, John would be ... until I cave."

Keith walks into the kitchen, stares at Laura, and says, "You started without me."

Laura says, "More like what did you give the kids to put them to sleep?"

"Mom's hot chocolate has a sleep potion. They played so hard I suggested a nap and then climbed on the couch." Keith gets a beer and motions if anyone wants one. "How did you girls make out?"

"Good." Laura nods toward Marilyn and says, "Nothing a month on some tropical island wouldn't cure. The doctor said no lifting for thirty days. Work on a nice tan, hook up with some rich guy."

"She's already looking for a life better than the farm?" Keith is grinning. "She hasn't received the full benefits yet."

Laura glares at Keith.

"Stop it, you, guys." Marilyn pinches her lips. "My hundred dollars and the hundred and fifty from his paycheck puts me in homeless status."

"They're supposed to arrest John tonight or tomorrow morning." Laura looks at Keith. "We'll move her stuff tomorrow morning. Jason would be happy to store it at his house; we can move it all in a couple of hours. Sid said they'll keep him in jail till late afternoon tomorrow."

"You're not listening. None of it can happen—"

Keith sets down his beer. Quietly he says, "It'll happen. Jason can help you move, and I'll take care of the lawyer." He loses his expression. "Jason's is a great place to store your stuff. Chill for thirty days, get healed up, start on a light work duty. Summer brings some great opportunity of twelve-hour days at a dollar an hour at the farm. You'll be rich." Keith swallows a mouthful of beer. "The end of the year, you'll be single, basking in a nice tan and ready to take on the world."

Marilyn cringes, holding back a grin. "There must be some miracle potion in that beer."

Keith gets a beer, a glass, and sets it in front of Marilyn. "The world will look better now." He pours her half a glass. "Keeps you within the weight restrictions." After a small pause, Keith raises his bottle. Laura raises hers. The room gets quiet. Marilyn looks at them both, picks up her glass. Keith says, "To a new beginning."

Laura says, "To a new beginning."

Marilyn touches her glass to theirs. "To a new beginning." She takes a small sip and wrinkles her face.

Laura downs her beer. "I'd better go. Don't need questions from Ace if he gets home before we do." She gets Chad up as he is rubbing his eyes. She keeps him quiet not to wake Johnny.

He gets to the kitchen and says, "I want to stay here with Johnny." He looks at Keith.

Laura says, "Sorry, you can't stay tonight."

Keith shrugs and gives him a hug. "We have more fun again soon." He's still pouting when they go out the door.

***

I tilt my head towards her. I'm serious about the lawyer. Drillman is a family friend and the best. I hold my hand up. "He'll bill me, and you can make installments."

Marilyn's lips tremble. "You hardly know me. I'll be lucky enough to scrape up money for daily expenses." She pours more into her glass. "That's sweet of you, but I can't accept your doing that for me."

"You think I'll guilt you into owing me?"

Her eyes widen. "No, I don't believe you're that kind of person." The room is silent.

"You're right. I would never do that. You trust me, and I trust you. It's a simple arrangement."

I open my address book, tucking Ginger's napkin under it. "I'll set up an appointment."

I dial Drillman's office. "Hi, Lisa, I need to set up an appointment for a friend—a PPO, and a divorce."

Seems like a long silence. Lisa comes back to the phone. "How about Friday at ten?"

I put my hand over the mouthpiece. "Friday at ten?"

Marilyn takes a breath, biting her lip, fear written on her face.

"That works."

"We'll need some more information."

"Hold on." I walk to the table. "She needs your information." I wink at Marilyn. "It'll all work out."

Marilyn slowly reaches for the phone. "Hello." She gives her all the information and hands the phone back to Keith. "She wants to talk to you."

Keith takes the phone. "Keith, you know better than to be involved in someone else's divorce. Everyone is looking for someone to blame. If it doesn't go well, they'll blame you, and you'll never see your money."

"Lisa, don't worry, I've known her since high school." I smile, "I'm not throwing them out in the cold."

"Them?"

"A four-year-old thinks I am superman. I know it's—"

"Keith, you can't have her staying there with her kid. The legal issues alone, not counting what could happen if her husband finds out. There is not much legal help when a father says he is protecting his family. Good guy or not."

"Don't worry, I heard it from Dad already."

I can see her shaking her head. "I'm not sure what you are thinking, but it's not reality. You're getting yourself into a lot of trouble."

"That's why I have an excellent lawyer. Make sure you send the bill to my address and not to dad's."

"Bill is not going to be happy."

"He'd should be ecstatic I'm scrounging up work for him. Goodbye." I grab another beer. "That's taken care of."

Marilyn slowly takes another sip. "You just have no idea how much trouble you are getting yourself into."

Johnny comes out rubbing his eyes, hugs Marilyn, she and says, "Did you have fun today?"

A grin takes over him. "Mommy, we were riding on a toboggan and went in a big circle till we fell off. Jake was chasing us until he got tired. We had homemade cookies. They were good, just like yours. Are you making cookies again?"

"Yes, someday, dear."

I say, "We are having roast beef dinner tonight, direct from the farm to the table."

Johnny looks back and forth between the two of us.

Marilyn says, "Go play. We're eating in about an hour."

We finish our beer, making sure not to wander into anything serious.

When I return with the food, Marilyn set the table and Johnny is waiting to eat. The beer helped Marilyn relax and Johnny was talking between bites of food. I rinse off the dishes when we finish as Marilyn brings the food and we put the leftover in the fridge. I take her hand. "I'll wash those up when I'm done feeding the cows. Relax and call your mom."

"Calling my mom is not relaxing, but I better ... before she sends out a search party." She looks up at the ceiling. "She checks so often she wouldn't know I've left, but John's been there promoting his caring ways."

The phone rings. "Hello."

"This is your buddy on stakeout duty while you have all the fun."

"Drinking beer and partying down." I smile. "And you are doing a hell of a job too."

"I saw Laura was at your buddy's earlier, but, interestingly, now John's parents are visiting."

"Okay, keep an eye on them. If they don't clean out the house tonight.

The girls are planning on moving Marilyn's stuff and storing it at your house."

"Can't believe you're not in the loop, Laura has already called, I've cleaned out the bedroom, and tomorrow if John is in jail were moving her stuff."

Keith says, "I'm glad to see you step up and help out."

"Yes, and once again you are the hero, and once again what am I getting out of this?"

"The nice guy status."

"Goodbye." Click

Twenty

February 13, 1984

The phone on the kitchen wall brings Marilyn anxiety back as she dials her mom. *I should inform the family I'm not dead.* "Good evening, Mom." She instantly goes into rambling and repeating seemly forever on how to fix her life. Finally, she interrupts, "Mom, I'm never going back. It's over."

"John is extremely worried and so was I."

"Do you have a place to live?"

"I'm staying with a loving family, and until my ribs heal, then I'll look for work and my own place."

"Your ribs, what—?"

"Yes, Mother from being kicked. I'm sure he told you everything."

The phone is silent.

"You can both quit worrying. Johnny has the run of the house. The dog is his new best friend, a teddy bear to sleep with, and a toy tractor. Friday morning, I have an appointment with a lawyer. I could drop Johnny off if you could watch him for a couple of hours."

"My hair appointment is on Friday—"

"Never mind, Mom, I have someone to watch him. The less you know the better it will be for you."

"Well ... we want to help. John said you got mad, throwing things and yelling, because he asked you to fix him something to eat."

"Mom, his dream world. When John calls and wants more information, tell him I moved to a safe house in Detroit, and you can't call. Now you do not have to lie. I'll stop by and see you soon. Thanks for everything. Goodbye." She doesn't wait for a response and hangs up.

Her heart is racing, her hands cold and shaking. *Concerned about John getting supper? What dream world she is living in.*

I dial my sister. "Good evening, Ann, this is Marilyn."

"I'm glad you finally called. Been worried sick. Expecting you to call since Saturday."

"Quit worrying. I am safe, somewhere John can't find me."

"Mom said you had another fight but wouldn't give me any details. Where are you?"

"In a private safe house, already have arranged an appointment with a lawyer on Friday. The restraining order will be processed next week and am working on some kind of normal." *My life, normal?*

"I'm glad you're finally coming to your senses about John. Raise your sights, find a man who has money, and it won't be in that town with all the hick farmers. Think of someone besides yourself, someone who can improve Johnny's chances for college."

Yes, Ann, I'm always thinking of myself, and Johnny's bachelor's degree is not the crisis of today.

"I'm proud of you. Finding a lawyer and a place to stay already. Sounds like you had a plan for once."

"It's day-by-day. They're arresting John tomorrow for assault. I'm calling to warn you when he gets out, he'll go after everyone, and he won't believe you don't know. I told Mom to tell him I moved to a safe house in Detroit, which is partly true."

"I'll give him a piece of my mind if he shows up here."

Marilyn is quiet. *I'm sure you will.*

Ann is laughing. "So, the real story is some hunk showed up in his four-wheel-drive truck and drove you off to his secret hideout."

Marilyn smiles. "I'm safe from the world."

"Oh, suppose it has a modern kitchen from the fifties, and running water."

"Ann stop it." She glances around the kitchen.

"We converted the garage to a cute one-bedroom apartment. Jeff's mom is living there." She lowers her voice. "This sounds terrible, but her health is failing, and she needs to be in a nursing home. Jeff is dreaming I'll become a live-in nurse and take care of her till the end, but it ain't happening. You can move here and have a real life."

"Thank you, sis, but I'm fine."

"Marilyn, a piece of paper does not keep him in line."

"The officer gave me her personal number, and they will arrest him ... if he tries anything."

"I'm still worried. How bad was the fight this time? Let me rephrase that.

How bad did he beat you?"

"Went to the doctor. She said I'll be fine with some rest."

"When are you moving from that damn dreadful town?" Silence. "Marilyn, are you still there? Give me a number where I can reach you."

She looks at the phone, with the number written on the dial. "I promised I wouldn't give the number out."

"Marilyn. I'm your sister. What if something happens?"

Marilyn pauses. "We'll have to take that chance. I gave ... them my word."

"You don't trust your own sister?"

No, and that's why I told a bunch of lies. "Ann, stop it. I can't deal with more stress."

Ann exhales into the phone and continues. "Well, I am glad you moved out. Now start feeling how you'd look in high heels, a slitted skirt, your hair, and nails professionally done. The goal. Find someone with money and a career."

"I haven't finished with this mess—quit worrying about me finding someone."

"The relationship was a dead end. You can't raise Johnny on an ordinary waitress salary. You need a man with a future. Make it your goal. It seems a little pushy, but I'm your sister—pushing you down a better path."

"Yes, sis. I can take care of myself and doing well considering."

"Sometimes you need a jolt of self-esteem. Love you."

"Thanks, goodbye, love yah too."

***

Marilyn makes her way slowly upstairs to her bedroom, and sorts more clothes, but her mind drifts. The peace and comfort could be gone in a moment. She pulls the curtain, looking at the huge tree, with a white blanket of snow covering the yard.

She hears Johnny say, "Hi, Uncle Keith."

She leans in the bedroom doorway, watching Johnny explaining to Keith about the new barn he built. Her eyes get blurry. *My whole life is a lie.*

Twenty-One

February 13, 1984

John arrives home from work, slides the twelve-pack into the empty fridge, and grabs one. The dirty dishes are stacked in the sink, and he hears her yelling. 'If you would've rinsed these off, they'd be easier to wash.' He ponders the thought as the loneliness creeps in. He wanders into Johnny's room. The closet door is open. He stares into the emptiness. *Selfishness, taking my kid.*

He proceeds to their bedroom, the bed still unmade, as he grabs his sweatshirt off the floor. Her top drawer is ajar. He pulls it open. Her clothes are gone. Opens each drawer, then the closet, each empty. *She was here today.* Slams his fist into the closet door, knocking it off the track. Laura is helping her. "Damn it." Miss Slut, the bar queen, talked her into leaving. Then the lowlifes at the safe house filling her head with shit. The modern freestyle life, toss 'em out and find the new one. There's a knock on the door. He rips the door open and freezes. "Yes, and what do you want?"

"The rent—you're three months behind. Remember?"

"Sorry about your luck, but the wife ran off with the money, the kid, everything."

"So, who's the liar? She said, you had money."

"Oh, and when did this happen?"

"Earlier today, and of course, like every lie, the other one has the money. Claims she doesn't reside here. Let me correct that, her friend told me." He pulls the eviction notice and hands it to John. "Pack it up and move it out, with no kids you better be out at end of the month or I'll be adding the court costs, too." He starts to leave but turns. "White trash deadbeats, that's all you are."

John yells as he is walking towards his car. "What did her new boyfriend look like?"

Stopping and slowly turning around, he grins. "She's not my type, but good looking. Yep, your wife ran off with another woman." He snickers as he turns.

"Asshole. I work every day. She spends every day." He slams the door. The bitch Laura always acts so tough. Her bar knowledge is Marilyn's gospel.

He sucks in a slug of beer, plops on the couch, rips her book in half, throws it across the room. More garbage of romantic crap she believes is true.

Where could she be? Bob claimed Laura had acted differently for a month, as if she were hiding something. Her mother was shocked when I told her she left. She must be staying close to sneak back today and get her clothes.

Maybe I should've added a kid when she mentioned it a few years ago. At least give her more to do. He drains his beer, makes his way to the fridge, and dials his mother-in-law. "Have you heard from her yet?"

"Yes, you kicked her. She has cracked ribs. She may be in the hospital."

"She was hitting me, and I pushed away; she tripped over the coffee table. You know how she exaggerates the fights. Is she okay?"

"Said she was."

"Did she say anything else?"

"No, not much."

"Where is she staying? I'll go apologize and make it up to her."

"She wouldn't tell me."

"Give me her phone number. I'll at least call her."

"She wouldn't give me a number."

"You are telling me she doesn't trust her own mother?"

"She is running away. Said she'd update me when she got settled. I may never see her again, just because you can't control your anger."

"Calm down she can't just run off. It'll be different, you'll see."

"I offered to let her stay here while you work it out. Said she's moving to Detroit."

"That's a lie she hates the city. She is hanging out with Laura. Next, she'll be at the bar trying to pick up some slob to take home, or she has already found one. You need to talk some sense into her. Have you talked to Ann?"

"Yes, but she hasn't contacted her either." She sniffles. "Said she'd call and keep me posted."

"Don't tell the police she called. I'll put out a missing person report, and they'll find her. She needs to come home, to where she belongs."

Her voice trembles. "Goodbye."

He slams the phone. Bob's twenty-dollar loan till the end of the week is not going to be enough for gas, beer, and groceries. It was stupid to throw the money at her.

He calls his mom, and she invites him over for dinner. He changes clothes, finishes his beer, and steps out the door.

A patrol car pulls into the driveway tight behind his truck.

They jump out. The passenger cop stands behind his door. The driver moves behind his truck and says, "John Desmond."

John spreads his feet and flexes his hands, glaring at them.

"We have a warrant for your arrest. Turn around. Put your hands on your head."

"This is bullshit."

"You can go peacefully, or we can add resisting arrest."

"Need to turn the stove off." *There're going to gun me down in my yard.*

"Stay where you are. Turn around; we'll check the house."

The passenger cop says, "Hands on your head."

"I need to call my lawyer."

"One phone call after you're booked." The police stay in position.

"This is bullshit, a family disagreement. You guys have nothing else to do except chase down innocent people minding their own business." He turns around and puts his hands on top of his head. The snow crunches as they run towards him.

They handcuff him, pat him down, and read him his rights. "Want to check the house?"

"No."

"Thought you were cooking."

"I was just leaving."

The driver says, "Which lie should we believe?"

The passenger cop says, "Where are you going?"

"None of your business. I want a lawyer."

They read him his rights and push his head downward, into the police car. They check the house door. It was locked.

***

It's nine o'clock before they let him have his phone call. He explains to his mom he'll use a public defender for the bond hearing but will need cash for the bond. Mom was unnerved when he didn't show up for supper and didn't answer the phone.

His mother's voice breaks up as she says, "We'll be there, and don't worry about the money."

"Okay."

Twenty-Two

February 14, 1984

Marilyn slides out of bed and tucks the covers tight around Johnny. She pauses at the top of the stairs taking in the play-living room. She pours coffee and unconsciously stares out the window, watching the smoke trail from the tractor. Jake comes up beside her as she reaches to pet him and lets him outside. "Thank you for playing with Johnny."

He is wagging his tail. Like he knows what she is saying. Her mind wanders to Laura's enthusiasm about John being arrested. Can it be possible for him to be out of her life?

Keith comes through the door with a grin and hangs his Carhart on the hook. "Happy Valentine's." He continues to the coffeepot.

Marilyn's afraid she'll burst out crying any second. She avoids eye contact and says, "Happy Valentine's to you. I forgot what day it was."

"Can't take credit. Mom reminded me, but she forgot a box of chocolates." Keith takes a sip of coffee and says, "I'll cook the steaks tonight to make up."

"That's a lot of extra work." She sets her cup down. *Can't believe he doesn't have a date.*

"Valentines farm style."

"At any moment I'll wake up from my dream and crash back to reality."

Keith talks through his grin. "This is it a normal day at the farm."

The small talk continues, as they go over moving her stuff and storing it at Jason's as if it was a normal. He calls Sid and verifies John was arrested and the earliest he will get out will be later today. Johnny wanders to the kitchen clutching his teddy bear.

Keith says to Johnny, "Remember what day it is?"

His eyes light up. He looks up, and Keith says, "You know where we hid it. Go get it."

He takes off into Keith's bedroom and comes out carrying a red folded paper and a wrapped-up cookie, handing them to Marilyn. "Happy Valentine's Day, Mommy."

Marilyn's hand is shaking as she opens it. "Thank you so much." She hugs and kisses Johnny. "I love you so much." Her eyes water

"Grandma G made them yesterday."

"That is so sweet of her. Did you thank her?"

Keith says, "Yes, we did and tested them to make sure they were good."

Johnny is nodding. "Mommy, why are you crying?"

"These are happy tears." She instantly wants to give Keith a kiss and a hug.

Keith grins. "Johnny, it's something a guy can never figure out. How about some breakfast?" Marilyn starts to get up, and Keith is already up and says, "Sit, it's Valentine's. I'm fixing breakfast." He sets the boxes of cereal on the table. "It's a tough meal. I'll cook eggs and bacon someday."

Laura shows up at nine, we all climb into her car, drop the boys off at Keith's mom, with Keith crouched down in the back seat we make our way to Jason's, a couple of hours later Marilyn's stuff is moved and we head back to the farm.

A quick lunch, Laura heads home, and Keith goes to the toolshed to work. Marilyn lays Johnny down for his nap in the waterbed. Marilyn tidies up the kitchen, hurting and exhausted she lays down on the couch, and falls into a dreamy romantic novel. *My sister's smirking and says, 'You're shacking up with a hunk with a four-wheel drive.'* Do girls really want it? Her fantasy disappear when she wakes. *Get to reality, sex with me? It would be pitiful.*

Keith washes up and looks around the kitchen. "You're supposed to be resting, not cleaning."

"I'm just trying to help out." She turns on the pan of potatoes. "It takes about thirty minutes."

Keith gets the steaks ready. "Make sure you don't tell Laura you are working, she'll give me hell."

Johnny is standing in the doorway staring at Keith and timidly says, "Mom never lets anyone in the kitchen when she's cooking."

"She didn't tell me. I'm in special-status range."

Marilyn kneels in front of Johnny. "He's cooking us steaks tonight. I will call you when it's ready."

"Time for a beer." Keith sets two beers and a glass on the table. "Few minutes. I'll put the steaks on."

Her heart is pounding as he pours some into a glass.

He halts. "You don't have ..."

"I've never had a relaxing beer before." Her dimples appear. "I told my mother and sister about this fantastic family I am staying with and how they are helping me."

The normal family farm."

"The story flowed out like it was real. Of course, I left out a few details of who was living here. Mother insisted on coming to visit not believing someone could be that nice. Then my sister has me moving in with her before she marries me off to a lawyer or doctor, being I haven't plan for Johnny to go to college."

"Family always gives advice." Keith checks the stove and puts the steaks on. He drains the potatoes and grabs a masher out of the drawer. Marilyn sets the milk beside him as he looks at her.

She raises her eyebrows. "You need to mix milk into the potatoes. It makes them creamy."

"Always wondered what the secret was."

Marilyn is setting the table and yells, "Johnny, go wash up and come eat." Keith brings the steaks over as they sit down to eat.

Marilyn fixes Johnny's plate cuts the steak into little pieces and takes a bite.

Johnny says, "Mommy, that's mine."

"You tested my cookie. I'm testing your steak ... Mmm, this is the best ... steak I have ever eaten." She smiles at Keith. "Steak at our house was rare, and only when it was on sale."

"The reward of farming, we eat first-class."

Marilyn quits eating and stares at Keith. "What's the secret? I know you don't add milk."

His eyes twinkle. "It's the corn, like cookies for humans."

Twenty-Three

February 16, 1984

I have my first cup of coffee before making my way to the feeding frenzy. Anticipating Ginger brings a rush; the modern woman wants a little fun. One more brief fling before spring. I finish feeding, check Marilyn's Pinto, and it starts right up before I go back in the house.

We sit sipping coffee and adding small talk. "I'm looking at new tractors today. I'll bring Johnny some brochures." My mind wonders whether she does or doesn't. Do I need them all?

Marilyn is pouring more coffee before I come out of my trance. "Thank you."

She comes back to the table. "If you have a roast in the freezer, I'll attempt to make it for dinner tonight. Looks like you have everything else."

"You're doing a great job cleaning. You want to cook too?"

"I'm still sore but getting bored reading farm magazines." She glares. "Besides, I'd like to add something to make up for my freeloading."

I bite my lip and swallow my grin. *I have an idea.*

She is studying my face and says, "I'm sure you're thinking of more cleaning projects?"

"Well, of course," I say as the grin forms, "although I can't imagine it's very dirty. I clean every Friday."

Panic flows from her. "I didn't mean ... A house always needs cleaning."

"You're being very diplomatic."

"I've seen worse." A smile appears as she looks away. "If you want us to leave for the night or ... don't feel obligated; we'll go to my sister's." She loses her expression and swallows. "You had a life before we came along."

"I've never realized the pleasure of a conversation over coffee in the morning." I hold back a smirk. "You'll be indispensable if you learn to drive a tractor."

"You're avoiding the subject, how we must be crimping your nightlife."

"I'm trusting you to keep a secret. The bar gossip has been known to exaggerate the truth. Farming is monotonous, the fantasizes keeps me sane."

"I'm amazed at everything, deciding what needs to be done, and how much to feed the cows. Did you learn that in college?"

"I learned to how to professionally party, some hard knocks about football when you're not the super stud, but farming ... not so much."

Her dark brown eyes look through me. "How do you decide when to buy a tractor?"

I break into a huge grin. "When a new driver shows up, it's time."

"Stop it. I won't be here sponging off you that long!" Her dimple emerges. "What time would you like to eat dinner tonight?"

"Dad feeds the cows on Thursdays so we can eat anytime, and I will be home before five."

Her face goes blank. "Will he—"

"Don't worry, he won't check on you. But Mom, is wondering what kind of stuff I'm filling your head with and may ask you over for dinner one of these days. Two taboo subjects not to mention the great sex you're getting, and new farm equipment."

Johnny was standing quietly in the kitchen archway. "Mommy, what is sex?"

She cocks her head. "I have no idea. I think we should have Uncle Keith explain it to us. He went to college." Marilyn turns towards me with a smirk. "And the story ..."

I cough. "It's something men try to learn to make women happy." I sip some coffee. "I went to college, but still can't figure it out. When you're older will discuss more details."

Johnny is quiet for a moment but ask, "Is that why Mommy likes you?"

Marilyn's blushes.

I rub my chin. "Must have something do with it."

We continue talking, after Johnny goes off to play.

Some guilt tries to seep in as I dress in my flannel shirt that Mom gave me for Christmas and tell Johnny goodbye. "I'll take you someday."

Instantly Marilyn's stern commanding tone says, "Johnny, no one can know we're staying here, remember?"

His sad eyes tear my heart out. "We'll take a tractor ride tomorrow while your mom's gone."

He scuffs off to the living room.

I make my first stop at the local John Deere store and pick up the planter parts and brochures. I asked Ralph, the parts manager, if I can borrow the phone, why he is getting my parts ready.

I call Jason and say, "We're exploring life in the city today. See you in about a half-hour."

"And you're not showing up," Jason answers.

"Figure about four hours."

"So, what secret are we hiding now?"

"Ralph is trying to weed in on my dates, so I can't explain."

"And the people at the house don't know what you're doing?"

"Hate to make people jealous."

"You are coming up to the bar tomorrow?"

"Yeah, have an image to maintain."

"With a family, it is hard to juggle."

"Goodbye."

***

I circle town before heading to Ginger's parents' house. Spot her husband's truck behind the bar. He's supposed to be out of town. Why would he be at a bar? I drive down to the party store payphone and dial the bar.

"Maggie's."

"Daryl, this is Keith. Is Pete there?"

"No, had a drink, met some burly guy. They talked for a bit. Pete downed his beer and said, 'I've got to go kick someone's ass.' And they walked out together. I jokingly asked Pete when he came in if he got fired. Damn near bit my head off."

"Thanks. Don't tell anyone I called."

I envision his smile. "To the grave."

"Especially Laura."

"Got it."

I dial Ginger's parents' house.

Ginger picks up on the second ring. "Hello."

"This is Keith."

"You're late."

"Pete's truck is parked behind Maggie's, and he's not there."

The phone goes silent. "He left for Flint an hour ago."

"He's left with someone from out of town. I'd drive around, but he'll be suspicious if he sees my truck by your parents'. Think he set you up?"

"That bastard. It's okay for him to fool around, but heaven forbid if I want some stud action. I hate him. The old man across the street has been keeping tabs on me, suspected he was reporting to Pete. Keep it hard until I work out another plan."

"Been working on equipment during the day with dad. I'll give you a call tomorrow midmorning and be at the bar on Friday night, of course."

"I'm going to go mess with him and lead them on a wild goose chase. See you tomorrow."

***

The forty-five-minute drive to Caro to price out the equipment was overwhelmed with the guilt of lying to Marilyn and the remorse of no sex. *I'm losing my edge.*

Ralph, the salesman, is excited to see me again. He promises the world half price, then adds the extras after he has you hooked. I grab brochures for Johnny and write the prices down on the sheets, makes me feel like I have bargaining power against a monopoly. Where else are you buying a John Deere? They give me the story about the excellent service, how they can match the delivery better than my local store.

***

I turn into the driveway. Dad is out feeding the cows already. I'm sure he's wondering where I've been all day. I feel good inside, even though I missed out. Who would believe that coming from me? Johnny and Jake ran to the door. I hand Johnny the brochure. "Go pick out a new tractor."

He carries them into the kitchen. "Look, Mommy, Uncle Keith brought us pictures of new tractors."

I sit with him explaining the differences, and he keeps asking more questions.

Marilyn looks over Johnny's shoulder. "Is that the price of the tractor?"

"Yep, sixty-five grand for the one we need or want depending on who you ask. The two-drive model is forty-five grand with less horse power. Course the bank would happily give us the money, but Dave, my brother-in-law, thinks I'm spending his inheritance."

"It has to be scary!"

"You can't score touchdowns being scared. Matter of fact, can't score at all if you're scared."

Marilyn looks away.

Twenty-Four

February 17, 1984

Marilyn pours her morning coffee with a quick glance out the kitchen window at the swirl of smoke that drifts around the barn. She lingers in her Cinderella dream as she sits at the kitchen table.

Keith says, "Everything okay?"

He stands, confidence oozing out each muscle, the coffeepot in his hand. Slides her empty cup to the edge of the table.

"You snuck in on me." She looks away. "I'm so out of it. Of course, you already know that."

"You've made significant progress in a week."

She grips her cup. "You realize the lawyer is another threat to John?"

Keith sits at the table holding his cup in both hands and says, "Can't be more than anything else."

"He'll wonder where I got the money. Why you are helping me—"

"Unless—I'm sleeping with you." Keith grins.

"Stop it; this is serious."

"Life in a hick town, fun until you get too serious."

***

Marilyn showers, digs out the only dress she owns that doesn't appear too short, puts on makeup, checks the bruise, and returns to the kitchen.

Keith sets eggs down for Johnny and stutters. "How do you like your eggs, Miss Marilyn?"

She mumbles, "It's ... too revealing..."

"No, no, honestly, you look ... good. Johnny, what do you think?"

Johnny stops eating. "Mommy, why are you wearing a dress?"

She smiles. "I have a meeting today with a lawyer, and you're staying with Uncle Keith."

He looks at Keith and goes back to Marilyn. "We're going on the tractor."

Keith winks at Johnny. "Tell her, Johnny, you're practicing how to drive."
Once they finish eating, Keith warms up her car and comes back in the

house.

They sit in silence, Marilyn says, "Guess it's time for me to go." She gives Johnny a hug and kiss. "I'm really proud of you." She glances towards Keith.

"Can't leave me out." He opens his arms with his sweet grin.

She squeezes him tight, her breasts pressing against him, ignoring the pain in her ribs, soaking in the security of his arm wrapped around her. *No one ever warmed up my car* The cold air hits her when she walks outside but she slides into her warm car. She grips the wheel and goes out the driveway.

***

The twenty-minute drive of provoking emotions. She swore off guys forever. Now, a simple hug has her in some teenage delusion. Her hands ache from the drive as she walks into the law office. The secretary introduces herself. "I'm Lisa, and you are Marilyn?"

"Yes."

"Nice to meet you. We're representing you on an assault charges, doing a PPO, and filing for a divorce?"

Marilyn's voice quivers. "Yes."

Lisa takes papers out of a folder and puts them on a clipboard. "Fill out everything as completely as possible."

Marilyn fills out the forms and leaves the address blank.

Lisa glances at the papers. "I understand the secrecy, but we need an address. What address did you use for the police report?"

"My girlfriend, but—"

"Put her address down. You can always change it. I'll make a note for you to come pick up the paperwork." Lisa tilts her head, trying to make eye contact. "You'll have to fix the address issue before the court date."

Marilyn nods. The waiting room brings calm. The greens and browns match; the carpet and wallpaper blend in such detail that it should be in a magazine.

After a few minutes, Lisa gets up. "Follow me." She leads her into Mr. Drillman's office.

The dark mahogany desk dominates the end of the room, and one wall is full of books, top to bottom. Could someone read that many books? He greets her with a gentle handshake and motions for her to sit down. Lisa closes the door behind her. The silence is unraveling the little confidence she has left while he's examining her file.

"Mrs. Desmond, it's tragic the wrong that happened to you." He looks at her and, with a warm, calming voice, says, "Everything we say here is confidential. The information is to find the best settlement for you and to do that we need every detail of what happened, good or bad." After another long pause, he adds, "Let's start with some basic information. How long were you married?"

"Almost five years."

"How long have the arguments been violent?"

"The last two years. Everyone told me it would happen, but I didn't believe them, of course. Another statistic."

"This is you, doesn't matter about anyone else's issues. When was the first time?"

She pauses. "Six months after we were married. It was a slap across my face. It scared me but comparatively, it wasn't much."

"What was it about?"

"He was playing poker with his buddies, which was okay, but he expected me to sit home alone. I was naïve. And shocked, no one had ever hit me before. I always believed he would see ... dumb but—"

"Mrs. Desmond, situations don't go away by themselves. We're here to help you correct it. So, what happened before when you called the police?"

"It was last summer. He hit me and knocked me down. When I stood up, he hit me again. I crawled to the bathroom and stayed there until he passed out. Called the police, went back to the bathroom, and waited. They took him to jail, but his parents bailed him out the next day. I moved to the safe house and then to my mom's."

"What made you return?"

"He would visit me at my mom's. He promised ... It's stupid ... I believed he had changed." She stops and mumbles, "I dropped the charges."

Drillman shows no emotion and says, "You said this started shortly after you were married. Has he always left bruises?"

"No, he would ..." She closes her eyes, sensing his beer spit spraying her face. "He would grab my hair, telling me to look at him, and scream how terrible and—"

Drillman holds his hand up. "I get the picture." Never changing emotion, he says, "How often did this happen?"

"It was mostly in the winter. We barely had enough money to pay the fuel oil bill and the rent each month, but he would still stop at the bar. Cooped up in the house with the heat turned down into the mid-fifties, wearing our coats, yet scared he would come home and yell at me for not doing enough."

He is writing notes on his pad. "Any man you know, someone he may have assumed was too friendly?"

"My social life consists of going to Laura's or Mother's for coffee."

"He was okay with that?"

"He blames Laura, so I rarely brought it up."

"She works?"

"She is the night manager and bartender at Maggie's."

"He works every day, correct?"

"Yes."

"Why did you quit your job?"

"John accused me of flirting with the customers. I was friendly ... I never ..."

He holds his hand up. "His opinion doesn't make it true."

"Skip, the owner, was going to tell him he couldn't come to the restaurant anymore, thinking he was helping. But I knew it would be a fight, so I quit."

"So how do you know Keith?"

"My girlfriend Laura and he are friends. I had no place to go, and..."

Mr. Drillman rose from his notes.

"He volunteered to let me stay, and he's been a perfect gentleman."

They went over more details about Friday night, and Marilyn adds how happy Johnny was living at Keith's.

"Johnny's your son?"

"Yes."

"Has John ever hit Johnny?"

"He'd yelled at him till he'd cry and run to me. Called him 'a wimpy ass kid.' I constantly threatened John with calling the police if he so much as touched him. He has always backed down."

"Do you have any romantic feelings for Keith?"

"I've only known him a week, but he's a very caring person." She pulls a Kleenex out of her purse and dabs her eyes.

He has a slight smile. "There are a few of us."

You mean the gentlest hugs I have ever felt in my life. "I'm not someone to take advantage of his generosity."

"Just asking the question. Your husband ... extremely jealous."

"Yes."

"So, what's the plan for your living arrangements?" He sits there staring at her. "With small-town gossip. If he is smart and talks to a lawyer, they'll play along. Then he'll testify that your son saw you naked in bed with Keith. Probably be more graphic."

"I would never—"

He continues. "Studying John's profile, he'll go ballistic, inform the court he knows his family is in danger, and tear into Keith. It may not be fair, but they'll overlook the wrong, as a father protecting his child."

She is dabbing tears to keep her makeup from running.

"Mrs. Desmond, we are dwelling on this a little more than we should, but I want you to realize they'll try to prove you're unfit. If you tell the court Keith is an upstanding person, do you think they'll believe you're not sleeping with him?"

She rubs her hand.

"What's the reason for leaving the safe house?"

"Johnny became unruly, being cooped up every day ... It felt like a prison. Even the counseling didn't help; it added to the depression."

"I still recommend considering it again."

"I know."

"Have you ever thought about moving back into your house, without your husband, of course?"

"The landlord is evicting us. We're almost three months behind."

He stops, and his green eyes laser through her. "You must realize your living arrangement is a no-win situation, and you have to fix it." He looks at the file. "Let's move on.

"We need a detailed list of your assets. Lisa has the paperwork when you leave. What loans do you have and cars do you own?"

"He still makes payments on his truck. My car is old; I got it from my mother."

"Do you have any savings or retirement?"

"No."

"Are there belongings still at the house?"

"I moved some things out earlier in the week. The rest, it doesn't matter."

"Even if it's what you have already, the court looks at it as equally divided and we assume your half should be more. How did you move your furniture? Police report says you have cracked ribs?"

"Laura and another friend of hers moved the stuff."

"You were with them, right?"

"Yes."

"Did you destroy anything?"

"No, why would I—"

"They're your belongings, and you can do anything you want with them. People break furniture so the other spouse can't have it. Legal, but not in the best light. Some major decisions, each change your life. I would recommend petitioning to keep everything, even if you sell or give it away." He flips over some pages. "When there're children involved, it's a minimum of six months for a court date from the date you file. With their wisdom, it may work out, and you just need time." He slowly raises his head.

"I am not changing my mind." A deep breath, aggravating the pain in her ribs. "Not this time."

He stays unemotional and says, "Did you talk to the prosecutor yet?"

"No."

"We'll get the report. One important point the restraining order is valid for a year. If they convict him, they will extend the restraining order. What are your thoughts on leveraging the assault to improve your divorce options?"

She bites her bottom lip.

"Think about it."

"We'll file for no visitation and build a case about his violence, leveraging how it spills over towards your son. Write down the details and we'll decide if it is relevant or needed. The Friend of the Court, with their grand wisdom, will allow him some visitation if he files for it."

He flips through some more papers. "The restraining order should be processed on Tuesday or Wednesday. Keep a copy with you. We'll put divorce papers and child custody together and have them ready by the end of next week. I want to remind you." He puts his hands together and his fingers point up. "The first time or anytime he encounters you, instruct him to leave, end of the conversation. If he wants to discuss anything, give him one of our cards. If he doesn't leave immediately, call the police. He has to realize you're serious."

Her heart is thumping in her chest. She pauses, avoiding eye contact. "I feel like a terrible mother."

"You're taking the steps. It is a proven fact that kids growing up in a violent household repeat it. They become their environment. It is not easy, but you're on the right path."

Marilyn closes her eyes and nods in agreement.

"When he finds you and says how sorry he is, and how much he loves you ... Remember, no conversation, you leave, no exceptions."

She mumbles, "I understand. I won't fall for the lies."

"Do you have any questions?"

She shakes her head.

He stands. "Keep us updated if anything changes."

She is shaking and almost loses her balance when she gets up.

He opens the door for her. "Why don't you sit for a minute? Lisa, can you get her some water?"

Marilyn says, "I'm fine, really."

Lisa comes around her desk and walks her over to a chair. She hands her some water and sits beside her.

After a few minutes, Marilyn stares at the greenish leather chair with metal bronze buttons tracking down the arm in such perfect order. She sips some water. "Thanks for everything. I'm okay and ready to go home."

Lisa touches her arm. "Fill these out." She slides papers into a folder. "Call if you have questions. Drop them off or mail them to us; there's no rush. Dear, lots of things to digest; take your time. You can do this."

She makes it to her car. Laying her head on the steering wheel, and sobs. *I'll never have a normal life. Who am I trying to fool?*

Twenty-Five

February 16, 1984

Marilyn eases the death grip from the steering wheel as she exits town, but another panic attack comes on and she stops on the snow-covered shoulder, barely off the road. Mr. Drillman advice of how to fix life from his desk that you could use for a bomb shelter, making over a hundred dollars in an hour.

Decisions. I can't even drive. Crying takes over as she rests her head on the steering wheel. Her mother's words screaming at her. "You should've gone to college like your sister. Then, with her next breath, John will protect you from the world." *My new reality. Sleeping with Keith can't be worse than John. Everyone ... would Laura sleep with Keith? Get real; you'll have to sleep with someone to afford a place to live.*

A car slows down and makes a U-turn and pulls up behind her. An older man walks to her window and says, "You need help?"

She cracks the window and mumbles, "It's a woman meltdown. Thanks for checking." She pulls out onto the highway.

Her fingers ache when she finally gets to the house. She drives straight to the garage. Hard to believe a car even fits. She stays close to the left side. *At least you won't hit his car.* The mirror barely clears. The driver's door won't open enough to get out, so she climbs over to the passenger side. *That's ladylike with a dress on.* There's a sizeable gap between the two cars as she quickly closes the garage door.

***

She hears Jake woof, and she can hear Johnny's footsteps.

He freezes. "What happened, Mommy?"

She forgets how bad her face looks. "I had a slobber moment, and it smeared my makeup. Come, give me a hug."

He wraps his arms around her. "Your eyes are all black."

"It'll wash it off. Don't worry."

Keith is standing in the doorway. "Should've warned you, Bill's a little direct."

She nods. “At least I held it together until I left.”

“Is the car in the garage?”

“Yes.”

“I forgot to tell you I’d put it in.”

“Didn’t want to leave it out.” *Take a breath; you’re safe.* Her heartbeat slows. “I managed no scratches or dents on the Vette.”

Keith breaks out with his patent smile.

“Let me change and wash my witch face. Then we’ll have some lunch.”

Keith says, “We voted for grilled cheese sandwiches.”

She furrows her eyebrows. *Johnny doesn’t eat grilled cheese.* “Okay. I’ll be right back.”

She stares into the mirror. The black-smeared cheeks, the puffy bloodshot eyes—*I look like a witch*. After changing into her favorite jeans, she takes her bra off it hurts tighten around her ribs. *He will notice*. She puts on her faded kitty sweatshirt and hears them laughing on the way to the kitchen.

Keith, without looking up from the stove, says, “One or two?”

“One’s plenty for me. I would’ve—”

“Relax, take a break.” He serves Johnny’s sandwich, cut in four exact triangles, and glances at Marilyn. “Any special requests?”

She is looking at Johnny’s plate. “No.” Her body quivers watching Johnny bite the first corner off each piece.

He places her sandwich on the table. “Dig in.” He finishes cooking and brings two more to the table.

Johnny has bitten each point and put them on his plate, making a circle in the center. Keith peers at Marilyn, who hasn’t touched hers.

Her eyes are watery.

Keith says, “They taste good if you eat the circle first.”

She takes a breath. “I see that.”

She finally takes a bite. “They’re excellent in halves, too.” She asks Johnny what they did this morning.

He gets excited telling her about plowing the snow with the tractor. He waves his hands, showing how they put the snow in big piles.

“I’m sure you worked really hard.”

“Mom, Grandma G is really nice.”

“Yes, I believe it runs in the family. Let’s go read a story and take a nap.”

When she returns to the kitchen, Keith has his checkbook, invoices, and notebook scattered across the table. She watches him for a minute in the doorway. "Figuring how much my stay is costing you?"

"No, you're cheap compared to these bills."

"The lawyer doesn't work cheap."

"The important point is he's the best."

"He went over the worst-case scenario and suggested using the assault to leverage John to not fight the divorce. The big issue was about my living here, and John using it against me." Keith shrugs. Marilyn continues, "Had to pull off the side of the road to regain my composure to drive home today. Then, someone stopped and asked me if I was okay, which freaked me out."

"Just a neighbor checking if you needed help."

She laughs. "I'm sure he was, but I looked pitiful, and another image you won't ever forget. No matter how much makeup or fancy clothes I wear, I find a way to be ugly."

"The girl this morning was a stone fox. Think about it. Last week you hit bottom, and a week later you were the hottest chick in town. Transformed right here at the old farmhouse. I'm impressed to be the first one seeing the new you."

"You continually say nice things to me. I hope ... Johnny is happier than he's ever been." Tears form. "You're his superhero ..." *And mine.* "I promised Johnny we'd find a nice place someday. I made it up, thought it would help, give him hope, but now he believes I found a place. He asked me yesterday, 'Why didn't we come here last year?'"

"You could have if you had wanted to." Keith winks. "Did you ever brainstorm any options?"

"No, too depressing."

He tears out a piece of paper and hands her a pen. "Spell out everything, even if it sounds crazy." His soft hazel eyes watch her.

She stares at him, her heart melting. "I can't believe you got Johnny to eat his grilled cheese sandwich."

"You turn triangles into circles, and circles taste better. Everyone knows that."

She laughs, and wants to give him a kiss, but starts writing. "Move to Port Huron with sister."

"Just write the ideas on the front, staying at some guy's house. Flip it over, evaluating side." Keith is grinning. "Write. Try it. Great idea."

Marilyn writes. *Stay at Laura's.* She flips it over. *But Bob—*

"He's on his way out next."

It's a short list. She sits in a daze.

Keith stretches his neck to see the list. "Ten minimum, twenty is better." He stares at her. She keeps writing the last issue on her paper. *Need a babysitter.*

Keith says, "Mom is a great babysitter."

"She hardly knows me."

"Johnny has sweet-talked his way into her heart. You don't think she makes me hot chocolate and cookies, do you?"

Marilyn ponders the thought, but doubt is her reality.

***

Keith goes to do the chores. The phone rings as Marilyn reaches to call her sister. She stares at it until it quits, then dials her sister, giving her updates of the great progress. Ann reminds her of the goal. Find a rich guy. She's interrupted from her list, with Jake's bark, a knock, and someone opens the door.

Marilyn tenses.

Laura yells, "Marilyn, it's Laura."

Marilyn takes a breath. "Hi, what's the matter?"

"Bob didn't show up. Guess he's not waiting until the end of the month to start screwing me around. I'll move his shit out on the porch in the morning. Can you watch Chad?"

Marilyn smiles. "No hot dates for me tonight. Did you try to call earlier?"

"Yes."

"I was afraid to answer."

"That's what I figured. I called back, but the line was busy. I knew someone was here. I am running late. How did it go with the lawyer?"

"Great, if I'm not inviting men over to the house for the next six months. I used your address for my residency. Hope that's okay?"

"Of course. Whatever you must do. Our new code consists of two rings.

Hang up and call back. If work slows down enough, I'll call you later. Depending on what Bob does, it may be Sunday or Monday before I pick Chad up."

Fear overtakes her. "What do I tell Keith?"

Laura gives her a quick hug. "Tell him no girls, no parties, for the rest of the weekend." She back out the door.

Marilyn stands with her mouth open, staring at the door. She picks up Chad's bag, feels the pain in her ribs, but carries it into the living room. The boys are already playing. *What do I say to Keith? We didn't ask permission.* She checks the roast and keeps glancing out the kitchen window, waiting for him to put the tractor in the toolshed.

Twenty-Six

February 18, 1984

Laura starts the bar cleanup, the waitress called in she was sick, Jason did a drive-by of her house and John's truck was back up to the door. The urgency rattles through the bar as Laura announces last call before the two-a.m. cutoff and Jason starts restocking the coolers. Ten minutes later, she shouts, "Drink it or lose it." She hears the stragglers grumbling but continues pushing them out the door. She has everyone out by quarter-after two and opens a beer, gets one for Jason and Sara as they're finishing the cleanup.

Jason goes and starts the cars.

Laura says to Sara, "We're finding another waitress. That's the last time she leaves us hanging. The busiest weeknight and Miss Prissy takes the night off."

Sara says, "She owes me a new pair of shoes, with as much running as I did tonight."

"Let's wrap up. I need to evaluate the mess at my house."

"What happened?"

"It's been shitty with Bob for the last month. His payback left me hang with no one to watch Chad tonight and has the weekend off but is moving out on a Friday night."

"That doesn't sound good. Call me if you need anything. It takes a couple of hours to unwind before I hit the bed, anyway."

"Thanks, I'll be alright." Jason waits for her as she locks the door.

"I'll follow you home." He grins. "And tuck you in."

"I don't ... It's my mess."

"You can take care of yourself, but ... moral support doesn't hurt. Nothing going on tomorrow or, more like, today, and I hate my friends drinking alone."

I want to be alone. "Okay."

***

She opens the door; the smell of stale beer hits her before she turns on the light. She scans the kitchen: cans are open, upside down, with beer dripping off the cupboards, toilet paper rolled through the wet mess on the table, countertops, stove, and floor. Her hand tightens into a fist. She sucks in a scream and looks at the note on the table. Written with one of Chad's crayons, in a puddle of beer with the key.

Mrs. Bitch.

Your key, for your next sucker. We would've cleaned up, but we ran out of shit paper.

PS: Hope you didn't want a beer!!!

She steps around beer puddles, wads up the note, and throws it at the sink. She continues to the living room, with Jason following her. *Why didn't I talk him out of coming? I don't want anyone to know.* The couch is gone, the coffee table and end tables tipped over, newspapers scattered, her albums dumped out, the TV stand gone. Her neck stiffens. Her bedroom door is open a crack. She pushes it open and turns on the light. The lamp is decorated with her bra and panties. They had opened each drawer and have thrown her clothes everywhere. The mattress leans against the wall with another note.

Ready to screw the next one.

"He is such an asshole." She slams the door closed.

Jason walks up behind her and puts his hand on her shoulder. "What is it?"

"He tore the bed apart."

He raises his eyebrows. "And the why?"

"When I moved in, I had the rails installed wrong. It fell apart the first night. He always bragged to everyone about how he'd rescued me from my blondness. With one last dig, he tore it back apart."

"Let's go to my house."

"You go; I'll be alright."

Jason, with harshness in his voice, says, "There's no beer. You're going to do a half-ass job and become more pissed. And I'm not leaving so you have a pity-party alone."

Laura wants a good cry, a beer, a cigarette. She gave up the cigarettes, the beer is gone, and she can't cry in front of Jason. Bob's room is empty with the vacuum parked right where he finished. She continues to Chad's room.

Nothing touched, *thanks for a small miracle.* Her eyes are watering; she leans against the doorpost. Without looking at Jason, she says, "You can leave. I'll sleep in Chad's bed and get an early start."

He doesn't answer.

She bites her lip. "Let me grab some clothes." She scrounges through the clutter and finds clothes, trying to stay in control. Jason has picked up the empty cans and is wiping the counter when she enters the kitchen. "Go on home? It's not your mess, and I'll handle it."

Jason grabs her bag and puts his arm around her. "We're going to have a drink, get some sleep, and later we'll clean up this mess."

Jason walks her out to his truck, as she is still in a daze. "Bob is nasty, but John in my house, touching my underwear and whatever else his gross pea brain might do ... I wouldn't put it past him to steal them so he could play with himself."

They drive slowly with the lights off by John's house. Bob's car is parked in the driveway, and John's truck is behind the house.

They walk into Jason's, he grabs a couple of beers as Laura goes to the couch, her face buried in her hands.

Jason continues to the stereo. "Rock and roll or something mellow."

"Any Pat Benatar?"

"Coming right up." Benatar takes over.

Jason raises his beer for a toast. "To our Miss Benatar."

She raises her head and returns the toast. "And his balls rot off."

Jason grins.

They sit, taking in the tunes. Jason grabs a couple more.

Through blurriness Laura is staring at her bottle. "Not sure when Bob become more of a pain than he was worth. Once I ... damn it. I became the maid. He would leave shit for weeks and wait for me to clean it up." *Why did I ... with a slob?* "What the hell ... Was I that desperate?"

"We've all been there. At least you're not married." They continue with the tunes blasting, each in a delusional world.

"I could've used being young and foolish, but the bartender, who's always in control..." *It never felt ... not like.* "Enough of my pity party. He took his best shot." She slugs the rest of her beer. "It will be a long day. I had better get to sleep."

Jason gets a blanket and a pillow. “I’ll take the couch. You can have the bed, even has clean sheets.”

“I’m not taking your bed, and—no, we’re not sharing.” Her green eyes expose a twinkle as she rips the pillow and blanket from him.

“If you slept in my bed, I could ...”

“You’re definitely hanging around Keith too much!” She walks over and gives him a hug. “Thanks for caring. Good night.” She touches his arm. “This is against your loyalty to Keith but would be a great favor if he didn’t know the details.”

He winks. “No problem, you just wanted someone to spend the night with and he’s busy.”

She is shaking her head and smiles as he heads to the bedroom.

***

Laura stirs and smells coffee. Jason is at the counter drinking a cup when the world comes into focus. She asks, “What time is it?”

“It’s nine-thirty.”

“Shit, wanted to leave by nine.”

“You needed to sleep. I’ll make eggs and toast quickly if you want to eat.”

“Beer and cigarettes will suffice. Just kidding. Toast and coffee are all I need.” She heads to the bathroom. Staring at the puffy, bloodshot eyes, she thinks how good a shower would feel as she splashes her face.

Jason has toast plus homemade strawberry jam as she sits on a barstool beside him.

Laura says, “Just drop me off. I don’t expect you to help clean.”

“It won’t hurt me to have a little cleaning practice.”

“Never took him for such an ass, but hanging around John why would I expect anything else? Should’ve moved his shit out in the snowbank.” She finishes her coffee. “Let’s go.”

She lies down on the seat as they drive by John’s house. Jason is scanning behind the house. “There both gone.”

***

Laura walks through the sticky floor and starts a pot of coffee. "I'd add Bailey's if I didn't work tonight." She digs out a bucket, Pine-Sol, a mop, and cleaning rags.

Jason reaches for the bucket. "I'll start in the kitchen."

She feels her eyes water. "The laundry is calling, I can't even imagine wearing anything without washing it first."

"Let me know when you're ready to set up the bed, I've heard you need help."

She smiles. "Smartass." She puts her underwear in the washer and then a load of sheets. It is after one o'clock, but the place has shaped up and smells of Pine-Sol.

Laura says, "Let's take a break and have lunch. I need to call Marilyn. She'll be worried and wonder what happened."

She dials and hangs up and dials back. Marilyn answers the phone. Laura says, "Hello."

"Hello, I was getting worried but didn't want to wake you."

"I overslept, then went to cleaning."

"Well, how bad?"

"The typical for the lazy slob he was."

"I'll come over and help."

"It's under control, and you need to stay hidden."

"It's my fault."

"No, you stay put. Going to be looking for a roommate. We'll discuss options that are within our budget."

Marilyn says, "Why don't you come over tomorrow and have dinner with us? No reason for you to eat alone. I'm preparing roast beef and chocolate sheet cake for dessert, and there will be plenty."

"You're impressing Keith with your cooking?"

Marilyn laughs. "I'm not ready for anything else. It's weird to dig through the freezer and decide what you want to fix, instead of how I am making one package of hamburger into two meals. My heart was beating out of my chest last night, when we were sitting around the dinner table with the boys, Keith carrying on a conversation, they're laughing and ..."

Laura hears muffling. "Are you crying?"

"The emotions burst out of me. I can't control ... It's the simple things he does."

"Hope you're keeping that in check."

She sighs. "Yesterday before I went to the lawyer, I squeezed him as tight as my hurting ribs would let me and had to force myself to let go. He's making grilled cheese sandwiches for lunch, which Johnny would never eat before. I didn't know they tasted good cut into triangles."

"Damn girl, don't be falling—he's wild, crazy, and looking for the next one."

"It's not the wanting ... I realize he's showing off." *But I tingle inside.* "How bad is the house?"

"I can live without his smelly ass couch. His big act of toughness. He drank the beer and poured the rest out. My screaming fit is over, and everything is under control. Tell Chad I love him and miss him. See you tomorrow."

"Okay, come anytime, planning dinner around two thirty."

She hangs up and comes back to the kitchen table. Jason had cleared the dishes from lunch and is finishing his coffee. "So, how is she doing?"

"She is cooking meals, and Keith is playing with the boys on the snowmobile."

"I keep teasing Keith about his new family life ... he likes it."

"I read somewhere that if you stop for a minute, the simple things make you happy."

"Keith's charm getting to her?"

She looks off into space. "I will kill him if he hurts her."

"The vibe I feel from Keith is taking care of her, and not the joking kind. His demeanor is completely different with her."

"I've noticed. I can't thank you enough for everything you have done. Keith gets the accolades and you move furniture and mop up messes." She smiles and stares into his brown eyes. "Please, let's keep this a secret between the two of us. Keith would never judge what happened, but I feel so disgusted. Letting Bob take advantage of me and Marilyn will find some way to blame herself."

"We all have our farm secrets." He pats the top of her hand. "I'll stop at the bar later."

"Thanks." Laura hugs him. "I'll be okay." She watches him and waves as he leaves. *He is such a sweet guy.* She closes the door as the tears start. She grabs a towel, breaking into uncontrolled sobbing.

The pity party is over. A shower and dress for work.

Twenty-Seven

February 22, 1984

Less than two weeks and a daily ritual, Marilyn pours her coffee, glancing out the window, watching swirls of smoke from the tractor and assessing how life feels secure. The inner joy of fixing meals, how happy they are joking and eating together.

Keith comes in from chores each morning, and we have conversations about life, with no arguments. The solidness of his convictions is the opposite of his playboy image. Her fears seems to be melting for the first time in her life. The PPO gives her freedom again, but she wants to stay in her cocoon.

Keith has cereal and goes off to the toolshed.

Laura is going to charge her a hundred dollars a month rent, which is a hundred less than she should pay, and justified it with Marilyn watching Chad and fixing meals. Marilyn argued without success that she should pay half, but Laura is not changing her mind. Then, Marilyn agreed to work Thursday and Friday nights. She'll need to overcome the fear of working at a bar, although it is connected to the bowling alley, and families come there all the time. The next crisis will be convincing Johnny they must leave. *Maybe I'm not in charge of my life.*

There is a knock at the door. Jake wags his tail and woofs, yet fear grips her. Johnny is staring at her as she slowly moves towards the door and opens it.

Jake squeezes between her. The woman reaches and pets him. "Don't mean to intrude, been waiting for Keith to bring you over and introduce us." She sticks out her hand. "I'm Gwen, Keith's mother."

Marilyn shakes and mutters, "I'm Marilyn, and of course, you know Johnny and Chad." She rubs the top of their heads. She steps to the side of the door. "Please come in."

"It's nice to meet you." Gwen bends down and gives them a hug. "And how are you boys doing today?"

Johnny says, "You want to see our barn? Uncle Keith helped us build it last night."

Gwen smiles and says, "Of course."

They make their way back to the kitchen, and Marilyn asks, "Would you like some coffee?"

"Yes." Gwen says as she sits down. "Johnny has made himself right at home."

Marilyn takes a small sip of coffee. "Keith is in superman status, with Johnny." The silence lingers as they both take a sip. "I'm not sleeping with him."

Mrs. Larson sets her cup down. "You've heard the rumors? Keith charms all the women." She bites her lip. "I condemn his free-living lifestyle." She freezes her stare. "You can't keep living here."

Marilyn opens her mouth.

Gwen holds her hand up. "If you need a place to stay, we have an extra room, not as private, but helps with the gossip, and morally the right thing to do."

"Thanks for your generosity. My restraining order is finally processed, and I'm moving to Laura's on Monday."

Gwen's face relaxes. "Did Keith invite you to Sunday dinner?"

Marilyn lets the breath out she has been holding. "No."

"I make dinner for the family every Sunday and apologies for Keith's manners, but you are invited."

"Thanks for the invitation. I was planning on fixing dinner for Laura, but I'm sure Keith would rather eat—"

"No, I don't mean to intrude. But remember you are always welcome."

Marilyn feels a warm glow. They continue with some calm conversation, and she finally starts to relax. Then spits out. "Keith has been honorable and a gentleman. You should be proud of him."

"I am but." Gwen finishes her coffee, "He is no saint." Touches Marilyn's arm. I'm here to help and a cheap babysitter."

She watches her leave and paces around the kitchen. Then the fear takes over. Keith going to be mad we're not going to his mom's. It's early for lunch but ... She sticks her head into the living room. "I am going outside for a minute."

They never look up and say, "Okay."

She is curious about what Keith is working on and how he manages the cold for hours at a time, but fear increases on her way to the toolshed. She opens the door of the toolshed, not feeling any warmth but hearing the roar of a jet engine, with some rock and roll trying filtering in the air. Least the kids won't be able to hear if he yells at me. She weaves by the tractor with a bucket, then the one that says 4020 on the hood, whatever that means. He's working in the far corner behind the planter. She smiles to herself, remembering him telling Johnny what the different equipment was. Some of it must have rubbed off. He still doesn't notice her, she walks closer, admiring him.

The awareness of the chilly air takes her out of a trance, and she asks herself how long she has been standing here watching him. She moves even closer and says, "How is it going?"

Startled, he looks up and waves, then turns off the heater and radio.

"Is something wrong?"

I need a kiss and a hug. "No. Wondered when you wanted to eat?"

He looks at his watch and weaves towards her.

"Didn't mean you had to stop."

"I hate missing a meal."

He puts his arm around her shoulders, guiding her between the tractors. "Your mom stopped and invited me to Sunday dinner."

"You sound excited?"

Her legs are losing strength. She looks up at him. "I said no because Laura was coming but you can still go. I'm sure her is much better than mine."

He grins. "You're not getting off that easy." Wraps his arm around and we head for the house.

Marilyn sets lunch on the table, Keith, Johnny, and Chad wash up together. Everyone sits down and doesn't take a bit, just watches Keith. "Laura called. The restraining order arrived."

Keith stops eating and looks up from his beef noodle soup. "The new life begins."

She bites her lip and nods.

"Going to miss ... my personal chef."

"I enjoyed ... I'll cook when I can—"

Johnny stops eating. "Mommy—how come you're not cooking?"

The silence fills the air. Marilyn finally says, "We have to leave."

"I don't want to go. You said—Uncle Keith, can't we stay here?"

Keith sighs. "Well ..."

Tears fill Johnny's eyes. He jumps up and runs upstairs, with Jake running behind him.

Marilyn moves to follow him. Keith touches her arm. "Give him a few minutes with Jake? He's a great problem-solver."

She sucks in her bottom lip. "I don't want you to see me cry."

He squeezes her hand. "I'm going to miss you, too." They sit in silence and clear the table together.

February 26, 1984

Keith does the chores and goes to restaurant on his normal routine. Marilyn getting the Sunday dinner ready, fighting the depression and returns upstairs to work on packing. She hears Keith, and glances downstairs, Johnny is sitting on his lap on the couch.

Dinner is enjoyable with the finalizing of it left for tomorrow. Everyone is gone Keith finishes the chores.

Keith sets down two beers a glass and waves her to the table. "To good times." He raises his glass. "I've truly enjoyed your stay, and welcome you back anytime, in case Laura gets to bosses." They toast.

Marilyn holds back her tears. "You have changed my life; I'm forever in your debt."

"Our little secret winter fling."

She smiles, and they sit quietly.

Twenty-Eight

February 27, 1984

Marilyn packs the rest of their clothes and moves them downstairs while Keith is doing chores. The code double ring and Laura verify John is at work and the move is a go. She has the timing routine organized, puts on the bacon waiting for the smoke trail to end before she starts the eggs.

Keith takes a couple bites of food before saying, “You put some extra sugar in these eggs today?”

Johnny looks up. “Uncle Keith you don’t put sugar in eggs.”

“Your mom puts some secret potion in them.” He glances at Marilyn. “Guy could get addicted.”

She bits her lip and blinks back her watery eyes.

The silence is stifling, as they fill her Pinto with clothes, and the rest in Keith’s truck.

Keith goes into the living room to retrieve Johnny, whose eyes are watery carrying the tractor and teddy bear.

Marilyn looks away to keep from becoming a sobbing idiot.

He’ll miss my cooking, but it won’t keep him home forever. Move on and let everyone return to their lives.

He sets Johnny in the car, and Marilyn squeezes him tight, holding back the tears. “Thanks for everything you have done.” She reaches up and kisses him on the cheek.

He holds her close; she smells the coffee from his breath, afraid to move. He tilts her head, and his lips touch hers with a magical tenderness. Her legs collapse, but he holds her tight. Still shaking, she staggers to the car. *Does he do that to all women? Do we have time before I leave?*

He grins, holding the door. “See you soon.”

Her body is tingling. *I want …* She manages a small wave and drives away.

When they arrive at Laura’s, Marilyn opens the car door for Johnny, but he doesn’t move, just stares at his toys. “Please, Johnny, I know it’s hard, but I can’t carry you.”

He shuffles out, staring at the ground. She grabs a small bag and takes his hand.

Laura helps with the clothes, then shows her where to park behind the shed. Laura sets two cups out and pours coffee. Marilyn is studying the set of old kitchen cupboards and the ugly green Formica counter.

Laura says, "You like him, don't you?"

She keeps looking at the cupboards. "No one has ever treated me with so much kindness." She scans the room. "I trusted him as if I had known him forever."

Laura sits, her head propped on her hands. "Did you sleep with him?"

Marilyn, under some spell from earlier today, answers, "No ..." *But.*

"I trust Keith too." Laura fades into space. "But ... you look like a starry-eyed teenager after the first time."

Marilyn smirks. "I wanted to ..." She rolls her lip behind her teeth. "I've never had such a desire." She tries to calm herself. *I would panic and ruin it.* "No one can know. Not even Keith."

Laura's green eyes dance and sparkle.

"I'm fighting this weird emotion but feel Keith has a secret girlfriend?

"Ginger is a fling and will be over."

"The weird feelings I wanted to one minute and then break out in anxiety and fear the next." Marilyn looks away. "He was vague about his girl relationships but mentioned his mother was trying to set him up with a Karla. When, or if, I ever find someone," Marilyn sighs, "I can't live near here. We all realize John will forever harass me."

The sound of a diesel truck takes over, and Keith backs up to the steps. Jason pulls beside him with more furniture. Like professional movers, they bring everything into the house. Keith is in the bedroom talking to the boys. Laura sets out bologna, peanut butter, and jelly for sandwiches and announces, "Lunch is ready."

Keith takes a slice of bologna and adds jelly to it. He watches Johnny while he cuts it into triangles and slides him a piece. "It's fantastic." He gazes at Chad. "You want a piece?"

Chad nods.

Marilyn feels her eyes water as Keith winks at her. *He's going to make me cry.*

Keith makes a second sandwich, sharing it with the boys, too.

Jason grins, glances at Laura, then at Marilyn. "You trained him to become a gourmet cook too?"

Marilyn blushes.

Keith says, "Eat up, smart ..." He looks at the boys. "They just don't recognize good eating, do they, boys?" They are both nodding with their mouths full. As they finish, Keith says, "We'd better get moving."

Jason says, "Remember, we'll go pick up the couch and bring it tomorrow."

Keith bends down and wraps his arms around both boys. "I'll see you tomorrow." They give him a hug and run to the other room.

Marilyn hugs him and mumbles, feeling like a slobbery drunk, "Thanks for everything. I'm going to miss ..."

Keith says, "May have to sneak around, and I promised Johnny a ride in the new tractor in a couple of weeks."

"Okay." Marilyn pushes Keith out, holding her tears.

Jason is out in front, but Keith turns and says, "You can come over anytime."

Marilyn's eyes are watering. *I would love to.*

Laura puts her arm around her as they watch them leave. "We'll make it through this." She nods toward the door. "With help from our macho friends."

Twenty-Nine

March 1, 1984

Marilyn sits with Johnny on the couch and explains to him about having a babysitter as Laura goes and picks her up. The rules. "Bedtime is eight o'clock. You do what Sis says, and I'll be home when you wake up."

Laura introduces them to Sis. She so youthful, with her bangs and long brunette hair blending into teenage body waiting to fill out.

Chad runs and gives her a hug. "Are you going to read us a story?"

"Yes, do you have one picked out?"

"I'll go get one." He runs off to his room.

"Chad, you let Sis do her homework first." Laura waves. "Got to go." And she is back out the door.

Johnny stands in a trance, and Sis squats in front of him. "Would you like me to read you a story too?"

After what seems like forever, he nods.

"Well, go pick one out."

Marilyn sucks in the fear of leaving him. "He's never had a babysitter before."

"I love watching kids. I'll keep them entertained."

"He's shy at first, but once he starts talking, he won't stop." Marilyn goes to the bathroom and finishes getting ready. Examines her favorite black blouse and how perfectly it fits. She unbuttons the third one, buttons it up, then a flashback. The night out with John. 'Button it higher,' rings in her ears.

Marilyn gets her coat and hugs Johnny. "I love you," she says as he pulls away.

The sitter smiles and grabs both boys' hands. "Let's see what you picked out."

Fear tries to overtake Marilyn as she walks out of the house. *I've never worked at a bar before. Are guys going to hit on me? What happens when John finds out?*

Her frenzy continues as she opens the bar door. The nightmare a few weeks ago and now the table filled with people laughing.

Laura waves for her to come behind the bar. "Follow me. I'll give you the million-dollar tour." She takes her to the office, gives her some papers to fill out, and shows her where to put her purse, the time clock, and the storeroom. Walks her through the kitchen, introduces her to the cook and where to put the food tickets. Introduces her to Sara, the other waitress, and gives her a mini apron, with order tickets. "Welcome aboard." Laura grabs Marilyn's hands and pulls her around, directly facing her. "You're going to be fine."

Staring at Laura's confident green eyes pulls her out of her daze. "I don't know ... Is it a dream or a nightmare?" Her eyes dart around the office. "I don't look too available, do I?"

"What? You look great." She unbuttons Marilyn's next button, pats her blouse, steps back. "Perfect. Remember you're working for donations, but it's not a church. Let go of the anxiety you have floating around inside your head, because it's history." They walk out of the office. "Write out the orders until you get the hang of it. The bowling guys are easy, they order pitchers and a burger occasionally."

They head to Marilyn's section, where some bowlers are waiting to order. Laura holds up her hand and says in her drill sergeant voice, "Okay, listen up." She waits a moment for them to stop talking. "This is Marilyn. Your new waitress, and her first night. I don't want to hear anyone giving her a hard time or messing with her, you will be shut off forever."

One of them tilts his chair. "You must have mistaken us for the Tuesday night league ..." And they all laugh. "Welcome to the Maggie's Bar and Grill, the nicest gentlemen you will ever meet."

A short guy with blond hair says. "We're positive she is nicer than you." And the laughing continues.

"Someone has to keep you in line."

Marilyn's heart is beating out of her chest. She takes a deep breath to calm herself. The bowling guys leave to bowl, and more people take their place.

Jason arrives and takes a stool at the end but leaves one stool open. Laura tells her to take a break.

She didn't realize three hours had gone by.

Laura sets a Coke on the extra stool by Jason.

Marilyn sits down. "I'm wiped out already, not used to working this hard nonstop."

"You must have it under control. No one has yelled for a beer." Jason sets his beer down. "Keith is having dinner with his parents tonight, may not show up."

"Not expecting him to babysit me."

Jason takes a sip of beer. "It's more about impressing the new waitress, can't let anyone get a jump on him." He smiles and turns towards her. "The family meetings are sometimes a little tense. He has a rule never to drink when you're mad."

"They weren't happy with me staying there, but Keith kept acting as if it were nothing. His mom came over and talked to me one day. She was nice, but direct." Marilyn gets up. "She notified me that her son is not a saint and that living there was a sin. Back to work."

The night whisks away as everyone is laughing, helping her relax. The end of her shift has arrived, and she goes to the office, counting her tips.

Laura comes to the office. "How's the income?"

Marilyn looks up. "Better than I expected." She has a small smile. "They were trying to impress me."

"Yes, they're not really that bad."

"I didn't have time to ponder who was looking or..."

"Don't let John's programming control your thoughts. They're men out unwinding, dominating their little world." Laura hugs her. "Go home, get some sleep."

Her mind races as she waits for the car to warm, then heads to Laura's, which is home, although it doesn't feel... She leaves the car running as she goes into the house and gently touches Sis's shoulder, trying not to startle her, but Sis jumps anyway.

She glances at Johnny, who is sleeping at the other end of the couch.

Sis is grabbing her schoolbooks. "Sorry about leaving him on the couch, but he was afraid you wouldn't come home. He insisted on waiting for you."

"It's okay. I try not to press it too hard." Marilyn drops her off and hurries back to the house. She tries to pick up Johnny, but instant pain shoots through her ribs. She tucks the blanket tighter, puts a kitchen chair next to him so he doesn't roll out, kisses his forehead, and whispers, "I love you."

He stirs but doesn't open his eyes. "I love you too, Mom."

She pushes a strand of hair from his face, then goes and takes a shower, washing the smell of the bar from her hair. She sits down at the kitchen table as the evening events rush into the quiet space. *A beer to relieve the anxiety?* She puckers as she takes her first sip; she has never drunk a beer by herself. With the noise still running in her head, she refills the glass, as it tastes better. *Keith's secret someone keeps haunting her.* She sips the rest of the beer, with relaxation and exhaustion finally taking over. She heads to bed.

It's past eight o'clock when she wakes up with a start, then tries to figure out where she is. Johnny isn't on the couch as she makes her way to the kitchen. The boys are eating breakfast.

Chad says, "We were getting hungry, so I fixed breakfast."

"That's very grown-up of you." She smiles at him. Day one, and she neglected the kids.

She fixes some coffee, making conversation as Chad is talking about everything, they did with the babysitter last night. There is an empty can sitting by hers. She washes up the boys' dishes and throws in a load of laundry.

Laura comes to the kitchen and gets coffee. "You're working hard already."

"Practicing for next week."

"You were great last night. It will be busier tonight; more people come in to eat then during the week, but you will handle it. Once the band starts, it will be drink orders. Don't wait for me to tell you to take a break squeeze it in when you can. Did you have any problems with anyone?"

"One guy was persistent, asked me out, wanting to know who I'm seeing. I'm kicking myself for being so nice, especially when he left me a fifty-cent tip."

Laura glares. "They all want you to believe they are God's gift and you can't live another day without them." The corner of her lip turns up. "Their qualifying standard is anyone that says yes. Another inside secret is I led them to believe Keith is the bouncer and we need to check with him."

Marilyn ponders and says, "Have to admit it wasn't as bad once I got into a rhythm."

Laura says, "Surprised Keith wasn't at the bar last night."

"Jason said he was having dinner and a budget meeting with his parents.

He mentioned it but was vague about the details."

"Keith wants to farm a thousand acres. His dad is old school and doesn't want to buy to expand." Laura smiles. "Don't ask me why or how either of them decides, but I had the impression they're very heated opinions."

"I was in shock. The tractor he is planning on buying is forty-seven thousand dollars." Marilyn sets her cup down, gathering her thoughts. "Confidence oozed out of him as he waved a wand, and my troubles were gone."

"A little dreamy-eyed feeling coming out." Laura is grinning. "I realize I have brought this up, but my issue of life. They have a brief fling, don't get all attached, and it doesn't put them in cheap status."

"Would you ... with Keith even if you knew it would end?"

Silence overtakes the kitchen. Laura stares intently. "And why do you ask?"

"My mentor for the correct answer." Marilyn breaks out with a smile. "My one-guy experience doesn't give me much to go on."

"Our secret. Yes. But once he saw my little tits, he would be looking for bigger ones." She laughs and shakes her head. "We tease each other about how good we are, but I hate when he tries to one-up me."

Marilyn is laughing. "You always make it sound simple."

Laura takes a sip of coffee. "Sounds like you're dreaming about it?"

The smile leaves Marilyn's face. "It's great to joke about, but ..."

Thirty

March 1, 1984

Cereal replaces my eggs at breakfast as I gaze at the empty chair, waiting for a profound tidbit from Johnny to lighten my morning. The living room ... with the toys still scattered, as Jake lies at the foot of the stairs. His ears perk up as I say, "Got pretty attached, didn't you?" He follows me to the kitchen.

I move the cab-less 4020 over to the barn at Dad's, making room for the new tractor. I stick my head in the door at my parents' and remind Dad about it; he seems overly calm. Mom asks if I'm coming for Thursday supper. *A real meal before going out drinking.* I dial Ginger, but no answer, and head to work in the toolshed.

***

I pull into the parents' driveway for supper, and Karla's car is sitting there. *What kind of bullshit is this? Should I leave? They manipulated something. Got the pastor on call. Why can't they stay out of my life?*

I give Mom her normal hug, but she doesn't make eye contact. Karla's face is white as she awkwardly hugs me and goes to help Mom. I began a generic conversation with my dad about farming. We say grace and fill our plates, but the tension ... I'm fighting to keep the anger from exploding.

Mom is carrying on with Karla about church stuff, as I hear bits of the conversation. Can't stand it anymore. "Karla, how's the dating scene?"

She stops eating. "Lots of old married farmers want to take me home for the night."

I grin.

Mom says, "That's disgusting and embarrassing."

I hold my smile and say, "Story I heard is they haven't seen or talked to a hot woman in years?"

"Keith." Mom glares at me. "I can't believe such words come out of your mouth."

Karla's face is red.

"I meant it as a compliment. You have them wishing—"

"Keith. That is not a compliment," Mom says. "No wonder the nice girls won't go out with you."

Karla bites her lip.

Dad, in his gruff voice, says, "It's all that bar trash talk."

I glare at Dad. "My interviewing system: explore what girls like at night and then get them up at four for chores, a test if they can handle life on the farm. They've all run out the door, and I go look for the next one." I smirk. "True what the old farmers say, can't find good ones anymore."

Mom says, "Keith James, my God, I raised you better than that. Stop it, or I'll find a bar of soap." She pushes away from the table but keeps glaring at me. "Could you apologize?"

When she turns to get the cobbler, I wink at Karla. "Sorry."

Mom's face is still red. "Let's have some of Karla's apple cobbler."

Everyone's mouth is stuffed. I glance at Karla and say, "I'm checking the box makes great desserts."

Mom glares, and the table is silent.

I must have a serious talk with this girl. *Was she in on this bullshit?* We talked before, but...

We finish eating, and the girls mill around, taking the dishes away. I feel the air through my nostrils. Dad makes small talk, bragging about the new tractor and how it will improving the farming. Yet he's been complaining for weeks. *Who's he impressing?*

Karla glances at Mom and says meekly, "Thanks for inviting me, but it's time for me to go home."

Mom gets Karla's coat and hat, gives me a death look.

The air goes through my teeth before I get up from the table and say, "Sorry, let me give you a hand." I pick up Karla's dishes.

Her fingers are shaking as she points to the cobbler. "I made extra. You can take it home."

"Thanks." I walk her out, holding the car door as she sets the dishes on the seat. I suck in my anger.

She turns with watery eyes, her voice trembling. "I'm sorry for the evening, your mom ... I thought ..." She turns away.

I reach for her arm. "Hold on—I didn't know you were coming—"

"No—my fault."

"Stop at the house. We'll decide who's at fault."

She stands there just staring.

"I'll be over in a minute. We'll have a back-of-barn meeting—no parents."

She doesn't answer and wipes the tears as she climbs into her car.

When I came back, Mom wrapped up the extra cobbler. Dad's gone to his lounger, watching TV.

I say, "According to your rules, I need help to find the right girl, but putting Karla in the middle of your family desires doesn't help."

Mom's voice quivers. "You need to be settling down, find someone with no ex-husbands or ... She is a nice church-going girl that comes from a good hardworking family."

"No baggage, right?" I pick up my cobbler. "Some insight into an arranged marriage. It went out of style like in the Shakespeare era."

"You might find it if you weren't trying ..." Tears come to her eyes. "Just go."

I kiss her on the cheek. "Goodnight, Mom. Thanks for supper." *I need a shot and a beer.* Karla is sitting in the driveway.

We stomp snow off our boots. I let Jake out. "Go make yourself at home. There's beer in the fridge if you want one." I stand on the porch waiting for Jake to check the car.

She's standing in the middle of the kitchen. I set the cobbler on the counter, open the fridge, and hold up two beers.

She waves her hand. "Not much of a beer drinker."

"Might have some wine." I hold up a bottle. "Someone left this must be good."

She says meekly, "A small glass."

I scrounge the cupboards to find a wine glass, grab my beer, and motion towards the living room. "Let's be comfortable."

She sits at the far end of the couch, examining the room. "Daycare services?"

"Part of my side job. Watching kids plus my niece, her kids love it, they don't have to put toys away. Keeps Mom happy, believes I'm looking forward to having a family soon."

She smiles. "I'm really sorry." She takes a drink.

"Don't apologize for my mother; she set us both up."

"I imagined—"

"She wants me married off to a nice, hardworking girl like yourself. She doesn't understand I like them ditzy. Easier to move on after ... Never mind."

"You don't have to explain. I'm not the sexiest girl on the block." She takes a drink.

"You are the sexiest girl on the block."

"Nice try. I'm the only woman for miles."

"There you are. I was being an ass tonight. Felt you were in on the setup."

She breaks out crying.

I get another beer, the bottle of opened wine, a box of Kleenex, and take a seat beside her.

She wipes her tears and regains her composure. "I knew you wouldn't let your mother set up a date. I should just go home before I embarrass myself even more." She takes another gulp of wine.

She pours more wine and takes another big drink.

"I knew your mother was setting you up. My make-believe world came up with the idea you were scared to ask me. My real world knows you've never been afraid to ask anyone out."

I grin. "I'm always scared, but ego assumes they all want me."

"And they do. On the other side of the road, where I live, no one wants me. I've made a big enough fool of myself for one night." She gets up but staggers.

I reach for her hand. "Sit for a minute. Too early to call it a night. Do you drink wine often?"

She plops onto the couch. "I don't drink because I make a fool of myself."

Karla has finished off the wine, and it is a little past nine. I'm smiling as I watch her stagger to the bathroom. "You're in no condition to drive or let your parents see you drunk."

"Then I'll walk. Remember when we were kids? We did it every day."

"Yes, the neighbor gossip sheets, daughter walks home drunk and crying. I'll drive you home, it's the logical answer, but to impress them with your party life, you could stay for the night?"

Her mouth drops open.

"Alarm goes off at four-thirty. Your turn to feed the cows." I laugh.

She is taking deep breaths, and a smile breaks out. "You got me drunk, so whatever your heart desires."

"I ..." *Can't tell; is she scared or does she want to?* "Don't take this wrong, but my heart feels as if you were my sister. And I could never ..."

Her eyes are watery. "I always felt—"

"I apologize for being blunt, just slap me when I cross the line. You're smart, dedicated, hardworking, a skilled cook, and better looking than you give yourself credit for, but you walk around in a bubble of depression because you missed out on the prissy gene."

She sits staring.

"Go ahead, slap me. My sister would."

Karla takes another drink, waves her hand back and forth in front of my face. "The gossip says you're wild and take advantage of women."

"You're turning this around on me."

"Yes, but they still want you."

"They claim there is the one. My problem, because of my low moral code, according to my parents." I pause. "I'm scared as hell. My friends are either divorced or wish they were." I take a drink and gaze at her. "Okay, enough of this shit about what's wrong with us. Call your parents, tell them you'll be home in the morning."

"It will be neighborhood gossip, but neither of them will want anyone else to know." She is breaking into a small smile. "You make everything simple. My parents are wondering why I'm not home already. I can guarantee they'll be afraid to ask."

"You can go home right after feeding the cows." I drink the rest of my beer. I leave her in the kitchen to talk to her parents and get pillows and blankets.

She walks into the living room. "I'll sleep on the couch."

"It's a nice warm waterbed and a little more private." I motion towards the bedroom.

"You know they're thinking ... You took advantage of me or they're having grandkids."

"The secret is women feel good after staying the night at the farm. You can put a notch on your lipstick case, seduced the homecoming king. The only problem I see now that you're—"

"Not a virgin—"

I almost spit out my beer. "You'll be hot, smiling and looking."

She stands in a daze, gives me a hug, holds up her pinky finger.

I bump mine against hers. "Secrets of the Hood."

"For the image of the hood. I won't let you down, but I need something ... in case I'm sick."

I get her a pan.

"If you hear me being sick, no trying to sneak a peek of me half naked with puke all over me."

Thirty-One

March 2, 1984

I'm awake before the alarm goes off as the night races, the urge, my mouth waters. This Mr. Right is bullshit. *Could've raised her self-esteem and made her feel good.* I drag myself out and feed the cows.

Karla's swollen eyes are staring at the wine bottle, when I return to have some coffee.

She says, "Was looking for the warning label. Do not drink in one sitting, causes a massive headache."

I grin. "You need wine-drinking practice."

She shakes the splash left at the bottom. "Hope I didn't make too big of a fool of myself."

"It's unwinding at the farm. Let me make some coffee."

"I'd better go. Heaven forbid the neighbors see my car. The rumors, the lectures, and the details of how easily you seduced me. I don't want to explain."

We still have time.

With a quick hug, she's out the door.

I sit with my coffee. *Okay, it was the right thing.*

The phone rings a few minutes after eight. It's the tractor salesman verifying the schedule for delivery at ten. Good, something I can deal with, but a hot spring fling would be great way to get the season started.

The tractor arrives and dad jokes with the driver about how he'll need a demonstration when planting season comes.

After he leaves, Dad gets quiet and rubs his chin. "You're tearing your mother's heart out with your immoral lifestyle."

After a ten count, I exhale. "Then you'll be glad I worked out a plan with Karla, and she is going to feed the cows at five a.m. on Saturday mornings. Meanwhile, I can spend more time with Miss Right, on Friday nights, no leaving her wanting in the morning or the one-night stand syndrome."

"Get your head out of your ass." He turns and walks away.

"Little trust in your son might help."

The rest of the day passes quickly. I talk to Jason, explaining why I didn't show up last night.

"I had a surprise supper from my mom. She set up a casual date with Karla, convinced her that I wanted to go out but was afraid to ask."

Jason laughs. "And you're not dealing with them two at a time anymore."

"My caring nice-guy image has me in monk status in case you haven't been paying attention."

"You'd better see a doctor. Something must be wrong. Your mother arranges a date and you couldn't talk her into a quickie?"

"Thanks, buddy. What would I do without such wisdom?" I hang up the phone before he answers, but I still hear him laughing.

***

My anxiety builds as I cross the street. *We're not dating. I helped her out. It was a winter fling, with no benefits. Move on.*

The bar has an early buzz. Game face. Her back is towards me as she's waiting for a drink order. I squeeze between my buddy and the waitress standing in the middle of the bar. I stick out my hand. "I'm Keith, and you are the new waitress."

She takes my hand and bites her lip, holding in a smile. "Marilyn."

"You look gorgeous." I look at her left hand. "We'll find some time and mingle."

"You sound awfully confident."

I wink at her. "Laura can vouch—"

Laura yells from behind the bar, "Keith—leave her alone. She's here to work."

"I'm here to help." I wave my hand.

Laura yells, "She doesn't need your advice or help."

I take an empty table in her section. Laura sets a single beer up at the bar station.

Marilyn brings it and, in a little louder voice than her normal timid one, says, "You must know the bartender."

"Lots of mutual friends here. It's family only better. We toss out the deadbeats. I lost my cook this week, so I'll have a burger and fries tonight."

"Thought you'd have a new one lined up?"

"You can't believe all the stories."

She looks up from her pad, with those dark brown eyes that melt my soul.

I whisper, "The tractor came today. Pick a date and we'll go for a ride."

She smiles, gazing across the bar before answering. "Laura's rules: tell them no the first time. No matter."

"Talk with her, and she'll give me high recommendations."

Her eyes get watery, and she leaves without answering.

As she sets down the food, I pat her hand. "You're supposed to melt at my touch and are forever in my spell." I grin and hold her hand.

Her dimple breaks out. "You're definitely a smooth talker."

I lean closer. "On Monday, bring Johnny we'll go for a tractor tour, some lunch, maybe a nice cozy nap."

Her eyes water as she walks away. Her blue jeans define the perfect sexual attractiveness and sweetness. Jason arrives as I take my first bite of hamburger. Marilyn brings him a beer and takes his order but never looks at me.

Jason says after she leaves, "What's up? She appears upset about something."

"Laura told her to play hard-to-get, so she's not coming over till Monday."

Marilyn brings Jason's order, and me another beer.

"Thanks." I nod. "She's after my heart already."

We finish eating between the small talk, tell Marilyn to cash us out, and free up her table. I add a twenty and we move to our stools at the end of the bar.

I watch her clean off the table, pick up the tip, and whisper to Laura.

Marilyn walks to our bar stools and puts her hand on my shoulder, whispering in my ear. "You don't need to do that."

"Wanting to make a great first impression."

She smiles with her dimple coming out again. "I'm impressed, but don't get any ideas. I'm difficult."

Jason breaks out laughing. "She's heard about you."

The normal Friday night gets in full motion with the band playing and everyone partying, but I have mellowed. My mind keeps drifting to Marilyn, wondering what she is feeling.

Jason points to the floor. "Gordy is hot on Marilyn."

"He was watching her earlier."

"I'll tell him she's taken."

"And explain to him how I got to know her so well, considering we met a couple of hours ago."

We slow our beer drinking to tortoise speed, just like the band, one per set. I study everyone in the bar, wanting to ask Marilyn to dance, and ponder who is watching her. I change a keg for Laura and ask her, "Does John know Marilyn works here?"

"No, but he will eventually find out, and she is worried sick he'll go after us, especially me."

"You should be careful and don't be afraid to call. I could teach him a lesson."

"He's underhand and makes up his own rules."

Marilyn mini-break she grabs a glass of Coke, leans against the bar, and say, "My feet are killing me."

I jump up from my stool and motion for her to sit.

"I didn't mean..." She hesitates but sits down. "Thanks, but you're a paying customer."

"Anything to impress you with my manners."

She pauses.

I say, "You're impressing Gordy."

She glances at the band. "He invited me to the after-party."

Keith says, "They're a little wild."

"Not mellow like yours?" Her eyes are twinkling. "Told him I had a curfew. If you remember, I'm taking guys out of my life, not adding them."

I touch her arm. "How's the main guy doing?"

She looks around, bites her bottom lip. "Adjusting. He misses ... I gotta go to work."

Jason says, "She was about to cry."

"I'll deny it, messes with my bachelor carefree image, but the kid melts your heart."

Jason takes a swig of beer and seems to drift off. The band starts the last set as Marilyn's shift ends, and she meets Laura at the end of the bar.

Laura says, "You did a great job tonight."

"Thanks, went better than expected." Marilyn gazes at her and says, "I forgot to tell you, Johnny was scared I wouldn't come home last night." She grabs her purse. "Good night."

I touch her arm. She turns around. "You're missing your goodnight kiss and hug."

She stares at me for a minute, then turns and runs out the door.

Laura's eyes are glassy. "I'll never forgive you if you break her heart."

"Promised I'd take care of her."

Thirty-Two

March 3, 1984

Marilyn tries to grasp some self-control on the ride home. *The heart wanted a kiss. You're a fool.* She pulls into the driveway, wakes Sis, who is sleeping on the couch, and takes her home. She parks the car behind the shed, finally takes a breath, and checks on Johnny, who's asleep in his bed, the teddy bear wrapped in his arm. *He thinks I have it under control.*

She heads to the shower, with blips of the ugliness trying to flash back as she indulges in the hot water. She wraps up in her faded old housecoat, wanders to the kitchen, and opens a beer. It tastes better tonight as she takes a sip from her glass. Then Keith's grins, the evening divulges into a music video, trying to find relevance, then flash, the moment gone. She smiles, finishes the beer, rinses the glass, and crawls into bed.

Guilt and desperation still waver as she picks up the cereal bowls the next morning and makes coffee. The boys are already in their room playing.

It's eleven. Laura joins her. They sit quietly for a while until Laura says, "You look worried."

"Still a lot of issues with no answers, and John could blow up at any moment."

"Make it simple. John is a done deal, history. It needs paperwork. The family should be ecstatic you are moving on in life. The money will be tight, but it's life." Laura tilts her head. "And the Keith issue. Take the plunge, or move on, can't answer that one for you."

Marilyn smiles, setting her coffee cup on the table. "You mean the uncontrollable emotions; one moment I want to cry and run away, the next I'm giddy, like a fourteen-year-old ..."

"We all want to find Mr. Right." Laura breaks into a smile. "And be wowed according to our dream fantasy?"

"Welcome to my fantasy world, a Friend of the Court hearing in two weeks. I'm going job searching this Monday and visiting Mom's on Wednesday, which is worse than job searching."

Laura takes a drink of coffee. "It's moving along and get over the guilt of

Chad fixing breakfast. Kids need to learn some responsibility."

"I know. Which reminds me, Keith is calling later and asking Johnny to go for a ride on the new tractor tomorrow."

"We're going to Mom's for dinner. Chad has to understand they can't do everything together."

"He won't want to miss out, and we can go early. Keith won't care. You can just pick him up there."

March 5, 1984

Marilyn goes to Skippy's and explains her new life without John. He has Saturday and Sunday mornings available, which she felt guilty for not telling him how late she gets out on Friday nights.

Saturday evening, when Keith calls, they make small talk about the bar and the weather, before Marilyn gets Johnny and puts the phone up to his ear. He listens to Keith, and nods, his eyes are glistening. Marilyn says, "He can't see you. Tell him yes."

She takes the phone, and Johnny runs off, telling Chad.

"Thank you again for doing this. He's off to tell Chad, hope you don't care if he comes?" Marilyn takes a pause. "And does ten o'clock work?"

"Anytime, sounds like a party."

March 6, 1984

The boys are running to the door, with Marilyn hardly out of the car.

Chad turns the handle.

"It's not polite to walk into someone's house—"

Chad says, "Mom never knocks."

Keith stands inside the door. The boys give him a hug. He holds out his hands. "Welcome back. You want a hug, too?"

She buries her face against his soft flannel shirt and holds him longer than a greeting hug. Then she blurts, "Hope it was alright to come so early, would've had to tie them up if I'd waited any longer."

"Well, of course, gives us time to ... catch up on the juicy gossip." Keith grins. "You boys go play for a bit." They run off to the living room, and Keith gets her a cup of coffee. "And how's the first week?"

"It was better than—"

"Than you worried about?"

"Yes, I know. Laura keeps telling me the same thing. Some guys were actually nice." She raises the corner of her lip. "It's a short list."

"You're still talking to me. Must have made the cut." He breaks into a huge grin and winks. "You're on the hunt. You need to expand your list."

What did I just say? "Yes, you're the ..." She feels her face turn red. "I assume my ex listened to his lawyer and is working on his best behavior, at least until next Monday. When we have the child support hearing. Mr. Drillman said he's filing for restricted supervised visitation, which will push John over the edge."

"Do you need someone to watch Johnny?"

"No, Laura's going to watch him. She volunteered to go, but the fewer people he sees helping me, the better. Besides, I need to handle my mistakes. I'm scared, but ... He goes into anger mode when there are no witnesses. Manipulates whatever so it appears I'm making it up."

"He gave me that impression when I met him at the bar."

"Makes me feel stupid, how I fell for his lies all these years."

Keith gets up. "We've all been there. At least you're moving on. The legal stuff, Bill is the best. Don't be afraid to ask if you need something." His eyes are twinkling. "Anything your heart desires."

She mutters, "Thanks. You have done so much already." She feels the tingling taking over her body.

Keith says, "You boys ready?" The boys instantly scramble for the door. Keith looks back at Marilyn. "Since you're missing out today, we'll schedule a private ride in the future." He breaks out his patented grin.

"It's okay, you boys go play with your new toy. I'm taking a nap."

"There's an extra pillow and blanket in the closet or help yourself to the waterbed it's more comfy."

Her eyes water as she bites her lip and watches them walk towards the toolshed, one on each side, both boys still talking. She sits at the kitchen table finishing her coffee and thumbs through the brochures. She never realized there were so many tractors.

The house looks clean as she pulls the blanket and pillow out of the closet. She stares at the waterbed and lies down. *Mommy, it's mushy.*

Jake woofs, and she jumps, checks the clock. It's noon already. Quickly, she tries to straighten the blanket.

"Is anyone home?"

It's Laura. Her heart slows a bit as she rub the sleep out of her eyes on the way to the kitchen.

Laura says, "Looks like you were sleeping."

Marilyn stacks the brochures on the table. "Don't you wonder why it's so relaxing here?"

"The farmhouse has a magical effect."

"I still can't get over how much the boys love it. Johnny hasn't talked to a man before, not even his grandfathers. He would cower away. Comes here, and Keith is his best friend."

Laura picks up the pot of burnt coffee, pours it out, and makes a fresh one.

Thirty-Three

March 7, 1984

Johnny takes his tractor as they go to Mom's. He's happy to show it to Herb. He acts like a caring grandpa. *Did he change?* Mom motions Marilyn to the kitchen and gets glasses for iced tea. Mom, as always, dresses in a thin, faded, printed cotton dress. They went out of style in the fifties.

Mom's judging eyes check her blue jeans. *Are they too tight for acceptance?* Marilyn blurts out, "I'm starting back at Skippy's in a couple of weeks and working at the bar two nights this week with Laura. Not the perfect job scenario, but income."

"Wearing those tight jeans, you'll have men—"

"Would a mini skirt be better?" Silence takes over.

Mom is staring at her glass and says, "You seem awful tense. Hardly know what to say anymore."

"No one wears dresses anymore, my jeans are not that tight, and I'm not a teenager."

Mom's eyes are watery. "Not a place for a soon-to-be-divorced woman to work. Guys assume you're ... easy."

"Mom, it's not some dive pickup bar. Families and women by themselves come in all the time."

After a seemingly long silence, her mother says, "John stopped by. He was in tears expressing his concern—"

"I don't care if he is concerned." The bile rises in her throat.

"You do overreact. He said he'd made arrangements to pay the rent, but you kept screaming when he tried to explain."

Her heart is pounding out of her chest. "Maybe he could have done that before he punched me, then threatened he was going to make Johnny watch if I didn't do my wifely duties and take care of his needs—and I don't mean cooking."

Her mom's face turns white. "Oh my God, dear. I didn't realize."

Marilyn wipes the tears away. *Can I go back to Keith's?* "Added to that, it will be at least another month before my cracked ribs heal."

"Why didn't you tell me?"

"Because I don't want anyone in town to know, especially blabbermouth Herb."

Her mother gets up and flutters around. "How about a cookie?"

"I don't want any."

Herb makes his appearance. "I'll take a couple." He pulls out a chair.

Was he invited?

Her mother gets out a glass and pours him some milk.

Herb says, "Thanks." He glances at Marilyn. "Having a tough time?"

Her mother gets a cookie and milk and takes it to Johnny.

Marilyn says quietly, "No, I am doing great since John is out of my life."

Herb sneers as he takes a bite. "Johnny seems content living in his make-believe world, with Jake as his best friend, pushing around the fancy tractor."

"Yes, he wanted to sleep with it."

"Kind of spendthrift for a girl with no money, to buy an original John Deere toy. They're not cheap. A Chinese knock-off serves the same purpose, kids don't know."

The plastic one you bought him is where? "If it is so important, a friend gave it to him."

His eyes stare with his slimy smile. "Jake must like the kid."

"Trying to cheer him up." Marilyn swallows a scream and says, "Jake is a very lovable family dog, but I'm not dating him. I want guys out of my life, which means you can stay out of it, too."

He glances behind her and says, "You don't need to have a hissy fit." He holds his hands surrendering as he makes a slight wave.

Mom says, "Herb, she hasn't found someone to move in with. It's only been three weeks."

"I'm not trying to suggest that, but John is convinced she was seeing someone. It's why she left."

Marilyn clenches. "He accused me of that a month after we were married. He lives in his own paranoid world. You're lucky he doesn't wonder about you hitting on me."

"Calm down, dear." Her mom touches Marilyn's arm. "Herb is stating things you need to know."

She feels her face getting red. "Nothing John says is the truth. He's a lying, despicable person."

Herb draws back his chin. "Sorry to rile up your hot little temper. You make it hard to have a rational conversation."

"If they convict John of something, hopefully he won't be getting visitation."

Herb says, "Not right to make up stuff just because—"

She jumps up. "Johnny, pick up your toys—we're leaving."

Herb chews his cookie and talks at the same time. "You still haven't learned to calm your temper, I see."

Afraid she'll break out crying, Marilyn scrutinizes the living room and the worn paint. "Johnny."

Johnny yells, "Hold on, Mom, I'm coming."

She glares at Herb. "If you could squeak out a small lie, to help your stepdaughter for once in your life, tell John you've never seen us."

Her mom is up trying to rub Marilyn's shoulders. "Calm down, dear. We're not defending John and won't tell him anything, you know that."

Herb tries to squeeze close. "I always think of you as my daughter."

Right as you gawked at us in our pajamas when we were teenagers. She hastily helps Johnny with his coat and boots.

He says, "You can't just snap because someone is giving you advice you don't agree with. We're trying to help, not that you realize it."

Mom's voice quivers. "We love you."

She grabs Johnny's hand and heads out the door. She is shaking as she slams the car into gear, spinning snow out of the driveway.

Johnny waves. She never looks. She parks at the stop sign, wanting to turn towards Keith's house. Tears are running down her cheeks.

"What's the matter, Mom? Don't you remember which way to go?"

She smiles at him and rubs his stocking hat. "I'm having one of my ..." She wipes her cheeks and heads to Laura's.

Thirty-Four

March 12, 1984

Marilyn scans the courtroom, the judge's bench, the tables, the railing, all matching wood. Fear tries to grip her. John's parents are sitting behind him. *It's child support and visitation. Why would they be here?*

"All rise."

Marilyn wrings her hands under the table. John's lawyer is giving the judge the made-up version of John's sick view of how he's such a noble father. Mr. Drillman delivers a rebuttal of John's uncontrollable anger outbreaks, and the voices banter about Johnny's life. She fades into a zone, studying the wood grain flowing across the table like a motionless river, the only solitude she can find.

Mrs. Desmond struts to the podium, answer the judge's question, and make a gagging statement about the care she adds to Johnny's life, then ending it with "Johnny's always been happy and likes to visit." Looks at Marilyn. "It won't change unless someone tells him lies."

Marilyn swallows in the scream. *No, what is happening?*

The judge continues, "I will award you time with your grandson every other Sunday noon to six." He looks at John. "You understand, sir, that I'm allowing you to see your son, with restrictions. I would recommend some anger counseling if you would like to see him more. Do you understand?"

His lawyer pulls his arm. He stands up, and John mumbles, "Yes, Your Honor."

His lawyer says, "My client understands and wants to do everything possible to mend this relationship."

The judge announces emotionlessly, "We have a court date set for October first, at nine o'clock. If some agreement comes about, we can change the date." He pounds his gavel. "Court adjourned."

John's voice pierces the fog. "Dear, we can work this out. You always said divorce doesn't fix anything." John's left hand, with a wedding ring claimed to be lost, blocks her path to leave.

Mr. Drillman interjects, "Mr. Desmond, have your lawyer work up a proposal, and we will get a settlement."

Marilyn feels John's breath. She cringes, closes her eyes—

"She's still my wife, and someone I love. We could end all this with a sit-down kitchen-table conversation instead of paying high-priced lawyers, like yourself, to talk for us."

Mr. Drillman leans in front of Marilyn.

John slides around the side. "You are my one and only."

Marilyn finally raises her head. Smugness is staring at her.

"Mr. Desmond, you are violating your parole and restraining order." When a police officer arrives out of nowhere, Mr. Drillman continues. "We have a restraining order against him."

The police officer says, "Sir, you need to leave the courtroom immediately."

John holds his glare and doesn't move.

"Sir. Now."

Marilyn mumbles, "John, please go. You'll be in more trouble."

"All because I love you." He turns and leaves.

The police officer turns back around. "Give us a few minutes. We will escort him out."

Mr. Drillman escorts Marilyn into the wide hallway, the clean shiny marble floors, the openness of the high ceilings as she tries to catch her breath. Nothing is in focus.

John's mother walks up with her brashness. "Marilyn, I want to apologize for my son's being foolish, but he is serious about changing his life. He's even promised to go to church."

Marilyn can't get words out and stares at her. *It's a lie.*

She continues, "I know you're having a hard time, but families struggle together, and we love together. Divorce is for weaklings and quitters and you're neither."

She wants to run, but her knees may collapse.

"Remember what guys want from a divorcee? And it's not to raise someone else's kid in a nice loving home. It's hard for kids to grow up without both parents. You said that yourself."

Mr. Drillman takes Marilyn's arm. "We'll contact you before the twenty-fifthfor the visitation arrangements." Mr. Drillman guides Marilyn towards the door.

Mrs. Desmond raises her voice, echoing through the hall. "So, you're going to repeat what your mother did?"

He opens the door and guides her out as the cold whips inside her coat. "Which way is your car?"

She looks around, seeing his hazel eyes penetrate her with such assurance. "Over there." She points off to the right. Her lips tremble. "I can't handle this. I want to run away."

"You must get John out of your life and your son's. There's no compromising a toxic relationship."

"Thanks for everything. Keith said you were the best."

"You have the judge working with you. Sunday afternoon visitation means he's not sure he'll get his act together. I don't want you to get your hopes up, but my guess is John will quit wanting to see him. Keep me posted, and document everything that is said or done, no matter how trivial it may seem."

Marilyn closes the door, but Mr. Drillman is knocking on the glass. She rolls the window down.

"Guilt only works if you accept it to be true."

March 13, 1984

Tuesday evening, she puts the boys to bed, savoring some time for herself, when the phone rings. Marilyn grimaces, takes a breath, and picks up the receiver. "Hello."

"Good evening, this is Keith. Thought I'd check on my favorite overnight guest."

Tears instantly form as she sits at the table. "Thanks for the sweet thoughts, but—"

"Thinking of my boys. You need to get out of the house. Breathe some good farm air. Why don't you come over tomorrow?"

"You don't ... want to be involved in my life."

"Too late for that, and you can't hold out the juicy details."

"You mean how my mother-law is telling me how I'm wimpy lowlife for not staying married to her son? And how guys think a divorcee wants and needs make her easy."

"Guys hope that about all women; we don't discriminate." He breaks out laughing. "The way it is you're sacrificing, you're stuck listening to some guy brag, so the kids have fun."

Her heart is pounding. The smell of his soft flannel shirt sends quivers racing through her body.

March 14, 1984

The fields are turning to mud so there are no tractor rides for the boys, but they are happy playing in the living room. Fear and depression stalk the edges of Marilyn's thoughts but seem to disappear with the afternoon kitchen table talk. She ponders on her way home how relaxed she was talking to him. She writes a letter to her aunt in Tennessee, which she has been going to do for six months to ease her mind about how she is doing, figuring her mother has probably put her into panic mode about the divorce. Her aunt's words, always subtle but ... 'We are all family and if you ever need anything, we're here for you.'

Marilyn is ready for work. Chad's ready for the weekend with his dad, when his dad pulls in the driveway, Chad gives Johnny a hug and whispers something to him. He grabs his bag and is out the door.

"It's time to pick up Sis to babysit," she says to Johnny, "Want to come?"

"No, I'll wait here."

It stops her. Has he already adjusted? A few weeks ago, he would never let her leave, even to go outside. "I'm really proud of you."

"Yes, Mommy."

"Give me a kiss and hug. I'm dropping Sis off and going to work. You be good."

"I will."

Marilyn gets choked up and mumbles, "I love you."

Johnny heads to his room.

She drops Sis off and heads to work, her new routine. It rips her heart but everyone else has adjusted. The afternoon mini nap hopefully helps the Saturday morning sleep time. If John stays working, the thirty-five dollars a week of child support and the twenty dollars of alimony will put her on the plus side of the bills.

The bar is hopping already when she enters. Keith and Jason order their burgers and fries in the same routine when they arrive. The guy from last week is back and takes a table in her section.

He seems pleasant, but his patronizing feels creepy.

"My name is Arron, and it is nice to meet you, Marilyn."

She feels irritated but makes eye contact. "Nice to meet you, Arron. Would you like some food tonight?"

"Yes, I'll have a burger and fries." He touches her arm and nods at Keith's table. "I have some competition for a date?"

"I'm not dating or looking."

"Did he ask you out yet?"

It's none of your business. "Yes, I turned him down, too." She stares at his hand.

He slides it off her arm. "I wine and dine with the best."

She tries to ignore him, but he asks questions wanting attention whenever she's close to his table.

He flags her over. "Not really a 'hang out in the bar' type of guy." Slips a ten-dollar bill in her hand. "Give me a number. We can have a conversation outside the pickup scene."

She's trembling but mutters, "I have a son that gets all my attention. Thank for the money." Her stomach churns as she sticks it in her pocket and walks away. She picks her shoulders up as she sees Laura watching her.

At the end of her shift, she talks to Keith and Jason, wishing she could stay and have a beer with them.

March 17, 1984

Saturday evening Marilyn arranged date night with Johnny. She finally asks, "You have questions about going with grandma D tomorrow?"

Johnny's eyes pierce through her. "Chad told me what to do."

How could he look like John? "I'm proud of you for being so brave."

"I want Uncle Keith to be my dad. Have you asked him yet?"

"Things take time—"

"You said you like him."

"I do—but we just can't move in with Uncle Keith. I'm still married to your father, so I can't live with someone else." *Uncle Keith is not going to ask me to marry him.* "When we get that worked out, we'll see. Your dad is living at Grandma D's now. You can have fun just like before."

Johnny sits staring out across the room.

"I don't want you to lie, but it's okay to tell them we were at a rescue place. Just don't tell them it was Uncle Keith's and how much fun you had."

"I won't, Mom."

Skippy is not thrilled with her leaving work early because the restaurant is still busy. She explains it's Johnny first time with visitation and she has be there to say goodbye. Laura has Johnny ready to go when Marilyn gets home five minutes before noon. And Mrs. Desmond pulls into the driveway, right at noon.

Marilyn is shaking as she helps Johnny with his coat.

Johnny says, "Mother, promise me you won't cry."

There is a knock on the door. "We'll be out in a minute." She hugs him. "I love you more than anything."

"I know, Mommy. Don't get all mushy."

She hugs him again and opens the door, the glares directly at her mother-in-law with a whisper. "You better make sure nothing happens to him."

Mrs. Desmond breaks out in the fake grin Marilyn has seen many times. "You're invited to come over at three for Sunday dinner." She looks at Johnny. "I'm sure you would like that, wouldn't you, Johnny?"

Marilyn freezes.

Her mother-in-law leers. "Sorry, wasn't thinking?" She glances at Johnny. "You have a date. Next time." She laughs, "Johnny, we are going to have so much fun..."

You're disgusting...

Thirty-Five

March 16, 1984

John gets into his routine on Friday nights, hanging out at Jack's after work. Takes a slug of beer and says to Bob, "My visitation hearing was Monday. I can't believe they make me pay child support and alimony because she doesn't have a job. Just not right; a woman leaves you on a whim. You pay or go to jail."

"Glad I didn't have any kids with my ex-wife. What's the next step?"

"Find her unworthy, take custody of my kid." His jaw tightens. "Someone had to convince Marilyn to leave. Nothing personal, but everything leads to that bitch Laura."

"I agree. She is a bitch, but damn, she was a good ride while it lasted." A grin spreads across Bob's face as he stares out across the bar. "She changed in the last couple of months, wouldn't talk. Her only statements, 'Not interested. I don't want to talk about it. Where's the rent money?' End of conversation."

"Wife will turn my kid into a wimp." John still stares at the neon sign. "Kid would run and hide when I came home."

"Yeah, gotta be tough to handle. What drives a woman to leave on the coldest night of the year?"

John takes a gulp of beer. "Is Laura seeing someone else?"

"I wouldn't doubt it."

"You're taking it a lot easier than I would."

"I could use some, but no ring, no money lost, watching a kid every night became a real pain, it was time to move on."

"They were planning this. Feel it in my bones."

"Marilyn is the new nighttime babysitter." Bob raises his eyebrows. "She still needs a daytime job to pay the rest of the rent."

"Someone gave her money. Wife has an expensive lawyer, moves the furniture, lives somewhere for three weeks, and Laura boots you out, all flows too sweet to be by accident."

"Did she go to one of those safe houses?"

"She hated it the last time."

"What about her sister helping her?"

"I'm sure she's involved, but why use Laura's address if you're moving to Port Huron? Besides, she loves living in this hick town." John slams his fist on the table. Everyone turns around. He holds his hand. "It's fine, everyone; I had a brain fart."

Bob squints. "What?"

John leans close to Bob, lowering his voice. "It's simple. She is hiding out at some guy's house, pretending to live at Laura's."

Julie stops at our table and rubs John's shoulders. "Relax will help you."

John closes his eyes and lets out a breath. "Thanks, I just realized how my wife made a fool of me."

She sits down.

"She never planned on fixing supper, knowing it would piss me off. Then drive to her boyfriend's and whines, and says to him, 'He just threw me out.' Blinking her conniving puppy-dog eyes, which I fell for a hundred times."

She squeezes his hand.

John returns the gesture. "You're the best."

She winks. "Bet you're damn good yourself, no matter what your ex says. Gotta run. Do you need another beer?"

"Give us a couple to go."

John motions to Bob. "Drink up." He guzzles his beer. "Let's go for a drive." Stick the beers in their coat pockets. "If I can catch her fooling around, she'll come crawling back and begging me to take care of her before she'll give up the kid." He's shaking his head. "She claimed I hurt his feelings, that's why the kid wouldn't talk to me."

They drive by Laura's the lights are on, but there's no car in the driveway. Bob says, "I assume the girl from down the road is watching Chad. Wait here. Let me sneak up to the house. The curtain used to be cracked. I might see who's there."

John waits in the dark, the thoughts racing, empties his beer, then drinks some of Bob's.

Bob opens the door with a shit-ass grin on his face. Turns up the heat, rubbing his hands together.

"Well?"

He says, "Your kid's there."

"What the hell?"

"Someone was on the couch. Guess it's Sis, the babysitter, but her mother wouldn't let her babysit on weeknights, because of school. If it's your wife, where's her car?"

"Might be in the garage."

Bob finishes his beer and flips the bottles out the window. "No, the landlord has it full of stuff."

They head to town and circle the bar parking lot. John points. "My neighbor's truck."

"That's Keith's truck parked beside it. They hang out all the time."

"I remember how much of a smart-ass he was. I would've liked to coldcock him."

"Keith is an ass, but you don't mess with him. He was a tough dude in high school, played nasty. Spiked one of my buddies in a game once. Keith stood over him and laughed."

"He appears to be the typical dumb football player boasting about his sexual exploits."

Bob points across the street. "Go down the alley. Keith has a farm on Stiles Road. He always brags about how hard he works but sits in an air-conditioned tractor during the day and spends his nights at the bar. I asked Laura how he was in bed. Denied she knew, of course." Bob smirks. "There's part of your answer."

John stops, turns lights off, and stare at Marilyn's car parked beside Laura's Cutlass. "Real convenient. She could be seeing anyone."

Bob says, "Keith hits on all the new girl, they become daffy; it's sickening to watch. Laura was always tight-lipped, like nothing was going on, but ... I've seen him in action. Let's go in and check."

"I'd love to do that, but they'd have me arrested if I went in and didn't leave. No, I am going to have a little chat with Ms. Bitch Laura. Maybe my old neighbor too. Wonder what stories he'll make up. I gave Aaron twenty bucks to snoop but haven't heard anything yet."

They stop at the party store to grab a twelve-pack before leaving town. They turn down the first side road, and Bob cracks a beer. Drives by Marilyn's parents' house.

Bob says, "Could she be staying there again?"

"No, the bedroom light was always on before. Her mother was shocked when told she left."

"Are you going to get back together?"

"As bad as she treated me, I ask myself why I'd want to, but we had some good times. Guy could do worse. If she is already tapping someone else ... how does a guy ...? It's ugly to think about." John's jaw tightens.

"Julie wouldn't be bad. She has a soft spot for you."

"Yeah, I've noticed, and something to tide me over would be nice."

"Couldn't we all use some?"

They drive slowly down the gravel road past John's old house. He slams the steering wheel, pointing at Jason's house as they drive by. "Never thought my neighbor. He knows Laura. He doesn't work during the winter. Could've slipped down to my house any time. Think about it. He sat there really quiet that night at the bar."

"It fits, Keith with his smart-ass quote about picking up lonely married women and taking them for a ride in the waterbed. Covering up for his buddy."

"No wonder I didn't like him."

"He gets that smirk look on his face. 'The fun of living in the eighties.' I've heard him say."

"If I find out he had anything to do with Marilyn I'll wipe that smirk off his face, maybe forever."

They pull up in front of Jack's. Bob says, "Going in for one?"

"No, I'd better get home. Mom will sputter about me having a beer."

***

John opens the door and hears Johnny Carson on TV. *Mother is up waiting for me.* Puts his beer in the fridge and grab one, ands sits in dad's chair.

Mrs. Desmond sips the last of her drink from the ice, shakes the court papers. "John, this is terrible what is going to happen. The lawyer needs to fix the visitation. If she moves, we will never see Johnny."

"Yes, Mother, she wants to destroy my life. And she'll do whatever."

She gets teary-eyed.

"It's my kid too. The problem is I'm not allowed to talk to her, so everything goes through the lawyers. I can't do much her lawyer is sucking every dime."

"It's hard to believe I won't be able to see my only grandchild."

"Quit talking like that," John says. "The lawyer passed it off as a normal ploy, and we can eventually get equal time.

"Lot of this doesn't make sense. We were out driving around, trying to find where Marilyn was staying. Low and behold, we found Johnny at Laura's with a babysitter, and Marilyn's car was hidden in the back alley at the bar."

"That's terrible. She out partying already?"

"She was parked among the workers."

"Either way, tell the lawyer she's hanging out at the bar, leaving Johnny with a babysitter. How could she find someone so fast if she wasn't—"

John takes a drink of beer. "Bob and I are going to stake out the old neighbor, find out what he's doing. Never told you this, but last summer I screamed at him for blocking the road. She went down the next day and apologized. Then convinced me it was to keep peace with the neighbors." He leans back in the chair. "After I thought about it, he kept looking at her ... something you don't notice at the time."

"Was she cheating on you?"

Thirty-Six

April 22, 1984

Anxiety overwhelms Marilyn, not seeing Johnny off for the visit with his father as she serves the next breakfast. But Johnny only concern was going to Keith's tomorrow. She drifts off the aura of Keith touching her hand, calmly explaining the disking, having her circle the barns, but because of the rain practice time, was limited. He squeezed tight to her on the tractor seat, telling her to relax. Every part of her tingled and frightened her at the same time.

"Order up." Skippy is staring at her.

April 23, 1984

Marilyn keeps trying to hush Johnny and Chad who were up early and remind them to be quiet. She fixes them breakfast but their excitement over rides most of the warnings. The next dilemma, wear her old, faded blouses and shabby jeans or the only nice pair? She'll need to wash each night. They are off to Keith's, but the kid's excitement is not taking away her fear.

Can I even do this?

Keith's laughter rings in her head. "It's only twelve feet wide, and a straight line." Then adding, "You're a natural." It's a sweet thought from him, but a lie to her.

As she pulls into Keith's parents' farmhouse, the boys jump out of the car and run into the house. Mrs. Larson greets her at the door with her warm smile. "Morning, boys, go get in my car; we'll drop your mom off." She hands Marilyn a thermos of coffee. "Let me know if you want more or less cream."

Her face goes blank. "I never thought ..."

"Don't drink too much. The bathroom is inconvenient for women. Guys have a tendency to forget that." She pauses and raises her head. I'll come back at ten. Okay?"

"Yes ..." Marilyn lets out a breath. "I hope the boys don't drive you too crazy."

"They're the fun part. Figure an afternoon break around three and Keith will pick you up around six o'clock. Not sure what you have planned, but you are welcome to stay for supper. Remember, you can't work all day and fix supper good supper."

"Thanks, Laura is off work today and is fixing us something tonight."

They make their way to Gwen's car. "Call me Gwen or Grandma G." Marilyn opens the door, and the boys scramble into the backseat. Gwen sits quietly for a minute with her hands resting on top of the steering wheel. "He's my son and I love him to death, but he must respect you ..." She gazes over and starts the car.

"You should be proud of him." Marilyn, flashbacks of the morning talks. "I've heard some stories, but he's been a perfect gentleman."

"Maybe some of my preaching sank in." They turn down the lane. "Working in the field is hard on your good clothes."

"My old ones are—"

"We'll see what we can do." She pulls up by Keith's truck and says, "Some womanly advice. Don't let them intimidate you. Their egos burst out of each brain cell, wondering who is the best." She pats Marilyn's leg. "See you at ten."

Marilyn smiles. "Thanks. See you boys. And be good." Marilyn jumps out and waves at them. She leans against Keith's truck, her heart pounding admiring how he keeps the planter in a straight line, which is even wider than the disk.

He swings the planter and struts towards her with his wide grin.

She is completely inside. "What?"

"You must have read a guru management book. They say, 'Dress for success.'"

She blushes. *The only ones ...* The tractor and disk, sitting like a gigantic statue sitting in the field raising her anxiety.

He reaches out his hand to help her up the ladder. *He loves this part.* They're squeezed together on the seat.

"It's time to show off."

She takes a deep breath. Trembling as she pushes in the clutch, and shifts into gear. The tractor jerks when she lets out the clutch, but they are off.

Keith points towards the barns and field. "You'll be able to see me. When we get down the row, you can see across George's farm, where Dad is plowing. Depending on where you are in the field, you can see one of us.

If you have any issues, stop and wave." He shrugs and grins. "One of us will come over."

He quietly gives her instructions at each turn, and with the calm in his voice, her heart has slowed a bit.

After the third time around, he quit talking. When they're almost at his truck, Keith says, "Well, you ready to spread your wings?"

She is gripping the wheel. "I'm not sure."

His grin takes over his face. "You'll be an expert by evening and bored to death." He leans over and gives her a kiss on the cheek. "You're ready now. I'll pick you up around noon." He shuts the door and climbs down.

Exhilaration overtakes her tingling body. The tractor jerks as she lets the clutch out too quickly again. She tries to focus as the thoughts race through her mind. *Am I lapped over enough? Where is the spot I'm driving to? Is it the right angle?* His lips tingling on her cheek. *Why didn't he give me the old tractor?*

She catches him in the mirror watching. She grips the wheel tighter and rechecks how straight she is going. Keith watches about halfway and then jumps into his truck and leaves. Still in disarray, she stops before making the turn, but after a few rows, she lines up parallel. She slows the tractor to a crawl, lifts the disk, hits the brake, and turns in one motion, although her fingers are cramping from her grip. The nightmare thoughts turn to accomplishment. She glances across the fields towards Keith and is instantly off course and misses a chunk. *So much for thinking you have conquered this.*

Flashbacks of learning to drive a stick. Laughing at herself. *Keith is definitely a better-looking instructor*. Each time some confident seeps in that she is lined up better.

***

Marilyn was happy to see Gwen, right on schedule, as fear started to overwhelm her if she had to go what would she do? She couldn't remember the last two hours. Then Keith is walking down the end to examine the rows. She checks her watch it's noon. Her stomach had barely quit churning and now panic mode again. She stops, drops the disk to the ground, and turns off the tractor.

His big smile is plastered across his face when he meets her at the bottom of the ladder. Dust matted on his face with a brown streak around his t-shirt collar. "Let's get some lunch."

She's mesmerized by his dusty face and huge smile. He wraps his arm around her shoulder, walking her over to the truck. *What does he think?* They drive over and pick up his dad on George's farm. She slides over tight to Keith, her leg rubbing his. She leaves it there for the ride.

His dad glances at Keith. "How's she doing?"

"She's not off much." He winks at Marilyn. "She's only getting about ten feet each pass, but she didn't miss any spots. I'm figuring once she gets some twelve-hour days in for a couple of weeks, she'll be halfway decent."

"Did you tell her she has to cook dinner?"

"Dad, let's break her into the twelve-hour days first."

"Your mom told me to remind you they have labor laws." Joy engulfs Marilyn as she see his dad's grin.

Gwen is putting sandwiches and potato salad on the table when they walk in. "Everyone get washed up."

Keith motions Marilyn to the bathroom. Johnny and Chad are talking to him when she comes out, explaining how they made no-bake cookies.

Marilyn's eyes water. The family issues seem to have disappeared, and everyone is working together. She has never felt such closeness.

Keith's dad winks at her as they sit down at the table. "Are you bored yet?"

"No, I'm still too worried about being in a straight line—"

Gwen says, "Don't worry. After a couple of days, you'll be bored, but as skillful as them. They want to make it sound hard."

"I hope ... I'm extremely grateful for what you have done for me."

"Dear, you are doing fine." Gwen sets the cookies out. "The boys helped me make these this morning." The boys sit with beaming smiles.

Keith takes one quickly and bites into it. "Nope, they're not very good. You boys better not eat them."

Gwen says, "Keith. You boys better get one before Uncle Keith eats them all."

He quickly grabs another one and starts laughing. Keith looks at his dad. "You feel all right, Dad?"

"Little heartburn from eating too fast, Mother would say."

Keith is staring at him. "Take a nap. We can't catch up to you, anyway."

"No, I'll be fine."

***

Marilyn is completely exhausted when Keith shows up at six. They switch, and he drives the tractor up to the barn, and she follows in his truck. His dad is feeding the cows already, and they head to his parents' house.

"You did great today." He squeezes her hand. "We're teasing about twelve hours a day. Normally we only work about eleven."

She bites her lip to keep from smiling as they pull into the driveway. "Is this farming boot camp to see if I measure up?"

"You passed day one." Keith's lip is twitching. "Mom may think it's too much on your first day, but we'll work on more than a quick kiss."

"Isn't that fraternizing with the help?"

"It's a bonus, and if you keep up the excellent work, there'll be more."

"I should've known." She jumps out, holds the door open, *wanting him to kiss her no matter who is watching.* "Your mom said I should tell you no."

"Oh, she did. Guess I need to have a talk with her about motivating the employees."

She holds the smile in and goes into the house.

***

Gwen has some jeans and tops laid out. "Take these home and try them. They weren't stylish enough for Jeanie when she was young, but they're comfortable. No reason to ruin your good clothes."

"Thanks. I'm worried about how decent a job I'm really doing."

"Remember, they'll never let you know and ruin their manly image. Plan on staying for dinner for the next couple of nights?"

Compassion seeps into her mind. "Thank you. Okay. Come on, boys, time to go home." The drive seems to take forever, as she is trying to stave off exhaustion.

May 2, 1984

By the third morning, Marilyn is experiencing some confidence.

Gwen drives her to George's farm this morning. "You and Dad are working here today. They are talking about rain tomorrow, so the guys won't be coming to the house. I'll bring them a sandwich, but you can come and eat with us."

"Thanks, I'll keep working."

Gwen's face glows. "You are taking a break."

"Thanks." She heads towards the tractor. Her mind drifts. *No morning kiss.* It's work, the fence is closer, focus on each turn, there's no leeway at the end. Marilyn is into a comfortable routine, keeping the tractor lined up and making the turns.

Gwen brings her back from lunch. "You're doing an excellent job. A secret between us. Paul is stingy with compliments, but you impressed him with your hard work."

"I took it as a compliment when they were teasing me about keeping up."

Paul has stopped. Maybe she wasn't paying attention. She makes another round. He still hasn't moved. Did he wave?

She stops and stands on the front tire, hoping Keith is watching. He returns the wave. She heads to the front of the field. Her thoughts are in overdrive. *Did I do the right thing? What if it's nothing, and I made everyone stop working?* But something doesn't seem right. Will Keith be mad if it is nothing?

She reaches the end as Keith pulls up. He jumps out and says, "What happened?"

She is looking across the field. "I didn't see your dad wave, but he hasn't moved in a long time."

"Jump in. We'll go check."

Keith is driving faster than normal. The truck is bouncing across the rough field. His muscles are taut, stretching his t-shirt, as he grips the steering wheel with both hands.

Marilyn says, "I hope it's not my paranoia, always thinking something is wrong."

Keith never looks over, and his voice tenses. "Dad probably stopped to take his nap, but we need to check."

The tractor is stopped. Ninety degrees from the row. The plow is still in the ground. Paul is slumped over the steering wheel.

Keith jumps out. "Wait here."

Thirty-Seven

May 2, 1984

I run to the other side of the tractor and race up the ladder. "Dad! Dad!" I push him back in the seat. I shake him. His head flops to the side.

I meet Marilyn before she gets to the tractor. "Call 911 and tell George to come help me move Dad out of the cab."

"Is he breathing?"

I look away. "Yeah."

She turns and says, "I'll bring your mom."

His glassy eyes stare. No pulse. "Dad!" He is cold. I lean against the front tire and break out sobbing. "Damn it, God. Why are you doing this to me?" I stare at the sky. "Okay, we disagreed, but—"

I wipe my face on my T-shirt, take a breath, and climb into the cab. "Damn it, Dad. What the hell am I going to do?" I check his pulse again. His hands are cold and getting blue.

Suck it up.

"Damn it, coach, it's not a game." His body is lifeless as I gently work him out of the seat, sitting him on the floor, his legs flopping over the steps.

George runs from his truck and stands at the bottom of the ladder and says, "Heart attack?"

I shrug. "He kept saying it was heartburn." I lean Dad to one side and climb out of the cab. "Let's get him down."

George climbs into the cab and checks his pulse. "How long has it been?"

I reach for his shoulder. "Too long. It was a couple of rounds when Marilyn noticed he'd stopped, and at least ten minutes for me to drive over here."

We slid Dad down as I stumble with him on my shoulder, and we drop to the ground together, resting him against the front tire. I move his head against the tire and close his eyelids. "He always said I was stuck in my ego, not paying attention. Guess he was right."

George squeezes my shoulder. "Don't start the blame shit. He wanted the best for you."

I'm kneeling on the ground in disbelief.

George wipes his eyes. "Life of a true farmer." He squeezes my shoulder again. "Farm till our last breath."

My pickup is racing towards us. I wipe my eyes again and take some deep breaths.

Mom jumps out of the truck almost before Marilyn stops.

I meet her in front of the tractor.

"Where is he?" She pushes by me, drops in the dirt, kisses, and hugs him. "Oh, my God." She screams through the sobs. "Please, no. God. Please."

A gut-wrenching pain I've never heard from my mother. I follow George to the other side and lean on the tire. Marilyn talks to the boys, closes the pickup door, and walks towards us. Moments later, a sheriff's car is racing up the path. Marilyn wraps me in a hug, sending a shiver through my body.

I motion to the other side of the tractor. One of them brings Mom over to us. I put my arm around her and walk her towards the truck. Marilyn embraces her, to hold her up.

Mom says, "It can't happen. He can't leave me."

The ambulance is bouncing through the rough field. The cop checking on Dad tries not to make eye contact with us and waves the ambulance towards him.

The ambulance swings around in front of the tractor.

Marilyn squeezes my arm. "If only I had seen him quicker. Maybe—"

"Where is he?" Curt is out first.

I point and mumble. "He wasn't breathing when I arrived."

Marilyn says, "Let me take the boys—"

"Drop them at George's. His wife can watch them until we leave."

"Okay." She touches Mom's arm. "I'll be right back."

They lay Dad on the ground. We wait in a silent daze until Curt heads towards us. "Sorry, Mrs. Larson. It was too late."

The officer goes to his car and then comes over to us. "Were you the first one here?"

"Yes."

He motions me away from my mother. "I'm going to need a statement. It's just routine when someone dies unexpectedly."

I just nod and shrug.

Another police car is coming up the path. It's Sid.

He walks directly to Mom and gives her a hug. "I'm so sorry, Mrs. Larson."

Mom's crying with her head on his chest. "It just can't be so."

Marilyn pulls the truck close to us. I'm looking out into nowhere, holding mom as her sobbing continues. Within a few minutes they load Dad into the ambulance.

Mom is sniffling now and holding back her crying. "I don't want to leave him yet."

The ambulance drifts out of sight. Sid motions for me to come over. I glance at Marilyn. "Can you give Mom a ride to the house?"

She puts her arm around mom and heads her towards the truck. I am still in a daze, and she says, "Sure, I'll come back and pick you up."

Disoriented, I don't answer.

Sid says, "We'll give him a ride."

George turns towards me. "I'll feed the cows tonight. Fourteen buckets, right?"

"Eighteen now."

"You go be with the family. I'll take care of the cows and the tractors."

Sid asks me if he had climbed out before I got there. We go into more detail. "Who shut off the tractor?"

After a long silence, I say, "It was off." *He knew.* We went over few more questions, they gave me condolences and I head to the tractor. My hands are shaking as I start it up and let the tears run down my face.

***

Tracks of tears are still on Mom's cheeks as she sits in a trance, staring at Dad's empty chair, when I finally make it to the house. Marilyn is sitting at the table with Mom and a box of Kleenex. Silence controls the kitchen as I motion to Marilyn.

The boys are wide-eyed, sitting on the couch with fear written on their faces. I give them both a hug. "Can you boys stay with Grandma?"

Still dazed, they nod.

Marilyn's eyes melt into my soul as she puts her hand on my chest. "What do you need me to do?"

"We need Mom out of the kitchen. She doesn't need to hear me tell every person what happened."

"Should I call Laura before she leaves for work?"

"Yeah, that's a good idea." I rub Mom's shoulders and say, "Why don't you go and watch the boys?"

Still in a daze, she heads to the living room and says, "You boys ready for story time?"

Marilyn takes her iced tea and the Kleenex. Mom sits on the couch.

The boys look at me as I nod, and they go sit by her.

Marilyn is on the phone. "I'll tell him." She hangs up and bites her lip. "Sorry, I ... Says she loves you. Sorry, I didn't know ..." Fear flashes in her eyes, the same as the first night I met her.

I furrow my eyebrows. "What?"

"I didn't realize—"

Squinting out aggravation, I say, "Explain."

Her eyes water. "I'm sorry, it's dumb ... She wanted to hear from you, not a secondhand friend."

I pull her tight, and she breaks out sobbing into my sweaty T-shirt. "Going to be a lot of messed up emotions, including myself." My eyes are blurry. "There's no secondhand friend bullshit." I tip her chin up. "We're all in it together." I wipe tears off her cheeks with my fingers. "Talking about emotions, a cold beer would be nice."

The stress leaves her face. She breaks from my arm and goes to the fridge.

"Don't bother; Dad gave up beer years ago. There's nothing in there."

"I'll go to your house."

I find a dusty bottle of Jack Daniels in top cabinet. "This will do for the moment." I dig out a glass. "You want some?"

She shakes her head.

"Hope you can hold it together. It's going to be some shit ... my bullheadedness, the extra cows. Dad always worried about how we're paying the loans. Not wanting employees is part of the reason I bought the tractor and now ..." I take a big swig. "The modern farmer gets bigger equipment and stays ahead of the bank loans, but you still need people."

Marilyn touches my arm. "You can't blame yourself. He was proud of you."

The burn holds in my throat. "My pain-in-the-ass sister won't be thinking that." Sentimentalism is seeping into my heart. "I'd better start making calls before ..." I hold up the glass. "Makes me a bumbling idiot."

"Your mom made a casserole. I'll put it in the oven. We'll need to eat later."

I dial my uncle.

Thirty-Eight

May 2, 1984

The boys are quiet on the ride home, a welcome relief to let Marilyn get her thoughts under control. The questions are hanging like fog. Exhaustion should put her to sleep. *They needs an explanation.*

Marilyn sends the boys off to brush their teeth. She sits on Johnny's bed and sucks in emotions and tries to put her thoughts together. She pats the bed beside her when the boys come in. "I'm proud of you boys today for sitting with Grandma."

Chad says, "How come Grandpa went in the ambulance?"

"He had a heart attack. They came to help, but it was too late. Now he has gone to heaven."

Johnny whispers, "Didn't he want to go to heaven?"

Marilyn smiles at herself. "Everyone wants to, but Grandma's heart is sad because she can't see him."

The whites of Johnny's eyes show. "Mom, I don't want to go to heaven if it makes everyone sad."

Marilyn sniffles. "That's very caring, but we don't decide when the time ... We just need to help Grandma's heart to heal by showing her extra love."

Johnny leans towards Chad. "I've never felt my heart."

"I've never felt mine either."

Warmth goes through Marilyn. "Well ... we say with all our heart as a loving expression of caring and because we need love the same as our heart."

Johnny raises his head. "Mommy, do you love Uncle Keith in your heart?"

Marilyn holds a smile.

Chad looks at Johnny. "Mom told me she loves Uncle Keith."

Marilyn stutters. *Oh my God, I didn't ...* "Yes, everyone loves Uncle Keith." Her hands are shaking. "Let me tuck you in, and we'll talk more in the morning."

"No, really, she said she loved him."

Marilyn indulges in an extra-long shower, trying to wash away the new fears. Stops at the boy's bedroom before she crawls into bed. *I'm so naïve.*

May 3, 1984

The clock clicks off the minutes till two a.m. Marilyn puts on her housecoat, grabs the old beat-up notebook, wanders to the kitchen table, and turns on the dim light above the stove. Starts scribbling.

Are Laura and Keith a secret couple?

Keith wants good sex. Can I be that good?

My tits, bigger than Laura but are they big enough?

I'm a dreamy eyed puppy-love teenager?

How will I make Johnny understand when it is over?

When will it be time to go?

Laura pulls into the driveway. Nothing makes sense, she closes the notebook, and buries her face in her hands.

Laura quietly closes the door and pauses at the table. "Having a heart-to-heart with yourself?" She continues to the fridge and sets a beer and glass in front of Marilyn. "One can't think without one."

Marilyn still sits in silence before she pops open the top. "Thanks. I can't imagine it will help. Writing it down made it worse." She takes a sip and glances at the glass. "Always wonder why people liked it so much, and now I drink one daily."

"Or the real question is, how does one live without it?" Laura takes a drink. "Must have been hell over there today."

Marilyn pours more into her glass. "The worst was Keith's mother screaming. I'll never get it out of my head. Keith was in a trance but calm and under control. The boys, being troopers, patiently sat in the truck out in the field when the police and ambulance came. I tried to explain after ... I'm sure they're more confused ..." Marilyn takes a drink. "The tension started when Keith's sister arrived. I'm working prepping stuff for dinner, wearing Jeanie's old clothes, Keith sitting at the kitchen table, drinking Jack Daniels and keeps talking like she not there."

"Now that had to stir some shit."

"Gwen was reading to the boys. Jeanie after introduction and a stare down move towards me whispering, wanting the details."

Laura gets out two beers. "And?"

"Jeanie nodded her head towards the living room. 'Where's the dad?' I glanced out the window took a deep breath. 'They have different dads, and I don't keep track of them.' She stomped away."

Laura raises her eyebrows. "Wow. What did Keith say?"

"Thought he was going to spit out his drink, but his mom walked in, and everyone instantly quit talking—"

"She can be overdramatic—"

"The next instant Jeanie hugging Gwen with tears rolling down her cheeks."

"Yep, that's the girl I know."

Marilyn empties her glass. "I never realized. I'm sorry you are his secret lover."

Laura pulls back. "What the hell are you talking about?"

"You've known him for a long time. You both were trying to help me, and I'm ... you said you loved him. I'm not getting between you."

"I do love him." Laura gazes out into nowhere. "Besides you, he is my best friend, but we're no couple or planning on life here and forever."

Marilyn's body quivers. "I'll get away from him—"

"You'll do no such thing—it's the game we play. For the security of someone. We dwell on moonlit walks, some kissy-face." Laura gets more beer. "Maybe have some sex, which messes with our woman's emotions. Our imagination says we find love and poof."

Marilyn says, “I’m beyond rational points.”

Laura’s eyes sparkle. “Good, get that shit out of your head. Do you love him?”

Marilyn sets her beer down. “I feel safe around him, and my heart ... his sister said to me while we were cleaning up the dishes, ‘You must be good if you lasted through the winter.’ I felt guilty at first. Then she adds, ‘He’ll still dump you.’ I let out a breath almost whistling, ‘But you don’t know how good I am.’”

Laura sits grinning.

Marilyn takes another drink. “I’ve never slept with him.”

Laura stares out into nowhere.

Marilyn’s hands shake. “Do you believe me?”

“Damn, girl, of course. You couldn’t lie if your life depended on it. Enough of that crap. What else happened?”

“Dave grabbed a glass and poured some whiskey and plopped into Paul’s chair. Keith jaw tightened, his knuckles turned white from gripping his glass. Kept thinking any moment Keith was going to drill him but he finally started breathing again.”

“Mr. Banker is an ass. When I was young, getting divorced, he led me on until dragging out my personal life, then with a mocking sneer, says, ‘What are your assets?’ Enough of that shit. How’s the tractor driving?”

“It's mentally draining trying to drive in a straight line in the middle of a field and make sure you’re parallel with the last row. At the end of the row, everything must be timed, raise the disk, hit the inside brake pedal, and turn the wheel. Did you realize that tractors have two brake pedals?”

“No, I didn’t.”

“Depending on whether you’re turning or stopping, which one do you use? I held my breath every time I got to the end of a row, but I finished the day with some deep satisfaction of myself.”

“I’d still be bored out of my mind.”

“I was in a trance.”

Laura nods. “When is the funeral going to be?”

“They’re making the arrangements in the morning. I assume it’ll be Monday or Tuesday at the latest.”

“We need to find a babysitter.” Laura downs the rest of her beer. “My mom can watch the boys, but it is a forty-five-minute drive." She throws her can in the sink. "We'd better get to bed. The boys will be up soon."

Marilyn grabs the edge of the table when she gets up.

Laura grins. "You need more drinking practice."

***

Marilyn is pacing, pondering the guilt-ridden conversation she needs to have with her mom.

Laura is ironing her work clothes. "You don't have to call her."

"No, she could at least pretend to be grandmother for once." Marilyn dials the phone. "Good afternoon, Mom."

Her first words. "Felt like you disowned us after your meltdown."

"I apologize; my emotions are all over the place. Juggling two jobs, *driving tractor,* the babysitter, dealing with John's visitation—I want to hide from the world. But I promise we'll come over soon and spend some time together."

They talk about the gossip of the family. Marilyn finally asks, "Could use a favor."

The phone is silent. "Marilyn, we don't have any extra money."

"Mom, I'm wondering if you would watch Johnny and Chad on Monday afternoon." Marilyn is taking long breaths ... "I know it's the last minute—"

"Must be something pretty important, or secret you're not allowed to trust your mother knowing?"

"A funeral for a friend. His dad died. The boys are too young to attend a funeral. Laura and I are both going, and our babysitter is in school."

"Was it Paul Larson?"

"Yes."

"I read that in the paper. Surprised he would hang out at the bar."

"Keith, his son, comes by regularly and ... He's always make sure no one gives us a hard time."

"They own that big farm. He is the kind of guy you should date."

"Mother."

"Is he still single? Paper didn't mention a wife."

"Yes, he's single." Marilyn closes her eyes.

"Quit acting like a nun. Put on some makeup. Do you have a nice dress to wear?"

"Yes, Mother, it's a funeral, remember?"

"Best time, you can comfort him. Bring extra clothes for the boys, and they can stay the night. In case you—"

"Thanks, Mom, but he has family he's spending time with."

"Use it as leverage against John, what he has to measure up to if he wants you back."

"Mom, under no circumstances let John know."

***

Marilyn tries to focus on work mode Thursday evening.

Mr. Straggle Mustache's gruff voice pierces her thoughts. "Sweetie, you're missing it tonight."

Marilyn glances around the table and realizes she is at wrong table. "You're delusional. I'm definitely not your sweetie."

Everyone laughs.

"Hurry, we are dying of thirst."

Marilyn straightens out the order.

She gives Mr. Mustache a glass of water with no ice. "Don't die here." She walks away. The table now is roaring.

Laura says, "What's going on?"

"He must be drunk, confused me for his sweetie and said he was dying of thirst. I gave him some water."

Laura grins and says, "You're getting some spunk."

Marilyn holds her breath. "Fighting demons, but I'm not winning."

Thirty-Nine

May 8, 1984

I'm groggy from the beers after the funeral home visitation last night. The guilt and thoughtfulness of everyone ripped the emotions out of me. The warmth of Marilyn and Laura was my refuge, I introduced them like family to everyone. There's a bond I can't explain in the moments standing with them, with my dad's soul watching in complete calm.

I eat up the stale Sugar Pops, seeing Johnny's face, realizing how much I miss him in the morning. Slap myself back to reality. My tie, the knot, looks like shit. I stick it in my pocket and go pick up Mom.

Mom says, "Where's your tie?"

I pull it out of my pocket. "Thought I looked better without it."

She takes it, ties it like she's been doing it every day. Pats my chest. "Much better. I am proud of you, how you've handled everything."

I stammer. "Thanks, Mom."

Her eyes are getting watery. "We'll get through this."

"I know we will. Dad wouldn't want us to sit around sulking. I'll go back to planting corn tomorrow. They are predicting rain on Wednesday, could set us back couple of days."

Mom holds my arm as we walk to Dad's truck. I can see a tear running down her cheek. "Dad always said, 'Good thing you can cook because you sure can't drive a tractor.' God rest his soul, he tried to teach me, but I never got the hang of it."

"Marilyn caught on quick."

"Dad said she did really well."

"Yeah. I told her you would watch the boys; assume it was okay."

"Anytime, they're sweet kids." Mom glances at me. "We need to get back to normal, whatever it will be. Also, I want to apologize for judging her so harshly. She's a nice girl."

I take a quick glance as my eyes blur.

***

I'm dazed through most of the funeral, as my mind fades to history. The pastor's fake words of wisdom anger me. Did he know my dad or fit the Bible story of the day? Okay, I should have more of God in my life, but the judgement of me by the ones who go to church sucks from my viewpoint.

I invite Jason, Marilyn, and Laura to the front table for lunch afterwards. Judging from my sister, it was the right thing to do. I take a bite of food, keep my stone-cold face, and lean over to Laura. "My sister thinks I'm a stud being able to take care of both of you."

"I'm sure you quashed that rumor."

I lean over and whisper in Marilyn's ear. "Don't look up, but my sister is telling Dave how hot you girls are and making him jealous."

Marilyn almost spits her food out, catches it with her napkin, and wipes her mouth. She leans towards my ear and whispers, "Nice try, but she thinks I'm some hussy after your money."

"The bank has first dibs. If I don't, get enough corn planted, Dave will send his management team to give me guidance. Next year I'll be homeless, eating in the soup kitchen, and drinking Boone's Farm."

Marilyn says between bites of food, "You're planning on me coming tomorrow?"

"Yes, Mom's looking forward to the boys." I turn with my eyes squinted a bit, taking a couple of breaths. "I'm supposed to pass along, Dad never got around to telling you what a good job you're doing."

Marilyn pauses for a moment and looks at Mom.

May 9, 1984

George feeds the cows in the morning, and I fuel up the equipment. He says, "I'll finish plowing that field this morning before I take Martha to the doctor, but between your girlfriend and me will work the fields so can keep planting."

I choke up, he sounds like dad's twin. I mumble, "Thanks."

He climbs onto the tractor.

Marilyn parks by the house with her thermos in hand and walks down the driveway towards me. Her dark brown shoulder-length hair is neatly tied in a ponytail; her blouse is tucked tightly into her jeans. She's the hottest farm fashion of the year. *We've got time for a quickie.*

She hugs me tight, then pulls away. "I'm sure the rumor wire is burning up today, which is life, but if my ex finds out ..."

I wrap my arm around her. "We'll keep them guessing, and quit worrying about your ex. We'll take care of it if he tries anything. Let's ..." I gaze towards the house. "We'd better go to work." I drive the tractor over to the field, and she follows me in the truck. I line her up in the front field, explaining the smaller fields and the different angles between the creek and the fence. "Remember, the turns are a little trickier, because it's not a square field."

George finishes plowing the field by ten and takes the tractor to the tool shed. The rest of the morning is gone when I see Marilyn has stopped. I finish the row and realize she has the disk caught in the fence. I jump in the truck and race over.

She caught the post, the fence tangled, ripping it loose from the other posts. The disk is wedged against the rear tire and a fence post. She is leaning against the tractor tire with her back to me as I walk up behind her. *She's crying.*

She blurts out, "You told me to pay attention ..."

"And the daydream was?"

She is standing between the tire and the ladder on the tractor. "I'm sorry, I didn't ..." She cowers away like a beat dog, breaks out sobbing. "Pay attention—when I backed up, it made it worse—"

I gently pull her towards me. "It's okay; we're planning on taking the fence out, anyway." I massage her shoulder. "If it hadn't hooked the post, you probably would have got loose."

She finally takes a breath. She keeps her arms between us and her head down.

I tip her chin up. "Let's go get some wire cutters."

I pull up to the toolshed. Marilyn is still in a trance as I grab wire cutters and gloves and throw them on the seat. I squeeze her thigh. "Miss Marilyn."

She puts her face in her hands. "I can't do anything right—"

"You're doing great. We'll find a rainy day and practice."

She straightens up. "Quit, I'm not some sexy hot babe. Just take me to bed and you'll see how unsexy I am, and you can check me off the list." Her face is red. "You can move on."

I put the truck in park and glance over at her. "I tease you ... it's the only

..." She finally looks at me. "I ... I ... You're a special girl that's touched my heart." I lean over, pull her head close, and kiss her.

She is shocked but returns the kiss.

"It's our secret." I break out in a cat-ass grin. "Break's over, no more trying to seduce the boss."

She's sniffling. "I'm telling your mother."

I cut the wire wrapped around the disk, coil up the extra, and move the tractor into the field.

I climb off the tractor. "Speaking of Mother." She is coming up the path with lunch. I wave and point towards the tree. Marilyn is still standing in a daze and I say to her, "Come on, lunch is here."

Mom drives Dad's truck and sets the basket on the tailgate. The boys carry the cooler with iced tea. They're all examining the fence. Mom smiles at Marilyn. "You started cleaning out the fence for him?"

"I told her it was next year's project." Marilyn is biting her lip. I'm not sure whether she's going to cry or laugh.

Johnny's traumatized. "Mom, what did you do?"

Marilyn cowers, holding in tears.

I smile at Johnny. "You know your mom thought it looked messy. Tired of driving around it, she just ripped it out." I grab a bologna sandwich and wink at Marilyn. Johnny and her still have fear carved on their faces.

Mom wraps her arm around Marilyn's shoulder and walks her over to the truck. "Everyone, grab a sandwich before Keith eats them all."

I lift the boys up into the truck bed, and Mom hands them their sandwiches.

She hands Marilyn one too. "He didn't yell at you, did he?"

Marilyn is shaking her head. "No, no ... I'm sure he wanted to."

"He'd better never. He wasn't raised that way."

"It's me ... I went into a complete meltdown. He ..." She raises her head, looking straight at me. "The perfect gentleman."

Mom pats her leg. "Dear, don't lie for him." She glances at me. "I know him better than that."

***

I spend every day that's not raining, planting. George and Marilyn are taking turns at the disk. I can see the end in sight as I'm starting the normal feeding of the cows. The last two weeks were hell, but the corn peeks through the ground, giving the inner reward of farming.

May 19, 1984

Marilyn pulls in, and the boys run with their bags and drop them inside the door. "Uncle Keith, can we play in the sandbox?"

"Sure."

They grab tractors.

Marilyn watches them run by her. "You boys ..." She looks at me. "They've already had their baths."

"I won't let them get too dirty."

I touch her arm. "You should plan on coming over on Sunday. I'll cook some steaks."

She answers just above a whisper, "That sounds nice."

"Is everything okay?"

"Yes." She turns. "I've gotta go to work."

I stand motionless. *Thanks, you are the best.* She makes a small wave.

You missed your kiss ... It's a no, she's had enough of my inflated ego.

The boys are chasing Jake around the sandbox. "Boys, I'm going to feed the cows, and then we're going to Grandma's for supper. Stay by the house, and don't get dirty."

They're both laughing. "Okay."

It's hard to imagine how well-behaved the boys are, for having deadbeat dads. I drop the silage into the trough. My mind goes to Marilyn. *Her emotions seem to come around and then crash into depression.*

***

Mom's quiet demeanor soaks into my heart, and she says, "Have you told Marilyn how much we appreciate her help?"

"Well ... kind of."

"Remember, you complained about Dad never giving you a compliment. You'd better tell her what a great job she is doing. We couldn't have done it without her."

I nod. "I will."

Mom quietly watches the boys finish their cake, looking at Dad's chair with sadness. "You boys run and play. Unless you want to help do the dishes." They scramble off. She exhales, her eyes misty. "Are you sleeping with her?"

I shake my head. "No, Mom. I'm sure it was the scuttlebutt at the funeral. But no."

"Promise me you won't take advantage of her. She needs help and time to sort out the pain in her heart too."

"Don't worry, Mom. She's going to make it."

"We need to pay her something. She can't work for free."

I roll my lip. "I paid for her divorce; she is working to pay it off."

Mom goes silent. "That was nice of you, and wondered why she wouldn't talk about it. You still need to give her some money."

"I know how it looks but made her promise, because I didn't want Dad..."

"I'm writing her a check the next time she comes over. Also, don't be worrying about taking care of me." She holds her breath. "I miss your dad more than anything. It's going to be a big change, but I'm more worried about you settling down, finding a nice girl and getting me more grandchildren."

I hug her. "I'll start working on it." I gather up the boys. Stick my head back in the door. "You want grandkids or a daughter-in-law first?"

"Keith!"

Forty

May 18, 1984

After supper, I help the boys build a tent, a sheet draped over the kitchen chairs on one side and tucked in the couch on the other. I grab a beer and turn on the TV and listen to the boys with Jake in their tent. The realization of such a sincere moment is more enjoyable than being at the bar. *Am I getting old?*

Jake comes out of the tent; his ears perk up with a deep growl. I peek out the window. It's Bob's Camaro in the driveway. *Why would he be here?* I open the tent and whisper, "You boys go to the hiding spot and don't come out till I come and get you."

They scamper off.

Someone is pounding on the door. "Open up."

Jake woofs but turns into a deep growl. We reach the door, his hair on his neck is standing up, and I flip on the porch light. John is standing back a couple of steps, rubbing his hands into a ball, while Bob stands motionless when I open the door and say, "Do something for you boys?"

John becomes rigid and says, "My wife's at the bar. My neighbor, your buddy, is at the bar. No one's at her house. Your home. Wonder who's watching my kid?"

I stand in silence; Bob's guilt and boldness is matching a hunted rabbit. John's veins are pulsing in his neck when he says, "All the roads lead here."

"So you're lost?" I glance at Bob.

John says, "No, you're playing dad and screwing my wife."

Jake is barking. I grab his collar. "Enough." I step outside, leaving Jake behind the old wooden screen door. He goes into a low growl. "You must be mistaken."

"No, I'm not mistakėn. We hang out here long enough, and she'll come pulling in the driveway. It was a family issue we could've worked out. If the gigolos weren't always out sniffing."

"I hate family disputes, but the story around town is you were using her as a punching bag." I suck in a smirk. "Couldn't believe, you seemed ... such a caring guy when we met."

"I've heard you're always chasing married women." John is moving, flexing his hands into fists. "It's time someone taught you about what happens when you screw with my wife."

"Didn't know she was available. If we're going to fight over her, I'll assume she is damn good, but—" I raise my hands but keep them open. "You should at least let me ... Maybe it's not worth fighting about."

"Your swanky, sick-ass words don't work with me." He licks his lips, and his body is squirming. "I figured it out. You watch the kid. She gets out of work. Comes by and takes care of you."

I glance over at Bob again, seeing his nervous twitch. "I've heard it works, right, Bob?"

John tries to talk through raging bull snorts. "You're such a lowlife setting up your buddy, or were you sharing?" He spits out. "What's his name, my neighbor? Oh yeah, Jason. I should've kicked his ass a long time ago."

I bite my lip to keep the smirk hidden. "You should've been a detective—"

He raises his chin. "Uncle Keith, the gig—it's a neat little scheme—but I'm the real dad, and I ain't leaving without my kid."

"You have a dilemma. As you heard, I'm every woman's dream, and I would be there tonight but for these sixteen-hour days. Even I have some limits." I turn toward Bob and say, "Take your buddy home, talk some sense into him before he does something stupid and gets himself hurt."

Calmly, I move to keep them both in front of me. "Some scenarios to consider. Jake's going to rip you a new asshole if you try to go inside the house. And me, on Friday nights, I used to run over two-hundred-and-fifty-pound linemen, sometimes two or three at a time. Tell him, Bob, you'll never grow up and be tough enough."

John says, "You're a washed-up pussy sitting around in a tractor all day. My kid is here. I can do whatever I want to protect him."

Bob glances at John, then at me and says, "John, we'd better leave. Remember what we talked about earlier?"

"You should be listening." I gesture towards Bob.

Bob makes a small movement towards the car. John bolts towards me linebacker style. I twist sideways. He whips by me and takes a swing with his left, which I duck away, taking a glancing blow but landing a kidney punch.

John is huffing and says, "A sucker puncher." His face turns into a mad dog.

Jake is snapping through the screen.

I reposition so that Bob is not behind me. "You'd better load him in the car before he gets hurt."

John lowers his shoulder and charges and tries an upper-cut but misses. I hit him under the chin and spin off the side as he takes another wild swing. Bob pulls me around. John grabs the other arm as I trip Bob to the ground. I punch John in the ribs, and he stumbles. They both regain their balance.

I position myself with my back towards the house. Jake is snarling at the screen. They both rush me, Bob a little behind, as John tries a low punch. I swing my knee up and at same time punch him dead in the nose, hearing the bone crunch and seeing the blood spurt. Bob makes a glancing blow to my eye, but he is off balance.

John is on his knees and tries to punch me in the groin, misses, but grabs my leg. Bob is now behind me and pulls me to the ground.

The screen door slams.

John punches me in the kidneys and ribs.

Jake is dragging John away as he is screaming. "Get off me, you damn mutt!"

I flip Bob over, landing a solid punch on his jaw, the other side of his head. He falls off me and staggers, trying to get up. *He's done fighting.*

John slams Jake into the car. Jake yelps and drops to the ground, whimpering, trying to move.

I'm moving closer to Jake, staring at John, and say, "Time to leave."

Blood, dirt, and drool are all over John's face. A bull at the end smells blood, not knowing it's his.

"Do I have my kid?" He charges me again.

I block his weak swing to my head and hit him in the gut. He takes another aimless swing, and I feel teeth cut my fist, but he staggers. The next right drops him to his knees. I stand over him. *One more punch.* "Next time you won't be so lucky." I turn away.

Bob is staring but not moving. I lick the blood from inside my lip. "You'd better drag this shit-bag out of here before I lose my patience."

I pick up Jake, and he squeals in pain. They drag themselves off to the car. Jake is whimpering, taking quick breaths. *Broken ribs.* They both crawl to the car. I carry Jake into the house and lay him on his bed, as they start the car and leave.

I head to the bathroom to assess the damage. My bottom lip is swelling from the cut on the inside. I rinse my face and wipe it with a cold washcloth. May have a small shiner starting below my eye, but I feel good considering. I make up a bag of ice and check on Jake, his brown eyes asking me to help him. I scoop water into my hand; he licks it. "Just rest, buddy."

I walk into the bedroom. "All clear, boys." Fear is engraved on their faces as they climb out of the closet. "Don't worry, everything is okay."

Johnny says, "Uncle Keith, what happened?"

"There's nothing for you to worry about."

Johnny's dark brown eyes consume his face. "He hit you, just like he did my mom."

"He won't be hitting anyone for a while; we'll talk more later. You guys go and play." I dial the bar.

"Maggie's."

"Laura, I need to talk to Jason."

"What's going on?"

"I'll explain later. You sound busy."

"Yes, we are slammed. Hold on." I hear the band playing.

"Hello."

"Jason, Keith. John and Bob just paid me a visit. They weren't happy when they crawled away and are in no condition to bother anyone but—"

"You're okay, right?"

"Yeah, only two of them."

"How'd he find out—"

"Not many Uncle Keiths in town. He thinks one or both of us are seeing Marilyn. So watch yourself. We're fine. I took a couple of wimpy punches. Jake jumped in and tried to rip John's arm off, which evened up the fight. Tell the girls we had words and came to a mutual understanding. I can't imagine they'll bother anyone else tonight. John crawled on his hands and knees to Bob's car, but keep a look out."

"Okay, I'll call you if they show up."

"Talk to yah."

Johnny has tears in his eyes. "Uncle Keith, what's the matter with Jake?"

"Think he has broken ribs. He needs to rest." My eyes are blurry. "We'll take him to the vet in the morning."

Streams of tears on both of their faces. Johnny says, "It was my dad. He hurt Jake. I could hear him yelling."

"He won't be bothering us anymore."

I sit in my recliner with the ice pack for my eye. "Go lie down in your tent." My stomach and ribs are feeling the blows.

***

Chad is pulling my arm. "Uncle Keith."

I'm startled awake. "What's the matter?"

"Jake threw up beside his bed."

I stagger, getting out of the chair, and Johnny is kneeling beside Jake, petting him.

I touch Jake, and he's not breathing. I wrap my arms around both. "He was a good dog and was trying to protect us." I grab an old towel and cover him. We sit, trying not to cry. I wipe my eyes with my sleeve.

"My dad killed him. I hate him."

"Your dad is a sick person."

"Why can't you be my dad?" He breaks out sobbing.

I gather them in my arms, and we sit on the couch together, not talking.

"Tomorrow we'll have an official ceremony and bury him in the farm cemetery. He will forever be part of the farm."

Johnny wipes his face with his pajama sleeve and says, "I'm really scared, Uncle Keith. I heard him saying he was going to take me."

"I won't let him hurt either of you. Go, guys, grab your stuff and sleep with me tonight?"

They grab the pillows from the tent, I lock the outside door for the first time in forever, and they follow me to bed.

Forty-One

May 18, 1984

Marilyn arrives at work early, although she ran from Keith's house as if she were late. She hesitates at the bar door, realizing how badly it needs repair. *It's all a mirage. No guy can be that perfect.* The noise and bustle of the bar overwhelm any thoughts beyond the next order.

The band starts the second set, and the place is jamming. The phone's ringing. Marilyn watches Laura answer the phone as she checks her drink order.

She holds the receiver up and yells, "Jason. Phone." She glances at Marilyn. "Keith."

Marilyn freezes and watches Jason talking on the phone. Jason watches her and nods. She picks up her order, trying to shake the fears. *Laura thinks nothing of it, and I'm paranoid.*

Eleven o'clock when Marilyn has time for a break and sits down beside Jason. "Keith getting bored watching the kids?"

He grins. "Keith always finds something to keep life exciting."

"I feel guilty for asking him. His first Friday night after finishing the planting."

Jason says, "He's watching Chad, and Laura's not feeling guilty. Besides, it gives him practice for the excitement of family time."

"I'm not sure he's ready for that. Is everything okay? Can't imagine he just called to check in."

He says just above a whisper, "John and Bob stopped by the house."

"Oh my God, what happened?"

The guys sitting in stools around the corner swivel their heads in our direction.

Jason leans close. "Said they had a man-to-man conversation—"

"John doesn't have civil conversations."

Jason says calmly, "John has surmised that you and I are the hot gossip of the town." A smirk comes onto his face. "It started when we were neighbors."

She leans her head.

"We were both home all winter. Great logic for a jealous husband."

"Why go to Keith's?"

"He was looking for Johnny."

"This is getting way too crazy." She is rubbing her hands. "You'd better be careful. He'll come after you."

"Nothing to worry about. He only scares people who are scared."

"Everyone says I overreact with him, but there is no such thing." She bites her lip and squeezes Jason's arm. "Keith said he is okay?"

"Said he worked it out." He pats the top of her hand. "And for us not to panic."

They are waving at one of her tables. "I'll be back."

She catches up with the drink orders and returns. "Did John go into the house?"

"No, they were out in the yard. Keith thinks he has been following you or me around but was guessing if Johnny was there."

Marilyn's anxiety is building as she fidgets, wanting to call Keith.

Laura asks her to work over an extra hour, robbing her of sleep or worry, not sure which.

She finally can leave. She quickly grabs her purse.

Jason touches her arm on the way out. "I'll follow you home."

"You're awfully nervous for everything being okay." Marilyn and Jason scan the parking lot walking close together. "He must know I'm working here." She says, "But goes to Keith's?"

"He wanted to meet Uncle Keith."

Marilyn stops and takes some long breaths trying to regain composure. "How bad was the fight?"

"Keith said, to go about our normal evening."

Marilyn shakes her head and climbs in the car. She blinks the lights on and off once she is home Jason blinks the head lights. Marilyn takes a long hot shower, but anxiety and anger won't leave. She needs sleep but craves a drink to numb herself.

May 19, 1984

I roll quietly out of bed at four-thirty but was awake half the night. My eye is puffed and turning black and blue, but the swollen cut lip doesn't look bad from the outside. I sit down with my coffee after feeding the cows. The phone rings. "Hello."

It's Jason. "How bad was it?"

"John got a cut lip, a busted nose and a nasty bite mark on his arm. I adjusted Bob's teeth. How did you make out?"

"Nothing happened uptown. I followed them both home and no sign of them. Marilyn was in panic mode, surprise she hasn't called already."

"She at the restaurant this morning. I landed solid blows on John's face. He is messed up, and crawled to the car. I wanted to keep punching until he couldn't crawl, but he won't be going after anyone for a few days. He slammed Jake against the car and killed him."

"Shit. What are you telling the girls?"

"The least I have to, but I have a small shiner."

"She'll panic and blame herself for everything."

"Yes, I'm pondering how to explain when she gets here later."

Jasons says, "I'll go for a drive to see where John slept last night. Guessing he didn't go home to Mommy's. Laura thinks Bob is renting an apartment in Peck. I'll do a little scouting."

"Keep me posted. We're going to bury Jake."

"Take care."

I call Mom and tell her Jake has died, with as few details as possible. After the kids are up and have breakfast, we load up Jake and go behind the barn at Dad's, where I buried Buster when I was a kid. "This is our doggie cemetery." Gently, I lay Jake in the hole I dug. "Pick up a handful of dirt and say your last words." I throw mine into the hole. "You were a great dog."

Johnny throws a handful. "You were the best dog ever."

Chad throws his. "Love you, Jake."

Johnny has tears running down his face. "I love you too, Jake."

I shovel the dirt neatly, take a stick, and hang his collar on it for the headstone. I kneel on one knee as the boys stand beside me, tears running down our faces. "Thanks for always taking care of us, Jake. We will never forget you."

***

Marilyn's alarm goes off at six. She hits the snooze for the second time before dragging herself out of bed. She gets to the restaurant still in a daze, punches in late, and feels Skippy seething in the pass-through. She is hoping for a break in customers so she can call Keith. The morning whizzes by with no time. At the end of her shift, she is exhausted.

Skippy signals her over. "I'm changing the schedule, but it is too busy right now to talk about it. Stop back at three."

She stands with her mouth open.

"Nothing serious, but ..." He never stops and flips over some eggs. *I'd love to because I have no life.* "Okay." She climbs into her car. Evaluating ... *I'm getting fired.* Someone blows the horn. She hits the brakes. He holds his hands up and shakes his head. *Why didn't Keith call me?* She death-grips the steering wheel, and her hands are cramped when she gets to Keith's. *It's my son. My ex.* She knocks and walks directly into the house.

Keith yells, "Come in."

Johnny says, "Hi, Mom," and turns away from her, taking his plate to the counter.

Keith is at the sink rinsing the dishes. "You boys can go outside and play now."

Marilyn makes her way to the table, and they scamper outside.

She pauses in the quiet. "What's going on?"

Keith faces her.

She runs to him. "I knew it was more than a conversation. Jason was acting too weird."

"We worked out the misunderstandings. I didn't want you worried."

She is rubbing his chest. "You okay? Did you put ice on your eye?"

"Yeah, a minor bruise compared to his broken nose and loose teeth."

She is patting his chest and looking at him for a flinch.

"Lower."

Tears are forming, and she puts her hands over her mouth. "Stop it. Why didn't you call me?"

"It looks worse than it is. Bob caught me in the lip." He rolls it out, shows the puffiness. "Not bad, no loose teeth. Neither of them knows how to land a punch."

She is pacing. "I'm so sorry. I knew he'd eventually find out. How are the boys?"

"They are doing good. They hid in the closet, and John was guessing about their being here. Johnny heard him yelling, but we talked about it afterwards. He's going to be fine. Let's sit. You must be tired."

He put his arm around her. She stops, and her face tightens. "Where's Jake?" Marilyn pulls her skirt down over her knees and tucks her legs under her. Facing Keith. Waiting.

Keith looks away abruptly. "Jake passed away last night. We buried him this morning."

She screams. "What? What else happened?"

Keith holds up his hand. "Calm down—"

"Well, quit treating me like one of your bimbos. Yeah, I know you are the big shining knight who swoops in and saves the girl and have the big ego reputation to live up to."

Keith's face is instantly flushed.

"Tell me. All of it." She is shaking inside.

He reaches for her hand.

She pulls away.

Keith says, "John kept running at me, flailing wild punches, and Bob kept trying to sneak behind me—"

"They both went after you—"

"Yeah, I landed a solid punch that broke John's nose. They pulled me to the ground and jumped on top of me." Tears form in his eyes. "Jake went crazy and grabbed John's arm, trying to rip it off."

Tears come down her cheeks as she sits staring.

"John slammed him against the car and broke Jake's ribs. Must have punctured a lung. He passed away later in the evening."

"And they just left?"

"They turned like they were leaving, and Bob wanted to, but your ex turned into a rabid dog."

Marilyn's eyes are watering. "He'll—never let it go if I stay."

"After that beating, he's not looking for more." He takes a deep breath. "I'm sorry, I should've called you last night, but ..."

"I worried all night. Then I overslept and was late for work. Probably getting fired. Skippy wants to talk me later this afternoon."

"Whatever I do is to protect you and your son." Keith takes hold of her arm and softly pulls her towards him. "You don't need all the gory details, but he crawled away because he couldn't walk. He won't try messing with you."

"I didn't mean to yell." She slides over to him. "I smell like bacon and eggs."

"That's supposed to be bad?"

She snuggles into his chest. The romantic aroma of him soaks into her. "Thanks for keeping Johnny safe." Exhaustion takes over.

She wakes up. She is covered on the couch. "How long have I been asleep? Where are the boys? What time is it?"

"Three-thirty." Keith motions towards the tent. "They took a nap too."

She jumps up. "I was supposed to meet Skippy at three. I'd better call."

"Skippy's."

"Hi, it's Marilyn. Is Skip still there?"

"Yes, hold on."

"This is Skip."

"It's Marilyn. Sorry, I lost track of time, and—"

"It's why we need to talk. I want to help—but I can't have you working half awake. Or worried you may never show up."

"I'm sorry, I've had ... Things will be better." She is pacing around the kitchen.

"I wanted to talk face-to-face. But I am taking you off the morning shifts."

She stands in a trance, looking out the kitchen window.

"I have Monday and Tuesday from four to close open if you want to work."

"Okay."

"Sorry, I still have a business to run. Figure a later shift you can be on time."

"Yes, I understand."

"Okay, I'll see you Sunday at eight and on Monday and Tuesday at four?"

"I'll be there." She hangs up, staring at the phone.

Keith walks over to her. "Not good news, I take it."

I had better call my sister.

Forty-Two

May 18, 1984

John grimaces, his hands over his face, as blood drips onto his pants.

Bob glances. "You're dripping blood on the seat." He stops the car at the corner, digs around in the back, finds an old T-shirt, and hands it to John.

"Damn, my arm hurts. That damn dog bit me hard enough to break my arm."

"You should go to the hospital. Your arm is bad and could be broke."

"That's a dumb idea. Mr. Jock will tell them we were trespassing, and we'll end up in jail."

Bob says, "You stretched the nice sociable talk to scare him."

"My kid was there. I saw him peeking out the window."

Bob rolls his eyes and continues in silence to his apartment.

John seethes in anger and goes into the bathroom to clean up. Screaming in pain, he realigns his nose and stuffs it with Kleenex. He examines his face, deciding it won't look worse than before once the swelling and bruises disappear. He opens the medicine cabinet, takes four aspirins, and makes his way to the couch.

Bob hands him his ice pack. "You need this more than me." He raises his beer. "You want one?"

"You got any whiskey?"

"Want ice?"

"No, straight up. I've got to kill this pain."

Bob pulls a bottle from the top cabinet and pours a third of a glass.

John sits on the worn-out flowery couch. "I've gotta catch her with one of them assholes."

"I thought the plan was to set up a stakeout position. Fill in the gaps, she leaves her car at the bar and goes home with someone." He sets the bottle on the counter. "It's going to be tough doing that now."

"Shut up. Bring the bottle. I need more than one sip."

Bob has a smirk as he sets it on the end table.

"Smart ass finishes it, told yah so, and all that shit."

Bob takes a drink of beer. "You learn the point the hard way. Keith isn't someone to mess with. He never tells. Women defend him, even after they break up. He was dicking Laura, but—"

"What—why the hell didn't you tell me?"

"I don't have any proof. It's a gut feeling after the fact. She shut me off a few months before she kicked me out. I told you that. Quit talking about much of anything no gossip from the bar and was late getting home regularly. It's the little things you never notice."

John pours himself more whiskey. "Kind of like the wife. She quit talking about anything. Unless it was the money." He takes another slug. "She would glare at me when she was mad but never look me in the eye when she was talking."

"No sense dragging it out. Time to move on."

"Easy for you to say. I'll have thirteen years of child support and alimony to pay," John says sarcastically. "Cheaper for me to let her work a part-time job and get some on the side."

"Sounds like a great plan. And you're doing this with the super charm gene that's been dormant?" Bob breaks into a grin.

John slowly swallows a swig. "A great friend you are."

"You aren't doing it with your good looks." Bob downs the rest of his beer and gets up. "You'd be a lot better off figuring out how to get your divorce settled. If she quits her job, you'll pay more alimony. I've heard of guys still paying alimony after their kids left because their wife shacks up with a guy, never gets married, and never goes to work."

John is staring at his drink.

Bob pulls a pillow and blanket from the closet and throws them on the couch next to John. "That's a fancy couch, so don't get blood on it. See you in the morning."

John hits the couch with his left fist. "That's it. That's how Marilyn paid for a lawyer, and Drillman doesn't work cheap."

Bob turns, frowning. "What are you talking about?"

"It's been bugging me how she found the money for the lawyer. No one gives you money if they barely know you. My lawyer wanted six hundred dollars up front and said it could be a thousand to fifteen hundred if we can't agree. She had to be seeing Jason all winter, so he gave her the money."

Bob grins before turning towards his room. "Yep, sounds possible. The kid takes a nap and so does the neighbor. It's the modern world we live in. For a treat, invite Keith over and have a nice threesome."

"You're such a dick."

Bob is laughing. "Yep, your best buddy, or your only buddy, explaining the facts of life to you and you call me names. Speaking of that, Julie is begging for some attention from you, but if you don't step up, I'm going to weed in, and I'm not a sharing guy."

Bob goes to bed, leaving John mumbling.

May 19, 1984

It's eleven o'clock when John gets up on Saturday, his head pounding. His forearm is black and blue with punch holes in the middle.

Bob has coffee made and sitting at the counter and says, "You were ugly before, but it will be weeks before you look human."

"And a good morning." He heads to the bathroom. Raises his face into the mirror and analyzes his swelling. *The war isn't over.* John digs in the fridge and gets out a beer. "I'm telling my parents his buddies jumped us outside the bar. At least keeps them off my ass."

"Sounds like a story, and your mother won't believe a word of it."

"Thanks for reminding me."

"Telling you how it is. Going to the store and doing laundry. Is there anything you need?"

"Get me a twelve-pack. I'm not going home until tomorrow."

Bob holds out his hand.

John shakes his head, digging out his wallet.

May 20, 1984

John assesses which story to tell his mom; his body hurts everywhere as he climbs in his truck. He ponders each scenario on the ride. He quietly opens and closes the screen door when he enters his parents' house. His mom is reading the paper at the kitchen table.

She drops it and says, "What the hell happened to you?"

"Some guys jumped me coming out of the bar."

"Right. At the bar? You pick up someone's girlfriend, that's what the fights are always about."

"No, three of them jumped me for no reason."

"John Robert Desmond, stop lying. Did someone call the police? Yeah, dumb question. No, you're not in jail. Who was it?"

Dad comes to the kitchen. "What's the yelling—what the hell—"

"That's what I'm trying to find out."

John continues to his room.

Mrs. Desmond says, "Might as well sit. I want the truth, not what you're telling everyone about how you took on three of them."

John looks at his dad and then at his mother. "Went to Keith Larson on the other side of town to have a conversation."

"Is he related to Paul Larson?"

"It's his dad."

Mrs. Desmond rubs her forehead, slides her chair back, reaches into the top cupboard for the brandy, and adds it to her coffee, still staring at John.

"It was a conversation. Little heated but no fighting, until he sicced his dog on me."

"Did you witness them in bed together?"

"No." John lets out a long breath.

"You're an idiot. How do you plan to catch her doing anything now? I hired a PI to watch her on the weekends and to check on her in the evenings. He went into the bar one night when she was working. The only strange thing is her old neighbor is always there, walking her out, and they stay out in the car. It was just a matter of time before he caught them—"

John says, "Damn it, why—"

"Because, Mr. Tough—you'd pick a fight with the guy." She sits there for a long time, her eyes squinted, burning lasers through him. "The PI didn't dare get too close, but what does your imagination believe they were doing, with her car parked where no one could see them?"

John says, "We can question Johnny, find a clue when she's going over again."

"I don't think she'll be waltzing around playing kissy-face now."

The silence becomes stifling. "We would've eventually caught them." His dad rubs his chin and says, "PI said they were always nervous looking around the parking lot."

His mom says, "I take it you're okay?"

John says, "I'll live."

"Let me see your arm." She holds his hand. "It punched the skin. Guess you didn't ask if the mutt had his shots."

"I'll make him pay."

"You're doing what I tell you." Her jaw is clenched. "First thing is to let everything settle down again. The second thing is for you to stay away from both of them." She refills her coffee and more brandy. "You better keep your temper under control. I am not losing a grandson to them damn Larsons."

Forty-Three

June 10, 1984

Sunday morning, Marilyn thoughts wander with the smoke trailing over the barn as she sips her coffee, remember Keith entrances. Then the smell of John's day-old beer breath, as he makes her kiss him, haunts her reality.

Johnny is the first to break the stomach-churning back-and-forth. "What's for breakfast."

She makes Johnny waffles and adds his favorite blueberry syrup. He is happy as can be and doesn't seem worried about visiting his dad today.

Marilyn watching him eat and says, "Remember, don't say anything about Uncle Keith's." Guilt as she realizes she wants her son to lie.

"I know, Mom." Johnny hesitates. "I only talk to Grandma she is not mean like Dad."

"What else does she know?"

***

John's mother shows up exactly at noon. Marilyn gives Johnny a kiss and a hug and helps with his backpack. Marilyn opens the door.

Mrs. Desmond, with her painted face, says, "How is everyone today?"

Tension hits Marilyn. "Fine."

She rubs Johnny's head. "Johnny, why don't you go to the car? I'll be right there." She turns on her sweetness. "I bought chocolate ice cream special for you today."

Johnny looks back.

Marilyn waves. "I love you."

"You too, Mom." He runs off.

Mrs. Desmond drops the smile. "Not really a smart thing to do, sending your boyfriends after John."

Marilyn pauses. "Sounds like John is living his normal screwed-up life, looking for a fight. Trying to prove how tough he is." She hesitates. "Is there anything else?"

She rolls her lips. "Believe me, dear, I'm envious." She lowers her voice as if someone can hear. "I want to see my grandson every other week equal time."

"That ain't happening."

"My dear, your troubles with John will all go away. I forbid my grandson to go anywhere near the Larsons." She blows her breath at Marilyn as if she is casting a spell. "I will make everyone's life a living hell, and John can take care of you once I tell him you were sleeping with the neighbor all winter."

Marilyn recoils. "What are you talking about?"

With a half-smirk, she says, "You don't lie well. See you at six."

Marilyn slams the door and stumbles to the kitchen table. She breaks out sobbing.

Laura is instantly in the kitchen. "What the hell happened?"

Blubbering, Marilyn says, "I was having an affair with Jason, but don't fear. She'll keep it a secret."

"She just made it up?"

"Same as the rest of it, somehow John will show up in court as a perfect father, and she'll have me as some unfit mother. She is a witch."

Laura stands beside her. "Is John going to be there today? "

"Don't know, Keith said he broke his nose. I can't—what if Johnny calls?"

"I'll be here. You told Keith a ride sounded good. I heard you say it. Let me help you get ready for your hot date."

"You know me; I'll be a basket case worrying about Johnny."

"Stop it. It's 1984 you have the right ... to sleep with anyone you want. The rule: no kids are allowed in the bedroom. Remember, you are living in America. Women have rights. Why are you so scared?"

"I've lived five years of hell with John, and he won't stop, and now his mother—she threatened to go after the Larsons." She looks away from Laura. "I talked to my sister last night. Her husband is working on getting me a job at the dinner club. When they have an opening."

Laura tugs on Marilyn's arm. "You're going to run away?"

"I'm trying to protect everyone. He's going to come after you too if I stay. I'll make good money and send you some to help with the rent."

"Listen, girl, you're not sending me money. Period. What about Keith? Have you told him?"

"No, I will ... Promise me you won't ..."

"I won't tell, but do you love him?"

Marilyn tenses. "I ... That's why I gotta leave."

Laura is shaking her head. "You're sitting around being a martyr, and John's laughing his ass off. You should be telling him how good Keith made you feel. Better yet when they bring it up quit talking and get dreamy eyed." She looks at her watch. "You have a date in thirty minutes. Go get some makeup on. I'll find you something appropriate to wear."

Marilyn, in a daze, goes to the bathroom and puts on some eyeliner. Laura comes in with a pair of short cut-off jeans and a paisley blouse.

Marilyn's eyes widen. "I can't wear that. It's what I wore when I was a teenager."

Laura is smiling. "You will fill it out a lot better now. Put it on; let's see what you look like."

Marilyn shakes her head when she comes out of the bathroom. "I can't go out in this."

"You're going to the lake, right?" Laura steps in front of her. "Needs some help." She pulls the front of the blouse out of her shorts, unbuttons the top button, pulls it tight, stretching the next button, and ties a little bow in the front. "Perfect."

"Hope it doesn't pop out." Marilyn stands stunned. "I'm going to find something else."

Before she can even turn around, the Vette rumbles as Keith pulls into the driveway. Laura turns her around and pushes her towards the kitchen door.

Keith knocks, and Laura keeps Marilyn from turning around. "Come on in."

Marilyn's heart is beating so hard she feels her breasts moving. *How much can everyone see?*

Keith breaks into a huge grin. "Wow, who is this girl?"

Marilyn feels her knees go weak and can't move as she looks at Laura.

Laura says, "The girl is a little stressed and needs to unwind. Find her a nice place to chill. Take your time and have some fun."

Marilyn steps towards Keith. "Hope you are not expecting—"

Keith winks at Laura and reaches out his hand. "A ride with the wind blowing in your hair, your troubles will fly away. I promise this won't be boring like the tractor rides."

His hand softly touches Marilyn's exposed skin on her waist as he walks her to the Vette. She grabs his hand, and she drops into the seat, still trying to catch her breath.

***

Marilyn sits quietly, feeling the wind blow across the top of her hair as they turn onto the main road. The desire to run is still haunting her, but the sensation keeps her quivering. She realizes she has never ridden in a Corvette.

Keith glances. "Too much excitement to talk?"

She quickly turns, staring at the road. *Don't look, you're too weak to resist.* "I'll say something stupid."

Keith puts in a cassette by the Cars and turns up the volume. She is holding back the tears, and she dabs them before they roll down her cheeks.

Keith reaches for her hand.

She lets it caress hers, focusing on the blue sky with its puffy white clouds. When they reach Lake Huron, they turn, driving along the shoreline, spotting glimpses of the water between the houses and trees.

He hits the brakes beside a small sign: Mom's Kitchen.

Keith parks and, instantly, opens the passenger door. "Heard they have great prime rib on Sundays. Been looking for someone to bring to see if it's true."

She swings her legs over together, takes his hand, and grabs the door. She blushes and pulls herself inches from his face and says, "Glad I didn't wear a skirt."

Keith takes her hand. "You handled it great."

A young girl seats them at a corner table and gives them menus.

Marilyn is looking over the top of the menu. "Thank you for getting me out of the house, but ... Johnny, and the hell he's going through when he's at his dad's occupies every thought. My company may not be that good."

"Your son knows you love him. If you learn to deal with it, he'll deal with it."

She finally smiles. "You make me feel good about myself, even if I don't believe it's true."

The waitress brings Keith a beer and Marilyn a soda and says, "Are you ready to order?" She looks at Marilyn.

Keith blurts out, "Get the prime rib." Marilyn is studying the menu. Keith says, "I'll have the prime rib, with the loaded bake potato." He glances at Marilyn. "You'll hurt my feelings if you order something cheap."

Marilyn blushes. "Okay, I'll have the prime rib." She tries to stop her dimple from coming out but can't. "I'm sorry ... I enjoy ... Mrs. Desmond was on one of her rampages today when she picked Johnny up, says she wants equal custody or else."

They bring their salads.

"Part of it is the made-up affair I had with Jason, but she threatened to come after your family."

"Where did that come from?"

"She heard about Uncle Keith." Marilyn studies the dark green walls with dark-framed pictures of the countryside. "It scares me." *It's why I have to leave.*

"Apparently, she is jealous of Johnny hanging out." Keith laughs. "Quit worrying."

They finish their salads, and Marilyn says, "Let's talk about you. What was it like having any girl you wanted?"

A grin slowly develops. "It's not the stories you heard. Girls want bragging rights too. Everyone thinks it's a guy thing, but for girls, it's a whole new level." He watches her. "I've turned some down, I've even had some tell me no."

She feels some relaxation seep into her body. "My girlfriends always thought you were hot and would've ..."

"What about you?"

Marilyn feels her face heating up. "Somehow, you are turning this around. I'm too messed up to even think about ..." She looks away. "You've helped me beyond ..."

"You needed help, I helped, but you proved you're not just a good-looking girl waiting for a free ride."

"I'll give you that I work hard, but I'm not that—"

"Sexy. You're not looking through my eyes—"

"Oh, stop it." Her face flushes. The rest of the meal is more emotional small talk, yet each word proves he isn't the shallow guy the world portrayed. His gentleman status continues as he opens the door, and she gracefully swings her legs in, he is checking but the attention feels gracious.

Keith starts the car and says, "There's a small park where we can check out the beach. It's rocky, but we can swim and hang out."

"I didn't bring a bathing suit."

"Details. The place is secluded."

A flashback from Mother. "Mom warned me about guys like you."

Keith drives slowly, looking at the road signs. "Not sure where it is." They pull into what looks like a driveway but open into a mini parking lot, with only two cars. Keith holds her hand as they make their way down the small steep path. Some adults are sitting by the edge of the water, with kids playing. They walk to the left and sit on a jagged rock overlooking the glistening sun on the water.

Calmly, he leans over and slowly kisses her.

His lips are soft as he holds the perfect pressure. She finally pulls away. "I ..." Her body quivers.

Keith says, "Strange how peaceful the water makes one."

Marilyn can't answer, trying to slow her heartbeat.

The overweight guy on the beach yells at them. "Hey, asshole, this is a family beach, not a motel."

Marilyn feels Keith's arm tighten, and she stiffens. "I'm sure he didn't mean anything."

Keith stares at the guy, not saying anything, until the guy turns around. Then, with a big grin, she says, "Guess he's jealous."

She's trying to calm herself.

Keith holds out his hand. "Let's walk down the beach and get away from Mr. Lard." They reach the edge of the water. She removes her sandals, and they stroll along the beach.

Keith pulls her close, touching her lips gently, and holds her.

Every part of her body has goosebumps. *I don't want to wait any longer.*

His eyes are twinkling. She wants to kiss him.

She looks away and catches her breath. Is it the water or is Keith overwhelming her every emotion? Her inhibitions are gone, and she pulls him close, pressing her breast tight to him. She wraps her arms around his neck, letting his tongue touch hers.

Keith is gazing at her. "I can go tell Lard ass he has to leave."

"Please no." She pulls away.

Keith's arm is around her waist as they move along the beach.

She feels his hand slide against her skin and doubts she can stand on her own. *Orgasms or panic?* They make their way back to the car, he gracefully opens the door, holds out his hand and she slides into the car. The trembling emotions are coming at her in waves.

Keith reaches over, takes her hand, and rests it on her thigh. "We have time before chores to stop by the house?"

Forty-Four

June 27, 1984

A different world for me, I set up a time to pick the boys' up tomorrow morning. Marilyn is distant since our date, although desire filters through the phone conversations. I've already kicked John's ass once, and if I need to, I will again. What is she scared of now? I warm up leftovers and call Mom, updating her as she adds a mini-guilt trip. She misses seeing the boys and what's happening with Marilyn. I changed the subject to the new puppy.

"That is sweet of you. I'll fix supper. Is Marilyn coming?"

"No, just the boys. She's working." I get ready to hang up.

"Keith."

"Yes."

"Nice girls don't jump in bed because of your male desires."

"Mother, I'm not trying—" *Damn it, Mom.*

"Give her time—treat her with respect. It'll work out. Remember, I love you, and I'm proud of you. Good night." Click.

I stand there looking at the phone before walking over and hanging it up. *Thanks for the guilt.*

June 28, 1984

I sit talking with my morning coffee until after eight before calling about the puppy. Amanda answers, and I verify we'll be over after ten. She wants to catch up on my life for the last ten years, joking about things she missed. I take a slight pause, gazing at the blue sky before climbing into the truck. The fields are turning green with corn and whispering in the gentle breeze. It'll be busy for the next few weeks repairing the pens and swapping out the next batch of skittish cows. It takes a few weeks for them to adjust.

***

When I arrive, the boys are outside and come running. Questions machine-gun style not waiting for answers unload as they follow me to the house.

With a quick knock on the screen door, someone yells, "Come in," as I'm stepping into the house.

Laura comes up and squeezes me tight. "Glad you finally got here, I was ready for a drink at eight."

Marilyn's hug is soft. She looks up and turns as I try to kiss her on the cheek.

Laura rubs her chin.

I swallow the emotions. "Did you boys bring some old clothes?"

They answer in unison. "Yes, we have them in our backpacks."

Laura sputters, "They packed their clothes. Hopefully, they have everything they need."

"Guess we'd better not waste any time." I slowly turn back and glance before going out the door.

Laura arms folded across chest smiling, and Marilyn in some kind of trance, and mutters, "Thank you for doing this. You call if—"

"John's not showing up. Quit worrying."

***

Laura was right about the boys being excited, still caring on as we took a gravel road, and turn into the driveway. "Remember, only one."

Amanda opens the screen door before we start up the steps. My eyes fixed on the silky-smooth low-cut blouse.

She instantly hugs me as my face rubs her cheek. Whispering, "It's been a long time." She backs up and studies the boys.

I move my hand towards each boy. "Johnny, Chad, this is Miss Amanda."

She bends down exposing the smooth curved breast and shakes the boys' hands. "Nice to meet you." Her hazel eyes linger upon mine, as she pulls me tight. "Let's go see the puppies." We are side-by-side country dance, making our way to the barn. "You're welcome to take two. I promised Steve, I'd find them homes. He wanted to ..." She bits her lip. "He is so uncaring. Glad there are only four."

"We are under strict orders, only one, but I'll spread the word you have more."

Amanda slides the barn door open, and we follow her to the back. She holds up her hand for us to stop, and we peer into the stall. "Penny, they're here to see your puppies." Penny's sad doggie eyes that melt everyone's hearts but glare at us. The puppies are curled up sleeping in the straw bed.

Amanda says to the boys. "Don't get too close."

Their eyes are sparkling, and they nod.

"Penny is not mean but has growled protecting her puppies. Which one do you like? I'll get it for you."

Chad points. "The black-spotted one."

Johnny points to the dark tan one.

She hands them the requested puppies. "Nice-looking kids. Didn't know you had children?"

I suck in a smirk. "Me either. I'm the uncle. Johnny and Chad are in my apprentice program, learning how to farm. Jake died, and kids need a farm dog to play with when they visit."

Johnny blurts, "My daddy is mean and killed him."

She flinches and squints at me.

My jaw tightens. I picking my words carefully gave her some background about their mothers, and the rumor mill.

She takes a deep breath, holds it, and nonchalantly looking at me says, "And which ones do you like?"

Johnny blurts, "I like this one, Uncle Keith."

"He definitely likes you as well." Amanda softly replies and pulls my arm tight into her chest.

Chad pets the brown one Johnny is holding. The puppy raises its head and tries to lick Chad's face. "Uncle Keith, he has smelly breath."

I grin. "It's puppy breath."

With some secret code, they swap puppies, and the brown one snuggles up tight to Chad. Gently, I take the black one from Johnny.

Amanda through a whispering breath says, "You must be the favorite uncle."

Johnny looks at Amanda. "He is, and my Mommy really likes him."

I grin. "My secret family was desperate for a role model."

She freezes a smirk. "Your mommy and you are very lucky." She moves closer, if that is possible with clothes on.

Johnny blurts, "We want this one."

The boys head towards the truck as I wait for Amanda to close the barn door. My mind running out of control.

She wraps her arm around my waist. "It's hard to believe somebody hasn't snatched you." Her breasts rub against me.

I stutter trying to find a respectable thought. "Farming makes it tough on social life, especially in the summer."

"The story was you know how to make a girl feel good." She reaches out and rubs my hand. "I can't believe you've lost your touch."

I swallow to keep from drooling, helping the boys into the truck and awkwardly move to the driver's side. "Lots of exaggeration from my football days." I say with my patented grin. "Sure, you don't want something for the puppy?"

She moves into kissing range. "You stop back tomorrow when we have more time." She looks past me. "Lots of details to go over."

I smile. "Need some detailed puppy instructions been awhile."

Her eyes flutter, and she steps away from the truck. "Yes, come early, it will take time."

"Ah ... thanks again," I dribble out, "for the puppy."

"I'm serious ..."

"Always pay my debts." With a wink, I back out of the drive.

July 23, 1984

We name the puppy Buddy. I limit the playtime so the puppy can sleep. He is almost potty trained, and I let him run around the house during the day. Replaced the screen door and hung up a sign. *Guard dog on duty.* Life is back to normal and Amanda could fill the desire until Marilyn is ready.

We have settled into a nice routine; I watch Johnny and Chad every Thursday night and Friday nights. Switching off with Mom's and hanging out at the bar. She brings the boys over during the day and we hang out, but she keeps waffling, wanting and then running as if I were a predator the next. It's time. I know she is scared, but John took his best shot.

Forty-Five

July 25, 1984

John sits to watch TV as Mom and Dad get ready for a rare evening out. The thought of whiskey mellows his brain cells.

His mother's wearing a low-cut paisley dress, her eyes waltzing through the living room. She says, "We'll be home by eleven. No partying or inviting girls over."

"Yeah, right, Mom." Yet he checks out the window, the flashbacks of his brother and him waiting to see what the choice of liquor would be. He pulls a bottle of Jim Beam out of his old work boots stuck in the rear of the closet and takes a swig before sitting in Dad's chair. He smiles at himself; at least he doesn't need to add water. The TV show begins and ends, but he can't remember what he watched. After a few more swigs, he dials the phone.

"Hello."

"Good evening. This is your husband." The phone is silent. He takes a drink. Waiting.

"What do you want?"

"Conversation, to air out our differences. This divorce is destroying our lives."

"It's ending something we should've never started."

"I keep asking myself, why would I want you? Then the next question comes to my confused mind. Why do I keep trying to protect you?"

"Protect me—from what or whom?"

"Have you seen your stud mad yet? I have a temper but wait until you piss him off with your constant nagging." He takes a drink. "It's going to become a nightmare for your precious little Johnny."

"You're lucky he didn't call the police for assault, trespassing, and killing his dog."

"We stopped for a friendly beer. He went off for no reason ... I keep pondering why? Oh, my kid was there, and he's doing my wife."

"What did you call for?"

"Partly to apologize for messing up your evening, but more to warn you.

I hear you are the hot new divorcee in town."

"Only in your sick, made-up world."

"Wanted you to know I recommended you for a one-nighter."

"Are you ready to sign off on the divorce?"

John grins at himself. "You give me full custody. I'll waive your child support. You could party with your friends whenever the whim hits you, a perfect world."

"My perfect world is you drinking yourself to death."

"Wow, a little feistiness dribbling out from your new tough boyfriend?" He pauses. "But who would send you the money?"

"I don't need your money."

"You gonna put it in writing?" The phone goes silent. "You still there?"

"You give up your visitation. Leave me and my friends alone."

"Messed up your pretty boy, didn't I?" He laughs.

Click.

John wets his lips and takes a slow drink of Jim Bean.

July 27, 1984

John meets Bob by his truck on Friday after work and says, "Passing on the bar but thought I'll come by later if you're going to be home."

Bob says, "Yeah, no problem. I'll be home by eight."

"Wanted to make sure I wasn't interrupting a hot date."

"Where'd this caring shit come from?"

***

John's mom is having her afternoon cocktail when he walks into the house.

She turns and raises her eyebrows. "Home on a Friday night. Without going to the bar. I'm proud of you."

"Yeah, well, everyone thinks I've lost my manhood."

"A few more months to stay low and keep the police from trumping up something else would be a wise thing."

"It's shitty just to see my kid two Sundays a month, while she lives wild and free."

"Go relax. Supper is in the oven; it'll be ready in an hour."

John's mom is giddy when they sit down for supper. "It's not the same for you as being with Marilyn and Johnny, but I enjoy having family meals together. Have you tried talking to her lately?"

"Yeah, I called her on Wednesday. Checked if she came to her senses and wanted to work out better visitation. She hung up on me."

"What did you say to her?"

"I was trying to warn her about Keith's temper."

"You think she is seeing him instead of Jason?"

"Can't decide, but she has to be seeing one of them, I assume, most of the winter. A buddy checked her out at work, said she would tease and flirt but shut him off when he asked her out." John stops eating. "Mother, to be honest, I want her out of my life. How proud can one feel when she comes crawling back to me after sleeping with half the town?"

"She has made it hard on you and Johnny, but you still need to fight for full custody. Johnny needs you in his life, especially when he gets older, and I want to watch my grandson grow up."

"They'll have him so brainwashed he'll hate us." John shakes his head. "Besides good luck getting any justice. Hope you're not still paying for the private eye."

His mother looks at his dad. "We have a retainer, and if needed, he'll be a witness in court. We'll take care of Johnny if you get custody."

When they finish dinner, John watches the news with his dad. His mother finishes the dishes and joins them. Nervousness overtakes him when the next game show comes on. He goes and takes a shower. Wraps an extra shirt around his waist before getting ready to leave.

His mother looks up and sets her crocheting on her lap. "You look very handsome. Remember, no drinking, and stay away from Marilyn."

"Yeah, yeah. I am going over to Bob's, may stay the night, so don't wait up."

***

John kills the lights and drives slowly on the rear side of the elevator, parks, changes into an old black T-shirt and hat, and slides between the buildings to the bar parking lot. Quickly, the deed is done, and he's back to his truck and puts the old clothes in a bag. He heads to the Peck party store, drops the bag in the trash, and grabs a twelve-pack. Thirty minutes, he knocks on Bob's door.

Bob yells, "Come in."

John puts the beer in the fridge and grabs one. Bob is already drinking. "This is tough, not having a beer in public." He sits on the couch.

Bob says, "Yeah, saves money, but hard on the social life. Julie has been asking where you've been."

"And your idea of fun is sitting with the parents watching game shows?"

A small smirk comes to Bob face. "So, how's everything else going?"

"The norm, wife's being unreasonable as hell." John stops talking takes a long drink of beer and says, "They're making fifty dollars an hour working on the oil rigs out in the Gulf. Plus, overtime. You can make two thousand dollars a week."

"Wow, that's definitely major money. But working with a bunch of smelly guys in the middle of the ocean." Bob is looking at the ceiling. "And no women for weeks."

"Yeah, and you're getting laid every weekend." John's crooked teeth spit out.

Bob gives him a finger gesture. "I'm working on it, at least."

John says, "Look at life in five years, I could be rich."

Bob smirks and says, "Marilyn, she'd love the money, but something tells me she's not waiting for her rich oil tycoon to come home."

"I'm working on a plan to get her off my ass."

"You have some magic fairy dust? My ex moved away. I haven't seen my kid in forever, and the court still makes me pay."

"I'm gonna mess with anyone that helps her and she agree to reduced support. I didn't tell Mom I'll give up visitation." John continues between drinks, "Do you know something else interesting? Jason walks her out of the bar every night."

"How do you know that?"

"My mom hired a private eye. Been spying on her."

"Wow, remind me never to piss her off."

"Add up the shit. Jason lives within walking distance of my house. He doesn't work all winter. He could've walked to the house anytime. The night she left, he could've driven there, put her car in the barn that night, and moved it to wherever the next day. I never drove by his house, always went the other way."

Bob takes a big drink of beer. "He doesn't seem like he has the balls, but he's silent and there's something sneaky about him."

John drains the rest of his beer. "Keith, his loudmouth muscle—" He crushes his beer can and throws it into the kitchen.

Bob says, "That's ten cents," and shakes his head. "It does fit together neither Keith nor Jason seemed shocked when you told them she left." Bob drains his beer. "Laura shut off any social conversation, but once Marilyn left, she turned up the bitch and wanted me gone. Think your wife was sneaky enough to move in with one of them?"

John grabs two more beers. "Interesting that if I mention either of their names to my kid, he freezes and quits talking." He guzzles a mouthful of beer. "They knew. Played me and you. They're going to find out about messing with me."

Forty-Six

July 27, 1984

The next morning, I call the trucking company and verified they're coming on Monday morning. They'll deliver the new cows on the eighth, which gives me five days to repair the pen and the auger. I'm writing it on the calendar like I would forget. Amanda's phone number glares at me. My adrenaline—I tuck it under the calendar page.

Coach recommended Kurt, a high school kid, as a part-time helper. Not a complete solution, but it'll help with the next few crazy days getting the cows changed over. Without Dad and Jake's help, it steps up the challenge. Few people are dumb enough to jump into a pen with twelve-hundred-pound beef cows in panic mode. I laugh at myself. Told Kurt it would be good football practice on how to dodge linebackers.

***

Mom is making meatloaf and insisting I come for supper on Friday, loneliness is in the air. I update her on the next batch of cows arriving and I cut back thirty head from what we planned before Dad passed away. We sit in eerie silence, knowing this, but if the price of beef drops much lower, we could lose money next year.

Her eyes are watery as she says, "It'll work out. Is everything going okay with Marilyn?"

"Well ... yeah, why?"

Her gaze penetrates my soul. "Then invite her over for Sunday dinner."

"Are you sure that is a good idea? It could be a heated discussion, with Dad not here, Dave will be pressing to lower the loan."

Mom puts her fork down and finishes chewing her food. "Forget about Dave. Marilyn seems a bit more special."

My heart jumps. "Yes, you could say that, but ..." I hold my gaze on her.

She says, "Time for her to know farming is a family, and we won't always agree, but we all pitch in no matter what." Mom leans ahead. "If you use your football mentality with Dave, he's on your team, blocking for you. He's not the linebacker trying to stop you."

I look across the kitchen.

She continues, "Marilyn needs to know the rosy picture you painted has some thorns."

I swallow my food. "She knows I've ..."

"Keith, I'm your mother, not a girl you're trying to impress. Dave is not running the farm. That's your job. There's no fighting over it." Mom is staring at me or through me. "Dad agreed; we need three hundred head for the best profit ratio. We may need to readjust the timeframe. You can't expect Marilyn to do as much work as your dad and to have devotion while you are out chasing other women."

I grip my fork like when I was ten and stuff my mouth full and wait for the rest of the tongue-lashing.

Mom's eyes are glassy, but with sternness, she says, "Be honest with her. You either love her, or you don't."

"I've been ... She's getting her life settled."

Her voice quivers. "If you're leading her on or ..." She wipes her tears and says, "You'll answer to God if you break Johnny's heart."

***

The bar is rocking. *Didn't they know I wasn't here?* I slid onto my stool at the far end of the bar beside Jason, but I feel invisible. Where has the nostalgia gone? Marilyn visits us on her break, enlightens us with gossip, but Mom's words engulf my thoughts. I take an extra breath. "Mom is inviting you for Sunday dinner."

Without hesitating, she says, "Do you want me to?"

"I don't want you to feel obligated or guilty if you say no, and before you answer, Sis and her family are going to be there."

She straightens, almost at attention. "Still the same question. Do you want me to come?"

"Yes, of course I do." I hesitate for a breath. "You saw a bit when Dad passed, but Dave and I don't have a blending personality. He has an indignant belief that his college education in higher finance is better than my simple, proven spiral notebook system."

Her expression disappears. "Can't be as bad as my family."

"Mom believes I sugarcoat the family farming, so you'll like me."

She gazes at me. "You probably did." Her eyes sparkle. "What should I bring?"

"Just you and Johnny, stop at my house around noon. We'll ride over together. We eat about one."

Marilyn glances at her tables. "I'd better get to work. Panic will start if they run out of beer."

Jason takes a slow sip of beer, staring at Laura, who's serving drinks. "So, it's a family, with an official date to be announced."

"No, asshole. Word of advice," I say, glancing over, "never let your mother get involved in your relationships. She treats Johnny as another grandkid already. Then lectures me about the proper way to treat women."

Jason is choking, trying not to spit out his beer.

The party is losing steam, and Marilyn has her purse in hand, getting ready to leave.

I volunteer to walk her out.

Marilyn says, "John has someone spying on me."

I set my beer down. "After his ass-kicking, he realizes the good guy has won."

"You're awfully confident." Marilyn rolls her lips under her teeth. "You promise to return and finish your beer, so they know you didn't take me home?"

"Looks bad for my reputation," I say, scanning the bar, "but I promise."

She walks ahead of me as I scan the cars in the parking lot and on the street. They all look empty, and nothing sticks out. Halfway to the back parking lot where her car is, I wrap my arm around her shoulders.

She opens the car door, trying to pull away. "No—he's watching."

I pull her tight, give her a hug and a kiss and say, "It was so quick, no one could have seen it."

Her dimple is still there when she gets in the car. "I hope so."

I can taste her lips. A peacefulness settles into me as I watch her drive away, and I casually return to my beer.

July 28, 1984

The phone rings. It's four-thirty in the morning. "Hello?"

"Keith, this is Jason."

"You're up awful early. What's up?"

"Truck sitting alongside the road with two flat tires. I walked home, figured no reason to get anyone else up in the middle of the night."

"It's morning for the real workers in the world. When do you want to change them?"

"Pick me up about seven-thirty, we'll grab Dad's spare. The gas station doesn't open until eight anyway."

After feeding the cows, I round up the four-way, a hydraulic jack, and some hand tools, just in case. A nonchalant Saturday morning drive, letting the air take our thoughts out the windows. I finally say, "Sort of an odd accident."

Jason says, "Yep."

We change the tires and set the flat ones on the tailgate. We stare at four nails stuck in a small spot, with a couple more sideways not punctured through. "Strange, all of them in a bunch."

Jason nods. "There're shingling nails, and no one could've dropped that many accidentally. We haven't been working on any roofing projects. Besides, it had to happen after I left the bar."

We close the gate and head to the gas station.

Clarence examines the tires when he puts them on the tire machine. "So." He stands with a huge grin. "You gonna tell me who?"

Jason says, "Why do you say that?"

He pulls out his pocketknife and digs one out. "Nail balls." He digs out more and shows us pieces of nylon under each one. "You wrap up the nails in a woman's nylon. Probably threw them under your tire when you parked somewhere. A mile or so and you have flat tires. The tires are junk. Can't patch that many holes in one spot."

We stand and keep looking at the tires.

He says, "Well?"

We look at each other before Jason says, "I'm not dating anyone."

I grin. "Feel like I've been in monk status, good as I've been."

We follow Clarence into the waiting room. "Well, it's no accident. One of your secret admirers is looking for revenge." He is still grinning. "We'll have the tires ready this afternoon."

We are silent for the first mile. Jason says, "You think John could have done it?"

"It fits the slime bag, little mind, believing Marilyn is so naïve and you took care of her all winter."

Jason closes the door and leans into the window when I drop him off at his dad's. "Well, smart ass, why go after you but wait to take revenge on me when I was sleeping with her in January? It's July."

"I was asking myself that question. He was bluffing, wanting me to admit something."

Jason is shaking his head. "And what am I getting out of this?"

I break out laughing. "The honor of being my best friend." I suck in my grin. "Marilyn is beyond stressed about him coming after us—"

Jason pats the door and says, "I needed new tires—no reason to bring up why."

"That's why we're buddies."

Forty-Seven

July 28, 1984

Marilyn opens the grungy curtains, and glances through the kitchen window. Looking for the boys, one finally runs out from behind the garage. Wondering how well they are following the warning. No climbing on the farm equipment. She pours coffee and makes out a grocery list.

Laura staggers into the kitchen, dressed in her thin old robe, which doesn't hide much. She sips coffee before sitting. "What are we pondering today?"

Marilyn glances at Laura's puffy eyes. *She always knows when something is amiss.* "Keith's mom asked me to have Sunday dinner tomorrow."

"She is playing matchmaker?"

"Or trying to convince the family to accept me is what crossed my mind. Keith's sister wasn't overly fond of me at the funeral, if you remember. I can't imagine anything has changed."

Laura quips, "Not your first time meeting everyone. Why are you so paranoid? Keith's mother is the perfect mother-in-law. And his sister—she's not high society because she's married to the local assistant bank manager. It's not New York."

"She'll find something wrong, the way I'm dressed, a hair out of place."

"You've gotta quit wearing those baggy work shirts that you call blouses. We will dig through my closet and find you something."

"I felt hesitation from Keith about asking me." Marilyn drums her fingers. "This time ... they're sizing me up. My goal is not to embarrass Keith."

"Your only concern, is he ready to be a one-woman man? Or are you ready to handle if he's not?"

"Can I even satisfy him is my thought." She bites her lip. "When I ... get dreamy eyes thinking about Keith, my nightmare ..." She is rubbing her arms.

"Oh my God, girl, you've pulled his heartstrings. Time to get naked. He'll take it from there. He's been different since he met you. If you noticed, he didn't talk to the hot brunette, which is completely out of character."

"I assumed she was—"

"That never stops him—it's more of a challenge. She made eye contact a few times. He doesn't miss the signs." Laura tilts her head and says, "What do you think of Jason?"

Marilyn flinches. "What do you mean?"

Laura sets her cup down. "He's been staying late to help close up." She glances away. "We've had some after-hours conversations."

She stiffens and doesn't blink.

Laura glares, breaking into a smile. "What? I know I swore off guys."

Letting a smile creep out, Marilyn says, "What else haven't you told me?"

"He's relaxing, and easy to hang out with."

"So, he's not suggesting to—"

Laura's eyes twinkle. "No, but he's still a guy ... a quiet Keith. I invited him over tomorrow for Sunday dinner. Thought I'd make a roast dinner. I'll give you extra money when you go to the store."

Marilyn breaks out grinning. "You're going to impress him with your cooking?"

Laura looks over her coffee cup. "You can help me before you run off, impressing your hot jock with how sexy you are."

She closes her eyes.

Laura says, "Does it seem possible we're talking about some kind of relationship?" They clink cups. "Whatever it is, sisters forever."

July 29, 1984

Marilyn helps Laura get the roast ready for the oven on Sunday morning. Then, like teenagers, they pick out a flowery blouse from Laura's closet. Then, she curls her hair, adds eyeliner, views herself in the mirror, and buttons the blouse to mother-approved status. She walks into the living room.

Laura is smiling. "I would say more cleavage, but it's mom-approved."

Marilyn feels good for the moment.

Johnny is talking non-stop on the ride and asks, "Mommy, why are we dressed up so nicely to go to Uncle Keith's?" The car gets quiet.

"We don't need to appear homeless." Delightfulness settles for a moment, but her stomach is churning. The reality ... *am I ready?*

She barely stops the car before Johnny leaps out. He opens the door, and

Buddy jumps on him as he picks him up. The dog is licking his face. She opens the screen door and glances at Johnny. He is chasing the dog around the yard. *Couldn't he at least wait until after dinner?* "Now don't get dirty." She meets Keith inside the door as he plants a heart-throbbing kiss on her.

Keith wraps his arm around her, and they make their way to the kitchen table, which is covered with stacks of folders and notebooks. He says, "Yes, the paperwork. I made iced tea. Would you like some?"

"You made it?"

"Yes, fill the jug full of water, add tea bags, and set it out in the sun." He winks. "More of my over-the-top talents." He pushes the papers aside and sets a glass in front of me. He motions towards the table. "My professional bookkeeping system." He explains the details recorded for each cow. He picks up a spiral ring notebook with *August 1983-August 1984* written on the front. "My personal notes."

Marilyn says, "I never realized you had to keep so many records. I'm impressed."

"Keep that belief. Dave will tell you I don't have a clue regarding record keeping. But I keep information about every cow."

"I believe you know what you're doing."

"The truth ... never mind." He winks. "Yes, I do."

She glances up but doesn't make eye contact. "Am I ..." Her heart is pounding. "...dressed okay?"

"You're looking damn ... Jeanie has a little jealous streak of someone outdoing her."

Marilyn slaps his shoulder playfully. "I want to fade into the background."

Keith holds his patent grin. "That's not happening. You're the star."

Her chest tightens. *Can I live up to their expectations?*

Forty-Eight

Aug 11, 1984

I drink my first cup of coffee, trying to clear the cobwebs. *A few too many last night?* The brunette from a week ago, with her green eyes, scanned the bar but intrigued me with the way she pulled her shoulders, elevated her chin, and stared. Then Amanda pressed her breast into me. Still makes my mouth water ... I haven't committed ... a little quickie to calm the body's desires? What could it hurt? Then Mom's righteous guilt trip filters into the conscience; she's not taking care of me.

I step into the cool morning air. The stars disappear as light cracks the edge—a cow standing in the yard. I open gate reposition on the other side of the lone steer, and he trots into the pen. I close it, examine the latch, and slide the pin into the hole. It had to be open all night. I glare at an empty pen.

We've had cows out, but not the entire herd. I quietly circle the barn and hear cows slobbering on corn, eating themselves sick.

I grab the old fence and posts ripped out of George's fence. I string it across the bunker opening. It'll hold the few cows in there eating silage, and if we don't spook them, they will stay put. I grab a leftover piece of cold roast beef and wash it down with coffee for breakfast.

I take a breath and call Mom. She answers after a few rings but says she was awake. Describing the issue, my voice shudders. "It's a mess. With enough people, we'll keep them from being scattered over the entire neighborhood."

Mom, calm as ever, says, "Get stuff ready. I'll make calls to the neighbors." She hangs up.

I'm chewing my piece of beef, waiting a dozen rings before Jason answers.

"Whoever this is, it better be damn important."

"This is your best friend and can't believe you're not awake receiving the last kiss and making sure she's home before daylight. You know how the town likes to talk."

"Asshole. You called to see if I'm getting any?"

"Assume you were but keeping it a secret from me."

"Well, assume no more. I went straight home. Alone."

"My interesting morning. The steers played in the cornfield all night—"

"What the hell."

"Yeah, that's part of what I said. It was an easy count of fifteen in the pen, two hundred and ten running around eating themselves sick."

"Shit. How did it happen?"

"A jealous husband comes to mind."

"Killing your dog, flattening my tires, and trying to kick your ass. We're going to visit this asshole soon."

"He needs to acquire a clearer message."

"I'll pick up Dad and be over shortly."

"Stop and grab a couple dozen donuts? Mom's contacting neighbors. I'm calling Curtis next. There will be ten or fifteen people."

"Are you calling the girls?"

"Probably ... later. Don't want to interrupt their beauty sleep."

"Thanks. You weren't worried about mine."

I take a breath. "It was latched yesterday."

"Awfully bold to walk in and unlatch it."

The phone is silent. "Not for someone who knew I wasn't home and no dog."

"See you soon."

***

I climb out of the truck, feeling the emptiness of the barnyard. *What a mess.* George pulls in. I motion for him to climb in, and we drive along the path towards his farm to evaluate the situation.

I break the silence. "The gate wasn't latched correctly, someone opened it. I don't want Mom worried, even if she thinks I left it unlocked ..."

"The guy you had the fight with?"

I shrug. We walk halfway up the fence line and find no tracks or corn destroyed, so they haven't crossed over to George's. We decided to cut a row of corn along the fence, opening a space.

George goes to cut the strip, blowing the corn back into the field. It's way too green to try to save it for feed. Carl arrives, and we move the wagons and the tractors in a line. The neighbors are showing up, and we're moving equipment and vehicles to make a funnel to the gate. Jason and his dad picked up the water tank from across the road and started filling it with water.

Mom made a large pot of coffee to serve with doughnuts and set it up on the picnic table.

I ask her, "Can you call Marilyn? Tell her I won't be able to take the boys for a ride today."

"You should've called her already. You go call her right now."

I trudge into the house. Still, *she treats me like a teenager* ... Each ring brings more anxiety. On the fifth ring, she answers.

"Hello."

"Good morning, this is your wake-up call."

"Nice try, but I was doing laundry."

"We have a minor crisis at the farm today." I pause. "The cows are out."

"What do you mean?" Marilyn's voice quivers.

"The gate came open sometime last night, and they are wandering in the cornfield."

"Oh my, how did that happen?"

"Haven't evaluated the how yet." *Change the subject.* I say, "We're having a cattle drive just like on TV, without horses. We're rounding up people instead."

"I'll get ready and come over."

"Before you jump in with such enthusiasm, these are seven-hundred pounds, wild, and unruly steers."

"You mean similar to the guys I know?"

"Thought I was a teddy bear? Anyway, going to be a crazy day and—"

"We're on the way." Click.

***

We polish off the rest of the coffee and donuts while we put together a plan. Curtis brings a couple of his buddies from the football team.

"Everyone, listen up." I choke while waiting for them to quit talking. "These are young wild steers, and unpredictable. So don't push them too hard. If one turns towards you, stop, and wave your towel. Normally they'll turn and hopefully head towards the barn. If they break out, don't try to stop them, move out of their way. It's not worth getting hurt. The important part is staying even with George and Carl in the tractors. They'll be able to see them and set the pace.

"The closer we get to the barn, Carl's side needs to slow down, and George's side pick up the pace, which will turn them into the pen. Mom is tending to the gate. You young guys on the outside, pay extra attention. There's more space between you and they'll try to break out on that side."

Marilyn pulls in as we're loading up. I wave for her to pull her car along the row with the rest. I tell the boys they must stay inside today because it's too dangerous. We load everyone into the pickups, Marilyn, and Karla in the front seat with me as we head to the back of the field I explain about the young steers and what to expect. Marilyn's face has lost all expression.

Karla reaches out her hand to Marilyn. "I'm Karla, by the way. Nice to meet you." They shake.

Marilyn says, "Nice to meet you too."

"Sorry. Karla lives down the road."

Karla says, "This is your first cattle drive, I assume?"

Marilyn says, "Yes, I've never ..."

Karla pats her arm and glances at me. "This is the biggest one we've ever had. You can walk next to me."

I say, "Stay focused. Whatever you do, don't turn and run. There're freaky big when you are standing facing them. Remember, stay still unless they charge you, which is rare. Then head fake, sidestep, let them go by you."

The girls are in the middle on the shortest side. The noise and the drive begin. They are bunching up good when some of them turn, but we kept moving together on our side.

I hear Marilyn scream and Karla yell, but I can't leave this side till we push them into the pen.

We close the gate; I run to check on Marilyn.

Marilyn glances up at me. "I'm okay."

Karla says, "Two steers came right at her." She smiles. "She sidestepped him like a matador."

"It was my fault I wasn't—"

"She handled herself great," Karla says. "Her scream sent them running."

We round up a few stragglers before lunch. I estimated about seventy wandering. Mom and the church ladies have lunch organized and, of course, bring more food than we can eat.

While everyone finishes eating, I have Jason lift me in the bucket, studying out over the field and planning stage two.

The circumstances are easier compared to the morning drive, although it'll be hard walking against the rows of corn, but we can push them straight into the silage bunker. We'll herd them into the main pen afterwards. I announce, "If anyone needs to leave, go ahead. I'm thankful for the help." No one leaves.

By six o'clock, all but four are contained. Everyone's face is dusty with sweat streaks, reminding me of all the hard work and great friends. The church ladies add more food. I stand in the pickup bed and announce, "Eat something before you leave." I thank everybody personally before they leave. One more cow wanders up to the water trough.

Thinking the boys should be paid, I meet them at the car and offer, which they refuse, but I hand them twenty bucks each anyway.

Curtis says, "I told them it's football practice with added pointers from the greatest player in Brown City."

They both step up and shake my hand. "He thought he was tricking us, but we're honored and glad we could help."

A lump forms in my throat as I thank them again.

One of them turns back. "We'd love to have you come to the locker room before the game. The other players would love to meet you."

Goosebumps run down my arms. "I'll set it up with Coach."

Mom found hay. They're dropping bales to cover us and are delivering the rest tomorrow. I don't bother to ask how much. The next crisis kicks in: how sick they are from eating the green corn and how long they will have to be eating hay to calm their stomachs.

Dave, Jason, and his dad sit on one tailgate, Karla, and Marilyn on the other. I grab beers. Mom and Sis are finishing cleanup. I say, "We are only missing three. Hopefully, by morning they'll find the water trough."

I give Karla a glass of iced tea, passed out beer to everyone else, and raise mine for a toast. My voice quivers. "To the best family and friends." We drink up, letting the day settle in with the sweet sound of wailing cows in the background. Karla and Marilyn are murmuring to themselves.

Jason's dad says, "Was the gate unlocked?"

I glance at Jason. "The latch was flipped up." I pause. "Damn cows."

"Did you have a pin in it?"

"It was hanging from the cable." I hesitate. "Not sure how it came out."

He scans everybody, holds his gaze at me, and says calmly, "You'd better call the police. He's becoming more brazen—kills your dog, flattens Jason's tires, lets the cows out—"

Marilyn slides off the tailgate. "What flat tires?"

I open my mouth, but nothing comes out.

"This wasn't an accident?" Marilyn's voice rises. "My ex—you didn't tell me?" Marilyn glares at me. "What other secrets haven't you told me?" She dumps out her beer and heads to the house.

Forty-Nine

August 11, 1984

Marilyn marches towards the house and pulls the screen open. Keith is holding the top of the door.

"It's not what you think."

"You didn't lie about the tires?"

"He needed tires—we didn't want you to panic."

"Because my ex flattened them. I don't remember hearing that." She holds her breath and says, "I should've been in the loop, don't you think?" Her veins pulse in her neck.

"We weren't sure it was him."

"Right, because other husbands want revenge too. How did he flatten the tires?"

Keith's eyes twitch.

Her jaw tightens. "You're not telling me?"

"Balls of nails rolled in pantyhose."

"That's him. The last time, he used me as the alibi. Tricked me into lying about it. Thanks for adding me to the list of your other trustworthy friends."

"I wouldn't ... I was—"

"You should've told me." She looks at his hand still holding the door. "I'm going home unless you have something else you should tell me?"

Keith removes his hand from the door.

Marilyn walks into the house.

Gwen asks, "What's the matter?"

"Did you know John flattened Jason's tires last week?"

She half-squints. "No."

"It's a secret, and only the privileged are allowed to know." She looks into the living room. "Come on, boys. Time to go."

Keith's mom wipes her hands on the towel. "Tell me what happened?"

"The condensed version of my Barbie-doll world. Someone opened the gate last night. Someone flattened Jason's tires." Johnny is in panic mode. "And whatever else may have happened. You can ask Keith for the details.

Maybe he'll tell you."

Marilyn turns to the boys. "You boys go to the car." She turns to Gwen and says, "Apparently, I'm too feeble to handle reality."

Keith's mom instantly hugs her. "We appreciate everything you have done; don't let his chauvinistic attitude make you feel bad."

Marilyn returns a quick hug, each heartbeat pumping anger and fear. She heads directly to the car, pushing the boys along in front of her. She opens the door. "Get in."

Johnny looks at everyone still sitting on the tailgates. "Can't we tell Uncle Keith goodbye?"

Marilyn doesn't look and snaps, "We don't have time." She pushes them into the backseat. Focusing straight ahead, she never stops before getting on the road.

Johnny says from the backseat, "Mommy, why are you so mad?"

"I'm not mad at you."

"Did Uncle Keith hit you?"

"He would never do that." Tears seep into her anger.

"But Mommy—"

"I'm mad at myself." Her voice is trembling. "We're not talking about it." The boys are silent for the rest of the ride home. They instantly scurry off to the bedroom as soon as they're inside.

***

She watches the light dim and fade into complete darkness. Helplessness and loneliness take over every thought. She'd cry, but anger won't let her. She checks on the boys. They've turned out the light and tucked themselves in. She grabs a beer, takes a drink. *Why am I drinking? To drown my reality.*

She finishes, gets another, dials the phone. "Hi, Sis."

"Good evening, and what is my hot single sister doing sitting at home on a Saturday night?"

"I have no idea what I'm doing." She reads the label on her beer bottle.

"You broke up with your farm boy?"

Marilyn smiles. "We dated. We didn't commit to getting married."

Ann is laughing. "I was expecting some juicy tidbits about your hunk splashing around in the waterbed?"

Marilyn doesn't answer.

"So..."

"Sis, I haven't ..."

"What do you mean you haven't?"

"It's not him. Besides, I could panic in the middle of it and ruin whatever dreams he's having about me." She takes a drink. "John let Keith's cows out. Half the neighbors, his friends, and I, we herded over two hundred cows loose in the cornfields."

"Don't tell me you've been trying to impress him by being a farmhand?"

"It was my fault. I need to do something."

"Damn it, girl, take him to bed, and if he can't stand up to John, he's not worth it, anyway. Move on."

"John is taking revenge on the people who helped me."

"You've got to move. The mother-in-law apartment is empty. He won't mess with you here. It is time. Pack your stuff and join the modern world."

"He ..." Tears well up.

"We'll get you a job at the Dinner Club somehow. I know what you're going to say, so save it. We're sisters; we're family; we help each other."

The phone goes silent as Marilyn stares into the dark.

"You still there?"

"Yes, sorry. Why can't I have a life without turmoil?"

"You can. What's holding you to that hick town? It seems scary, but it was one of the best decisions I made to leave there. You want to be Mom, sitting around in a worn-out housedress, watching soaps? What about Johnny's future? You'll be able to enroll him in kindergarten. He'll meet kids to play with and will forget about cows and tractors."

"Please, Ann ..." Marilyn pulls the label off her beer.

"You going to wait for something worse to happen before you move?"

Tears drip off her cheeks. "I'll need help to move."

"Jeff can get his boss's truck, and we'll come over on Saturday. John won't bother you over here."

"You're right. But—"

"You're improving your life and Johnny's. Ten years from now, they'll still be chasing cows, with manure on their boots. No more talking. I'll see you on Saturday. Love yah." *Click.*

"Love you, too." Another beer emptied watching the news about the winners in the Olympic Games.

It's not Keith in love but sympathy for me. Johnny Carson's monologue drags into the night. *Karla knew exactly what to do today and would make a perfect farm wife.* She downs the beer. *Is she waiting for him to get his wildness out? They have a secret, and I know nothing about farming, even less about sex. In my fantasy, I can take care of Keith, but in reality...*

August 12, 1984

Marilyn is cold and her body is aching as she realizes someone shut the TV off and she is covered up.

Laura says, "You're not made for cattle drives and partying all night?"

Marilyn slowly sits up, trying to get her bearings. Her head is pounding.

Laura sits beside her. "Did you get them all back?"

"All but three, and they're hoping they'll wander in before morning. The whole thing was my fault."

"Stop it. Shit happens."

"I've made a mess of everyone's lives."

"I can't believe John hasn't come after you too. Or has he, and you didn't tell me?"

"No, he wouldn't dare. Why do you ask such a question?"

"Jason's tires had nails in them—that's why he got new ones."

"He never said why ... assumed they—"

"They led us to believe that they were wore out. John did it. They couldn't be repaired. Excuse me." Marilyn runs to the bathroom, grips the sink, and examines the person in the mirror, trying not to see the swollen bloodshot eyes and a face smeared with misery, dust, and old makeup. *Suck it up.*

She gargles, brushes her teeth, and splashes water on her face, wiping it on the towel.

Laura has her feet resting on the coffee table.

Marilyn makes her way to the couch. "There goes my Barbie-doll image."

"I'll never tell."

"None of this would've happened if I'd left like I should've. Let's face some facts. He feels sorry for me, and maybe would like to take me to bed, but it's not some romantic love story. He will be on to someone else as soon as I'm gone."

Laura puts her feet on the couch. "You're letting John screw up your life." She rests her head on her knees. "We all care about you."

"So, I let everyone suffer because of my wimpy ass. I'm going to move."

Laura slowly straightens. "Keith can handle it—"

"Handle it—why I sit around drinking beer pretending I'm some special dame? Or wait for John to kill someone because he thinks he is a boyfriend?"

"He's not—"

"I've decided—I'm leaving. I talked to my sister, and I can move on Saturday. Everyone's life can return to normal. Sis said I don't need to pay rent, so I'll send you money for rent and drive over and work till you find someone." She puts her hands over her face, hiding the tears.

"Stop it. You're letting John run your life."

Marilyn wipes the tears on her sleeve. The silence consumes them, and they go to bed. She throws her dirty clothes on the floor and sits on the bed in her underwear; she needs a shower. Could she stand long enough?

***

Marilyn wakes around eleven, still feeling sick. She stumbles out of the kitchen. Laura is already up and dressed. She holds back a smirk. "The first hangover is always hell."

"And my last. As I wallowed in my screwed-up life. Promise you won't tell anyone the stupid stuff I said and did."

Laura says, "Sister pack, remember. I'm off to get groceries. You don't look like you're in any condition. Let me fix you some toast before I leave."

"I can't eat."

"It'll help."

"Everyone is expressing their sorrow for helpless me."

"You are not helpless." Laura sets the toast down. "Eat and go rest. The boys are outside playing. Everything is fine."

"I'm serious about leaving."

Laura says, "We'll talk later."

She leaves, and Marilyn nibbles away at the toast. *Keith let me have my tantrum. He didn't yell, he didn't hit me. It actually felt like he wanted to hug me.*

She dials. No answer and heads to the shower.

Fifty

August 13, 1984

I let Buddy out for his morning duties, finish a cup of coffee and head to the tool shed. No calming morning sun but wailing of sick cows.

Two cows are standing outside the water trough. I grab the gate and drag it across the opening so they can't wander off. Then I break bales of hay into the corn trough. Putting some bales in the tractor bucket, I drive along and spread the hay by hand in the trough. It's after eight o'clock before I finish. Frustration has moved to anger, and the extra hours for who knows how long will not help me calm down. *He is going to pay.*

Buddy is whining when I open the door.

"Hold on, we're all hungry." I set his puppy chow down, call the vet, and start cooking breakfast. *Marilyn penetrates my soul telling me to go sit down.* The phone rings, snapping me out of my trance. I move the pan off the fire, and the toast pops up. "Hold on." It's still ringing. "Hello."

"Good morning," Mom says. "How is everything?"

"We're not set up to feed hay. I just finished took an extra hour."

Mom calmly says, "It's just temporary, and it's not harvest season. When is the vet coming?"

"Around ten. Jason and Curtis will be here shortly, and we'll put the sickest ones in your barn. We shouldn't have mixed them together, but there was nothing we could do. The stupid animals would eat themselves to death. We'll need more hay."

"They're saving some for us. I'll have him deliver it tomorrow."

"Put it in your barn. Hopefully, we can get these back on silage at the end of the week."

"Did you contact the police yet?"

"No—don't say it, I'll call."

"They are open twenty-four hours. You can call anytime."

"I wanted to talk to Sid."

"This is a gentle reminder. Don't plan on taking care of it yourself."

"It would get better results."

"Revenge is not who we are. Report it to the sheriff."

"Yes, Mother." I grimace, hang up the phone, and try heating the eggs and butter my cold toast.

Curtis and Jason arrive, I pour coffee, and we lay out the game plan for moving the sick cows.

The smell of sick cow shit hits me, before I even start the wallow around in the pen pushing them into a four-animal trailer. We reduced it to three at a time after almost getting shit on trying to get the fourth one in the trailer.

We break for lunch and set the boots outside. The scrumptious leftovers and the grimace on Curtis's face brings a grin and the want to vomit. "No matter what anybody tells you, stay away from girls for a few days."

He smells his arm. "It's soaked into my skin."

Jason breaks out laughing. "Curtis, you must be mistaken. Look at these huge farm families — six, eight, kids—women must like it." He nods towards me. "Keith, inside secret, he dabs some behind his ear before he goes to the bar. He's always had women wanting him."

I flip Jason off. "Curtis, I hope you have some better friends than this."

We're all laughing, choking on our food until Jason says, "John has to pay."

"I was pondering another ass-kicking, the broken-bone kind. Then Mom called first thing this morning, reminding me to call the sheriff and how we are this upstanding family. But, guess for everyone's sake, we should wait. The rumor I heard from a reliable source is he picked up a prescription for syphilis last week."

Jason is laughing. "It happens when you go to the city for a quickie."

Curtis puts his sandwich on his plate. "You're saying someone let them out on purpose?"

"Marilyn's ex-husband."

"Where does this guy hang out? I'll take the football team. We'll teach him a lesson."

"No." I put my hand on Curtis's shoulder. "Thanks, but we need to keep any blowback to a minimum." I look around as if someone can hear us. "We'll bide our time and find something to improve in his life. This secret farm knowledge."

Curtis nods. "Got it."

We slither in cow shit all day, but the worst ones are in the pen at Dad's. The vet gives them shots. We finish our long day loading hay into the pickup, then drive along breaking the bales and dropping them in the fence line. I grab three beers. I hand one to Curtis; he breaks into a grin. "I think you earned it, and I won't tell Coach."

Jason downs his beer quicker than normal. "I'm going home to scrub this shit off me. Reminds me why I went into construction and not farming."

"Don't lie to us. It's so you can suck down the couch money all winter." I grin and grab the empties and walk them to the door. Curtis waves on his way out.

Before Jason heads to his truck. "I'm going to drive by John's parents' house."

"We definitely need to keep track of the boy."

***

I peel my clothes off on the porch and throw them with my boots. Grab Buddy's bed and take it into the kitchen. I finish my shower, take a drink of beer, and flip the recliner lever. The smell still lingers. The phone rings. Back to the kitchen. "Hello."

"Hi, this is Karla. My dad has a cow corralled in the barn."

I blow out a breath. "Unless I miscounted, that's the last one. You want me to bring the trailer down and get him?"

"Dad gave him some hay. It will wait until morning."

Relief runs through me. "Thanks. Just finished my shower and threw my nasty clothes outside. I can't express what your help means to me."

Karla's voice lowers. "We're glad to help. How sick are the cows?"

"Vet didn't think any of them would die, but we are feeding in two different pens."

"Lots of extra work. How much does it set you back getting them ready for the market?"

"At least a month, for most of them."

"And the loan is due before."

"Yeah, the joys of farming. I'm sure my brother-in-law will remind me why I took on extra cows this year. And add a 'told you so.'"

"I forgot about him ... If you want a day off or a weekend, I remember how to feed cattle. I'll come and feed them for you."

I say, "Thanks for the offer. Also, thanks for helping Marilyn."

Karla's voice is hesitant. "She worked hard—"

"Her outburst was my fault."

Karla pauses. "Some neighborly advice not all women are naïve and we can handle the truth?"

I'm nodding. "Sorry, I did ... that to you."

"I'm too wimpy to say anything."

"Thanks again. Good night."

"Good night." *She would've made a good wife.*

***

Sid and Les, his partner, arrive on Monday before lunch. Turn the car around to face the road. We sit at the kitchen table with fresh coffee and exchange some light small talk. Mostly he is updating Les on my love life, which is nonexistent but sounds like I'm getting it every night.

Sid pulls out his little notebook and straightens, squaring his shoulders. He licks his pencil tip. "Start at the beginning."

I walk him through the fight, Jason's tires, and my synopsis of the cows getting out. Sid's eye twitches when I explain about Jake jumping through the screen door. They sit emotionless, as if we were in some cop show. My thoughts keep drifting. An hour later, the pot of coffee is gone. We walk out, and they exam the gate latch and the trampled corn. Les takes pictures.

Sid says, "How many acres of corn did you lose?"

I shrug. "At least five."

We stroll outside. Sid stops, his eyes narrowed, nods at Les, and puts a hand on my shoulder. His partner climbs in and closes the door. Sid gives me a police stare-down as we walk around the car. "Off the record. Have you threatened or sent anyone to visit him?"

"No, although we should've when he—"

Sid retorts, "We'll handle it."

"Marilyn doubts I'm tough enough to handle the issue."

"She said that?"

"No, doesn't have to say it."

Sid is shaking his head and opens the car door. "Mr. Macho, if you'd called us when you got in the fight, you'd be living happily ever after, raising all the farm kids you're dreaming about."

I rub my hand on my face with a smirk, my finger up.

"We're paid to handle shit like this. Let me know if anything happens instantly, not weeks later." Sid grins and glances over at Les. "And if you need help with your love life, Les here is single, he'll come give you some pointers."

I'm shaking my head, observing Sid shit-ass grin as he climbs into the car.

Fifty-One

August 13, 1984

On Monday morning, Marilyn scrubs the worn kitchen floor, trying to erase Keith's dejected face. She opens Laura's liquor cabinet door, staring at help to relieve the nightmare.

Johnny ambles in with his teddy bear under one arm, rubbing sleep from his eyes with the other. She holds out her arms, pulling him onto her lap and cuddling him tight, resting her chin on his head. "You're getting so big." A few minutes, Chad is shaking off his sleep. She pulls him tight to her. And says, "Would you boys like some pancakes this morning?"

They both nod and say, "Can we pour our own syrup?"

"I suppose, but not as much as the last time."

Marilyn works on breakfast with the guilt seeping in about how they will adjust without each other.

Johnny stops stuffing his mouth and says, "Mommy, when are we going to see Uncle Keith?" They are both looking at her. "He was taking us to explore the woods."

"I don't know. Keith is extra busy right now, with the cows getting out."

Johnny looks at Chad and says, "How did they get out?"

"Your ... We don't know."

"Why can't we go?"

"Uncle Keith has extra work. We're not going over there and bothering him."

"But Mommy, he told us we could come anytime, even if he didn't have time to play. We could—"

"We are not going. Finish eating, make your beds, and get dressed. Unless you want to help with the dishes."

They waste no time finishing and getting changed and are outside before Laura sits down for coffee.

She slips out a smile. "You look a little livelier than yesterday."

"That was a dumb thing to do. Yet I had to fight the urge to drown it all out again today."

"I smell the Pine Sol, and you've scrubbed the floor so hard there is no shine." Laura stands laughing with her hands on her hips. "What did Keith say when you called?"

"There was no answer."

"He's there. Drive on over. He could probably use some housecleaning."

Marilyn moves the bucket and continues wiping the cupboard doors.

Laura grabs her hand and the rag. "You're wearing the paint off."

Marilyn stops. "I can't ..."

"Dammit, girl, he likes you. Drive over there and—"

"I've tried to call—he doesn't answer."

"You're not getting out of this, change your clothes, put on some makeup, and tell him you're not the mollycoddling type. Johnny will be fine even if it takes all night."

Marilyn's short breaths halt her answer. She finally spits out, "I'll dissolve into some wishy-washy blob, which proves he is right—I can't handle anything."

Laura laughs. "I'll finish cleaning." She grabs the bucket.

Marilyn shakes her head as she goes to the bedroom.

She dumps the water outside and rings out the rag.

She picks out clothes and lays them on the bed. This low-cut top she puts on. *Not for social visits.* This outfit is for church, and this one is to become a maid. She is staring at what else? *Work clothes it's what you always wear.*

Laura walks into the room. "What's the holdup?"

Marilyn reached for a favorite blouse. "I'm trying to decide—"

Laura exams the clothes on the bed. "This top looks good." She walks over and picks out a pair of mini shorts.

Marilyn is trying them on. "They're too short."

"Great, you won't need to talk. Go, you're not procrastinating out of it."

"I'm planning on apologizing, not seducing him."

There is a knock at the door. They look at each other, and Laura goes to answer it. Marilyn leans against the entryway to the kitchen.

A plump woman in her forties holds up an ID badge. "I'm Jean Bain from Child Services, and this is my partner, Barry Feldman. We are looking to talk to Marilyn Desmond."

Laura answers, "Do you have an appointment?"

She slides beside Laura. "I'm Marilyn."

They both stare at her. "Can we come in? We have a few questions to ask you."

Marilyn steps forward, glances at Laura, and opens the screen door.

Laura says, "You may want to call for an appointment the next time." She stares at them.

Marilyn points to the chairs and asks, "Would either of you like some coffee?" She glances at Laura and whispers, "I am okay." Laura goes to the living room. They decline the coffee.

Mrs. Bain opens her notebook, exposing a yellow pad. "There is nothing to worry about, Mrs. Desmond, a few quick questions. Is Johnny here?"

"Yes, they're outside playing."

"We'll need to talk to him before we leave."

Marilyn folds her hands together. "So, why are you here?"

"Verifying Johnny's sleeping arrangements and a safe home environment."

She raises her voice. "Who complained?"

"Anyone can file a complaint. We are concerned with the child's welfare, I'm sure you understand that."

"It's—John, isn't it?"

Mr. Feldman says with a commanding voice, "We can't disclose that information, but if someone is harassing you, having a satisfactory visit on file helps protect you from further complaints."

They ask about the living conditions then jump, "Who is Uncle Keith?"

"A friend."

"And not family-related?"

"No."

"Do any men live here or stay overnight?"

"No."

"Do you and your girlfriend sleep together?"

Marilyn crunches her eyebrows. "No, what kind of question is that?"

"We need to cover all the bases." Calmly, she says, "Why does Johnny call him Uncle Keith if he's not family?"

She feels her chest moving up and down. "I thought it would help Johnny adjust to men in his life. His dad made him so fearful he would cower from any man that was near him."

"Did this help?"

"Yes, he gets along with him well. He's still scared of men, especially his dad, and consequently, his dad is not allowed unchaperoned visitation."

"We show that Mrs. Desmond, his grandmother, who picks Johnny up for visits. How is that working out?"

"I fight with Johnny each week that he has to go because of some court that has no idea—"

"We have studies, children adjust better when they are allowed to see both parents. What is your relationship with this Uncle Keith?"

"We don't have one."

"Have you and Johnny been alone with him?"

"No, the point you want is I have not slept with anyone, with Johnny present."

Mr. Feldman's eyes tighten. "We're here to verify the living condition."

"Then you'll be glad to know that Johnny sleeps through the night. With no more nightmares or someone dragging him out of bed."

They're both staring at her.

"You're not writing that down?"

Laura walks out and is eyeing everyone.

Marilyn continues, "John would threaten or drag him out of the bed, every time we had a fight." Marilyn stands up. "Are there any more questions?"

Mrs. Bain folds her hands in front of her. "We need to talk to Johnny."

Marilyn takes a deep breath. "And what if I say it's not necessary for your report?"

"We'll have to call the sheriff and have them take him to child services. Mrs. Desmond, I don't mean to make this hard. You have a pleasant home here. We just have to verify he is okay."

Marilyn nods. "Okay, but Mr. Feldman will have to wait in the car."

He jerks his head back. "What?"

"He is scared to death of men. I told you that."

Mrs. Bain looks at him. "It's alright, Barry, you can go to the car. It will only take a minute."

Laura says through clenched teeth, "I'll get him."

Mr. Feldman is peering back but follows Laura out.

Mrs. Bain says, "We understand this is hard to deal with, but we're on your side. I need to verify where he sleeps."

They walk into the boys' bedroom. She says, "Kids with their beds made."

"They make their own beds before they go out to play."

She smiles and writes it down.

"In case you need to report to my ex."

"Please. We check on the children's welfare, not the relationship issues."

"He's such a considerate dad, he would give up his rights to see Johnny if he didn't have to pay support?"

She never acknowledges Marilyn.

They make their way to the kitchen. "Does that sound like a caring dad?"

"Many dads have issues with the support, but that doesn't mean they are not caring. You look like you're—"

"We're sorting clothes—if you must know my complete personal life. We were trying to decide whether it was appropriate to wear in public. And by the looks of Mr. Feldman invading our household, I would guess not. But in your personal judgment, is this okay to wear around my five-year-old?"

Mrs. Bain pinches her smile away, flips over the page, and writes in the notebook.

Fifty-Two

August 13, 1984

Fear breaks out as Marilyn holds the Social Services card in her hand. Then … "How did they know about Keith?"

"It makes no sense," Laura replies. "John is smart enough not to harass you if he wants you to sign off on his support."

Marilyn says, "You would think so."

"Another thing before I forget again. You do know that even if you agree with John for no support payments, the court won't allow it. Unless you prove you're wealthy and you don't need the money."

"I've heard that, but he knows everything, so there's no reason to tell him." Marilyn takes a long breath. "I keep wondering, did he know the boys were at Keith's, or was it a lucky guess? If I thought I could control my anger, I would drive up to John's work and read him the riot act in front of his so-called work buddies."

Laura smirks. "That's a great idea. Offense, as Keith would say, can't win playing defense. We'll put a plan together and do it tomorrow when he gets out of work."

"It's just an idea, of a demanding ex-wife."

"Oh no. I'm going to Mom's with the boys. You're going to Keith's, spend the night in the waterbed, make him late for chores."

Marilyn shakes her head slowly. "You make it sound simple."

Laura pats Marilyn's arm. "You need to find out, or it'll haunt you the rest of your life. You want the memory no matter how it works out in the forever."

Marilyn pauses and says, "I'm scared as hell."

A smirk comes to Laura. "We're all scared."

Marilyn changes her clothes, letting the blissfulness soak in as she gets ready.

Laura sticks her head into the bedroom. "The Sheriff Patrol is here."

"They're here to take Johnny—" Marilyn gasps and runs out to the living room. "How can it be that quick? And for what?"

There's a light knock on the screen door.

Laura is instantly there. "Can we help you?"

The officer in front says, "I'm Sid Avery, and this is my partner Les Simmons. Is Marilyn Desmond here?"

Laura stands in the middle of the doorway as Marilyn walks slowly towards them, her mouth dryer than Sarah Desert.

She slides beside Laura with some relief when she sees who it is. "What's the matter, Sid?"

"Can we come in?"

She pushes the screen door open. "She promised—"

Sid pulls back a bit and looks at the other police officer. "What are you talking about? We came from Keith's." He dips his head down but holds eye contact. "The cows getting out."

Marilyn lets out a long breath. "Come in." She motions to the kitchen table.

Laura says, "Would you like coffee?"

Sid says, "We're over our limit today." He sits calmly with his hands folded, his gaze on Marilyn. "Something you should tell us?"

Marilyn is rubbing her mouth, chewing on her lip. She shows him the business card. "Social Service just left. Said someone complained. Questioning whether I was a fit mother."

Sid nods. "That's what happens. A jealous spouse complains, and they follow up. You have nothing to worry about. If they had thought it was serious, they would have put us on notice before they even came. Has John had contact with either of you in the last few months?"

They both shook their heads. Marilyn adds, "Just his threatening phone calls."

"Write down what he said every time. We are here about the cows getting out doesn't appear to be an accident. And you both know Jason Edwards and the tires?"

"Yes."

Marilyn tells them the details of the first time John had nailed someone's tires. She tells him she was upset with Keith not telling her about what happened.

Sid draws a slow smile. "He didn't tell us either maybe the rest of it wouldn't have happened." Sid looks at his notes. "I gave him hell if it's any consolation for him not calling us."

"I've cause everyone enough trouble." Marilyn leans back in her chair. "I'm moving to Port Huron at the end of the week to live with my sister. Hopefully, everyone can return to a normal life."

Sid holds his gaze at them. "We're going to keep digging."

Les pipes in. "Something else?"

Marilyn shakes off her daze. "The people that help me who needs protection." She turns to Laura. "Even after I leave, it's a matter of time before he does something to her."

Laura shakes her head. "Quit worrying; I can handle an asshole like him."

Stoically, Sid says, "We need a contact number." He puts his hand on Marilyn's arm. "You have to trust us."

Marilyn gives him the new address and phone number.

"Call day or night, someone will answer." He holds a card until Laura makes eye contact. "Call about anything out of the ordinary."

Laura says quietly, "Thanks."

Marilyn extends her hand. "Thank you but there's not much anyone can do."

"We'll catch him. Justice always takes longer than we want it to." They turn and head to their car.

Marilyn and Laura lean against each side of the screen door in eerie silence until they leave.

Laura says, "I'll go get the boys."

Marilyn cannot move as the guilt seeps into her. *I'm leaving her to fight alone.*

Laura comes around the corner of the garage. "I can't find the boys."

Marilyn runs out to meet her. "Another thing I messed up, making Johnny scared of the police."

"Let's try the barn." Laura glances at Marilyn. "I realize they're not supposed to, but ..."

Laura slides the barn door open and shouts, "The police left. You can come out." Silence rips through the barn. Laura yells louder. "Chad, remember, we are going to Grandma's. Everything is safe."

They leave the door open and sit on the old farm equipment at the edge of the yard. Marilyn looks across the open space. "At Keith's, they had a game of secret code words and a secret hideout." A lump forms in her throat. "When I asked Johnny about the fight at Keith's, he crossed his arms, 'We had a plan.' It shocked me he's more under control than me."

Laura says, "For Keith such a bachelor image, the kids adore him. Whenever Chad goes over there, he comes back so excited."

The boys peek out around the barn. Marilyn says, "The police are gone, boys. They're not taking you away."

They walk sheepishly towards them. Marilyn and Laura give them a hug and walk silently back to the house.

***

Laura and the boys leave. Marilyn paces and finally puts on her favorite jeans and a plain blue blouse. She grabs the steering wheel with a death grip, but it keeps her hands from shaking driving to Keith's.

Keith's truck is gone. If she remembers correctly, it's Curtis's car in the driveway. She knocks. "Keith, are you home?" Silence yells back at her.

She says again, "Anyone here?" Silence. Dirty dishes are stacked on the counter. She checks the tool shed and looks out across the fields, the trampled corn glaring at her. She walks around the barns, and a peacefulness sinks in as she realizes the cows are quiet. She goes back into the house. Picks up the empty beer bottles, washes the handful of dishes, glances out the window. Her imagination sees the boys in the sandbox.

She flips the pages on his personal phone book, wanting to ... Picks up the notepad and a pen as a torn piece of paper, falls to the floor. She picks it up, a phone number with a heart at the end. Her eyes water, and her hands are shaking as she stares at it. *It's none of your business.* She lays the note on the stand and sits at the kitchen table.

Dear Keith,

> I am so sorry for my temper tantrum. It was uncalled for, no matter what kind of excuse I made. Your patience in dealing with my radical emotions comes from the depth of your soul. You and your mother took me in as if I were family, loved me more than my

mother. And the love you gave to Johnny I'd only dreamed could be possible. Your caring carried us through this difficult time in our lives. You'll forever be in our hearts.

Then the reality of getting you involved with my ex, knowing it would turn out bad, is unforgivable on my part. John will leave no one alone. I am moving to my sister's, hopefully that will help. This is totally my decision for the wellbeing of everyone, and I hope you can forgive me someday. You will always be my knight in shining armor. Hopefully, the next damsel won't have so much baggage.

Johnny wants to see you, but the pain of his saying goodbye would be too much. If you want more explanation, give me a couple of weeks to get settled and give me a call. With the aggravation I cause, I'm taking responsibility for everything that has happened. If you hate me, it is justified, and I understand if you don't call. I missed my chance for the rest of you, but life doesn't always give us what we want, especially not mine.

Love, Marilyn, and Johnny XOXOXO

PS: Left my sister's number on the pad by the phone.

Her eyes water as she tears off the page, folds the note, and writes "Keith" on the front. Tears drip off her cheeks and stain the paper before she can wipe them off. She squares up the pad on the phone stand and writes her sister's number on it. She carefully lays the other folded paper back where it was.

She exams the living room with the mismatched furniture, extending the warm aura she had, which, although short, will be forever. The Lincoln Log toy barn is right where they stopped playing, and the sheets for the tent are piled in the corner. Bracing herself at Keith's bedroom door, she retains the moments, wishing. She rushes in, sets the note on his nightstand, and runs out.

Her heart is beating out of control. She races out of the driveway. Never even a glance as she drives by Keith's mom's house. Tears are flowing when she gets to Laura's and starts packing.

Fifty-Three

August 14, 1984

John's anxiety peaks as his boss walks towards his workstation and comes to a stop. He keeps his head down while he continues to work.

"John, come with me," his boss bellows. "Tim is going to cover for you."

Everyone's air gun stops.

John's neck tightens as he slowly turns toward them.

Tim, who is standing behind the boss, shrugs, and wrinkles his forehead.

The boss, with his bulldog stance and gruffness to match, is looking around at the coworkers. "You guys and girls can keep working. John is taking a break." He motions for John to follow him.

Someone yells, "Glad to work with you, John."

John waves at them. "What's going on?" He glares at his boss's black busy eyebrows.

He remains silent walking to the front offices as everyone secretly glances. He opens the conference room door. "Some friends are here to talk to you."

John walks through the door. The police. His fists clench. Sid Avery and Les Simmons rise and flash their IDs, introducing themselves.

Avery motions to the chair at the head conference table and says, "Have a seat."

"What's this about?" John stays standing.

"Some routine questions. If it's more convenient, you can punch out and we'll go to the police station."

He clenches his jaw, holds his glare, but concedes and sits at head of the conference table. The silence lingers before John says, "You're changing tactics, harassing me in front of my boss and co-workers? For the record, if I lose my job, you'll be the first name on the lawsuit."

"Your boss was generous to let you stay at work. You may want to thank him."

"For letting me sit in these plush office chairs instead of my duct-taped stool. I feel the caring seeping out of my jeans."

Avery gets out his notebook. "It's a few questions; it won't take long." Avery eyes his notes and lets the silence linger.

John leans forward with elbows on the table. "Well?"

Simmons breaks the silence. "Your wife is Marilyn Desmond. Is that correct?"

"You make this grand appearance to ask me who my wife is?" With disgust, John turns to Simmons. "You don't have her name and phone number in your little black book? Everyone else does."

Avery says, "To continue, we're verifying information. She has a restraining order on you?"

"I haven't been close to her. What lies did she come up with?"

"Will take that as a no. When did you see her last?"

"I haven't bar or her house."

Avery props his chin on his hands and stares. "On Friday evening May nineteenth, can you explain what happened and with whom?"

John holds the glare on Sid Avery.

Avery doesn't move.

John breaks the silence. "I was checking on my kid. I suppose there's a law against it?"

Simmons adds. "Your son's name is Johnny Desmond. Is that correct?"

John never turns his head. "When are we done with the stupid questions?"

"Did you know Keith Larson?"

"Mr. Big Shot."

"What disagreements did you have with him?"

John's neck tightens, and his eyes dart, cop-to-cop. "Mr. Macho is screwing my wife. He glares at Simmons. "You must not be in the loop." Turns back to Avery. "And—I wanted to know if my kid is not with some sicko."

Avery leans forward in his chair. "We can end this conversation. Handcuff you and take you down to lockup. Nice ride in a police cruiser always helps clear the mind."

John leans back in his chair and takes a deep breath. "What is he accusing me of?"

"We are verifying information, not accusing you of a crime. Or have you committed one and want to confess?" Avery pauses, "Did you plan on doing bodily harm?"

"Funny. Again, he is sleeping with my wife. According to my kid, they call him Uncle Keith. Isn't that sweet? Family." John squints. "It's disgusting."

"You confronted him?" He flips pages in his notebook. "On May nineteenth?"

"I stopped to clear the air, to reach some understanding. Without warning, he sic that damn dog on me. It tried to tear my arm off." He holds his arm towards their faces. "Got the scars to prove it. Then, next thing, he's punching the shit out of me."

"Did you kill his dog?"

"It whined and growled at me when I left. So—no."

"Was someone with you?"

John's eyes wander at both cops. "Bob drove me over. I told him to stay in the car."

Avery glances up from the notebook. "And Bob has a last name?"

John lets out a long breath. "Kirkman. He'll verify what happened—if Mr. Macho doesn't want to let this rest, perhaps I should sue. Hire him to work the farm for me."

The lunch whistle blows as they finish details from the rest of the night. Avery says, "Let's move on to the evening of July twenty-eighth."

"What about it?" John asks, with his defiant emotion.

Slowly, Avery raises his head. "When was the last time you used nylon nail balls?"

John's face squints. "I don't know what they are."

"You are stating you never took your wife's old nylons and filled them with nails, and put them under someone's tires?"

"This is getting ridiculous. Maybe I should call my lawyer before answering any more questions."

"You get a phone call right after we book you." Avery stands and reaches for his cuffs.

"What other stupid question?" John leans back again. "Or what else are you trying to pin on me?"

Avery sits down. "Do you know Jason Edwards?"

John takes a few breaths before answering. "He's my old neighbor." His eyes dart to each cop. "Talked to him a few times." He takes a long pause. "They're cooking up a lie, I suppose?"

"Can you verify where you were on the evening of July twenty-eighth?"

Avery keeps writing. "With your friend Bob?"

"Yeah. So what of it?"

"Seems like an accomplice ... Was he with you on the evening of August the eleventh?"

John ponders the date. "Yeah, it was Friday, so what of it? We hang out on Friday nights. Has that become a crime too?"

"Where did you guys go?"

"Nowhere—we were at his apartment. You picked out these random dates to find one I don't have an alibi for?"

"We're following up on some issues that seem to involve you. Trespassing, intent to do bodily harm, killing someone's animals. Could be angry emotions in the moment but still serious." Avery leans across the table. "One could do time in the state pen."

John leans toward him, practically touching him. "I have no idea what you're talking about."

"What do you know about letting out Keith Larson's cows?"

"Someone else doesn't like him." He smiles and relaxes in the chair.

Avery holds his stoic expression. "We're verifying anyone who would have a reason. You understand fitting the profile. It seems easy for both of you to drive through town, see Keith's truck at the bar, drive out to his house, and let his cows out."

"I don't have any idea about his damn smelly cows." John pushes his chair away from the table. "I'm not answering any more dumb questions about make-believe stuff I could be accused of without a lawyer."

Avery slides his card across the table. "In case you think of something."

"I thought of something. Why aren't you arresting the slime bag for stealing my wife?"

John picks up the card. "I tried to protect her from the sweet-talking bullshit." His voice trembles. "She never believed me. Guys are only nice for one reason. Guess she is going to learn the hard way."

John walks out first as they exit the room.

Avery says, "Make sure you notify us if you plan on leaving town."

John never turns around. "You'll be the first ones I call."

***

John is third in line to punch out, goes to Bob's car, and rests on the hood. A couple of coworkers stop. "You okay?"

"The normal cop-harassing day."

They slap John on the shoulder. "Good luck," they say and walk away.

Bob walks up. "What was that about?"

John stands. Little above a whisper, he says, "Cops didn't talk to you today?"

"No."

"Something happened Friday night with Mr. Macho's cows."

"So?" Bob opens the car door and rolls the windows down.

"They think we did it."

"The night—the girls came over and we—" John smiles.

"Yeah—I didn't tell them." He bites his lip. "It's better the wife didn't find out."

"Got to admit, it's the perfect alibi."

"Yes, but would like to keep it a secret." He watches more workers pass and avoids eye contact. "They asked about the fight first, but whatever happened Friday night sounded serious."

Bob leans against his door. "But why didn't they get me to verify what happened?"

John steps away from the car. "That's the puzzling part. Cops don't ask questions for no reason." He shrugs. "I told them you stayed in the car when I got into the fight."

Bob nods faintly. "They're fishing, or they would've been asking me questions."

Fifty-Four

August 16, 1984

My four-thirty morning cup of coffee instantly becomes repetitious of thoughts. I reread the letter, ripping my heart, but it's time to move on and get back to work. *She is another girl; there'll be more girls, move on.*

I feed the main lot of cows, then go to Dad's. One more week before I can switch them to silage, but their growth rate is a major setback. May have to leave them here till next year. *Thanks ass hole.*

The auger wagons and the chopper need repairs, but the gut tells me to replace them. We need something to keep up with the bigger tractor capacity. I make a list of parts in my notebook. The chopper, from what I can see, needs a new set of knives, a drive chain, and belt.

Our long-term goal was to build a bunker across the road, add fifty head, and a self-propelled chopper, which may never happen now. "Come on, Buddy." I slap my knee, and he comes running. *A mirage, two boys running with him.*

I load Buddy into the truck, least I'm not talking to myself. We're off to Jamison's Farm Equipment. I'm carrying Buddy and head to the counter when a girl comes out.

Her face lights up. "He's so cute." She reaches out to pet him.

Her auburn hair, tied in a neat ponytail coming out of a New Holland ball cap, makes my mouth water as Buddy wiggles out of my arms. "This is Buddy, my sidekick." I hold him on the counter. I reach out my hand. "And I'm Keith, not that it matters."

She grips my hand, holding her perfect smile. "I'm Cindy."

With a little extra loudness, I say, "Bout time they got someone to improve the customer service."

Phill walks out behind the parts racks and says, "Cindy, watch this guy." His old crusty grin lights up as he says, "He missed his calling as a politician or a gigolo, not sure which."

She shakes her head. "I watch them all." But she is still smiling at me. "What do you need?"

"See, Phill." I hand her my list. "She knows how to help a guy." I wink at her.

"Could've had it half done while you two were playing kissy face."

I laugh and say, "I've got lots of time."

"Now that's a lie. He usually wonders why we don't remember every piece of equipment he bought from us, ready and laying on the counter when he struts in." He shrugs and says, "He's the only farmer in the county needing parts."

Cindy is smiling, pretending not to hear us, and studies the parts book.

Phill drops the smile and says, "Sorry about your dad. How is everything?"

"We adjusted, changed life a bit." I say, "Sleepovers can stay the night. There's no leaving at four in the morning."

"See, Cindy?" Phill points at the list and says, "I'll get these. What did I tell yah?"

She rolls her eyes but giggles. "Does it come with breakfast?"

I nod and grin. "And fresh hot coffee." I check her out as she turns, walking down the parts row.

Phill shakes his head. "All the bullshit aside, if you need something, don't be afraid to ask. It has to be tough."

"Thanks, yeah, it's ... but ... Could use someone for a couple of months in the fall if you hear of anyone. My part-time kid is playing football."

"I'll let you know." He turns away. "Let me go give her a hand."

"I'm going to see Ken." We catch up about Dad and what is next. Then he nonchalantly walks by the hydraulic dump wagons and he adds the benefits of them over the auger ones. Getting back to his office and he figures out the cost of a better chopper and the wagons.

I return to the counter. Cindy is double-checking the list. I'm enjoying her fresh smell and trying to...

"Always have cold beer in case you need to unwind from working with Mr. Grumpy."

She is grinning. "I may take you up on that."

"Phill, you should have her do PR to show your customer how much you care, and I'd show her the farm hospitality."

Cindy is grinning at me.

Phill says, "Cindy, this guy has so many lines, surprised he hasn't written a book yet."

"They're secrets." I wink at Cindy. "I never tell." We get the stuff loaded. I look at Buddy, and his ears perk up. *What is getting married and living happily ever after bullshit, anyway?*

He wags his tail as we pull up by the toolshed. Buddy curls up, setting the list down on the table and what is the next step. A smile comes over me. The women in my life. It's more fun when you're not supposed ... then the ... *It was a fling, but no nakedness.* My eyes water ... enough wallowing.

August 17, 1984

The next morning, I sit with my coffee. *Was it love? Hell, a few kisses don't make it love.* I walk to the tractor. Damn kid. *I miss Johnny asking his thousand questions.*

I line the wagons up and get to work repairing the auger systems. The sheriff patrols pulls in and drives beside where I am working. I'm trying to read Sid's face as he gets out of the car. Good, bad? Cop emotion they teach them, you can't tell.

Sid says, "Glad to see you actually working." He breaks out in a grin, with the corners of his lips turned up.

"Yeah, does happen on rare occasions."

Sid grinned. "Got a few minutes?"

"Yeah, let's get some iced tea." I break the ice cubes from the tray. "Well?"

Sid wipes the sweat off his glass. "This visit is strictly off the record." Relaxation sucks out of the room. "And never to be repeated, especially not to your girlfriend."

"This needs beer," I say slowly, "and you're mistaken about the girlfriend part. She is moving."

"She told me and added some reasons why. I want to help get this guy out of her life, but John had an alibi for Friday night. Arranged, planned, or luck, we'll never know, but Bob said they had women visitors that stayed the night. The women didn't want to admit it but said they were there."

The silence hangs. "Leaving a dead end."

"Proof-wise, yes, but Mrs. Desmond has issues." He fidgets slightly. "The intuition of years on the job, your dad and I hanging out together—it's all connected."

"Dad knew her?"

"We never talked about it, but ..." He holds his gaze on the glass of iced tea and says, "I'm only telling you this because your dad was a trusted friend. We interviewed her. She talks as if she barely knows you, but the laser eyes would've burned holes through me if it were in a science fiction movie. Mrs. Desmond had a kid she put up for adoption or had an abortion. She's the only one who knows." Sid glares and says, "She accused your dad of it being his kid. He detested the woman, but she spread the rumor. There're people who believe it's true."

"I knew this needed beer."

"My theory is she always wanted revenge, but her grandson hanging out with Uncle Keith, has pushed her to find a way." He cracks some emotion. "I have to admit that was clever, being the kid's uncle. My partner verified the woman has an obsession, but we can't arrest her for it."

Stunned, I'm rubbing my chin.

"She made a complaint to the Friend of the Court." He is still glaring at me. "And more you can't tell, and it doesn't prove anything."

I lean forward.

He sits up, exhales, and says, "Mrs. Desmond has this elaborate story that Marilyn and Laura are sleeping together and making out in front of the boys."

I close my eyes. "Marilyn is running to protect us?"

"She's scared, for everyone, but Mrs. Desmond won't let it go." Sid stands and says, "I'll keep working on it. If we press the fight, he'll find a lawyer and sue you for the dog bite; he has a nasty scar, and it's their word against yours."

"Yeah, part of the reason I didn't call."

Sid says calmly, "You don't want to hear this, but Marilyn moving is going to help the situation."

I roll my bottom lip under my teeth, sucking down the lump in my throat. "She wasn't too excited about farming, after the cows getting out mess." I turn away. "Glad you came by." I stand in the doorway watching until he's out of the driveway. Wipe my eyes on my sleeve and head to the toolshed.

***

I finish the chores, warm up leftovers, and wash the dishes, including the ones from breakfast, before grabbing a beer. When the phone rings, I say, "Yeah."

"Well, what's been up?"

"Been working my short twelve-hour days. Glad you called to check."

"You became a monk, is the rumor, but I'm sure it was a lie."

We banter back and forth, and then Jason asks, "You coming to the bar tomorrow night?"

"I'm not sure how welcome I'll be."

"It's her last night. She is training a new girl." The eeriness of quiet filters through the phone before Jason says, "You should talk to her before she goes."

I take a sip.

"What Laura filled me in on, she's a mess, blaming herself for everything that happened to us."

"Adding to the mess, her ex has an alibi for Friday night."

"It's another page of life, not the end of the world. You should let her know."

"She'll blame herself even more. Then, Johnny—what can I add?"

"You're lovesick—and afraid of a five-year-old?"

"Better to end it nice and clean, not all the sappy talk about love. She believes she is protecting us. Next month, I'll be playing in corn stalks and won't have time to—never mind."

"Be hard on your reputation if everyone found out you give a shit?"

"Thanks, I need that."

"Go see her." *Click.*

I hang up the phone and sit in silence with my beer.

Fifty-Five

August 19, 1984

Marilyn sits with her morning coffee, enjoying a bit of peacefulness. She dreams of a house in the country as she watches the rays of sunshine reflect on the dust through the window. *Keith's face, he loves me.* She sips her coffee. *You're dreaming, girl.*

Laura plods out, her eyes puffy from the lack of sleep, her auburn hair matted and sticking up.

"You don't appear ready to get up." Marilyn stifles a grin.

"Who's ever ready at this ungodly hour?" Laura pours her coffee and sits in her normal spot at the table. "I adjust quickly from Mr. Slob to Mrs. Neat, doing the housework, and morning coffee ready." Her eyes twinkle. "You're going to make a good wife someday."

"I was envisioning life as a fashion designer in Paris, with one of those fancy apartments that comes with a gourmet cook and butler."

"Girl." Laura's lip turns up. "Our Prince Charming is going to be wearing a stained, faded t-shirt for work with non-stained ones for dressing up."

Marilyn laughs. "How to ruin my excitement in Paris? Tell your best friend." Instantly she reminisces about Keith's old T-shirts before washing them. "Before I leave for Paris and the day overtakes us, my sister is not charging me for the mother-in-law suite. My income should be twice what it is now. John will keep paying until after the divorce, trying to impress with his good-dad status. I'll send money to help you with the rent until October."

Laura cuts her off. "You are not sending me money. It's my fault, letting Bob talk me into leasing this place. I'll get a small apartment when the lease runs out." Her jaw stiffens. "You have enough stuff to worry about. Did Keith call you last night?"

Marilyn's voice trembles. "No, I left him a note and my sister's phone number." She takes a sip of coffee and says, "He doesn't owe me an explanation or a reason to ever talk to me again. John, with his screwed-up thinking, believes he has won and hopefully leaves everyone alone. It hurts like hell, but there's no other way."

Laura peers over her cup. "Did you ..." They hear a truck pull into the driveway

Marilyn glances out the window. "It's time."

Laura says, "Let me get dressed." She takes her coffee to the bedroom.

Jeff, Ann's husband, is surveying the yard. Marilyn sticks her head out and yells, "Back the truck right here," motioning alongside the house. He comes to attention and salutes.

Ann looks irritated walking to the house.

She hugs her and says, "Is everything okay?"

"Everything is great. Jeff's having a whiny kid attack. He had to give up his precious golf game today and spend the occasion helping family."

"I'm sorry for—"

Ann points her finger. "No. We're family. He can give up one Saturday of golf."

Marilyn grimaces. "Let me wake Johnny. Wanted him to sleep as long as possible." She leads Ann towards the living room. "My plan was to load everything here and on the second trip go direct to Jason's. He lives on the other side of town."

Ann says, "We're spending the day getting you settled and figured it would take more than one trip."

Marilyn leads Jeff and Ann to her room. "These boxes and everything except the dresser. Johnny's room contains only the bed and dresser." She paints on her cheerfulness and enters Johnny's room. He is already awake when she sits on the bed. "Wake up, sleepyhead, we have a big day."

"I don't want to go." He sits up in his bed, holding Keith's teddy bear. He stares and blurts, "Chad and I want to move to Uncle Keith's."

Marilyn says, "Keith has farming to do and can't be taking care of us, too."

"But Mom, we could help. He said he needs a cook, and you're cooking, anyway. I'll take care of Buddy. He told me that in a couple of years he'd show me how to feed the cows. Aunt Laura could serve Uncle Keith beer. There're extra bedrooms if you didn't want to sleep with Uncle Keith."

"You boys devise a great plan." Marilyn pulls the covers open. "Did Uncle Keith say it was okay?"

Johnny says, "Yes." And Chad is nodding.

She hides a smirk, "We are moving to Aunt Ann's, till the divorce stuff is worked out. Then we'll see what we can do."

Johnny is still pouting as she leads them both to the kitchen where Laura makes them breakfast. Jeff instantly goes to work on Johnny's bed, and the house takes on an eerie silence, with Ann blipping out one liner's that no one acknowledges. Her life is loaded in the truck and Marilyn gives Laura a hug, never making eye contact, biting her lip, and they head to Port Huron.

"What's Love Got"—she shuts the radio off, continuing the last twenty miles in silence.

The silence continues as Jeff and Marilyn set up the beds and Ann makes lunch. The boxes are stacked against the wall in the living room and look like some new wall design.

It's after one, when Marilyn kneels in front of Johnny. "You play with your cousins. We're going to get the rest of our furniture."

Johnny still pouting and never looks up. She kisses him on the forehead and turns quickly away. Jeff makes small talk, prying for details and adding advice, on the drive to Jason's house. She is nauseous by the time they arrive.

Marilyn gives Jason a hug, and her voice trembles when she introduces Jeff. Jason moved most of the stuff towards the door before and they load the truck quickly. Marilyn stands in the doorway with sadness overwhelming her. "Thank you." She gives him a hug. Jeff is sitting in the truck. "Tell Keith ... I at least could offer an official apology." She turns to leave and stops. "You both be careful. John will still want revenge."

Jason is nodding. "We can handle it." A smirk seeps out. "Remember us when you become rich."

"I will." She bites her lip.

The ride to Port Huron starts out quietly until Jeff finally says, "Jarrod, one of the partners at the restaurant, and my best friend, is a meticulous go getter. Some say he has eccentricities, but he was impressed with you. And believe me, he doesn't impress easily."

She shakes her head. "I'm not here to impress anyone."

"A little extra ... you'll be wined and dined with the best people." He glances over when she doesn't answer. "The opportunity and dreams coming true."

Marilyn watches the last bit of countryside whisk away. *You have no idea what my dreams are.* She says, "I'm not rich man hunting." She glances at him.

"I want Johnny settled into school and John out of my life."

He glances over and says, "Ann's not going to let you become a hermit."

I can hardly wait for her to fix my life.

***

They unload the truck, stack the boxes with the others. Johnny comes from playing with his cousins and quietly sits on the couch with his tractor. Marilyn sits beside him feeling like her chest is going to explode. "I know it's hard, but we had to move." She takes his hand and sits in quietness.

Ann knocks on the door, pokes her head in, and says, "Jeff is making cocktails, and I made enough spaghetti for everyone, it'll be ready shortly." She steps into the room, peering at Johnny. "Cheryl is excited about having her cousin to play with." She glances around and says, "The bed has clean sheets, and the unpacking can wait till tomorrow. Come enjoy supper."

Marilyn says calmly, "Thanks." Ann is already out the door. Marilyn stares at her life packed in boxes, and finally comes out of her trance, grabs Johnny's hand. "Let's eat."

She closes the door in the hall slowly, and they make their way to the main part of the house. Ann's fake, bubbling teenager persona is in full swing, informing Marilyn of the correct wine with spaghetti.

Marilyn takes a drink of wine.

Ann tips her glass slowly to her lips. "You must sip, just a taste on your lips. No gulping, you're not drinking beer."

She smiles to herself. *According to Keith, if you can't take a swig, it is not worth drinking, and beer goes with everything except ice cream.*

Ann raises her wineglass. "Welcome home." They toast. "Go collect everyone. I'll take the garlic toast out of the oven."

They all settle in to eat, Jeff summarizes the proper rules at the dinner table. "Kids should only talk when asked a direct question."

Ann says, "Dear, some other time."

Marilyn's anxiety peaks. *We're not eating meals together.* After they finish eating, Megan and Cheryl drag Johnny off to their room. Jeff gets himself another drink, and the TV comes on in the family room. Ann bustles with nonstop chit-chat while Marilyn quietly helps her do the dishes. Without taking a pause between sentences, Ann pours more wine into their glasses and drags her off to the family room.

Jeff, in his recliner, sips his bourbon on the rocks. A smirk develops. "Ann was saying you found a stud farm-boy. Your face says you're missing him?"

"I'm thankful to you and Ann for getting me a place to stay, but we are sad about having to move." Marilyn squirms. "He was a sweet guy. Johnny and Chad had worked out a plan for us to move to his farmhouse."

His eyes squint. "Hope you're not listening to a kid. You'll have great opportunities to meet Mr. Right, and Johnny will adjust." He flips his hands open. "And no smelling cow shit every day, gotta be worth a million bucks."

Marilyn exhales through her nose. *You can do this.* "Apparently, you are out of touch with modern farming. The tractors have air-conditioned cabs, stereos, and the best feature is the air-ride seat. More comfortable and peaceful than your fancy recliner." *What did I just say?*

Jeff lets out a chuckle. "Air ride ... how was it?"

"Jeff, stop it. We're not guys sitting around talking about our sexual fantasies." Ann's eyes bug out. "You're a crude ass some days." She continues to glare at him.

Marilyn gulps the rest of her wine and stands, never making eye contact, and says, "Thanks for everything. I'm calling it a night. We have another long day tomorrow."

Jeff pulls back his smirk. "I apologize. It's family." He raises his hand. "You got some. It's the eighties. It's not a sin."

She sucks in a breath ... and goes down the hall to Cheryl's bedroom. The kids are sitting contentedly on the floor, coloring. "Come on, Johnny. Time to go."

Johnny turns towards Cheryl and says, "I have to go."

Cheryl keeps coloring. "Okay."

Hand-in-hand, Marilyn leads him through the kitchen, down the small hallway, to their apartment door.

Just what I need. First day we're discussing the sex life I don't, didn't, and won't have.

Fifty-Six

August 20, 1984

Marilyn's early-riser gene has her digging through the kitchen boxes finding the coffeepot but grogginess from the wine and the reality she wants to just have a good cry. Waiting for the coffee, she opens the living room curtains that almost look new and views the backyard, with a lone swing set, neatly mowed grass, and a freshly stained wooden fence. The separate driveway off the side of the house gives her some privacy, but knowing her sister Ann, she'll keep a running tab on everyone who comes and goes. It's only eight o'clock in the morning when she starts unpacking.

Johnny still looks asleep when he wanders out at nine, holding his teddy bear.

Marilyn says, "Good morning."

He walks past her and sits at the end of the couch.

She finishes up one more moving box, makes toast, sets cereal and bowls on the table. and says, "Johnny, come eat. I got Sugar Pops to celebrate our first morning." Ann, always planning, had filled the fridge with basics.

Johnny is whispering to the teddy bear sitting on his lap and stays in his world.

She sits beside him, feeling the warmth of his small body next to hers, and takes his small hand. "I love you very much, and this is hard right now but will make our lives better, and we can visit once the divorce is final."

"When are we seeing Uncle Keith?"

With every nerve tense, Marilyn pauses. "Remember, I want to see Uncle Keith too. It'll take some time, but ... I promise ... you'll get to see him." She stands up and takes his hand. *And how am I pulling that off?*

After a few spoonfuls of cereal Johnny says, "There's no place to play. We're not allowed outside the fence. We can't climb the tree, because of the flowers, and there's no sandbox."

"There are different rules compared to the country. You never had a swing set before ... it'll be fun to play on." She tries to keep her voice from trembling. "Once we get settled, I'll talk with Uncle Jeff about a sandbox."

Johnny stops eating. "Cheryl said her mother won't allow one because she not having sand tracked in the house."

Marilyn rubs her face impatiently. "We'll figure out something. Moving is always hard at first, but that doesn't mean it's bad. You'll start school in a couple of weeks and make new friends. You'll have lots of fun things to do."

"I'm not going to school."

She gathers her thoughts and says, "All kids go to school to learn new things. You have to learn to read and write, learn how to add numbers."

"Grandma G was teaching us already. She would teach us more if we still lived there."

"And that is really nice of her, but she can't teach you everything you need to know. Uncle Keith went to college to learn." She feels her heart beating out of her chest. "Pouting will not fix it, and you will be dumb if you don't go to school. Now get dressed and brush your teeth. You're visiting Grandma Desmond today."

Johnny trudges off, and she opens another box.

***

Marilyn hates herself as she coaches Johnny on the way to Laura's about what not to say when he visits Grandma Desmond's.

Johnny answers angrily, "I just won't talk."

"Grandma always has fun things planned."

Johnny doesn't answer.

When Mrs. Desmond arrives, Marilyn kneels and gives Johnny a hug. "I love you."

He frowns. "I know, Mom." He trudges out to Mrs. Desmond's car.

She blew him a kiss, but he turned away. Tears are running down her cheeks as she goes inside. "Hopefully, this is the last time. When she drops him off, I'm telling her, she can't see him. I can't stand the agony, and I'm a basket case all the time he's gone."

"It's hard for kids, but he's dealing with it. You have to deal with it."

"I hate myself. I made up this elaborate story that if he wanted to farm, he'd need an education and college."

Laura says, "A stretch, but he's still a kid and lots of them say they don't want to go to school."

She closes her eyes. "Said he'd be dumb if he doesn't and then promised he'll be able to see Keith."

Laura smiles. "What did he say?"

"Said he didn't care, and Keith could teach him how to farm. The intriguing part?" Marilyn grins ruefully. "The boys have devised a plan for how everything would be perfect if we move in with Keith."

"What?"

"Yep, I'm the private chef, and you're the bartender. When Keith comes in from feeding the cows, we'll be there to wait on him." Marilyn bites her lip as Laura tries to stifle a laugh. "The juicy part is we both have permission to sleep with Keith, in case we're afraid to be upstairs by ourselves, and they'll sleep in the tent."

"Did you tell Keith?"

Marilyn's smile fades. "No, I'm not calling him."

Laura gets up and dials the phone.

"What are you doing?"

"This is enough of you two not getting your shit together." She hangs up. "He must be outside. Grab your purse; we'll go find him."

"I'm not going—I have to visit Mother and quit stringing Keith along. He can do better than me."

"I can't believe—you don't want to know?"

"Know *what*?"

Laura's mini crow's feet appear. "Girl—how is he?"

"Stop it. I've messed up his life enough."

"You're scared to death."

Marilyn scans the beat-up cupboards. "What if I am? I'm still not going." She lets out a long breath. "Please let it go. I'm off to Mother to deal with that issue. She'll be outraged, I didn't bring Johnny to visit. And of course, it's my fault she hasn't seen Johnny, although she could've come over anytime to visit the last few months."

Laura folds her arms across her chest.

Marilyn continues with more confidence as she gets it out. "Mrs. Boss will go ballistic when I tell her it was her last visit unless she drives to Port Huron. But I'm done feeling guilty for either of them."

***

Marilyn and Laura sit at the kitchen table after she returns from her mother's and says "I'll miss our Sunday afternoon talks.

Laura says, "I'm breaking the rules but been spending time hanging out with Jason." A cat-like grin consumes Laura's face.

"I was thinking he was hanging around more than normal."

"We worked out some rules." Laura gets a beer. "You should have one."

"I don't dare." Marilyn looks at the clock. "She'll be here anytime."

A car pulls in, but it is Chad as his dad drops him off early. He gives Laura a hug and shows her his new toy.

Laura says, "It is really nice. Now, go and put your clean clothes in the drawer. Johnny will be here shortly, and you guys can play for a while."

Mrs. Desmond arrives, and Marilyn sucks in a deep breath. "Wish me luck."

"You've got it under control; just walk away when she starts shouting."

Marilyn walks calmly out to the car as Johnny runs by her and into the house.

Mrs. Desmond squints at Marilyn. "Glad you came out. You have manipulated Johnny so bad he doesn't even talk and cowers from his own dad. It's horrible what you have done."

Marilyn's heart is pounding. "Yes, it is horrible, the fear with which he has lived. When Johnny is older and decides he wants to visit, we'll contact you."

Mrs. Desmond's neck is strained tight. "You can't do this—"

"Because John messes with everyone's life he touches, we're moving away from him as possible. We will call you about visitation."

"You can't shut us out—I'll drag you through every court in the land—tell them how you slept with every farm boy in the county." She breaks out her big fake grin. "And how you do really like women."

That's why Child Protective Services checked my lifestyle. "You're despicable, the same as your son." Marilyn straightens her shoulders and walks away calmly.

"You bitch—you're going to pay for this."

"Yes, I'm doing them all." Marilyn doesn't look back.

Laura is staring as she moves towards the fridge. "That was quick."

Marilyn says, "The first time I've ever stood up to her."

Laura holds up a beer. "One to celebrate is in order."

"I'd never make it—home." Marilyn opens the beer.

"The boys love sleeping together, and I heard we already slept together." Laura cracks open her beer, raising it for a toast.

Fifty-Seven

August 20, 1984

John gets out two beers, hands one to his dad, and plops down to finish watching the baseball game as Mrs. Desmond takes Johnny back to Laura's.

Dad says, "It's breaking Mom's heart the way Johnny is rejecting her."

"He's a kid believing the propaganda Marilyn is feeding him." John's jaw clenches. "She had him hating me for years." John whistles out a breath. "I'm planning on moving to Texas."

His dad takes a long drink and slowly stares at John. "Mom will be pissed."

"The cops visited me at work. They are trying to hang me with something, and we all know they'll keep making it up till they do."

The TV goes to commercials.

John continues, leaning forward in his chair. "Can you imagine bumping into that smirky asshole Larson? Dad—it won't be just his dog the next time. And now his police buddies are checking everything I do. I'm afraid of having a couple of beers after work. After the stunt, with the police, my boss is being an extra prick. Then deal with Mother on her revenge campaign. She said to herself, 'You've got to wait.' The cops are setting a trap. Just not sure what it is."

"It'll take time to blow over," Dad says, taking another drink. "Mother has a vendetta against the Larsons. Now they're stealing her grandson, I've never seen her on such a revenge trip."

"In a couple of years, the cops will be on to someone else, and if Marilyn spends time with the asshole, she'll get a taste of his egoistic, lying self, although she may still be too dumb to realize it. But it won't do me any good," John says. "He was the most coveted guy in high school and ten years later, still single and looking. The jock mentality—never satisfied, always looking for the next score."

Dad nods. "Never thought about that."

"He'll dump her in six months, and she'll be added to his list."

Dad cocks his head to one side, listening. "Sounds like Mother's home."

"This is between us. I'll tell Mother when I know for sure."

Mrs. Desmond slams the door and screams, "That bitch. She is moving."

John jumps up and meets her at the kitchen doorway. "What?"

She grabs the whisky from the cupboard. "Says I can't see Johnny anymore unless I drive to Port Huron."

"Her sister lives there."

"Whatever." She pops some ice cubes out of the tray and says, "Well, she strutted her hot little ass out to the car to tell me with a big smirk on her face. I wanted to slap off." She takes a swig of her drink. "Hanging around the Larsons, she is already becoming like them. Cocky and conceited."

"Yeah, that's what I've been telling you."

"You'd better call your lawyer in the morning to fight for more visitation. People told me that parents split equal time, and I can take care of Johnny during the day, and it'll reduce your support payments."

"Yeah, I'll see what I can do." John gives her a hug. "I'm going for ride."

"Don't do something stupid and get yourself arrested," she calls after him, taking a slug of whiskey.

***

John parks at the other end of Laura's road, where he can see if anyone leaves. Then once it gets dark, he drives by Laura's with his lights off, feathering the gas on the truck to keep it quiet. Marilyn's car is in the driveway where it always is. He drives to Bob's, his mind racing. John knocks, turns the doorknob, and walks into Bob's living room.

"I thought you had the kid," Bob says, picking his head off the couch.

"I did. He went home, remember? No overnight stays."

"Yeah, I forgot." Bob gets up. "You want a beer?"

"Yeah."

Bob pulls a beer from the fridge and hands it to John. "So, what's up?"

"Mom is on the warpath." John guzzles half his beer. "Marilyn told her no more visitation. She is leaving town."

"Whoa, she's moving in with Keith?"

"Not yet. I've been checking on her, and this last month she has been working or at Laura's. Least, that is where she is parking her car."

Bob sits back down on the couch, putting his elbows on his knees. "Maybe Keith got her a place somewhere?"

"Keith can't move from his precious cows."

"Well, he gets her an apartment for six months, the divorce is over, and she moves in with him." Bob smiles ruefully. "Or she found a good job somewhere?"

"That's it. Her sister." John slams his beer down onto the end table. "She hates me and was always coaxing Marilyn to move even before we got married. Let's go for a ride and check out the neighborhoods."

Bob grabs two fresh beers as they head out. They drive by Keith's house first, his truck in its normal spot with a dim light on in the house. They throw the cans out along the road to Jason and drive by Marilyn's mom's house. Everything appears normal on a Sunday night. John buys more beer at the party store and makes another pass by Laura's before they go to Bob's. "I'm calling her at least to rattle her cage."

John finishes another beer before he dials Laura's house. When he hears the click that someone picked up, he says, "Is Marilyn there?"

The phone is quiet, but it's not hung up. He stands and waits as his lips twitch.

Marilyn answers, "Hello."

John says, "Mom said you're leaving."

"I am."

"So, should I assume you notified the court, and their lack of caring forgot to notify me?"

"I'm doing what is best for Johnny, and too bad about manly ego."

"You're such a fool. Your macho boy just wants steamy sex."

"You are so sick."

"You want me out of your life?"

"Forever."

"Here's the deal." He blows on the mouthpiece.

"Yeah, what is it?"

"The blunt truth."

Silence.

"You're not that hot, and in three months he'll dump you." John smiles at himself. "Want me to drop my visitation? It's simple. Find a way. No support.

Otherwise, no deal."

"That's the miraculous deal you dreamed up? You must have forgotten what they said. I don't have input for the amount of money you pay."

John grins. "The part they didn't tell you: You prove enough income and don't need my help, they'll change it. With your new swanky lifestyle with Keith, it shouldn't be hard to show how much he's paying you to sleep—I mean, work on his farm."

"I'm moving to my sister's, not sleeping with Keith. If you must know."

John is silent.

"I'm leaving this town forever."

"Getting one of those fancy jobs you always talked about, making the big bucks. However, you do it, quit charging me support, I'll move to Tennessee, and you'll never see me again. If not, I'm going to request every other week visitation. The lawyer says it's the new fair way to settle divorces. Mom already volunteered to watch Johnny while I work. I'll be better off than I was taking care of your ass."

"You're so caring."

"At least I'd toughen the kid up. Explain to him about women. Add some facts about his mom. I can't stand living here and watching you turn him into a sissy."

The phone is silent.

John is grinning. "It's a deal you can't pass up. Get back to me when your caring heart sees reality, but don't wait too long. May just pick Johnny for a visit, and you'll never hear from us again." He hangs up.

"You're smooth." A smirk drips off Bob's face. "Think you can pull it off?"

"Somehow, I don't dare move to Texas without the support lockup. My biggest problem is keeping Mother from harassing everyone, so Marilyn will settle."

"Good luck with that."

"Working on making Mom to believe the week-on, week-off visitation may be possible."

Bob is rubbing his chin. "She seems way too clever to just go along."

"Yeah, it'll take some doing. I'll rumor around about Tennessee. Mom knows I won't go, but it may jolt Marilyn."

Fifty-Eight

October 1, 1984

Marilyn sips her coffee, letting the taste linger, reminiscing about her life, how it has changed in six months. Keith continually joking about life, and his confidence brought joy to her day. *Why didn't I say yes, at least ... the ultimate of his naked body*. Her body tingles.

Johnny wanders out, holding Keith's teddy bear, and ends her dream world.

"Good morning, sunshine," Marilyn says as he continues to the couch. "Are you excited about school today?"

"No, I'm not going to school."

She sits beside him. "Why don't you want to go?"

"Zach teased me, saying I lied about driving a tractor."

"He's probably jealous."

"He said I was making it up. Called Keith dumb and said farmers don't have Corvettes."

"Don't let it bother you."

Johnny is staring at the wall. His head moves up slightly. "He said guys only have Corvettes to get laid. What does laid mean?"

"We'll it's ... how some men trick women into ... liking them." She pats his hand. "Let's eat."

"Did you get laid by Uncle Keith?"

"No." She's trying to catch her breath. "It's not something ... Uncle Keith ... It's not something nice men do with women."

"I'm going to punch him if he says anything bad about Uncle Keith or you again."

"You should tell the teacher and not get in a fight." She sucks in a breath. *It is what his dad would do.* "He's teasing you. Just play with other kids."

Johnny eats his breakfast slowly in silence, then takes forever to dress.

Marilyn is staring at the clock. "Hurry, you're going to be late for the bus." She pulls him along as the bus waits for them. "Now remember, no fighting." The driver smiles at her and closes the door. Johnny never looks back. "I love you." It's only eight o'clock and she feels completely exhausted.

***

She takes her shower and puts on her only royal blue dress, studying herself in the mirror. The V-cut neckline never seemed so low before. Too sexy. She digs out her dark blue skirt and a plain light blue blouse. The faded blouse makes her look like her mother. *I hate it.* She scans the closet and concedes plainness in court.

The drive to Sandusky has her heart racing. The divorce agreement, John giving up visitation is too good to be true, and Mrs. Desmond didn't even make an argument, something is not right. Her neck is stiff and fingers ache when she finally reaches the courthouse.

***

Marilyn finds a wooden bench outside the courtroom, away from where everyone enters. She keeps her head up and glances at the people coming in, hoping for Mr. Drillman to arrive shortly. John enters, making her wish she wasn't so early. He is decked out in a cowboy shirt, tight-fitting blue jeans, and new cowboy boots. With a fresh haircut. *Wonder where he got the money to buy that if he's so broke?*

She refrains from looking over. His warped mind would think ... if he saw her looking. Why didn't she bring Laura? She'd know what to say. Her hands are sweaty as her mind wanders. Keith drifts into her consciousness and the want of him. He's never called, answered the letters, or cashed the checks.

He's moved on.

John is standing in front of her with his feet spread. Vibes flowing as if he had just won a boxing match.

In shock, she looks up. "What?"

He tucks his thumbs into his belt loops. "Heard you were looking for a cowboy."

She is shaking. "Your dream world. Leave me alone."

He stands up straighter, looking down at her. "A close-up of what you're missing. I can read your mind. Wanting one more fun ride?"

Marilyn's heart is pounding as she looks towards the door. "You are sick. Get away from me." She wants to run, but she'd have to touch him to slide by.

He smirks, with a puffy grin. "One to remember us by."

"You are violating your court order." She closes her eyes.

He doesn't move.

"Sir, you need to move out of her space." Drillman is half John's size pushes between them. "I will have you arrested."

John spouts, "She motioned me over here. Like always, the guy gets hassled." He turns. "Thank you for helping us work out our problems." He laughs as he leaves and whispers, "Asshole."

Drillman says, "You alright?"

Her chest is pounding. "Yeah." *He always gets the last dig.*

He sits beside her. "You should've yelled. Someone would've helped you."

She glances at him and says, "I didn't want to make a scene. He was standing in front of me and caught me off guard. It's what he does when you're least expecting it. If I'd yelled, he would've acted like he did nothing."

"It's almost over. Let's go in."

***

"All rise."

The judge comes through a side door and says, "Please be seated." He pounds the gavel. "Court is in session." He flips through the papers, and the court is silent. He looks at each lawyer. "We have reached an agreement with the divorce and support. Is that correct?"

Each lawyer stands and answers yes.

The judge unemotionally glances at Marilyn and says, "You've agreed to awfully low support for your son. Do you have a plan to maintain his well-being?"

Drillman turns towards her. "You can answer."

Marilyn stands. "Yes, I do, Your Honor. I have an apartment suite beside my sister with minimal household expenses. My sister and I share any babysitting requirements, and I obtained a good job. The increased income and the decreased expenses more than offset what we had when we were married."

The judge nods and turns to John. "Are you concerned about the quality of life your son will have without your support?"

"The extra dollars—"

His lawyer turns and whispers.

John stands, glances around the courtroom. "I'm devastated over this divorce ... I came from a family that works together in tough times, unlike hers." He stops talking and takes another breath. "Johnny is five years old, and she's taught him to be afraid of me. He would run to his room when I came home from work." John gets choked up. "I love my son and only want the best for him, even though ... I will do the best I can for him." With some tears flowing, he sits down.

Marilyn grits her teeth and starts to rise from her chair when Drillman reaches out.

Stone-faced, the judge keeps looking at John.

John slowly rises back to his feet. "Sir ... in a blunt term ..." He looks over at Marilyn, "She exaggerates simple disagreements, makes it hard for a man to do the right thing."

The judge holds out his hand. "Mr. Desmond, this court is concerned about what's best for Johnny. Both of you as his parents have a moral obligation to support him until adulthood. The court hopes you will not let the other disagreements sway you from that obligation."

John sits down.

The judge continues staring at John. "I strongly suggest setting up a savings account for your son to help when unforeseen things happen."

John slouches and his lawyers stand up. "We will, Your Honor."

The judge nods. "I hereby declare you legally divorced. I will sign this and send it over to the clerk. You should see your paperwork in the mail in ten days." He pounds his gavel. "Case dismissed."

"All rise."

Drillman is studying the paperwork on the table and doesn't move. Marilyn feels John's glare but doesn't look.

When the thump of boots fades away, Drillman says, "I'll walk you to your car."

"I want to tell you how grateful I am for everything you have done for me."

"You're welcome, and I'm glad I could help, but Keith is the one you need to thank. How is the boy doing anyway?"

Marilyn looks at the light clouds. "He's my knight, that's for sure."

Drillman holds open the door of her car. "He has a good heart. You'll settle him down."

"Thanks again."

Her eyes are blurry as she drives to Laura's. The fight of emotions, wanting to see Keith and wrap herself around him. But the reality: it was a winter fling, with an extension into summer, a memory, but over.

Laura meets her at the door and gives her a big hug. "Congratulations. How does it feel to be wild and free?"

"It hasn't sunk in that I am actually single."

"When is your first date with Keith?"

She bites her lip. "He's never called." Silence fills the space. "I sent him checks to pay my loan. Added a letter telling him ... never mind." She dabs her eyes. "I can't just show up."

"He's not John. I've lost my temper with Keith lots of times. He doesn't take it personally." Laura rubs her lips together. "He likes you too much not to call."

"Which proves maybe he doesn't. Besides, I can't go without Johnny, especially now. I would become mushy-faced, and then the guilt, it would be terrible. I wrote for him to call and talk if he wanted."

"You had some effect on him. He hasn't been to the bar. Jason said he is working nonstop. He always squeezes in time to chill out. The stress with his dad and—"

"My temper tantrum is no excuse for not helping."

"Give him a call early in the morning. He's up and drinking coffee. And just tell him you are coming. How is the job anyway?"

"Easier than I expected Jarrod the owner gave me a personal introduction to everyone. My boss Allan goes with the flow and is great with the waitress syndrome, about who is the most important. Sherry's jealousy tries to run everything, and I took her job. The girls tease me about how hot Jarrod is for me."

"He's probably more affluent than the guys we hang out with?"

"Stop it. It's pick on the new girl. None of them are sitting around drinking beer, besides he's not my type."

"What is your type now that you are free and single?" Laura laughs as she hugs her.

***

Marilyn's thoughts of Keith instantly consume the moment of silence. *Was he, my type?* The remorse still lingers when the school bus pulls up.

Johnny doesn't look at her and stomps towards the house ahead of them.

Cheryl is talking about her day at school. Marilyn says, "Sounds like you had fun today."

"Yes, school is fun." Cheryl opens the door, and they go into the house. They look at the drawing she brought home. "What's the matter with Johnny?"

"He can't go out for recess for the rest of the week."

Marilyn makes her way down the hall to her apartment. Johnny is sitting on his bed. She asks, "How was school today?"

Johnny rolls his lip out. "I hate school."

"So, what happened?"

"Zach said I smell like a cow and tripped me on purpose. So, I punched him."

"Didn't we discuss if he was picking on you to tell the teacher?"

"She never does anything. He always gets away with stuff."

"Go change your clothes and go outside and play. We're having dinner at Aunt Ann's tonight, and I'm cooking a roast. We'll talk more later."

Ann pounds on the door. "Put some clothes on. Your sister is here checking on you." She comes around the corner with two glasses of wine. "How does it feel?" She hands Marilyn a glass.

"It hasn't sunk in yet."

"Cheers to your new life in the city."

They touch glasses, and Marilyn says, "Thanks."

Ann sets her glass down. "Miss your farm boy?"

She raises her head. "Yeah ... it will pass."

"Don't dwell on it. It was a fling. You both had a good time."

"Yeah, probably right." Marilyn examines her wine. *Why am I drinking this?* "Did they call you from school?"

"Oh, yeah, nothing to worry about. It's boys being boys."

"Maybe, but it's kindergarten."

"Quit, you're making a big deal about nothing," Ann says. "We're celebrating tonight and have a surprise visitor."

"Who?" *Keith?*

"I promised not to tell."

"Ann, you're my sister."

Ann grabs her glass and laughs as she walks out the door. "See you in an hour."

The anxiety keeps churning. She checks the roast, and it is done. She turns the oven on low and gets dressed. She fights with herself over what to wear. Instead of the tight-fitting blouse, she puts on a plain one. Her heart is fluttering. She wants it to be Keith ... but something says no.

She washes Johnny's face and lays out school clothes for him to wear.

Johnny says, "Mommy, why are we getting dressed up?"

"We want to look nice. Other people are invited." She carries the roast still in the pan, and they head down the hall. Johnny goes off to Cheryl's room, and Ann is getting the rest of dinner.

They're both busy in the kitchen when the doorbell rings.

Ann says, "You answer it." She bites back a smile.

Marilyn tentatively goes to the door. Jeff sits forward in his recliner with a smirk on his face. She opens the door.

Fifty-Nine

October 1, 1984

John drags himself out of bed and goes to the shower. The anger and blissfulness keep crashing, as he ponders life after divorce. He dresses in his new Western shirt and new cowboy boots Jeanie help him pick out and struts out to the kitchen,

His mother perks up. "You must've gone clothes shopping. You look stunning."

"Thanks, Mom. Not sure how much it will help." He sits down as she is already up getting him coffee.

She rubs his shoulder. "I realized we talked about this, but ... Your lawyer is wrong about not having me testify. We can take care of Johnny and teach him what a family should be."

John looks out across the room. "We've made the proposal with the divorce. The judge can agree it's the right thing for Johnny or send it back to Friend of the Court."

"Don't sign off on the divorce till it's worked out. The court wants it settled and off the docket, and they don't care about it being fair."

The tension surges in his neck. He gulps down the rest of the coffee. "I want the divorce completed. Today."

His mom's face tightens, and every muscle strains as she says, "Marilyn will concede if you get your lawyer off his ass and fight for your rights."

"The guy always gets screwed in the divorce, Mother. The lawyer is saying I'm lucky to get the support that low."

Mrs. Desmond is shaking her head. "I don't like it. You're settling. Where are your Desmond balls?"

He says, "She'll squirm from her guilt by the end of the day." He gets up from the table.

Mrs. Desmond gives him a hug. "Do the best for our family."

The cool autumn air feels good on his face. He waves back at Mom before opening the door of his truck. He stops at the corner before pulling out onto the main road and grabs the bottle of whiskey out of the glove box. *A new life.* He takes the last swig and throws the empty bottle into the ditch. He licks the last taste of whiskey from his lips.

***

He looks around the courthouse parking lot and sees Marilyn's Pinto parked over in the far corner. He examines his cowboy boots, puffs out his chest, and makes his way to the courthouse. Once inside, his mouth waters as he spots Marilyn away from everyone. He ponders her sitting alone and smirks at himself. *What's going through her little mind?*

John walks quietly over to Marilyn, satisfaction oozing out of himself, and stands inches from touching her. *You'd like it. Wouldn't you?*

Drillman slides between them. "Sir, leave now."

John's lawyer is shaking his head when he reaches him. "Not a smart thing to do. They can get you for harassment."

John raises his chin. "I was thanking her lawyer for helping us work out our disagreements."

His lawyer maintains his unemotional posture and says, "Whatever you do once we get in the courtroom, stay humble in front of the judge."

"You're saying he doesn't like cowboy attire?"

The lawyer let out a breath through closed lips. "I have no idea. Everything is ready, except the judge's signature. If the judge doesn't sign it, your support will be at least double the amount you are paying. Did you convince your mother not to come?"

"Yes, I assured her you had everything handled. I hate it, but ..."

His lawyer nods. "Good, we have a deal. Let's not give anybody a chance to make it worse. I've never seen one get better. Now, the judge likes to ask and give advice. Whether you agree, don't argue with him. Just tell him you will do your best and thank him for his advice. Let's go in."

John holds his emotions but stares at the judge throughout the trial. He gags when he tells the judge he will put money away for Johnny.

When the judge pounds his gavel, dismissing the court, John glares at the judge as he walks out and then fixes his eyes on Marilyn. He walks straight towards her.

His attorney grabs his arm, turns him, and walks him towards the door, whispering, "Don't be harassing her. They'll come down on you with a vengeance."

"Can't be much worse than it already is. The cops harass me all the time."

"Document it each time. I can get them to stop, but it takes details and stops you for no reason, it is harassment." He reaches out his hand. "It's been great serving you, and if anything, else comes up, let me know."

John shakes his hand. "Thanks." He heads to his truck.

***

Four miles out of town, John turns down a gravel road, and two miles later pulls into the parking lot at the Hideaway Bar. He takes a stool close to the door, letting his eyes adjust, and sees two customers and the bartender at the other end. He has a graying goatee and ponytail. They exchange glares, and John says, "Shot and a Budweiser."

"Draft or bottle?"

"Draft." John lays a twenty on the bar.

He ponders why he put up with her for so long. Her constant complaining would drive any man to drink. The bartender sets down the drinks and takes the twenty. John downs the shot. His throat burns and his guts churn. The desire to kick Keith in the nuts and take his adulthood races through his mind. His jaw tightens, but there's satisfaction in the thought.

Jeanie comes in, gives him a kiss on the cheek, and sits beside him. "Relax, it's finished. Time for a brand-new beginning."

John holds up two fingers as the bartender grudgingly moves towards the beer tap and pours more beer.

Jeanie rubs his arm. "How did it go?"

"It was wham-bam and over. Seven years flushed down the toilet."

The bartender takes money from the pile and leaves.

"I'd like to see asshole Larson pay for messing up my life."

"Has to feel good getting her out of your life."

"Yes, it does." John takes a sip of beer. "The problem now is when my mother finds out I gave ... they took custody rights away."

"You didn't tell her?"

"Didn't lie but swayed her into believing the lawyer had it handled."

"Your ex has made your son hate you. It's terrible, but there is little you can do. One must get on with life."

"According to what my dad knows or would tell me, Mom has had a lifetime feud with Paul Larson, Keith's dad. It was something that happened in high school she would never talk about. Dad doesn't have a clue, but when she found out Johnny was over there, she went berserk."

"You loved your son but sometimes letting it go until he wants to know who you are is the best thing." Jeanie downs her beer and holds up the empty glass. "Why don't you stay at my place tonight?" She rubs the top of his thigh. "I guarantee you'll be dragging into work, but you'll forget the troubles of yesteryear."

John's thoughts go to last Saturday and her sitting naked on his chest. "You definitely have the skills to make a guy forget." He points to his pile of money for the bartender. "The ex was so frigid. I wonder some days how she got pregnant."

"You don't have to worry. You'll be begging for mercy when I'm done with you."

John smiles. "I'm not dwelling on it, but ... Last winter she was doing the neighbor, no wonder she didn't want any. Makes my skin crawl."

"My ex cheated on me for over a year. It's over but I still hate him. You're free and ready for the ride of your life. We're going to celebrate. I forgot to ask about the job in Texas."

"They're sending the hiring paperwork. I should have it this week. When Mother realizes I'm planning on taking the job, more shit will hit the fan."

"So, you're going to go?"

John stares at the rows of whiskey bottles and the top of her face in the mirror. "Is there a reason to stay?" She closes her eyes. He sits there watching her in the mirror. A mumbling voice adds to the eerie silence. "You want to go?" Slowly he turns, with a smirky squint.

Her eyes are glistening, and the corner of her lips rises slightly. "Yeah, why not? Never seen Texas, and my life is a dead end living here."

She raises her beer. "To Texas." They clink glasses.

Sixty

October 1, 1984

Marilyn grips the door handle to keep from running.

Jarrod produces a persuasive smile, pulls flowers from behind his back. "Congratulations." His eyes examine her.

She mutters, "Thanks ..." His solid square jaw and erect stance make him appear like a modern-day duke, transformed from some fairy tale.

Beside her, Ann says, "Come in." She takes a bottle of champagne from his other hand. "Dinner is almost ready."

Jarrod slides his hand in the center of Marilyn's back, and they all walk into the dining room. "Tell me the truth, Miss Organized. Who were you expecting?"

Marilyn's face flushes. "With everything going on ... I hadn't thought about it ..." Her legs are wobbly. "It was nice of you to come."

Ann sets out champagne glasses, while Jeff pops the cork and pours everyone a glass. They toast and Ann says, "To a new life and a bright future." They all smile. Ann's eyes are glimmering. "Dinner will be ready about twenty minutes, including Jarrod's favorite, glazed carrots, and some mashed potatoes, of course." Ann smiles at Jarrod. "And Marilyn's slow-cook roast beef."

Marilyn grips the counter to keep from shaking.

Ann says, "I'm proud of you going after the top bachelor. No second-rate guys for my sister."

Marilyn is shaking her head. "I never—he's one of the owners. I can't go out with him."

"There's no can't. Jump—doesn't he make you wet?" She says through a smirk.

"Stop it." Marilyn slowly let out a breath. "I'm not ready."

Ann grabs her shoulders, scans the room, and shakes her at the same time. "Pay attention. This is your golden ticket. Ride it and suck him in."

Marilyn is still dazed, and what clue did she miss?

Ann grabs her chin. "If I weren't married to Jeff, I'd be dragging Jarrod somewhere for an appetizer, then after-dinner dessert sex he would never forget. Lose the nun ideology to get a man. It is 1984 show him, make him addicted, so he can't live without." She pauses. "I'll get you some of Jeff magazines so can update on the modern sex."

Marilyn forces a smile. "It's been an emotional day."

"I'm sorry." Ann hugs her. "That part of your life is history. Now focus on opportunities. He wants to help you relax and enjoy the evening. Your old life of wiping up stale spilled beer, smelling cow shit, with a night out for pizza and beer is history. Buried history. Now, the future—summer hangout on Lake Huron in his boat, swaying in the waves, snuggled up to his hairy chest, dinner at the private marina." She scans the wall. "For Johnny, the opportunities could be unlimited. Otherwise, what chance will he have to go to college? Now focus."

Marilyn takes a breath. *It's your dream world.*

"You're rubbing shoulders with the elite of the city. Get out of your beer-drinking lowlife rut." Ann gives her a hug. "It will work out. The inside scoop on Jarrod: He likes decisive people and hates beer."

***

Jeff sits at the head of the table. Ann is on one side with her girls. Marilyn on the other side between Jarrod and Johnny. Ann adds another toast before everyone digs in to eat.

Jarrod says, "This is delicious, girls."

Marilyn feels his leg touch her. She takes a bite of the beef, trying to ignore it, and whispers to herself, "It is tougher than ..." She looks at Johnny and over at Ann.

"Sis, forgot I should've told you to go to Daryl's meat market instead of the grocery store."

Johnny blurts out, "Mommy, this doesn't taste like Uncle Keith's."

Jarrod tilts his head towards Johnny and says, "Kid knows the finer cuts of meat already." He pats Marilyn's hand.

Marilyn blushes, trying to keep her chest from moving.

Jarrod leans close to her ear. "Guy impressed your son too?"

She looks across the table. "He was a good friend and—"

"Don't be embarrassed. Ann said the guy was hot for you—I understand why."

Marilyn's stomach becomes a knot. She studies everyone as they finish eating wondering what else they have planned.

The girls pick up the plates and set them on the counter.

Jarrod leans towards Johnny. "How do you like school?"

Johnny sits there, and Marilyn clears more dishes. "Johnny, it's not polite not to answer."

"I hate school."

Jarrod breaks into a broad grin. "I feel for you, kid. I hated school too."

The adults stay at the table, and the kids go off to their bedrooms.

Jarrod, rubbing his chin, says, "Has some anger built up inside him."

Marilyn glances at everyone. "It's been hard, and he misses his best friend, and now a boy at school has been bullying him."

Jarrod glances at Jeff and says, "Boys have to learn to get tough quick in the modern world. My dad would toughen me up. He'd grab me by the collar and take me to the closet, standing me in front of the belts. 'Pick one out.' If I didn't stand up for myself."

Jeff says, "Modern kids get away with everything nowadays, even if they're caught. Just go home to their mommy, and she feels sorry for them."

Ann pipes up. "Johnny is only five years old. Let's not send him off to delinquent school."

The men finish their drinks and filter into the family room. The TV comes on, making background noise with the added clank of dishes. Ann gives a synopsis profile of Jarrod. Adds details of his square shoulders and arm muscles and says, "What do you think?"

Marilyn stiffens. "About ..."

She flips her hands. "Jarrod, Mr. Right."

"He seems nice ... I'm not ready for a relationship."

Ann washes the last pan and says, "He is a sweet guy and wants a dedicated and caring woman. His eyes were shining tonight every time he looked at you."

"He wasn't checking out my intelligence."

"You're playing it perfectly, showing some cleavage differently to pique his attention. Add the cooking, and how organized you are. Keep building on it."

Marilyn dries the last pan. "I'm not—"

Ann pulls Marilyn's chin up. "The past. Bury it—elevate your head, soak those dark brown eyes into his and catch Mr. Right." She pours more champagne into their glasses. "Come on. Time for some schmoozing."

They join Jeff and Jarrod in the family room as they gossip about work. They're laughing and enjoying their drinks as Marilyn silently reflects on her day. She looks for a polite moment to leave.

Ann finishes her champagne and gets up.

Marilyn takes her half-glass and follows her to the kitchen. "Thanks for the enjoyable evening, but I need to get Johnny ready for bed."

Ann leans into her face. "You haven't said two words. What's going on? You look bored to death."

Marilyn says, "Been a long day. I'm not in a socializing mood." *I want a beer and a good cry.*

"You should've finished your champagne. It helps you relax. I hope the hell you're not still dreaming about your farmer boy?"

"Please, I need sleep."

"He hasn't called. He's moved on. No reason to sit and mope. Leave Johnny here and—"

"No—" Marilyn sets her glass on the counter. "I'm not socializing."

"It was awful what you lived through." She leans close to Marilyn. "The best way to put it behind you is to go after the wonderful opportunity. He won't be waiting six months or a year."

Yes, Mother. She goes to the bedroom.

When she comes out, with Johnny in hand, Jarrod is casually leaning against the kitchen cupboard, leftovers in one hand and the flowers in the other. Ann is standing behind them, satisfaction beaming from her face.

Jarrod says, "I'll walk you home."

Marilyn turns down the hallway to the apartment. Johnny pulls his hand out of Marilyn's and opens the door.

She raises her voice and says, "I will come read you a story in a few minutes. Remember, there is school tomorrow."

Johnny never acknowledges her and then scurries towards the bedroom.

Jarrod grins. "Little jealous, a man talking to his mother."

"I'm sure that is part of it. He's having a tough time adjusting. The kid bullying him, everyone says it's nothing, but it has me stressed." She puts the leftovers in the fridge, eyeing the beer, and moves to the living room towards the outside door.

"It has to be tough, no man in his life." Jarrod hesitates. "What does the kid like to play with? Airplanes, race cars, a tricycle?"

"He has his favorite tractor and a sandbox. He misses Chad, as they used to chase each other around."

"Don't worry, he'll adjust."

"He's shy around men. I'm surprised he talked at all." She rubs her hands together. "Don't have much to drink." *Too bad you don't like beer.*

Jarrod reaches for her hand and lowers his voice. "We'll help you settle. This is a pleasant neighborhood, and he'll meet other good kids."

She keeps standing by the door.

"You've impressed people at work." He winks at her. "You've made me look like a genius for putting in a word to hire you. Hope I didn't scare you with my surprise visit, just wanted to cheer you up. Part of your new life."

Marilyn pushes out a smile. "Thanks for coming." The chilled air hits her as she holds the door. Goosebumps are forming everywhere.

"You have all kinds of potential." He glances at her chest. "We'll keep this on the hush. No sense adding to the work gossip."

"Yes, of course, thank you. It was a lovely evening." She initiates a hug but keeps her head down to keep him from kissing her.

Jarrod releases his hold and says, "I'm going on a business trip this next weekend, but the following Sunday, set up Ann to babysit. We'll spend a nice relaxing Sunday afternoon, take a ride, view the fall colors, and have a cocktail. I know a special place that serves the best prime rib dinner."

I've been there. She doesn't glance up. His stare penetrates her bra. "It sounds great." Marilyn whispers, "Sorry, I'm still trying to process everything from today."

"It's understandable."

She closes the door, holding in the scream.

Sixty-One

October 3, 1984

The cows are fed for the evening. I sit down with my leftover soup and crack another beer. I clean up the table, grab another beer, and let Buddy outside. It's almost nine o'clock, and I finish another beer, staring at the stack of letters on the phone stand.

I dial the phone as my heart pounds. It goes to voicemail. "This is the Lang residence. We are glad you called. Leave your number and we will call you back."

"This is Keith, calling to congratulate Marilyn on her divorce. Hope she didn't party too much. The farm is in full harvest mode, although they're predicting rain tomorrow, which will give us a break from our twelve-hour work schedule. Tell Johnny I said hi, and if you want, I'll take you out to celebrate. No strings." *Miss you.* "Call me when you can. Talk to you soon."

Seems odd her sister is not home. I grab the letters and sit at the table. Maybe she'll call tonight or in the morning. I take a long drink as depression flows through my veins. I pull the letter out of the envelope again. The twenty-dollar check falls out with it.

September 2
Dear Keith,

> We are getting adjusted. Johnny hangs out with his cousins, Megan, who is seven, and Cheryl, who just turned five. They have a fenced-in backyard with a swing set. Jeff, my brother-in-law, is going to make them a playhouse of some kind next spring. There's plenty of room, but of course, Johnny wants to play in the woods beyond the fence. He's signed up for kindergarten and starts on Monday. His biggest worry is about recess time, and the yard is not big enough.
>
> John has been on his good behavior. As I planted the seed, I won't go after more support or alimony. All I want is for him to leave everyone alone. Laura said he has faded away, which I was

hoping he would do with me leaving. He is more worried about money than about getting revenge. A small accomplishment for the disruption I brought to everyone's life.

My days are spent in the morning getting Johnny on and off the bus. Ann gets home in the early afternoon and tucks him in each night. I'm out at eleven so get most of a good night's sleep. We have a door between the house and the garage made into an apartment. Ann leaves the door open and checks on him before she goes to bed. He still snuggles up to his teddy bear every night. He has regressed to carrying it or his tractor everywhere again. I keep sewing up the teddy bear and promise to get it back to you, although it is threadbare.

I'm getting adjusted to working in such fancy surroundings. Everyone pretends to have money, but it doesn't help their manners. I'm happy with the income, but Johnny and I miss everyone.

Your payment is not what I was hoping to send. Long story but Jeff insisted I pay rent, which is the right thing to do but not what we agreed on. Add my working on making a deal for no visitation and John paying less child support. My income is not what I budgeted, so the phone still has to wait. They're extra busy at the nightclub in November and December, and that increases my income. I promise to send more.

How is the farming going? Hope you find someone to help.

If you are still reading my rambling life, I want to tell you how truly sorry I am for my temper tantrum. All the trouble I caused you. And how I let you down when you needed someone to help. Getting my emotions calmed down. You were only trying to protect me, which you did from the day I met you, and you've never wavered. You never played the guilt card, although I feel like I deserve it. Everyone tells me it's not my fault, but I knew John and his evil was my fault for bringing it into your lives.

Johnny misses the farm, Buddy, and you the most. I'm deeply thankful for how much you cared for him and for everything else you added to my life. They all tell me how strong I am, but the secret is you gave me strength. I'm sorry for not telling you in person.

Thanks for everything. And hope to hear from you.

Marilyn XOXOXO

I neatly fold and stuff the letter in the envelope and stack it with the others on the table. I thumb through the rest of the unopened letters. It's going on two months. Which one is Dear John? I don't need to hear, you were a nice guy, and I love you like a brother. I down the beer. *She's working on her next hero. Get over it.* I'll cash the checks someday. "Enough wallowing." Buddy rubs up against me as I pet him and head off to bed.

The rain is coming down as I finish up the chores. I sit around and brood until about eleven. I grin at Buddy and say, "Let's go. Doesn't look like my girlfriend is calling. Let's go see your girlfriend and check on the parts for the chopper."

Buddy runs behind the parts counter, looks down the aisles, and runs back to me.

Phil laughs. "She has the day off and ran off with another guy."

"Story of our lives, right, Buddy?" I explain what is happening with the chopper. He digs around in the parts book, writes a list of everything we need, and figures out the cost.

Ken, the salesperson, says craftily, "Think how much extra beer you could've been drinking if you weren't working on the old equipment."

Phil looks up. "About five hundred dollars for the parts and a week plus to get them."

Ken's face lights up. "Sounds like you need that new forage chopper for tomorrow."

I glance at Phil. "I swear you guys are in cahoots." We head to Ken's office.

He knocks eight hundred dollars off the price, which is still not as much as if I could wait till winter, but they'll deliver it in the morning.

***

I pull into Mom's before going home, leaving Buddy in the garage. "Sorry, Bud, you can't track through Mom's house. She would kill me." I slip off my boots.

Mom gives me a hug. "I am glad we got rained out. Everyone needed a break."

I gaze across the room. "Expensive day off. I purchased a new chopper. I could hear Dad saying, 'Make them wait.' But we should've done it at the start of the season."

Mom turns from her cooking and says, "Dear, don't be like your dad and work yourself to death to save money. If the farm can't support us, we don't farm."

I freeze in an emotional trance.

"It has been a tough year, but we have overcome it." Mom takes my hand. "Not you all by yourself, but our family, our friends, and God will help us through. Whether you want to believe or not." Her eyes are watering. "I'm making shepherd's pie and will drop some off later."

I mutter, "They knocked eight-hundred dollars off. I'm sure they are motivated not to sit on it till next year. Tomorrow I'll go to the bank and have Dave give us a six-month note, and we'll pay it off when the next batch of cows goes out." I give her a hug.

She tilts her head. "I didn't think we would be harvesting corn tomorrow. I told Sis I would watch the baby. We're ready for a little mini-break."

"Yes, I agree, but it won't be too wet on the back forty. I'll start plowing."

I get back to the house, wipe Buddy's paws off, get my coveralls, and go feed the cows.

Light rain is coming down, making it miserable but the smell of Mom's warm food helps me forget the dampness in my bones. "Shit." The letter's lying in plain sight. I take the letters and put them in the drawer in my nightstand. One should throw it away. Quit sulking. Farming is almost done for the year. I can switch focus and find a new winter fling. I crack a beer, turn the oven off, and dish the food onto a plate.

Continuous mist and gray sky are raising the moisture in the corn and halt the harvest. It's after ten the next morning when I connect the plow. "Dad ... I'm not hungover." *It's a mirage.* Tears drip off my cheeks. "*Farm, be proud. It's what we are born to do.*" The diesel hum fills the air.

Sixty-Two

October 19, 1984

I've moved the tractor up two gears, running the same rpm, and it seems like we are flying compared to the old machine. The farming dilemma continues as we need another tractor driver or dump wagons that unload faster. We'll need to pile the silage quicker, which means a bigger tractor.

Mom is helping Sis with the new baby, adding to her schedule. The good news is Rob, my football buddy, found me someone who needs some extra cash for a few weeks—it fixed the crisis at the moment, and he's getting the hang of it. Nonstop harvesting can wear on any person, no matter who you are. I've woken up still in the recliner a few mornings. Next year, we need some management improvements.

George is feeding the cows tonight. I've finished my shower and knocked off early today, so I can get ready for the ten-year homecoming reunion. I came up with excuses not to go, but someone was always reminding me, adding guilt, and saying, "You can't let everyone down."

I am getting my suit on when Mother stops over to inspect.

Mom checks my suit fit and fusses with the lint roller and says, "How is Marilyn doing?"

A lump forms. "She's moved on."

Mom still hasn't looked at me. "Do you love her?"

"I'm not talking about it," I spit out. "We have to live with it."

She pulls the lapel of my jacket and turns my chin around, facing her. "Get off your ego trip and tell her."

Damn it, I'm not a six-year-old. "I called her, if you must know. She's never called back."

Mom waves me over to the blank wall for a picture, acting as if she had never heard me. She finishes the picture taking and stands quietly. "You loved the cheering, but it's time for a genuine loving relationship."

I suck in my grin. *It was the day.* The flashback of how everyone loved me, and the uncontrolled testosterone teenagers winning a football championship ten years ago, and it brings joy to my soul. *Well, not my soul.*

Mom's getting ready to leave. I say, "I haven't talked to or seen Sandy since I walked off the stage at graduation. Life moved on. You didn't make a big deal of that."

Mom brushes my jacket again. "Remember, you represent the Larson family, and we are proud of you." She opens the door to leave. "I love you."

Did she hear me? "I love you too, Mom." I bite my lip. Buddy sits watching me with his head cocked. "Yeah, I'm confused myself." I fire up the Vette and head to town. My heart is pounding. Ten years ago, I would have played and ridden myself of this guilt adrenaline. The breakup with Sandy stemmed from one of her jealous rages. I laugh it off. It was high school. I had a championship to win, and lots of girls wanted me. Yet that little thought creeps in. High school sweethearts growing old together? Does it happen in the modern world? The breakup was devastating, but the consoling from ... it was forgotten. Who has one girl for life? You move on.

I've been working so much, I haven't even gone uptown for a beer. I park the Vette at the school and am chauffeured to the parade's start point, and back to the school, just like some celebrity.

I go to the locker room, and the coach quiets everyone.

Coach takes a deep breath, and his two hundred and fifty pounds engulfs the room. "For any of you still learning history, this is Keith Larson. He is responsible for a lot of school records and trophies in his four years, but the biggest one, the state championship trophy, would've never happened without him. He had exceptional talent and a work ethic above anyone I have ever coached, making everyone better. The overused cliché, but he is why they say it. One of my greatest honors, not because of the trophies, is what he brings to everyone he knows." He looks at me with his steely eyes. "Keith Larson."

Everyone claps, with a few hoots.

I step closer, giving him a half hug, shaking his hand and whispering in his ear. "I feel old." Turning, I scan everyone's eyes. "I wrote down a few thoughts of great wisdom I could bestow on you. They're wadded up in the corner by the kitchen wastebasket and reminded me why I didn't play basketball." I pause and see the smiles. "The cliche is that team toughness makes you a winner. We glory hounds in the backfield loved that saying. We rode behind the linemen, the hottest girls wanted us, high-fives from everyone, sometimes we'd get a grass stain on our uniform, and bragged about how we were the greatest."

I walk in a line in front of them. "Red Right 34, my favorite play, Rob our right tackle cleaned out the biggest toughest guys, Neal the fullback popped anyone dumb enough to step into the hole that I was coming through and we took no prisoners. The bodies brushed against me, grabbing in desperation as I waltzed into the end zone. Ten years later, I miss the adrenaline rush, but regrets linger for not thanking from my heart the guys who made it happen." I choke up. "They're the ones who make it."

They are all quiet.

"Enough about me. There's a drifting rumor that you are the underdogs today. I want you to ask your heart, do you have enough want, discipline to prove they don't know shit?" I stop talking, staring at each one by one. "Don't leave the field with regrets or blame. The lie you tell your girlfriend to make her believe you are the coolest guy doesn't matter. Don't lie to your teammates, prove to your teammates that you left it all out there."

Curtis stands and stares at me. "I want to add a confession to my fellow teammates." He scans the room. "I had the privilege of working with Keith this past summer." He swallows. "Everyone knows how humble I am."

Smirks filter through the air.

"To save you from embarrassment, don't challenge him. He humbled my ass." His voice trembles. "One day I'm bragging about my skills and explaining to Keith that if I had teammates like his, we would be winning our division. Keith ripped into me a tirade of my lack of respect." He bites his lip as he scans the room. "Blaming my teammates, my best friends, who put up with my ass, makes me lower than dog shit." The locker room is deathly silent. "You guys are the best teammates I could ever have, and I'm proud you let me play with you and promise I will do my best and you'd better be kicking my ass." He sits down. I can see tears running down his cheeks.

They all stand up and clap.

I motion everyone to sit down. "One last little thought. I have trophies of world greatness, but true greatness is earning the respect of your teammates. If you live by it, you'll win by it."

They are clapping and cheering for me as I walk out. The coach follows me and says, "Thanks for coming by. The modern kids and teamwork sometimes make me think I've lost my touch to motivate them."

"There're kids struggling along. Hope what I said helps."

"Curtis had a new attitude this year. Now I know why." Coach pats me on the back. "Thanks for coming. Go have fun. Hope we can win one for you."

"You can tell them. I didn't come to see them lose."

***

I rode with the assistant coach over to the parade cars. Sandy is sitting on the backseat deck with a blanket wrapped around her. Her face glows the same as in high school.

I take off my black dress shoes and step into the sixty-four Bonneville convertible and sit beside her.

Sandy grabs my hands and gives me a light kiss on the cheek. "You look debonair."

"I'm impressed you added French to your seduction."

The blanket falls off her shoulders.

The dark blue, silky, low-cut dress displays above it a pearl necklace that drifts into her auburn hair, a twinge of ... The body's desires ... "Definitely a glimpse of gorgeous, but I should check details. We have a few minutes, so we could slip down the alley."

"I fell for that line." She leans close to my ear. "I loved it."

I break out a grin. "Trying to keep half of the world happy."

Sandy turns her parade face on and is ready to woo the crowds when we start down Main Street. She says, "We were the center of the rumors. You haven't told me who the secret girlfriend is?"

"I thought I was still looking?"

She is waving to the crowd. "My source says you quit chasing women."

"It's been a ten-year party. Is it supposed to end? Had some setbacks at the farm this year, now this fall rain and—"

"Sorry to hear about your dad—stunned me. I called my dad and had a long-overdue heart-to-heart conversation with him the next day." Holding her movie star face, she says, "I should've come and ..."

"It was all a blur. See your family sent flowers, thanks, but it's brought new life changes. Then those deep regrets in life, as we'd argue daily, who worked the hardest. It's what killed him." I let breath flow through my lips and put my parade face on. "So, what's your story?"

"I partied the first year of college, wild and free in the big city." She is turning her head towards me with her evil grin. "The streaks of blonde moments carried over to college. Gary was the first guy I met who didn't try to take me to bed on the first date. We actually talked, and I wouldn't have gotten through college without him." It gets quiet, and she is staring at me. "You were a stand-up guy. They're glorious memories."

I glance at Sandy. "They're better than the trophies," I grin, and ... stand holding her hand.

She stares at me. "You're off the subject. Trying to be ahead of the latest scoop of the *Banner*. Football hero hangs up his spikes and gets attached."

"You have to be glad you didn't wait." We turn into the football stadium.

She keeps her painted-on smile while looking at the crowd and says, "I still wonder, but Gary and I are very happy."

"I owe you a sincere apology ..."

"We were kids." She squeezes my hand. "We were the king and queen in 1974." She turns towards me. "Our secret life."

I wink. "Our secret, but it is time for me to get serious in life."

"All the girls still dream about you." We turn down the side street towards the field.

She reaches up and kisses me on the cheek. "It's a great memory, and on with the rest of our lives."

I grab her tight and kiss her on the lips. "Yes, it is."

Her eyes are glowing. "Behave."

"Always." I see the driver watching us in the mirror.

***

I sit with Rob, Jason, and others from the team. We study the first half, dissecting every play as if we were playing. I drift off into my world, feeling the adrenaline, knowing the hole is going to open, hitting the last guy at full speed on the way to the end zone. I leave them planning the second half strategy and meet Sandy. We made our presentation at the fifty-yard line to the new king and queen.

They win the game by a touchdown, and the coach looks up and points at me in the stands on his way out. The bar is packed with people from the football game. We reminisce about history as the band plays, and we swap out our greatness with people we haven't seen in years. I keep having thoughts of Marilyn, wishing ...

We party into the night, a slow song from the past. Sandy asks me to dance, pulls me tight, spurring the memories. I can't remember the dance steps.

She says, "You'll make some girl a great husband."

"Farming has replaced a wife. I feel guilty not working tonight."

We walk off the dance floor. "You are different in there." She pats my chest. "Someone has your heart."

I suck down the lump in my throat. "Don't be spreading that around. I have one."

"We were young, but it is in there, and you could find it if you weren't still scared to death."

I circle the bar, having mini conversations, stopping to say hi to Laura.

She says, "Thought you became a monk?"

"Cows are the love of my life. I spend every waking hour making sure they have food to eat. It doesn't give me time for conversation."

"Jason said you are working yourself to death."

"Spent over twenty grand on a new cutter. Took all my beer money."

She motions me close. "The bar gossip is that John left town after the divorce. Rumor has it he moved to Texas."

I stand in silence, holding my beer.

"She misses you."

"Who?"

Laura loses her smile and grabs my arm. "Quit being an ass and call her. I don't know if she knows."

"I've left messages." My focus is on the bottles of whiskey behind her on the counter. "Called and congratulated her on the divorce. Would've invited her to homecoming. She's never called back." I suck in my anger. "One assumes she had had enough and moved on." I walk away.

Sixty-Three

December 22, 1984

Marilyn walks Johnny over to meet Ann and the girls, after dealing with another of Johnny's mini tantrums. Christmas shopping today. "It's tradition," Ann says. Marilyn disagrees but concedes.

Marilyn kneels in front of Johnny and zips his coat. She waits for him to look at her and says, "Behave." She stands and whispers, "Good luck," to Ann.

Ann smiles and winks. "Come on, Johnny, let's go have fun."

Marilyn waves goodbye, overwhelming the silent anxiety as she closes the door. She flips open her mini phone book and dials the phone. Each ring compounds fear. *What will I say? What if someone else answers?* After ten rings, she hangs up, wipes her tears, and calls Laura.

Marilyn wants to pour out her heart, but it's long-distance, so she keeps it short. After saying the hellos, she says, "I promised Johnny I would try to set something up with Chad so they could get together and—"

Laura says, "Great, come over early Sunday? Keith is taking the kids snowmobiling in the afternoon. You know Johnny would love it, and we can celebrate New Year's Eve."

"I have to work."

"Okay, I'll come pick Johnny up, and you pick him up on Monday. You want to see Keith too, right?" The phone is silent. "Sounds like a yes. We'll go on Monday."

Marilyn holds back a sobbing fit. "I did try to call him."

"On Monday, you're coming over and we're going to get this shit worked out. No more wiffle-waffling. Do you have to work Monday night?"

"No, not till Wednesday."

"That's great. You can sleep on the couch ..." She giggles. "Or share Keith's warm comfy waterbed."

Marilyn bites her lip, but a smile creeps out. "Stop it. Everyone's trying to run my life."

"I'm telling you how to fix your life. Living on a farm isn't a glitter life, of fancy dress and gorgeous guys drooling over us at exotic parties, the

Barbie-doll dream world. But a simple life with someone you love is not settling."

Marilyn lets out a breath. "Mine is never that simple."

"You need to go find out. Check it off. You had the best in town, pack it in your memory. And quit this 'I call and he called' shit."

"Laura, he's never called."

"Seriously. Said he did, he wasn't joking."

Silence before she answers. "I'm afraid it would make it worse."

"For Johnny or you?"

She examines the wall as if the answers are written somewhere.

"You still there?"

"For both of us." The vibes filter through the phone.

Laura says, "Merry Christmas. I'll pick Johnny up on Sunday about nine."

Ann never mentioned he called.

***

Marilyn wraps Jarrod's tie. Ann helped pick it out last week. It seems generic and expensive. *Of course, how would I know? Never knew anyone who wore a tie.* Ann claims, "He'll love it." The least she can do for Jarrod. He has been a gentleman, taking her to a fancy dinner, and the theater. *The good night kiss was ...*

She keeps apologizing to Jarrod for Johnny not interacting with him. The secret of her past and the nightmares that still haunt her on occasion. He has improved her life. Everyone says it just takes time for kids to adjust, but it's awkward. Johnny rejection makes Jarrod squirm and doesn't know how to handle it. She wants to tell him about her scary past and the ugliness of it all, but ... It's a secret she wants to bury. She's declined the subtle invitation to see his house. Fear overwhelms the next step.

***

The weeks of working at parties, sometimes two a day during December, are over. Management closes the banquet and restaurant, leaving only the bar open until after Christmas. A weekend off comes with the employee

Christmas party on Friday night across town and then getting ready for Christmas on Monday. The lack of a paycheck is offset by her four-hundred-dollar bonus for only working three months, which was more than she expected. Marilyn gives up fighting with Ann about driving her and picking her up.

Marilyn says, "I'm not a teenager and I'm not drinking."

Ann replies, "You need to go and enjoy yourself."

Marilyn lets out a long breath. "It will be work the whole night." She puts on the jade green puff shoulder blouse and the necklace Ann loaned her. Although no cleavage is showing, it seems provocative. The Christmas party glitter is taking its toll. She wants it to be over. And a traditional Christmas with a few friends watching the kids play.

***

Ann is excited as she pulls up in front of the restaurant. "See you at eleven."

Marilyn reaches for the handle but turns before sliding out. "Did Keith call me?"

Ann jerks but says calmly, "He called to congratulate you on your divorce." She flips the back of her hand. "Sorry, I forgot all about it. It didn't seem like much. He didn't say to call. Just wished you well. I should've written it down."

"I'll be ready at ten." She shuts the door and heads into the party.

Some of her work comrades are sitting together and evaluating how ... they could go home with Jarrod. Interesting each adding comments about things they would do if they got him alone. *I'm naïve.* He dances with different girls, each flirting for his attention.

I don't want to be Cinderella.

Jarrod dances with a few girls and walks by others to Marilyn's table. He holds out his hand and says, "Would you like to dance?"

Marilyn's lips are stuck together. The girl beside her kicks her under the table. She pushes her chair back, observing eight spiteful eyes staring at her.

He holds out his hand and leads her to the dance floor. He rests his hand softly on her back and takes the other one in hers. "Wanted it to appear everyone has a chance."

He moves smoothly as Marilyn tries to follow the easy flow, and she says, "They definitely believe they have a chance."

Jarrod looks down at her with a smirk. "You won the lottery before it started."

He pulls her a little tighter and whispers directly in her ear, "Your unaware innocence is part of your uniqueness."

The anguish is attacking her, but she says, "Ann keeps telling me to get with the modern lifestyle." *There must be something wrong with me not wanting the hottest man here.*

He looks down at her as the song ends. "Ann said you needed a ride home. Thinking of leaving about eleven."

Marilyn stops in the middle of the dance floor. *He's taking me to his house for the night.* "I'm ... I can't ... Ann is—"

"Ann ... didn't tell you I was taking you home?"

She catches her breath. "No."

Jarrod keeps his arm around her and says, "Ann assumed you would be more relaxed not worrying about driving home."

"She is always trying to be thoughtful." *Sis set me up.*

"I've known her and Jeff for a long time. She is just looking out for you. I'll keep an eye out when you leave, but if you leave before me, the Cadillac is in the reserved spot, unlocked, and the key is in the sun visor. Get it warmed up." He winks at her. "I still have work issues to check on yet. Later."

One of the bartenders she has seen at work introduces himself. The conversation is small talk, she hopes. Everything is becoming more of a blur. She walks outside at ten, standing at the entrance. *Ann, you forgot, I said ten.* She realizes she doesn't have a coat and goes back in.

It's almost eleven when she looks around for Jarrod, retrieves her coat, and goes to the car, just like she has been told. The Cadillac is running as she tentatively opens the passenger door.

Jarrod's grin is plastered on his face. "It's not right for the hottest girl at the party to get in a lonely, cold car." Marilyn closes her eyes for a moment and slides in on the warm leather seat. He pats the top of her hand. "Relax, it's early, we can enjoy the rest of the evening."

"Sorry, I was planning on going home." She glances but stares out the window.

"Something I said?"

"No." She tries to say calmly, "So, what is the rest of the plan that I wasn't told about?"

His mouth opens. He glances quickly. "No, it's ... we, I believe you could use a night to relax and enjoy yourself. I wanted it to be a regular date but feared the scuttlebutt would dominate the party. You're not the kind of person to take advantage of my position, but the optics of it ... You've been lucky to avoid it."

And according to your status, everyone wants to sleep with you.

The ride seems forever, and Jarrod spends time apologizing. She sits with her arms folded across her chest. He puts the car in park and quickly reaches over and takes her hand. "I'm honestly sorry for the misunderstanding."

She turns slowly towards him. "It was very unexpected, and I haven't worked out my fragile emotions from my divorce. I feel manipulated."

He squeezes her hand gently and says softly, "I wouldn't play games with you." He raises his tone of his voice. "I would hope you'd think more of me than that."

"I'm sorry, I didn't mean ..." Marilyn glares out the windshield. "My emotions are not ready for a relationship." She slows down her breathing. "Thank you for my generous bonus, which I assume you had some input on. It was way more than—"

"I make the checks out myself. No one else knows."

Marilyn's face becomes flushed. *It was four hundred dollars extra.* "Thank you. It was extremely generous."

"You're special to me, and I want you to believe it without any doubt left in your heart."

Marilyn's eyes concentrate on him longer than she ever has, but she opens the door.

He meets her in front of the car and wraps his arm around her waist, and they walk to her apartment. He faces her, pulls her intimately to him, and rubs tight against her.

Marilyn can feel ... *It doesn't seem right, but Ann picked guys better than me.*

"You have a special air of sweetness that is part of you. Hope you believe me. There was no manipulation. Ann was thinking you need a party to calm your stress, and I volunteered to bring you home. It wasn't a thought-out plan."

"I'm sorry. You could've taken other girls home tonight and had a fun night."

He raises her chin and kisses her.

She holds it a little longer than the previous ones before pulling away.

"My plan was for you to have an enjoyable evening."

Her voice sounds hollow. "And it was enjoyable." *It feels wrong.*

He stares at her and pulls her tight to him again.

She puts her fingers on his lips. "You have been wonderful to me. I am sorry—"

"Giving me the sign-off?"

"No, please, it's ... it's moving too fast. I'm still dealing with my issues, and it's no fault of yours. I have to prove to myself my self-worth."

"You're beautiful." He releases his tight hold and looks down at her. "I like your confidence." A grin beams through the dark. "Am I still invited to Christmas?"

She smiles. "Yes, you have been extremely patient, and I appreciate your caring for me." She unlocks the door. "Thanks for the ride home."

He reaches for her arm and kisses her.

"Good night."

He stands dazed and says, "Good night."

She walks into the house. Closing the door behind her, she locks it and waits for his car to leave.

A dim streak of light shines through the half-open bathroom door, and she makes her way to the bedroom. Shaking still, she strips off her clothes in the dark, throws them on the floor, and digs out her favorite sweatshirt and sweatpants. She goes to the kitchen, pours herself a beer, and sits at the table in the dark. *Hunger was in his brownish eyes. I felt him when he pulled me close ... I didn't panic, but ...* Cold and loneliness seep in. She gets a blanket and another beer.

Sixty-Four

December 25, 1984

Marilyn is drinking her coffee, wondering why Johnny isn't up and excited about opening his presents, at least, the few she could afford. She feels lonely but calm about a more normal Christmas morning. Keith and her last words sneak into her thoughts. Why hadn't he ever called?

He found someone else.

Johnny slowly walks out of the bedroom, and he slides onto her lap. He hugs her as they hold each other. "Merry Christmas."

She shakes the sadness and finally says, "Let's see what Santa brought you and have hot chocolate."

She has cleaned out a small corner in the bedroom, so Johnny has a place to play with his new Lincoln Logs. She hates it, but it's what he asked for. The memory of Keith scattered all over the living room will haunt her every day.

She opens the gift Johnny made in school. It was a picture of a house with a barn. In the front he has drawn them holding hands with Keith. The resemblance is heart-stopping. She finally stutters out, "It is perfect." She gives him a hug. "Do you want Mommy to find someone to be your dad?"

"I want Uncle Keith to be my dad."

"Relationships don't always work out the way we want them to."

"You said—We should've never moved away."

Her body wants to go into panic mode and run. *Why can't he let it go?*

She puts on a cheerful face as they make their way to Christmas dinner and somehow she becomes the door greeter. Cheerfully, she opens the door for Jarrod, dressed in his designer shirt, with a smile to match. Marilyn returns a kiss on the cheek, and his hug seems caring today. Mom is giddy when they introduce her to Jarrod and asks every question about him when they are in the kitchen getting food ready. Ann fills her in on a detailed history.

How does one become so perfect?

They are almost ready for everyone to eat. Mom slides close to Marilyn and whispers, "Sorry for not believing you could find Mr. Right. Jarrod is a real hunk. Ann says he's going places in the world."

"Mom, we are not in a serious relationship. He's a friend of Jeff's. We've had a couple of friendly dates. He's one of the bosses, being nice and helping me."

"He was eyeing you as more than a friend. Don't let him slip away."

They finish Christmas dinner, rinse the dishes, and go to open presents. Jarrod bought Johnny a space rocket and Marilyn a set of crystal glasses. Ann bought Marilyn silk pajamas with a matching housecoat. *They don't seem very practical.*

Jeff opened a second bottle of champagne to drink with their dessert.

Mom and Herb are saying goodbyes, but Herb wants to extend the hug and whispers, "You found yourself a hunk, girl."

Marilyn drags away from his hold. "Good night." *I can't imagine what your stories about me were.*

They clean up the dessert dishes. Marilyn says to Ann, "You shouldn't spend that much money on Johnny and me."

She cocks her head. "You need something to perk you up."

"You promised you wouldn't ..."

"I know, but the transition needs to be worked into your heart."

Marilyn puts her coat on and walks Jarrod out to his car. "Thank you for the gift. I had a nice day. Hope my mother or Herb didn't annoy you too much."

"They're just parents, wanting to make their kids look good. Mine are on a cruise, then staying in a condo in Florida and won't be back till spring, so you won't hear the stories they embarrass me with." He kisses her good night. "I enjoy families getting together. Take care, see you later."

Marilyn relaxes. The day went better than she had feared. *Glad he didn't walk me to the apartment and want to talk more.*

***

Marilyn helps with the last of the cleanup and rounds up Johnny.

Ann, calm as can be, says, "Put Johnny to bed, get your pajamas on, and return at eight for a nightcap. It's the Lang's nightcap tradition."

"I don't—"

"Stop—wear your new pajamas." She gives her a hug. "See you at eight."

Marilyn gets Johnny ready for bed, puts on her new pajamas, and tucks him into bed.

Johnny says, "Your pajamas are slippery."

"Yes, your Aunt Ann always buys fancy stuff. Did you have a nice Christmas?"

Keith's teddy bear is held tight to him. "I can't wait to go see Uncle Keith and ride on the snowmobile."

She brushes his hair. "Did you like your presents?"

"Yes, Aunt Ann wants me to show off my new pajamas. I'll be gone for a bit. Tomorrow you can play with your toys." She gives Johnny a kiss on the forehead and wants to have a quiet beer, but the buzz from the champagne has calmed her. *Ann, can't we just end the day?* She washes her makeup off. *Wonder who Ann thinks I'm going to impress?*

She knocks and walks in, hearing Ann yell from the other room. "Come in." She meets her in the kitchen wearing her new pajamas and housecoat. Instantly, she is glad she left her bra on. Ann grabs the chilled bottle of champagne and pours some into the empty glasses.

Jarrod and Jeff are sitting in the loungers with big grins.

"Jarrod—"

They pick up their glasses and say, "Merry Christmas Evening."

Marilyn is shaking so badly she almost drops her glass.

Jarrod has also swapped his clothes for tan silk pajamas, which seem a little revealing. He examines Marilyn. "You look silky sweet after the long day you've had."

Ann says, "You needed the little extra to cheer you up."

Marilyn plops onto the couch, afraid her legs will collapse if she tries to run.

They're joking about Herb and laughing about the day as Marilyn keeps her fake smile. She wanders in her thoughts. *This needs beer.* She takes a sip, knowing she can't leave until she is finished but can't get done too quickly or she'll keep pouring more.

Jeff gets bourbon and fills both of their glasses as Ann tops off hers and pours more in Marilyn's.

Jarrod is staring, giving her childhood flashbacks of Herb. *Did they expect me—why my sister didn't tell me? I was set up again.*

Ann raises her glass in a toast as she waits for Marilyn. "To family."

"Cheers."

Ann looks at Jarrod with a smirk. "And Jarrod has one more surprise."

Jarrod gets up and kneels on one knee in front of Marilyn. He slides a narrow, long box and hands it to her. "Merry Christmas."

"You bought me something already." Marilyn shudders and glares at Ann.

He says, "Something for bonding friends."

Her hands are shaking as everyone watches her unwrap it and open the box. It's a necklace, a heart surrounded by diamonds. "It is beautiful." Her eyes fill with water. "But I can't accept this."

"Jarrod, it is beautiful," Ann says and turns to Marilyn. "Stand up, let me help you put it on."

Jarrod is smiling as Marilyn tries to hold in her screams.

Ann nods towards Jeff. "You should talk to your best friend to see if he remembers how to make a woman feel good."

Jeff says, "You're getting a special gift—don't you worry."

Ann lifts her head. "I expected something sparkly."

A car rumbles past the house. Jeff says, "The neighbors are out racing again. You'd think they could at least take Christmas off."

She is still listening. "And how sparkly is it?" She holds Marilyn's hands. "You're allowed to be happy."

Jarrod moves close to her, and Marilyn whispers, "Thank you."

He pulls her tight and rubs—the silk. She's gasping without looking up at him. "You really shouldn't ..."

Jarrod straightens his shoulders. "It's time to feel good about life, and I'm here to make that possible. Add to that, you need somewhere to wear the necklace. Tomorrow we will have a catered lobster dinner, and next week I've secured tickets to the opera in Chicago."

Marilyn keeps her head up, glances at Ann, and says, "This is so overwhelming—I can't ..." She keeps staring at the curtain rods.

Jarrod reaches for Marilyn's hand to help pull her up and walks towards the door. "Merry Christmas." He kisses her. "Enough emotion for one day. I have some work to do tomorrow morning, but we'll spend the evening at my place." He scoots out the door.

Ann is beaming as she walks Marilyn to her apartment door. "Glad you had a great Christmas." She puts her finger on Marilyn's lips. "Don't talk. You are glowing with happiness."

***

She closes the door, wanting to drown her thoughts. She is beyond holding herself together. She takes the necklace off and throws it on the table. Streams are running down her cheeks, but she doesn't even wipe them off. *Doesn't anyone listen to me?* She buries her head in the pillow and cries herself to sleep.

Sixty-Five

December 25, 1984

The cold air nips my face as I walk towards the tool shed. Another winter day, dealing with the hassle of frozen silage. Mom has guilted me into taking her to church. *Dad's job.* At least not as bad as Sis, who has the hassle of getting a baby and a three-year-old up and dressed for church. It seems like more aggravation than it's worth. Mom is gleaming with pride as we take our seats. At least we're in the back half of the church.

I live through the sermon of what I should do for my wife and kids. Anxiety controls the moment, and I have no idea of the point. *I was good according to the rules. Well, most of the time. What did that get me?* The busybodies check off another year. Still not attached. Karla, with a new hairstyle and boyfriend. We exchange pleasantries.

We shake hands. "I'll put you on the list for backup farm help."

Karla gives me a hug and a kiss on the cheek. "Thank you."

The eye contact between Mom and her other friends the gloating if she does such a thing. *It's once a year and small thing to do for her.* We make our way home with the normal small talk until she asks, "What's Marilyn doing for Christmas?"

I suck in my emotions. "I'm not sure."

"I bought Johnny a Christmas gift."

So did I. "My guess? They're having a family get-together, and I wasn't invited."

She sits with her arms crossed the rest of the way home. I pull into the driveway, but she doesn't move.

She turns towards me. "For ten years, I have never pried into your personal life. I want you to call her and invite her over. If she can't come today, which I understand at the last minute, have her come Sunday. I will fix a family dinner."

"Mom—"

"You either promise to call and talk to her or give me her number—and I'll invite her and Johnny to dinner without you. They lived through a lot, and Johnny needs someone besides his mom for Christmas."

I can feel the veins in my neck. "I'll call her, but don't expect her to be waltzing over here. Feels like she has a new boyfriend, if you insist on knowing."

She closes the door; I watch her walk into the house. I put the truck in reverse, creep down the driveway, and pull up to my house across the road. I sit in a comatose thought, slam the door, and stomp into the house, ripping off my church clothes. Done with guilt for another year.

I reread the card from Marilyn.

Dear Keith,

We are having a small Christmas dinner with my sister and her family. Mom and Herb are coming over. It will be good to see her. We don't get together much, as you know. I'm not sure how to ask, and there's no right way.

We are planning a birthday party for Johnny on January thirteenth, and he wants you to come. My fault for putting you in this predicament. My apology should have been more than writing a letter. And here I am, asking you to bail me out one more time. If you have moved on, I understand. I'm only asking because of Johnny. Jason and Laura are bringing Chad. I promise you don't have to talk to me or explain anything. This is for Johnny, and I hope it helps him adjust. He misses you. We will be sending an invitation but wanted to send advance warning.

Hope you have a nice Christmas, and I want to wish you, your mom, and your family a very Merry Christmas.

Love, Marilyn & Johnny XOXOXO

Might as well get this over with. My hand is shaking, punching in the number.

"Merry Christmas, the Lang residence," Ann says. Her joy bounces through the phone.

"Merry Christmas to everyone there, too. This is Keith Larson."

She lets out a long breath, and in a low-pitched voice says slowly, "It's nice to hear from you."

I can feel my heart pounding. "Called to wish Johnny and Marilyn a Merry Christmas. I assume she hasn't got her own phone yet."

"No, Miss Thrifty always trying to save money, although she is doing very well with her new job."

"That is good to hear. I'll hold if you want to get her."

"I know how much you cared about her, but ... well ... she really is grateful for all you have done for her. And we can't thank you enough for having my sister happy again. I'll let her know you called, but she wants to put the past behind her."

"Tell her she can call collect."

"Keith, it's not the money." She is silent. "Why ... she hasn't called. How do I say—"

"She found someone?"

"Well, nothing official, but Jarrod is a long-time friend of my husband, has taken a real liking to her. Marilyn is cheerful and enjoys life again. He's a hard worker and has some great business ventures developing."

I squeeze the phone. My knuckles are hurting.

"She is always saying how you took care of her like a big brother." She pauses. "We are extremely thankful for what you done and hope you have a nice Christmas. I'll pass on that you called."

"Thanks." I wait until she hangs up before I slam the receiver. I sit staring at her card, still lying on the table. *Why was I waiting? A brother.* I reread the Christmas card and put it with the other unopened envelopes. *Which one is a lie?*

I pick up the presents for the family and head to Mom's for our Christmas dinner. Johnny's present stares at me. Should've just driven over and dropped it off. I already filled out the tag. From Santa.

I hug Mom when I walk in the door.

She whispers, "Did you call?"

I nod my head. "Yeah, talked to her sister—" My niece, Brittany, comes running up to me. I pick her up and give her a big hug. "What did Santa get you for Christmas?"

"I got a teacup set with dishes and my own table and chairs."

"You've been extra good this year—getting all of that stuff."

Sis rolls her eyes.

"Chad is coming over on Saturday. We're going to ride on the snowmobile, have hot chocolate—"

She turns around in my arms. "Mommy, can I go?"

I'm grinning.

She is shaking her head. "We'll work something out."

Christmas dinner ends as we try not to think about Dad, but we left his chair empty. Dave and I walk to the living room and have a sensible conversation as we wait to open presents. Mom's rule is no drinking on Christmas, and Dad let such a rule become a tradition.

Brittany keeps wondering what she could have in such a small box. Her tricycle is in the bedroom. We have a great time teasing her. My mind lapses. Kids make this moment and take some of the empty feeling away. I've never had such a thought. Brittany opens her gift and tries to ride the bike in the house.

I hug everyone goodbye and leave to do chores. *Sometimes it works in your favor.*

I hang the new flannel shirt Mom got me and pace around the house. I open the cupboard and stare at the whiskey. "My house, my rules. Mom won't know." Buddy's pathetic eyes are observing me. "Quit it. You're going to tell? Nothing more I can do."

I stop at Johnny's present and read the tag. *To Johnny. From Santa.*

"Bud, let's go for a ride." He wags his tail and goes to the door.

Sixty-Six

December 26, 1984

Johnny is playing in his room when Marilyn wakes up feeling the effects of the champagne. Processing the Christmas emotions overtaking her, she opens the velvet box and neatly hooks the necklace. The diamonds sparkle even in the dim light from the stove. She drifts. *What's life without worrying about money?*

Johnny is standing beside her and says, "Can I open my other present now?"

"What present?"

He runs to the tree and brings his present over. "Uncle Keith brought it last night. Said Santa left it at his house. He made me promise to wait for you before I opened it."

She sits stunned. "Why didn't you come and get me?"

"He said you might be mad."

Johnny opens a John Deere tractor and is bouncing with excitement waiting for Marilyn to get the ties off and remove it from the box. Marilyn says, "It's just like the other one."

"Mom, this is a 4640." He runs and gets the old one. "This one is a 4020." He explains every unique detail about them.

She is glowing inside herself. "You are really smart."

Marilyn finishes her coffee and gets dressed. "Johnny, I have to make a phone call."

"Okay, Mom."

She heads over to Ann's, and hopefully with some luck she'll be sleeping off her hangover.

Ann is sitting at the bar counter reading the newspaper, tipping it down, exposing her puffy eyes. "Good morning. You're looking happy today."

Marilyn stops, takes a breath, and says, "Ann, how many times did Keith call?"

Ann loses her smile. "Why are you back on that subject? I told you—"

"Did you lead Keith to believe I found someone?"

"I told him you were doing well." She rolls her lips. "And adjusting to your new life." The red lines brighten in her eyes. "Johnny could've spent the night, and you could've—"

"Given Jarrod some sex so everyone would be happy. Right?"

"It's not just sex—he really—"

"Loves me—did you know Keith was here last night? We could've invited him over for our pajama party. The noise was Keith's truck. He made a Santa delivery of a toy tractor to Johnny, made sure my kid had a Merry Christmas."

Ann pulls her head back. "You're feeling guilty because he bought Johnny a present?"

She freezes her glare. "There is some strange reason Keith believes I have a serious relationship, so he didn't stay. Wonder where he got that idea?"

"Well, if he really loves you and is so tough, as you say, he wouldn't let what I said stop him from seeing you."

"Well, I'll ask him." Marilyn takes some long breaths. "Either way, I'm calling Jarrod and giving the necklace back."

"Marilyn, you can't!" Ann shrieks. "You could screw up your life, and what about Johnny's life?"

"I'm thinking about Johnny. And the next time I screw a guy, it's because I believe we have a chance for a bonding, loving relationship, not to improve my social status."

"Calm down. It's not what it looks like. Jarrod loves you. Why do think he gave you the necklace?"

"How many times?"

Ann sits with her mouth open.

"Excuse me, I need to make a call." Marilyn opens her address book and dials Jarrod's private office number.

"This is Jarrod Raymond."

"Jarrod, this is Marilyn. Sorry for calling you at work."

"Is everything okay? You sound stressed."

"A little, but I need to cancel our dinner tonight."

"You are standing me up?"

"It's something important—it can't wait."

"I can't think there could be anything more important than a nice quiet dinner."

Who are you showing off to?

Ann's cobra eyes are glaring at her.

Marilyn takes a deep breath and says, "I wanted to tell you in person, but I'm returning the necklace. It was a gracious gesture, but I can't accept such an expensive gift. Maybe we could meet later in the week before I go to work, and I'll explain what I'm feeling."

"There's another guy?"

"I'm not ready—for a relationship till I—"

"You've been two-timing me?"

"No, Jarrod, I'm working on some personal issues—"

Click.

Ann grabs her by the shoulders. "What is the matter with you? Do you realize what you're doing? What you're giving up?"

"You mean my trip to Chicago, strutting with diamonds, drinking fancy wine, and screwing him all night, and the morning hangover of an expensive whore."

"So, you think I screw Jeff because I owe him?"

"I don't know and don't care." She moves away and dials Keith, but there is no answer. She hangs up and flips to the next page of the address book.

Ann is glaring and says, "No wonder you ended up with such a lowlife as John. You don't recognize a great guy when you finally meet one."

Marilyn dials Jason's house.

"Hello."

"Hi, Jason, sorry I'm calling so early. Is Laura up?"

"Yes, it's almost ten. We're drinking coffee and talking about how to fix our families."

Marilyn glares at Ann and says, "Hope you're doing a better job than me."

"Hold on." The phone goes silent.

Laura says, "Good morning, and how was your Christmas?"

"Depends on who you ask. Will you watch Johnny today? Also, we may need a place to sleep tonight, if that's okay?"

"Yeah, of course. What the hell is going on?"

"I just tried to call Keith, but there was no answer—"

"We'll go find him. He's around somewhere close."

"Thanks. This is something I need to do that's long past due."

"Soooo, what happened?"

"I'll explain when I get there. I'll see you before noon. Goodbye."

Ann is staring at her and says, "You're telling me you're canceling an evening with Jarrod to go play around with that farm boy again because he bought your kid a tractor?"

Marilyn closes her book and tilts her head. "I'm going to apologize for my uncaring behavior. And thank him for the love he gave to my son."

Ann tries to hug her. Marilyn pulls away and says, "We were young and naïve when you convinced me against my heart to marry John. 'You can mold him into a good husband,' you said."

"Settle down—"

"I'm not blaming you. I wanted out of the house." Tears are running down Marilyn's face. "Ann, do you have any idea of the anxiety, of never being able to say no? To spread your legs open and tell him you liked it, because it's better than—"

"I'm so sorry. I—"

Marilyn holds her hands up. "No, you're going to hear the ugly truth. The last time after John beat me, he threatened to drag Johnny out of his room and make him into a man if I said no. The fear, the hate, the mental anguish, I lived with it every day."

Ann starts crying. "Why didn't you tell me?"

"Because I don't want everybody scrutinizing my nauseating life," Marilyn mutters through her tears. "My five-year-old knows about love from the heart. He loves Keith and I'm going to tell him what's in my heart. No matter how he feels about me, hopefully, Johnny can still have an Uncle Keith." She storms past her. "Don't wait up."

Sixty-Seven

December 26, 1984

Marilyn walks through the hall, enters her apartment, and slams and locks the door. She hears Johnny talking to himself in the bedroom and makes her way to the bathroom, wiping her tears from her bloodshot eyes. She strolls into the bedroom. "Johnny, we're going to Aunt Laura's. Pack your overnight bag. Some play clothes, your winter suit, and pajamas."

Johnny jumps up. "Can I take my new tractor?"

"Yes, of course." She stares at the front of her dresser. *What about my overnight clothes?* She adds extra underwear, a clean sweatshirt, and her favorite flower pajamas. *You're not turning on any guys with this wardrobe.* Her heart is pounding as she presses her hand against her chest, trying to slow it down. She fixes breakfast, cleans up the dishes, and makes the beds, as Johnny has his stuff piled by the door, waiting.

Marilyn heart is pounding as she swallows the lump in her throat. *How does Laura handle the emotions?* She keeps wiping her blurry eyes trying to hold it together.

Johnny sits quietly with his tractor on his lap and finally says, "Mommy, I'm so happy we are going to Aunt Laura's."

She glances over at his bubbling dark-brown eyes. "Me too."

After a long silence, Johnny says, "Are we seeing Uncle Keith too?"

"Some things I have to work out first, but I promise you will see Uncle Keith soon."

She knocks at Jason's, and Laura yells, "Come on in."

Marilyn is trembling as Laura hugs her. Chad runs out Johnny shows him the tractor and drags off to his room. Laura watches them and says, "A new tractor."

Marilyn says, "My Christmas present."

Laura's eyes squint slightly. "What?"

"Keith delivered it last night. Told Johnny Santa had the wrong address." *I'm the one with the wrong address.*

Jason gives Marilyn a hug. "I'll leave you women to straighten out the world." He gives Laura a kiss and makes his way out the door.

Laura pours coffee.

Marilyn lets the silence linger before she says, "The condensed version, my sister told Keith I had a boyfriend. A serious boyfriend. And failed to mention to me that Keith had called ever. She never did confess how many times."

Laura's cup thumps the table. "Why would she do that?"

"She was playing matchmaker. Hinting to Jarrod, the managing owner of the restaurant, how much I care about him, but I'm such a shy and naïve girl, he would have to coax me along."

Laura is static. "Wow, what a mess."

"Yeah, and me in my Cinderella world playing along, with an arranged family adult pajama party and, to my surprise, Jarrod was invited last night. Keith stopped at the same time delivering Johnny's Santa present." Marilyn takes a drink of coffee. "I asked Johnny why he didn't come get me. He said Uncle Keith thought I'd be mad. So, he left." Marilyn sets her hands on the table and leans forward. "Laura, I may be blabbering idiot, but ... I'm telling him the truth."

Laura smirks. "About time, sounds like a party."

"Well, not sure that is likely. I'm over playing kissy face with my boss. Who out of the kindness of his heart bought me a diamond necklace and arranged a weekend date in Chicago, all expenses paid, including the opera." She takes a breath.

"You must've impressed the guy."

"My sister impressed him, telling him I was hot for him but so inexperienced and bashful, he would have to guide me along."

"I'm surprised Keith didn't come join the party."

"My sister admitted she told him I had moved on in life my guess, he believes it is true."

"You want me to go with you?"

"No. This is a mess I made, living in my ugly secrets."

Laura breaks into a grin. "Keith loves you. You won't need to prove—or—"

"Sleep with him."

"No, not until you're ready." Laura's face goes blank. "It's different when love is real. You want the best for the person. I know the difference." She pauses. "One bartender secret: he hasn't gone out with anyone since you left town."

"You are my best friend forever." Marilyn's eyes are watering. "No more waffling."

Laura gives her a hug. "Quit being so scared. Keith is gonna laugh and say, 'That was yesterday.' Tell him you need a beer."

A small smile takes over Marilyn's face. "You're awfully confident." *Why does it feel different when she says it?*

***

She is gripping the wheel, trying to calm every emotion, as she pulls into the driveway. Keith's truck is sitting in its normal spot.

Don't say, just do. What if I can't?

She enters the porch, knocks, and hears Buddy make a slight woof as she cracks the door. "Keith, are you home?" She bends down and pets Buddy.

He is wagging his tail and jumping around.

"You have gotten so big. Anyone here?"

There is no answer. She puts Buddy back in the house and fights the urge to run. Picks her head up and heads to the tool shed. She hears the radio competing to be heard over the mini-jet-engine heater, the winter work routine.

She makes her way over to the corner where Keith is working. She leans against the front rib tire on the tractor, pressing against her butt. She hears Johnny. *"Mommy, it has four-wheel-assist, that's why the tires are different." My kid knows more than I do. The want ... what if he doesn't ... am I letting a different guy run my life?* She puts her cold hands in her pockets, realizing she should have worn warmer clothes.

He stops working and is gazing at her. A grin finally takes over his face as he walks towards her. "You found my secret hiding spot." He opens his arms.

She jumps into his arms, taking in the smell of his bib overalls. "I'm so sorry." She feels her eyes getting blurry.

"Hold on." He shuts off the heater and radio. "Let's go into the house. I'm assuming you didn't drive all the way here to work on tractors?"

"According to Johnny, I need to learn about tractors." *Plus, other things.*

Her legs are trembling as Keith wraps his arm around her waist and guides her to the house.

Buddy is jumping all around as Keith grabs some cups, pours coffee, and gets some creamer. He tastes his. "Not sure you'll be able to drink that."

Marilyn tastes it and pours in more cream. "It's perfect."

"Right, for a cowboy in the middle of Wyoming."

She pushes her cup away and gazes at him. "Might as well go right to beer."

A grin seeps into his face. "Two beers coming right up." They toast, and he says, "To the truth of it all."

"There's so much to say, but what you did for Johnny—it was beyond caring." She takes a swig of beer. "You're his idol." *Mine too*. Her voice quivers. "You never wavered."

"Well, you don't need to apologize. I—"

"No, I'm still a mess." She takes another drink. "I'm not promising I can ever make logical decisions." She looks towards the wall. "But I'll not keep any secrets from you. As you say, everyone's playing the game. In some fake twisted reality, I was winning, only to find out I'm fighting bigger demons."

"It's easier to fight them together." He drains his beer, grabs two more. "Let's go where it's more comfortable."

He takes Marilyn's hand. She is shaking.

He positions his arm gently on her back, and they start into the living room.

He's taking me to the bedroom. Marilyn grips his shirt, and her legs wobble.

Keith looks down at her and turns towards the couch. "You okay?"

She is completely numb, pressing against him. In a complete daze, she stares across at his bedroom. "I never slept with him."

Keith laughs. "Well, you haven't slept with me either."

Marilyn breaks out with a smile, sets her beer on the stand, and rolls her head against his flannel shirt. "I'm scared ..."

Keith takes a drink. "I've been—"

"Out with other girls. It's your secret before me."

Keith says, "I know about making love, not sure I know how to be in love.

It's scary." Calmly he continues, "I think I'm still teachable. If you want to take on the challenge?" He pulls her tighter. "We have fences to be torn out, and you're damn good at that."

Marilyn dabs the water from her eyes on his soft flannel shirt.

Sixty-Eight

December 26, 1984

Marilyn wakes with Keith holding her and a blanket wrapped around her. She tries to blink the sleep out of her eyes. "What time is it?"

He grins calmly. "Time to do chores, I was worried you would sleep through it."

They sit holding each other as Marilyn stares at his bedroom. "I have changed since my escapade in the city, but I'm not doing chores."

Keith pulls back. "Wow, that's awfully demanding. Guess you think you can strut around on your good looks?"

"Well, according to my sister and ... they all want me."

"Didn't take long for you get a city attitude." He lights up his peacock grin. "You sit here and be pretty, and I'll do the chores and we'll work out more of the details." He kisses her.

Marilyn calls Laura and tells her not to expect her till tomorrow. "I'm still scared, but I have this overwhelming emotion but I need to know."

Laura says, "Relax and just let it flow."

Marilyn gazes out the kitchen window and can see the lights on the tractor moving between the barns. She starts cleaning the counter and washing a few dishes. She takes some leftovers out of the fridge and warms them up when she sees him put the tractor away.

Keith grins and compliments her about nothing, but it raises her spirits. They spend the evening in serious conversation about life. Marilyn's anxiety keeps creeping, and she needs a couple of beers to relax her. She can't say no this time and ...

Keith gets up and goes to the bedroom and brings out a blanket and pillow. "Since you are being so demanding about chores, you get the bed and can sleep late."

She bear-hugs him and finally looks into his eyes. "I want to—"

"When you're ready, we will."

She helps herself to one of his flannel shirts, stares at the nightstand with her letters lying there unopened and smells him as she lays her head on his pillow. Her body tingles. *I'm ready.*

***

When she gets up in the morning with such calmness of life, thinking it must be a dream, she goes to the bathroom and there is a new toothbrush lying on the sink.

Johnny and Chad spend their week of vacation most of the time at Uncle Keith's.

January 1985

The new year, Laura and she must work on New Year's Eve, so Keith and Jason are partying with the boys. Marilyn's has a phone installed, and she calls Laura and Keith and gives them the number. Jarrod stops at the restaurant but goes directly to the office and disappears shortly afterwards. When she comes in on Thursday, she is called to the office and informed she will be cut to one day a week.

Paul, her boss, adds, "You are a great employee, put me down for a recommendation." He hands her a card with his personal phone number. "We'll keep that between us."

In the silence, she says, "Thank you. You have been great to work for."

The weeks seem to drag. Conversation with her sister pertains to who's watching the kids. Marilyn takes each morning to look for another job, but her experience and winter job availability are not turning up much.

February 1985

Marilyn enjoys Keith's frequent trips for pleasant lunch dates, afternoon conversations, and the afternoon matinee while the kids are in school. She is overwhelmed by the depth of carrying on conversations. They picked out new kitchen cabinets. Jason is planning on putting them in before spring.

Keith keeps asking her about the money, and she has stretched the truth; she is doing fine, refusing to take money. Her old-fashioned beliefs about relationships. *We're dating; I am not letting him support me.* He keeps her supplied with beef, slips in extra groceries and Johnny's Sugar Pops.

Marilyn finds a side evening job at the local grocery store. She looks at nursing, which she wanted to learn before she became pregnant with Johnny. She has become self-sufficient, although barely, but is she conquering the demons?

Laura said she could use someone four hours a night during the bowling rush, but it wouldn't be worth it to drive from Port Huron. She dropped a hint to her mother about moving to her mother's house but is glad it was ignored.

Curtis is working after school, doing the evening chores twice a week. Keith takes the opportunity to play with Johnny in the evening, tucking him in for the night, the only time he goes to bed without a fight. Marilyn wants—no—Johnny might wake up. Keith's patience lets her snuggle up and holds her.

Gwen calls and invites her to Sunday dinner. Keith is adding snowmobile rides for kids only. Johnny's excitement is beyond anything since they moved to Port Huron. Anxiety creeps into Marilyn as she drives, realizing she'll spend time alone with his family. *Will they still be judging?*

Gwen asks when they're alone, "How are you making out? Keith said they cut your hours."

Marilyn hesitates. "I saved money knowing it would be slow."

"I do have some old-fashioned rules, about living together." Gwen reaches for her hand. "But the offer to stay here still stands. But only if you want to do that."

Tears are flowing as Marilyn hugs her. "Thank you again. I would like that."

March 24, 1985

Keith is having a steak party before the actual spring work begins. He tells Marilyn to come at eleven to help but leave Johnny at his mother's. Gruffness in his voice, Keith says, "It's something important. I need to tell you in private."

She has worked herself into a nervous wreck, trying to put on her eye liner. She is tremble as she nervously pets Buddy and says, "Good morning."

Keith gives her a light kiss. "Morning in a city but afternoon in farm country." He scoots around and slides out a kitchen chair, motions for her to sit, and pours coffee, asking if he is serving correctly.

Marilyn's eye's are darting around the room. *He's being weird* She stumbles out. "You plan on taking up serving for a side job?"

With the grace of a ballroom dancer, he swoops down on one knee and opens a small box. "Will you marry me?"

Marilyn is trembling. Her mouth opens, but the words don't come out.

He lets the grin fade. "It can be the history of 1984 if you want to say no."

"I .... But what if I can't ..."

"Love on the farm, you've been trying to resist it has a secret magic, and once the fairy dust takes over, you won't be able to stop."

She holds out her left hand as tears stream down her face.

He slides the ring on her finger. "I love you." He lowers his voice and drops his smile and says, "My one and only forever."

He helps her out of the chair. They hug and kiss. Marilyn says, "I love you too." Her fears evaporate as he embraces her, still feeling too weak to stand but the joy of who she has to hang on too.

***

Jason and Laura arrive first for dinner.

Marilyn holds out her hand.

Laura screams! And both hug each other and are crying.

Laura wipes her eyes, gaining some composure. "The night he picked you up at the bar, my heart knew. But I was afraid I'd mess it up if I ever said anything."

Keith's mom adds more tears and says, "I prayed everyday he'd realize how much you loved him."

Johnny pulls on Keith's arm and whispers in his ear, "Are you going to be my dad?"

"It's you and me, bud."

Johnny jumps up and squeezes Keith, he's choking him.

Don't miss out!

Visit the website below and you can sign up to receive emails whenever JC Akends publishes a new book. There's no charge and no obligation.

https://books2read.com/r/B-A-SFTAF-VTBZI

BOOKS 2 READ

Connecting independent readers to independent writers.

About the Author

The journey; at four years old, home, a gas station in Brown City, Michigan. Characterized as no stop-light town. Passion and life experiencing the power of the Dodge R/T in the sixties, and incredible loss of the true muscle car in the seventies. The next stop Flint, Michigan; living with the heart ripped out of GM as factories closed, and Pontiac and Oldsmobile no longer exist.

Each stop buried with secrets of life intertwine with automobiles, divorces, business closing, and job losses. The stories and pain are deep in the heart but chasing the American dream, and the words begin to unfold, with sunshine. life in The Villages, Florida.

Previously published short stories in the FWA collections; 'What to Wear' in volume nine What a Character, is out of print. A second place in volume ten Were your Muse Lives with 'Eggs over Easy'.

Email: jcakends@houckpublishing.com

Web Page: http://jcakends.com

Read more at https://houckpublishing.com.

About the Publisher

Promoting words and thoughts for the world to enjoy and ponder.

Blog: LwCS coming May 2026

(Life without Common Sense) http://houckpublishing.com

Read more at https://houckpublishing.com/.

www.ingramcontent.com/pod-product-compliance
Lightning Source LLC
LaVergne TN
LVHW100512110826
845146LV00002B/601

* 9 7 9 8 9 9 5 4 2 7 9 1 9 *